NO SECOND CHANCES

ALSO BY RIO YOUERS

Lola on Fire

Halcyon

The Forgotten Girl

NO SECOND CHANCES

A NOVEL

RIO YOUERS

WM
WILLIAM MORROW
An Imprint of HarperCollins*Publishers*

This is a work of fiction. Names, characters, places, and incidents are products of the author's imagination or are used fictitiously and are not to be construed as real. Any resemblance to actual events, locales, organizations, or persons, living or dead, is entirely coincidental.

HarperCollins books may be purchased for educational, business, or sales promotional use. For information, please email the Special Markets Department at SPsales@harpercollins.com.

FIRST EDITION

Library of Congress Cataloging-in-Publication Data

Names: Youers, Rio, author.
Title: No second chances : a novel / Rio Youers.
Description: First edition. | New York : William Morrow, [2022] | Summary: "From the acclaimed author of Lola on Fire comes a blistering novel of action, intrigue, and suspense about a down-and-out actor suspected of killing his wife, a wannabe starlet new to the L.A. scene, and the vengeful drug dealer they both dare to cross" — Provided by publisher.
Identifiers: LCCN 2021033809 (print) | LCCN 2021033810 (ebook) | ISBN 9780063001053 (Print) | ISBN 9780063001060 (trade paperback) | ISBN 9780063001077 (Digital edition)
Classification: LCC PR9199.4.Y667 N6 2022 (print) | LCC PR9199.4.Y667 (ebook) | DDC 813/.6—dc23
LC record available at https://lccn.loc.gov/2021033809
LC ebook record available at https://lccn.loc.gov/2021033810

ISBN 978-0-06-300105-3

22 23 24 25 26 LSC 10 9 8 7 6 5 4 3 2 1

NO SECOND CHANCES

PART I

CANARY

1

NEW L.A. WOMAN

Her favorite time, her favorite place. Nighttime on Sunset—the vibe, the opportunists, the neon signs throwing dreamy color. Everything about it made her feel alive. And at twenty-four, Kitty *wanted* to feel alive. It was why she had moved here.

She put her skateboard beneath her and rolled, breathing warm, tainted air. A smile—as wide and sweet as a slice of orange—broke across her face. She smelled exhaust, peppered steak, vape perfumes, a blend of colognes. A street performer played "What a Fool Believes" and high-fived her between chord changes. Her wheels thumped off the sidewalk.

Kitty Rae had been in Los Angeles four months. It still moved her, and her heart still made a hopeful, tinkling sound when she walked. She'd gone from waiting tables to bartending to selling Jell-O shots at Spearmint Rhino, all within a space of eleven weeks, then Kris "Sly Boy" Streeter had discovered her. Sly Boy was not the talent scout she'd been hoping for, but he lined her pockets in exchange for easy work. It was a start.

It also allowed her to move out of shared lodgings in MacArthur

Park to a smaller—but all hers!—apartment in Silver Lake. It was several steps shy of the L.A. residence she'd imagined for herself, but she *loved* being on the third floor, where the rugged, hypnotically moving tops of the fan palms were at eye level. Even better was the way the setting sun caught her street and splashed the buildings with mauves and oranges. Passion Hour, she called it, even though it lasted only minutes, seven at the most.

Where I live, she'd posted on Instagram, beneath a photograph of her street draped in those rich colors. Her friends back in Louisville had commented: OMFG!! and, Sweeeeeet!! and, Yo still Kentucky bitch. Her mama—whose cheekbones Kitty had inherited, as well as her propensity to dream—had added, So beautiful babygurl but have U met any CELEBRITIES yet??

Well . . .

She'd seen Caitlyn Jenner at a photo shoot at the Getty, and Ezra Faustino arguing with a valet attendant outside a restaurant in North Hollywood ("*I will fuck the fuck out of your shit!*" Mr. Faustino had screamed). All that was lit, but what was *totally* lit was the fact that she lived opposite—*opposite*—Luke Kingsley.

Mama: *Who?*

Luke Kingsley, the troubled star of *Ventura Knights* and *A Bullet Affair*. Kitty told her mama this but Mama didn't know those movies, so Kitty told her what Luke Kingsley was *really* famous for.

Mama: *Oh shit!*

He'd gone from a beautiful house in Sherman Oaks to a two-bedroom mission revival in Silver Lake. Kitty could stand at her window and look down into Luke's living room—could see him watching TV in his boxers and eating Cap'n Crunch right out of the box. And okay, it wasn't as cool as smoking weed with Seth Rogen or bumping beautifuls with Jamie Foxx, but—like working for Kris "Sly Boy" Streeter—it was a start.

. . .

Kitty picked up the goods from the trunk of a Cadillac parked in Norma Triangle (same Caddy every time, different location), then took a bus to East Hollywood and went to work. Twenty minutes in, she made Angelo's drop: an ounce of crystal packed into the false bottom of a Starbucks cup, tossed into a trash can outside Slick's Coin-Op Laundry on Melrose. Angelo's boy arrived moments later. He dug through the trash can and removed the drop. Kitty snapped a photo from across the street—making like she was taking a selfie, although there was no reason for her, or *anyone*, to take a selfie in this neighborhood. She needed the photo, though, as proof the pickup had been made. Kitty had no dealings with the money side of things. She delivered the goods, that was all. She supposed Ruben—Sly Boy's muscle, a man-shaped iron girder—collected, and God help the cranker who didn't pay.

Kitty pocketed her phone, put her board beneath her, and skated away. She'd pushed once—rolled maybe ten feet—when Angelo stepped out from the doorway of Gray's Marketplace, right in front of her, and she would've taken a spill if he hadn't grabbed her upper arm.

She flipped the front of her board up, caught it in her right palm while trying to pull her left arm loose. But Angelo dug his fingers in and grinned.

"You gotta be more careful, girl."

His real name was Salvador Gallo, but he had earned the nickname Angelo because of his soft black curls and doll-like good looks. He'd appeared in commercials for Gap and Tommy Hilfiger in the early 2000s, and was a semi-regular on the short-lived ABC sitcom *Almost Always*. Then his drug usage went from recreational to obscene, and that was the end of his career. Now his curls were laced with dirt and he had black grooves between his teeth. There was a canker on the side of his nose that never healed.

"Hands off, Angelo."

"Or what?"

Sly Boy had warned her not to engage with the buyers. "Every degree of separation is a degree that will keep you out of prison," he'd said. "You don't want these people getting to know you. They will fuck you over if they get the chance." Most of Kitty's drops were clean. No contact. But a buyer would surface on occasion, assuming their presence was welcome.

Angelo, for example: "Why you always so quick to be gone? Don't you know we could have a good time, me and you? We could take in the city. Do it all."

She pulled her arm, but he held on.

"I know a man can get that face on the cover of a magazine. You want that, girl?" The lesion on his nose looked wet and sore in streetlight. "Your face on the cover of a magazine?"

"Just get your dirty fucking—"

Angelo suddenly let go, his hands raised like someone had pointed a .45 at him. It had nothing to do with Kitty struggling to free her arm, or anything she said, and everything to do with the sage-green Mustang—vintage Detroit muscle—cruising toward them. It slowed as it approached. The passenger window buzzed down and Kitty saw the Viking for the first time. He was comfortably into his twenties, ugly-handsome, with a crooked nose and narrow forehead. His long beard was fashioned into two points, a darker shade of blond than the hair that fell to his shoulders.

Kitty heard Angelo say, "Shit," under his breath, then he turned and ran—bumped into an older lady, who called him a son of a bitch in Spanish and swiped at him with her purse. Angelo was out of range, though, scooting along Melrose with his dirty curls bouncing.

The Mustang voiced an oily, predatory snarl and rumbled on. Kitty watched its taillights for a moment, then skated to her next drop. And that should have been that. End of scene. Fade to black. Except she saw the Mustang again not forty minutes later, at a red light on Beverly. Kitty put it down to coincidence, but logged it.

She made her delivery (an eight-ball stuffed into a Taco Bell wrapper) at a nearby bus stop, photographed the pickup, and checked her backpack. Three drops remaining, then home.

A third sighting of the Mustang—on Sunset this time, ten minutes from her apartment—put her on alert, which developed into a deeper concern when the vehicle started following, then drew alongside her. It matched her speed for fifty yards, give or take, with Kitty looking dead ahead, playing it cool. Maybe the driver would get bored and floor it if she didn't react. Instead, the passenger window rolled down and the Viking's voice rose above the engine's steady rumble.

"You can really shift on that thing."

Kitty ignored him. She zigzagged between pedestrians, lithe as a ribbon. Farther along Sunset, a siren whooped three times, like the call of some exotic bird, and acoustic music strummed from a late-night café.

"I'd like to talk to you," the Viking said. "If you have a moment."

"I don't." Now Kitty looked over. "And stop following me."

Was he an undercover cop? Had he been watching her all night, or for *weeks*, and was now moving in for the bust? Kitty didn't think so. She'd be more likely to get busted at the beginning of her route, with a backpack full of product. Or maybe they wanted to use her in a different way—to take down Sly Boy, perhaps. But even then, they would arrest her first, then turn up the heat.

No, she wasn't getting a cop vibe. The Viking image didn't fit, nor the late sixties ride. And although Kitty couldn't see the driver sitting beside him, she *could* see his hands on the wheel. They were covered in tattoos—too much visible ink for a cop, even one deeply undercover.

"C'mon." The Viking smiled. Maybe he didn't mean to disarm her, but he *did*. He had a charming smile. "Two minutes. That's all I need."

If he wasn't a cop, then his business was on the other side of the thin blue line. A pusher, perhaps, or a pimp. A lawbreaker, for sure, and one of renown, judging by the way Angelo had taken to his heels.

"Not interested," Kitty said. The Micheltorena intersection was just ahead, where she'd usually turn right, skateboard partway up the hill, then hang a left onto her street. She wasn't going to lead these goons to her apartment, though, which meant she had to lose them.

"I don't give up easily," the Viking persisted. "Also, I'm not following, I'm *scouting*."

Two options: she could skate through a late-night store, exit via the back door, and shake them in the narrow residential streets north of Sunset. But even if she managed to give them the slip, how long before that old muscle car pulled alongside her again? They knew her face, after all . . . her route.

Her second option—to put a serious scare on the motherfuckers—would be more effective.

Kitty once saw Ruben Osterfeld take out three guys without losing a drop of sweat. She didn't know him as well as she knew Sly Boy, but he'd passed along his number in case she ran into trouble on the streets. "You look like you can take care of yourself, but if you need some heavyweight backup . . ." Ruben was a former UFC contender who'd taken Prince Santana the distance in the Octagon, and Kitty was grateful—now more than ever—to have him listed in her contacts.

She hopped off her board, pulled her phone from the back pocket of her jeans. The Mustang slowed to a crawl, then picked up speed and turned north on Micheltorena. The angry sound of its muffler faded into the Silver Lake ambience. It would return, though. Kitty was sure of it.

No answer from Ruben. Voice mail.

"Shit."

Fusion 44—Sly Boy's jazz club—was a few blocks north of the lake in Echo Park. Kitty could be there in fifteen minutes. Sly Boy preferred his runners didn't drop by unannounced (he didn't do *any* business at the club; it was strictly for jazz) but that was where she'd likely find Ruben. And if not, Sly Boy would know how to handle the Viking.

Kitty turned her board around and rolled down Sunset. She slowed where the pedestrian traffic was heavier, weaving between groups of people, sometimes hopping the curb and skating the bike lane. Her heart jumped. Small tears flashed from the corners of her eyes. Cool under pressure had always been one of her superpowers—the Coolest Kitty in the City, her girls back in Louisville always said—but this had set her on edge.

The Mustang passed her, circled, then passed her again.

"Motherfucker," she hissed. "What *is* your problem?"

Ten minutes of this, then she committed to the bike lane, blazing through every intersection. Traffic stopped for her—abruptly. She was nearly hit by a city bus at one point. It swerved across the bike lane to make its stop and she leaned a hard left, seeing nothing but the full-moon shine of its headlights. She ollied onto the sidewalk, caromed off a parking meter, and wiped out. Kitty knew how to fall, though, and how to get back up. She did so now, brushing grit from her grazed elbow, then retrieved her skateboard and ran the rest of the way.

El Picador Avenue, seventy yards of blacktop edged with magnolia trees and trash, home to office and apartment buildings, a yoga studio called Nirvana Flow, and Fusion 44. Its peacock-blue awning reached over the sidewalk like a sheltering wing. Frankie, the bouncer, stood outside, impressive in stature, disinterested in demeanor. He barely looked at Kitty as she swept inside.

The bar area was illuminated by soft yellow globes, but everywhere else was dipped in mood lighting. There were maybe twenty patrons sitting at tables in front of the stage, where a trio dressed in white suits played crime jazz. A half dozen more bodies propped up the bar. Kitty recognized Cal Schifrin, one of Sly Boy's new hires. He took care of the books, but he could also take care of himself.

"Should you be here, Kitty?" he asked. "I didn't see your name on the list."

"Looking for Ruben." Kitty breathed heavily and wiped sweat from beneath her eyes. "I got some creep following me. I didn't want to lead him to my apartment."

"Ruben's with the boss. He'll be down soon."

"I'll wait." And to the bartender: "Water, please. Lots of ice."

She was halfway through her drink when the Viking entered the club. He stood out, even in the gloom, a tall guy—six-two, easily— wrapped in lean muscle, an ornate tattoo on the left side of his neck. More dark ink decorated his forearms. He noticed Kitty and smiled, twisting the prongs of his beard.

"Shit," Kitty said. "That's him."

"That fucking guy?"

The Viking's driver stood just behind and to the left of him. He was thick-bodied and looked dangerous, as if missing a critical element that made him all the way human. An animal—a jackal, maybe—that would eat his own young to stay alive.

Cal put his drink down and got to his feet. "I'll take care of this prick," he said, striding past Kitty with his chest puffed out. Cal had once told Kitty that he used to train SWAT team members in close-quarters combat.

He and the Viking met at the end of the bar. Kitty might have heard their brief conversation, had the band been between numbers. Not that she needed to hear anything. Cal gestured toward the door. *You're not welcome here. Kindly leave.* The Viking twisted his beard and nodded toward Kitty. *Not going anywhere. I want to talk to her.* Cal said something else, puffing his chest out a little more. He prodded the Viking with his finger, which ended all dialogue.

The driver stepped forward and drove his fist into Cal's face. It was a quick attack, and devastating. Cal's nose broke open with a staccato pop. He wobbled on his heels and raised one hand, perhaps in some feeble attempt at defense, or to cry uncle. Whatever it was, it didn't work. The driver grabbed him by the hair and introduced his face to the wall. Not once, but three times. The impacts were solid enough to halt the band. A flower of Cal's blood bloomed on the rustic brickwork. One of his teeth hit the barroom floor and skated all the way to where Kitty was standing.

"Ain't that some unhappy shit," the pianist grumbled into his microphone.

The driver let go of Cal, who dropped into a loose heap, his days of eating solid food behind him, much like his days of training SWAT team members in close-quarters combat. His face was a broken mess.

The Viking examined his fingernails—indifferent, cool—and tipped Kitty a wink. At that point, Sly Boy and Ruben appeared, bursting in from the back of the club where Sly Boy kept an office. Kitty wanted to vault the bar and hide. Shit was about to go down, and it wouldn't just be *unhappy*. There would be guns. There would be bodies.

Or so she thought.

Instead, Sly Boy adopted a cautious posture, his eyes peeled to full circles. "What the fuck, Johan?" he said, and uttered a nervous laugh. Even Ruben appeared reluctant to venture too far forward. He looked like a scared two-hundred-and-sixty-pound boy.

"Kris," Johan said calmly. "It's been a while. You look good."

"Yeah, it's been . . ." He shook his head, getting back on track. "What the fuck, man?"

Johan—the Viking—gave his beard another twist, then pointed

at Kitty. "Her." He offered his disarming smile. "I want just a moment with her."

All eyes on Kitty. She stood in the yellow light, her legs trembling. "I didn't do shit." She looked from Sly Boy to Johan, then back to Sly Boy. "I've never seen this guy before. He just started following me."

"Scouting," Johan corrected her. "This is Los Angeles, after all, where fortune favors the ruthless."

An uncharacteristic hush descended on the club, broken only by creaking chairs and Cal's tuneless wheezing. Some of the patrons had vacated, but most were old jazz guys. They'd seen this—and worse—before. They looked put out, if anything, that their evening's entertainment had been interrupted.

Sly Boy nodded at Kitty—more with his eyes than with his head. Kitty frowned, not certain she understood the gesture. He clarified.

"Go," he said.

"Go?"

"With him."

"No." A coldness washed through her. It had the paradoxical effect of increasing her jitters, yet making her firmer inside. "I don't want to."

Sly Boy turned his lips down. He swallowed hard, straightened his sleeves—impeccably arranged, as always. The eight-hundred-dollar haircut. The suit from the House of Bijan. It was all about outward appearance with Sly Boy, but was there anything inside?

"It's easier for everyone," he whispered, "if you go willingly."

He had educated Kitty about not talking to the customers, distancing herself from trouble, maintaining the degrees of separation that would keep her out of prison. She had thought him savagely smart, but maybe he was just gutless. Either way, Kitty no longer felt protected by Sly Boy, or by Ruben "take my number" Osterfeld.

She left the club with the Viking, feeling suddenly and overwhelmingly alone.

Johan Fly exuded strength and confidence, and Kitty, to her surprise, felt safe in the short time they were together. They walked down to Sunset, then slowly east. Johan talked about how his father had crossed the ocean in 1977, from Denmark, and was now one of the wealthiest men in the city. He said that it had been that way with his people, his bloodline, for hundreds of years. They traveled to foreign lands. They took what they wanted. They prospered.

"What about you, Kitty?"

"What about me?"

"What do *you* want?" Johan had stopped, framed in that moment by a towering ficus tree. He looked similarly robust, with his carved, narrow forehead and skewed nose. "Wait, no. Let me guess. You're new to the city, flew in from—oh, that accent—somewhere in the South, but not *too* far south. Virginia, maybe. Or Kentucky. Mama's back home, missing her little girl. But she's proud of you, Kitty, chasing your dreams in L.A. And it could happen at any moment. That skin, those cheekbones. It's just a matter of time before somebody discovers you. Then you'll show everyone back in Jerkwater, Virginia, how high you can climb."

Kitty opened her mouth to respond, but a bubble of emotion had risen into her throat. She managed to breathe. Only breathe.

"All those hopes and dreams." Johan spread his arms, then drew them in slowly. "Yet here you are, with a backpack full of junk, skating from trash can to trash can."

His assessment was close, but it wasn't *that* neat a trick. Clearly, he was familiar with the streets and the people who worked them so knew that she was fresh on the scene. Her accent had a southern flavor, but it wasn't deep-fried. Virginia/Kentucky was an educated (or lucky) guess. And what pretty person didn't arrive in Los Angeles without at least one eye on the stars?

Still, he'd evoked emotion, partly resentment at being packaged into such a trite little box, mainly a blue, singing disappointment in herself.

"Is that what this is about?" she asked. "Why you followed me—*stalked* me—from Melrose Avenue? Why your boy put a hurting on Cal? Just so you could degrade me?"

"Not at all."

"Oh right. You're *scouting* me."

"I want to elevate you." He twirled the prongs of his beard again. "Take you closer to where you want to be."

Kitty tried looking away from him, but her gaze kept snapping back, drawn by some illogical science. He must have recognized this, and wanted to test it, because he walked on, his shoulders arrogantly lifted. Kitty turned back the way they'd come. She saw the driver propped against the Mustang's rear fender. He regarded her with his jackal eyes. Kitty sighed, then proved the science. She tucked her skateboard close and caught up to Johan.

"Who are you, exactly?"

"An entrepreneur, a social media sensation." He shrugged, as if who he was defied explanation: a box without sides. "Look me up: the Cali Viking. My accounts are verified."

It was close to midnight but this stretch of Sunset was still lively. Music boomed from a neighborhood bar and from passing cars—hectic blasts of sound, a mosaic of genres. Ringtones chimed. A homeless woman screamed something about Jesus Christ. Kitty and Johan walked to the corner of Echo Park Avenue. A mural covered the exterior of the building across the street, amplifying the Latino vibe. Johan took out his phone and snapped a selfie with it. He uploaded it to one of his social platforms with a few deft clicks, then waited a beat, nodded, and slipped the phone into his pocket.

"Five hundred likes already."

Kitty said, "What do you want from me?"

"Presentation is everything," Johan said, removing a strand of blond hair from his shirt and letting it float away into the night. "This skateboarding soul-diva vibe you've got going on: beautiful, strong, but with an appetite for fun . . . that's exactly what I'm looking for. I'd like you to work for me."

Kitty recalled the solid thump of Cal Schifrin's face meeting the brick wall at Fusion 44, and the way his bloody tooth had skated across the floor toward her.

"No," she said. "You're too dangerous."

"Dangerous?" Johan mocked a frown, pretending to consider the adjective, before coming up with another. "I prefer *persuasive*."

"No," Kitty said again.

"Listen, I'm talking about you doing the same thing you do for Sly Boy." He used his smile again. "No trash cans, though. A different product. A higher class of clientele."

Kitty opened her mouth to tell him that she wasn't interested, but the words weren't there. She stammered for a second, surprised at her hesitation.

"They say Los Angeles is the city where dreams come true. You could be waiting tables one moment, walking the red carpet the next." Johan made a camera out of his hands and mimed snapping her picture. "That does happen, Kitty. But not often. For every one dream that sparks to life, twenty thousand crash and burn. They should call this the City of *Broken* Dreams."

"Tell me something I don't know."

"How long are you going to be scratching around for Sly Boy? How long before that brightness inside you fades, and you find yourself on a flight back to Jerkwater?"

"I don't quit easily."

"I can keep you dreaming." He pointed northwest, at the Hollywood Hills perhaps, or at the few stars winking gamely through the light pollution. Then he pulled his cell phone from his pocket again and thumbed the screen. "Six-K likes."

He showed her: the Cali Viking in Echo Park. A filter emphasized the blackness of his tattoos and the brightness of the mural behind him. Kitty glanced at it, but only for a second. Her gaze snapped back to the man himself. To his blue eyes and slightly skewed face. She couldn't look away. That illogical science.

The snarl of a muffler did it. Kitty blinked and stumbled back a step, looking up to see the Mustang pull a U-turn and rumble up to the curb.

"My ride," Johan said, and brushed past Kitty. "Think about what I said."

"Sure, whatever," she said, but her words were lost beneath the Mustang's growl.

"And don't worry about trying to find me." Johan dropped into the passenger seat, then closed the door and looked at her through the open window. "I'll find you."

Another snarl, and the Mustang pulled away. It rumbled northwest on Sunset, out of sight before it was out of earshot. Kitty stood in one spot, swaying in a light breeze, only moving when a piece of trash tumbled across the sidewalk and got caught beneath her sneaker.

2

SUICIDE

Kitty got back to her apartment at 1:47 A.M., wanting only to sleep, to fall into a dreamless, concrete state and not wake until the date had changed.

It had been a long night. And *fierce*. The Viking had gotten under her skin. She closed her eyes and he was there. *I can keep you dreaming*. So arrogant. So self-important. Of all the things he'd said—and the violence she'd seen—this was what bounced around her mind and kept her from sleeping (from *dreaming*, ironically).

She lay in bed, watching the clock on her cell phone tick off the minutes: 2:28 . . . 2:29 . . . *I can keep you dreaming* . . . 2:30 . . . 2:31. A radio played in a neighboring apartment, at a volume she would never have picked up during the day, but in the still of night it came through clearly. She heard Young Thug and the Weeknd and Roddy Ricch. A breeze meandered through the urban hillside and shook the palms beyond her windows.

2:55.

I can keep you dreaming.

3:16.

"Get him out of your head, girl. Come *on*."

At 4:06, Kitty grabbed her phone, thinking she'd call her mama—7:06 in Louisville, Mama would be awake, making breakfast—but instead she found the Cali Viking on Instagram. Three-point-two million followers. She saw the selfie he'd taken with the Ricardo Mendoza mural in Echo Park, now up to 14K likes. There were hundreds of other photos: a gallery of vanity and entitlement.

She didn't click "follow."

4:42. Kitty put her phone down. She'd decided not to call her mama, although she wanted to hear her voice more than anything. Kitty was too tired to make any sense, though, and Mama would only worry.

The neighbor's radio had been switched off. It was as quiet as it ever got in this part of the city. The palm trees rattled, the traffic rumbled and hissed. Kitty would prefer the roar of the Pacific, or the coyotes howling in the hills, but she could live with this for now.

And eventually, yes, the ambience lulled her, and she slept, but not for long, because the sun had barely colored the horizon before she was woken by crashing and thumping sounds from across the street. Kitty rolled out of bed and staggered to the window, where she saw the actor Luke Kingsley, emptying his garage.

"You have *got* to be fucking kidding me."

6:53.

She longed for Kentucky.

There was no orderliness to Luke's process. He just threw shit onto his lawn. Boxes, flowerpots, recycling containers, a push mower, a faded yellow cooler. Kitty thought that, maybe, with times being hard, he was prepping for a garage sale. But when the framed *Ventura Knights* poster—signed by the whole cast, including Travolta—came crashing out, she knew he meant to kill himself.

. . .

Kitty had revisited a couple of Luke Kingsley's movies when she discovered he lived across the street from her. She'd also dug around online, and beyond all the vicious Reddit threads and bloodthirsty sensationalism, she found a 2018 HFPA red carpet interview, in which Sonny Mankowitz candidly asked Luke which beloved thing he would rescue first from his house in the event of a fire. "Wow, a fire?" Luke had replied, flashing the smile he'd purchased from Dr. Rick Glassman, dentist to the stars. "Not to tempt fate, but I'd have to say . . . yeah, I have a custom-framed one-sheet for *Ventura Knights* that's probably my most prized possession. It's signed by everyone—J.T., Emma, Reese, even Jimmy, the director. And sure, I own more expensive items, but *Ventura* holds a special place in my heart. Maybe because I had such a great time on the shoot. Maybe because it was my first big picture." By *big*, Luke meant that it was his first movie with an eight-figure budget. *Ventura Knights* underwhelmed at the box office, though, marginally recouping its costs.

The question was a setup, of course, because Hollywood dined on fresh meat, and Luke's stormy relationship with his soul singer wife, Lisa Hayes, had recently furnished the gossip magazines. Having received the kind of reply he expected, Mankowitz followed with: "A poster? Really? Most people say their partner."

"Right," Luke said, looking momentarily uncomfortable. "My wife. Yeah. Absolutely." He rolled back on his heels and brandished Dr. Glassman's smile again. "I'd probably grab her next."

The *Ventura Knights* poster exited the garage in spectacular fashion, bouncing off one corner, the glass exploding from the frame. It traveled end-over-end a couple of times before settling facedown on the lawn.

At this point another neighbor blustered into the street, dressed in boxers and flip-flops, his face a struck match.

"Hey, motherfucker. What the fuck?"

A box torpedoed from the gloom. It hit the lawn and split open, spilling paperbacks and comics.

"You want to quit with the goddamn noise?"

Now Luke emerged from the garage, carrying an Adirondack chair in both arms. He was also dressed in boxers, but with a baggy Black Sabbath tee that dropped to his ass.

"Almost there, muchacho," Luke said, and launched the chair. It landed on top of the *Ventura Knights* poster. "One quick minute."

This exchange lasted another twenty seconds, give or take, with Luke and the neighbor snapping at each other like small dogs. Then the neighbor retreated to his poky little house and slammed the door. It would have been amusing at any other time—these two men sounding off in their underwear—but Kitty couldn't get beyond the obvious: that this was the actor in the final moments of his life. Unless, by chance, the neighbor's intervention had somehow derailed his plans.

But no.

Luke had thrown his belongings onto the lawn, and kept the driveway clear, so that he could drive his car—a dented Dodge Caliber, not the Tesla of yesteryear—into the garage. He did so now, buzzing the driver's-side window down as he pulled forward. Kitty watched from her third-floor vantage point, one hand covering her mouth, as the Caliber rolled into the freshly cleared space.

The brake lights flared briefly. The tailpipe trembled and fumed.

Kitty imagined Luke reaching for the clicker clipped to the sun visor, activating the garage door, wiping tears from his cheeks with his other hand. The picture had no sooner entered her mind when the door started down on its tracks.

"Oh man. This shit is *happening*."

The bottom of the garage door met the flagstone driveway, forming a near-perfect seal. Kitty pushed away from the window, still tired but decidedly *not* tired. Adrenaline for the win!

"I can't even," she said, but she picked up her skateboard and went to him.

Luke's house in Sherman Oaks had an eight-foot steel gate with an intercom system, but here his driveway met the sidewalk like every other schmuck's. Kitty took it at speed, bending her knees to absorb the uneven surface through the wheels of her skateboard, adjusting her balance to account for the slope. She hopped off at the bottom, kicked the tail of the board, and caught it beneath her arm. The garage door was windowless, buckled at the bottom where Luke had doubtless thumped his car into it. Kitty heard the Caliber's poisonous engine grumbling on the other side.

"I don't need this shit, Luke," she said.

Although it occurred to her that maybe she *did*, because the Viking had been knocked off the top spot in her mind, and that was a good thing. She could take control again, get this day—her sense of self—back on track. Jesus, she might even *sleep* later.

But first, she had to save this washed-up actor's life.

Kitty walked around the side and here was the door. It had a window in it, and she peered through to see Luke slouched behind the seat of the Caliber, his eyes closed. She tried the door. Locked, of course. Without hesitation, Kitty thrust the nose of her skateboard into the lowest part of the glass. Her first attempt put three deep cracks into the window but didn't break it. Her second—a harder strike—did the trick. Kitty jumped back as the glass gave way. A large shard dropped like a guillotine blade, hit the ground, and shattered.

The stink of carbon monoxide and other chemicals wafted out, and Kitty spluttered, reaching through the broken window to unlock the door. She pulled it open. Another hazy cloud of poison pushed past her. Kitty dropped her skateboard, covered her mouth and nose with her forearm, and ventured inside. She noticed the garage door opener on the wall and punched it with the side of her fist. The door rattled up on its tracks, an ugly but immensely satisfying sound.

Two long steps, and she was at the driver's door. Luke's head rolled loosely. His eyes fluttered. Still alive. Kitty yanked the door open, wondering if he would put up a fight. He certainly wouldn't *thank* her. It was his decision to die, and she—a stranger—was taking that away from him, at least for now. But what else was she supposed to do? Luke had involved her from the moment he woke her up. Stupid jerk should have stuck his head in the oven . . . *quietly*.

Kitty grabbed his upper arm and pulled. He flopped out a little way, but that was all. She adjusted her grip, pulled harder, and met the same resistance. Kitty then noticed the seat belt latched across Luke's chest. A goddamn *seat belt*.

"What kind of idiot—"

Okay, buckling up was likely an automatic action. Muscle memory. But Kitty wondered if it was a subconscious thing. Perhaps, deep down, he didn't want to die. Maybe, after the smoke had (literally) cleared, he would thank her, after all.

His head rolled to the other side. He muttered something, then exhaled wheezily as Kitty leaned across him. She saw the keys hanging from the ignition and gave them a counterclockwise twist, shutting off the engine. She had Luke's seat belt unclipped a second later. He slumped forward, allowing her to grab him beneath his armpits and pull.

Luke had fallen on hard times, and the stress had obviously taken its toll on his body. He was a little north of six feet, and she'd seen him shirtless in movies. He had a good body for Hollywood. Not ripped, but lean and strong, like a young Eastwood or

McQueen. Kitty expected to feel firm slabs of muscle beneath his T-shirt, and thought she'd have to put her own muscle into hauling him from the car and into the clean air outside the garage. But this wasn't the case. Luke was thin—*too* thin—and Kitty moved him without difficulty. She dragged him alongside the car, avoiding the broken glass, and out through the main door.

"Urrggh," he groaned, opening his eyes wide, then screwing them closed again.

Kitty lowered Luke gently and rolled him into the recovery position. She was about to slide her phone from her pocket and call for an ambulance when he sprang to his knees, crawled a short distance, and collapsed against one of the boxes he'd thrown from his garage. He wheezed something, flapping one hand at her, then whooped and hacked from the depths of his lungs. This was encouraging, Kitty thought. Coughing—clearing out the toxins—was a positive sign. She held off calling the ambulance. He likely didn't have insurance anyway.

Luke retched like he was going to puke, but produced only a sticky, grayish thread of bile. It hung from his lower lip, swinging in the breeze.

"Gaaagh," he said. He spat between his hands, then wiped his mouth and looked at Kitty through whirling eyes. "Who the fuck are you?"

"I'm Kitty Rae," she replied, and pointed. "I live across the street."

The Viking had called Los Angeles the City of Broken Dreams. A reasonable moniker, all things considered. But Kitty reflected on the past ten hours and some of the people she'd interacted with: Salvador "Angelo" Gallo (creepy meth-head), Kris "Sly Boy" Streeter (full of shit), the Mustang's silent driver (would eat his young), Johan Fly himself (arrogant, *dangerous*). And now there was this guy, Luke Kingsley, in his dirty boxers and scruffy heavy metal

T-shirt. Yeah, sure, Los Angeles was the City of Broken Dreams for some, the City of Angels for others, but Kitty thought a more accurate, encompassing epithet was the City of Fucked-Up Men.

"Right . . . right." Luke nodded, spluttered again, then pushed himself to a sitting position. He looked at Kitty with a trembling smile. "How're you doing, Kitty? I'm—"

"I *know* who you are," Kitty interjected. She planted her hands on her hips and curled her lip with disdain. "You're the son of a bitch who killed his wife."

3
SOUL MAN

S hit, dog. What were you thinking?"
   Floyd had taken a turn for the worse. His skin had faded, the whites of his eyes had a distinct yellow tint, and there was a fractional delay between his mouth working and the words coming out. For the first time since his diagnosis seven months prior, he was showing the advanced signs of his sickness.

"Some days are harder than others," Luke replied, tilting the bottle to his lips. The beer was cold and good. "Felt like the right thing to do at the time."

"*Tsk-tsk*."

"I'd been up half the night, looking at old photos. Then I watched the first ten minutes of *Without Sin*. Huge fucking mistake." *Without Sin* was the big-budget Netflix original Luke had been signed to star in, only to be fired after the shitstorm hit. They gave his part to Walton Goggins. "It was all downhill from there."

"You said it."

Three P.M. on a Thursday afternoon. They were in the back corner of the Melody Bar & Grill, a cool, soulful establishment a stone's throw from LAX. Luke considered it his local, even though he lived twenty miles away—never a quick drive in the Los Angeles traffic. It was worth every minute of the journey, though. Floyd Tallent was his best friend, perhaps his *only* friend. They'd been meeting at this joint every month for the past eleven years. Floyd had stood by Luke through all the trouble.

"I can see you ain't exactly on cloud nine," Floyd said, pointing at the ceiling with one wavering forefinger. "But all things considered . . . you doing better?"

"For now." Luke shrugged and drank from his bottle. "Maybe cloud three."

"Well, shit, nobody ever wrote a song about cloud three," Floyd said, and a dusty chuckle broke from his chest. "It ain't so bad, though, and it's sure as hell better than the morgue."

"I guess you're right—"

"You know I *am*. And someone cared enough to save your ass, so there's that."

"Kitty," Luke mumbled, and finished his beer. One bottle. That was all he'd allow himself. The cops in this city couldn't slap a murder charge on him. He wasn't going to give them the satisfaction of a DUI. That single beer had gone down smoothly, though, and the company was good. The atmosphere was good, too. There was a feeling of neighborliness at the Melody Bar & Grill. The air buzzed with conversation and laughter. Soul classics pumped steadily from the sound system, appealing to the clientele, which, at this hour, was mostly older African Americans. Luke—forty-two and white—looked both out of place and entirely at home. It was a unique and heartening vibe.

He pushed his empty across the table and motioned to Vernon, the bartender, who brought over an ice-cold glass of water, because Vernon knew.

Jimmy Ruffin came on. "Gonna Give Her All the Love I've Got." Luke sipped from his glass and gestured at the music.

"You play on this?"

"This is Motown," Floyd replied, smiling and frowning simultaneously. "I was on the Atlantic side. You know . . . Aretha, Otis, Wilson Pickett. Shit, man, I *told* you that—"

"Right, right—"

"I knew some of those Motown cats, though. Benny Benjamin, Pistol Allen, Bongo Brown . . . most of the Funk Brothers. This"—Floyd touched his ear, indicating the music in a more intimate way—"is Jimmy Ruffin. I kicked around some with his little brother, David, and yeah, I played with him on one occasion; I happened to be in town when the Temptations were down a guitarist, so I grabbed my Gibson and stood in."

"Wait," Luke said. A smile touched his face. "You were a Temptation?"

"You should've seen me back in '65, with my conk hairstyle and sequin jacket." Floyd dropped a wink and looked, for one second, like his old self. "Man, I was *always* a temptation."

It didn't last, though. Floyd got to coughing and tears trickled down his cheeks. Luke rubbed between his shoulder blades, which helped, but not as much as the booze. Floyd downed the remainder of his bourbon and wheezed for a time, then breathed easier. He wiped his mouth with a trembling hand and blinked his jaundiced eyes.

"Well, shit."

"You okay, Floyd? You want water or something?" Luke proffered his glass.

"Shit, no."

The doctors had been forthright with Floyd about the likelihood of chemotherapy being successful, and Floyd had been forthright in return. To hell with the chemo, he'd said to them. He'd lived longer than he had any right to, given his habits and transgressions, and considered himself blessed. He would live out his days not in a prison of drugs, but in the freedom of friends and music. Even so, Luke was about to ask if he needed to go home and rest when Floyd, with a single word, deflected the attention elsewhere.

"Kitty."

"What?"

"That's her name, huh?" Floyd's chin quivered as he spoke. "The girl who saved your ass."

"Oh. Yeah." Luke nodded, scratching the back of his head. "Kitty. Right. My neighbor."

Another soul classic fluttered from the speakers.

"I played on this," Floyd remarked, touching his ear again. "Now tell me about her."

Luke did. He thought it would take all of thirty seconds, but he kept finding more to say. "She's been living across from me for . . . Jesus, I don't know . . . for *weeks*, I guess." He'd never noticed her, which surprised him, because she was easy to notice. "Young. Mid-twenties, I'd say. Beautiful. Kindhearted. I mean, she recognized me—everyone's favorite wife-killer since O.J.—but wouldn't leave my side until she knew I was okay. She even helped me pack my shit back into the garage."

Kitty had wanted to get him to a hospital. She'd pay for the Uber herself, she said, but Luke refused. He claimed to have a phobia of medical facilities and white coats in general. A lie, of course, and the frown on Kitty's face said she knew it. What he *really* had a phobia of was paying thousands of dollars to be hooked up to a ventilator when he could get oxygen for free—albeit a smoggy, less concentrated form of oxygen—in his own front yard.

So Kitty stayed with him while he inhaled deep lungfuls of air, gradually restoring the toxins in his blood to a manageable level. He coughed copiously to begin with, but this eased as the time ticked along. The fog in his head cleared, too, and the smoky taste in his mouth faded. Luke tried standing after twenty minutes or so, but his legs weren't there and he sat down again hard. Kitty perched on a cooler at the edge of his driveway and said calming things to him. "It's all good, man, just breathe . . . in and out . . . you've got this." And having her there—having *someone* there—felt novel and lovely and possibly more than he deserved.

She went into his house—a shithole; he hadn't cleaned in three weeks—and returned with a cold, wet cloth that she drooped across his forehead. It was invigorating and he brightened immediately.

"Thank you," he croaked.

His gratitude was sincere, not simply for the cold cloth, or the care, but for her having dragged him from the fumy precipice of death. Jesus, what *had* he been thinking? He couldn't die yet, with so much left unresolved. And suicide was a damn good way of making himself look guilty. Or *more* guilty.

Kitty swept up the glass from the broken window, backed his car out of the garage, and started to clear the items from his lawn. Luke—upright but still woozy—helped with some of the lighter things. She told him to rest but he assured her that he was feeling better, which was true; he only wobbled a little when he walked, and the nausea had mostly passed. If he'd been in that garage any longer, though . . .

When only a few bits and pieces remained, including his ruined *Ventura Knights* one-sheet, Kitty picked up her skateboard and shuffled up the driveway. She turned back to him, hooking a thumb toward the block of apartments across the street.

"I didn't get much sleep last night," she said. "So, I'm—"

"Yeah. You go. I'm . . . yeah . . . it's all good."

"You're not going to try that shit again?"

"Christ, no." Luke still had the cloth pressed to his forehead. It was warm now, but it felt good. He wished he had pants on, though, which he supposed was another sign that he was feeling closer to his normal self. "It's . . . I'm good. Really. Thank you."

Kitty nodded. She sidled past his car to the end of his driveway, dropped her board, and placed one colorful sneaker on top of it. Luke called after her.

"It was nice meeting you." Standing there in his boxer shorts, like an asshole.

"Right," she said.

And then Luke blurted something he hadn't for at least two and a half years, because he was tired of saying it, and nobody believed him anyway.

"I didn't do it, you know." He lowered the cloth and looked at her with tired, bloodshot eyes. "I didn't."

Kitty nodded, then she was gone, just the sound of her wheels on the asphalt.

"This was, what . . ." Floyd mumbled. Vernon had refreshed his bourbon and he took a sip now. "Two weeks ago?"

Luke nodded. "Two, yeah . . . shit, nearly three weeks ago."

"You seen her since?"

"It's not like that, Floyd. Jesus, she's young enough to be my daughter."

"That's not what I meant." Floyd reached across the table and clutched Luke's bare forearm, his fingers still strong, despite his sickness—fingers that had glided up and down guitar necks in the company of Aretha Franklin and Ray Charles and Dr. Martin Luther King Jr. "I'm thinking you need more people in your life. More *friends*."

Luke shrugged. "I have you."

"For now." A frown ran all the way from Floyd's eyebrows, over his bald and beautiful head, to the fuzz of silver hair at the back of his skull. "But we *both* know you're going to want a more long-term arrangement."

This prompted a moment of silence between them, inescapably

somber despite the joyous soul music on the sound system. Luke looked away from his friend, his gaze drawn to the posters tacked to the deep red walls, and the cheery faces punctuating both sides of the bar. This was where Luke had met Lisa. She'd been singing backup with a band called Generous Joe and the Breathers. Luke had approached her after the first set, told her he liked the sound of her voice, and that she could breathe for him anytime. Lisa raised one eyebrow in a way that was endearing then, but would irritate the living shit out of him in later years, and suggested he work on his pickup lines. She let him buy her a drink at the end of the night, though, and then take her to dinner at Taix French Restaurant the following week. And that—to sorely misquote the great Humphrey Bogart—was the beginning of an occasionally beautiful friendship.

This place had memories, many of them colored by alcohol, his fondest involving Floyd. He and Luke always sat together, and throughout the years had talked about everything: music, sports, politics, film, history, life and death, black and white. They shared stories about growing up in Macon, Georgia (Floyd), and Madison, Wisconsin (Luke). They talked about old dreams and new hopes. Most importantly, Floyd had offered a shoulder to cry on after Lisa went missing. He'd been there when every other face had turned away. They were solid friends, thirty-nine years apart in age, different colors, from different histories, but together they formed a perfect shape.

And for every conversation, every smile, and every tear, there'd been music playing. Usually classic soul. Luke would never tire of the way Floyd's eyes sparkled when some old hit came through the speakers, and he'd touch his ear delicately and say, *I played on this.*

But now his eyes had lost their brightness, and his body—storied and ragged—was almost at an end.

"Well?" Floyd asked, and again, his voice and the movement of his mouth were subtly out of synch. "You seen her since?"

"Kitty?"

"Yeah, Kitty. Shit, who else we talking about?"

Another smile found Luke's lips, but it was touched with sadness. He watched as Floyd let go of his forearm, withdrew his hand, and took another hit of bourbon. Elsewhere, a cop car flashed noisily down Sepulveda, and the music switched to Stevie Wonder singing "A Place in the Sun."

"Yeah, I've seen her." Luke ran a hand across his face, not surprised to find his eyelashes were damp. "She checked on me later that afternoon, to see if I needed anything—"

"And to make sure you weren't hanging from a rope in the basement."

"Well, maybe. I'd actually spent the day cleaning the house, getting my shit together. I also lined up some voice work—another goddamn video game—and booked an appointment with my shrink."

"Good."

"Yeah. I'm on new meds now. They're . . . working." Luke drummed a finger off the side of his head. "Cloud three, brother."

"Better than the morgue."

"Anyway, as a thank-you, I took Kitty over a couple of tickets to the Egyptian Theatre—you know, that art-house place on Hollywood Boulevard. She thanked me, but didn't seem too impressed." Luke considered this for a second or two, then shrugged. "Maybe I should have got her an Amazon gift card."

Floyd rolled his eyes and chuckled.

"We talked for a short time. Neighborly small talk. Then I saw her again earlier this week. I was heading to West Hollywood to audition for some Peacock animated thing. Kitty was meeting a friend in Fairfax, so I drove her." Luke nodded and drank water. "It was nice. She's a sweet girl—a sweet *woman*, I mean. Jesus."

"Well, that sweet woman must believe you didn't kill Lisa," Floyd said, slurring just a little. "Otherwise she'd never have gotten into that car with you."

"I thought the same thing."

"All right, then. Sounds promising."

"I don't know," Luke replied, and sighed. "I've lost a lot of friends recently, and I'm finding it hard to make new ones. Besides, she's *young*. She doesn't want to kick around with a middle-aged has-been like me."

"Age doesn't matter when it comes to friendship," Floyd said. He finished his drink and set the glass down with a shaky hand. "We're proof of that."

"We are." Luke nodded. "But this . . . shit, I don't know . . ."

"No excuses." Another cough rumbled from Floyd's thin chest. He covered his mouth, waited a second, and continued. "Whether it's Kitty or someone else, you need to make new friends. What's more, you need to rediscover your sense of purpose."

Purpose. The word ghosted through Luke's mind, leaving a cold trail. Similar words followed: *ambition . . . desire . . . motivation.* These had all been in abundant supply when, at the age of twenty-two, Luke left Wisconsin for Hollywood. Tall, square jaw, great hair, he believed the roles would fall into his lap. This wasn't the case. He auditioned for commercials, TV shows, music videos, voice-over work, TV movies, independent movies, and all-out blockbusters, working two jobs—washing cars and waiting tables—to keep a roof over his head. It took three years to score anything. His first acting gig was a commercial for Delta Air Lines. (He flashed a bleached-white grin while another actor, dressed as a flight attendant, handed him a fake magazine.) Commercials for Burger King and Head & Shoulders followed, then an under-five in the NBC family drama *The Natural Way.*

His sense of purpose never faltered. That breakthrough role, he assured himself, was only an audition away. It finally came in 2012, ten years after landing in Hollywood: costarring in the acclaimed HBO thriller *A Bullet Affair.* Doors opened more readily after this. People knew his name. He was invited to parties and premieres. His agent went from calling him once every three months to twice a day.

More TV work, on notable shows: *Reno and Down*; *Retribution Gulch*; *Chain Lightning*. Then it was on to the big screen: *Out of Midnight*; *Red Town*; *Ventura Knights*; *Never Always Comes*. These pictures were not blockbusters—not even close—but Luke's star power was bolstered, for better or worse, by his tumultuous marriage to soul singer Lisa Hayes.

Everything changed after Lisa. Doors weren't simply closed. They were slammed shut. His agent and his management team parted company with him, and he was scratched from two projects at the pre-production stage—both with the kind of A-list talent attached that would have propelled him to the next level.

"Purpose," Luke murmured, recalling the past three years in a series of deteriorating snapshots. "I hear you, Floyd. I *do*. But my life is in the shitter, and no one is giving me a chance to get out."

"You make your own chances," Floyd said, forming a loose fist, thumping it once, lightly, off the tabletop.

"Not that easy. I can't land an audition for anything but low-end voice work. And I won't score a big role without an agent."

"Purpose doesn't need a goddamn agent," Floyd snapped. "Start a charity, read to old folks, write a novel. Jesus Christ, do *some-thing*."

Luke reached across the table and placed his hand on top of Floyd's, signifying that the message had been received, and that he was grateful. Floyd's reaction to Luke's attempted suicide had been exactly what Luke needed, neither too damning nor overly mawkish.

There was more to it, though. Luke looked at Floyd's softly trembling mouth, then into his discolored eyes, and accepted the truth he'd been avoiding for the last hour or so—that this was their final afternoon together. Floyd's discourse wasn't just the wisdom of a man who'd been around the block a few times. It was a parting lesson. A loving goodbye.

An understanding passed between them. It came in silence, and Luke found comfort in it. He didn't give voice to the many sorrows chasing through him. The only thing that mattered was that moment, and holding on to it, somehow.

"To hell with it," he said, his hand still placed on top of Floyd's. "I'm going to get another drink. A *real* goddamn drink. You're welcome to join me."

"Aw shit, I shouldn't," Floyd responded. "But this late in the day, what difference does it make?"

Luke went to the washroom, using those few minutes away from Floyd to shed a few tears. On the way back, he ordered a pitcher of beer and two large bourbons—to hell with driving; he'd Uber home and pick up his car in the morning—and the two friends drank together until early evening, talking only about the things that complemented their shape.

And as always, classic soul filled the background. Floyd's eyes occasionally glossed over and he would gently touch his ear, indicating not just a top-ten hit or a musician, but a lifetime of harmony and achievements and love. The music of living.

"I played on this."

4

MAKING MOVES

"You lonely, baby girl? You can come home anytime."

She was two thousand miles from the people she loved, from the neighborhoods, the scenery, the comforts (and *dis*comforts) she had known for all of her twenty-four years. Not a day went by when Kitty didn't think about going home.

"You hear me? *Any*time."

"I hear you, Mama."

Kitty had gone from calling her mama once a week to every other day. Homesickness, that was all. But there was a reason she'd moved west. Louisville—for Kitty, at least—was a dreamless place. Going back, she would assume the role that had been scripted for her by the neighborhood she lived in, the name on her birth certificate, and the color of her skin. Her potential could be packed into a small box, whereas in L.A., there *was* no box.

"There was a tornado in Bullitt County the day before yesterday," her mama said, sensing Kitty's emotion and kindly steering the conversation elsewhere. "Twister touched down."

"Yeah? Anybody hurt?"

"No, but Muncel Stevens says she saw that mean ol' thing and ran like her ass was on fire."

Kitty's new life was large and intimidating, but it was hers to script, and whenever that felt like too much, she would remember the dreamlessness and the small box and, most importantly, the boy she had left behind.

Kitty told her mama that she loved her and ended the call, then sat on the floor and gave in to a moment of self-pity. Mama had asked if she was lonely. Kitty wasn't, but she often felt *alone*, and there was a difference. She'd met a few people, of course. The neighbor directly below—Sophia—was ten years older, an ER nurse originally from Tennessee, and far too busy for anything more than an occasional coffee. There were a couple of women at Kitty's yoga class that she had friendly conversations with, but again, their busy lives had prevented them from getting together socially.

Then there was Johan Fly. Kitty hadn't seen him—or his Mustang—in the three weeks since their encounter, but he'd called her. She didn't know how he got her number, but supposed he had no problem getting what he wanted.

"You're still working for Sly Boy," he'd noted. It was the first thing he said when she answered. "Hopping between garbage cans. My little raccoon."

"I'm not *your* little anything," Kitty responded, and then, as if she needed to explain herself: "It's easy work. Good money."

"You deserve better."

"It'll happen."

But would it? For all its life and color, Los Angeles was still the City of Broken Dreams. Kitty had pondered this notion since Johan had introduced it, and found it helped to approach it from a different angle: that dreams—all dreams, not just hers—were broken on arrival, and that only those with the tenacity to rebuild, one tiny piece at a time, would achieve success. Her resolve would be tested, but she had to believe, to *trust*.

"I can do that," Kitty whispered to herself.

She got up from the floor, deciding that was all the self-pity she could handle for now, and crossed the room to the window. It was just after five, still a few hours from sunset, when her street would be struck with passion colors, which always filled her with warmth and appreciation. No passion now. An elderly neighbor was practicing kung fu forms in his front yard, and Luke Kingsley was sitting on his front step, eating a banana.

She waved but he didn't see her.

Kitty had turned the internet over in the days following their eventful meeting. She read accounts and interviews, watched news stories, scoured forums, viewed countless photographs. The most haunting—and damning—was Luke's shirt, splashed with his wife's blood. Kitty recalled the depleted look in his eyes (although that may have had more to do with the carbon monoxide poisoning) after she'd dragged him from his garage. *I didn't do it, you know*, he'd said, and there'd been such a sadness—such a desperate quality—to his voice that she wanted to believe him.

Detective Tera Montecino of LAPD's Missing Persons Unit had not been of the same mindset. "We're following multiple leads, questioning witnesses," she'd said during an intense and emotional press conference. "If Lisa Hayes is alive, we'll find her. If she's dead . . . we'll find her. And then we'll bring the guilty party to justice. I don't care how many movies he's made."

This was three years ago. So far, neither Detective Tera Montecino, nor anybody else in the LAPD, had found Lisa Hayes.

But did Luke kill her?

The sadness in his voice was one thing, but that bloodstained shirt was tough to overlook, not to mention the tabloid-fodder nature of Luke and Lisa's relationship. They had argued constantly, colorfully, publicly. There was cell phone footage of them being ejected from Musso & Frank's, with Lisa taking open-handed swipes at Luke while calling him a "small-dick motherfucker." One night, Lisa called the police to their house in Sherman Oaks, claiming Luke had tried to drown her in the pool. Luke insisted he was trying to *save* her. Both were drunk off their asses.

"He doesn't look like the killing type," Kitty said to Connie, her older sister, during one of their weekly Zoom chats.

"They said that shit about Ted Bundy," Connie replied. "Motherfucker was a killing *machine.*"

"I know, but—"

"Woman goes missing, you can bet your sweet ass her man is behind it," Connie interjected fiercely. "Same when they're killed. Ninety percent of the time it's the husband or boyfriend. Maybe ninety-*nine*. That's some factual shit."

Female homicides connected to a significant other were closer to fifty percent. Kitty had already looked it up.

"You stay the fuck away from him, Kitty."

Her sister was not one of the world's great sages, but Kitty thought this was good advice. She intended to heed it, too, yet found herself, just two days later, sitting in the passenger seat of Luke's Caliber, en route to Fairfax. She'd told Luke she was meeting a friend for drinks, but was in fact going to collect six thousand dollars' worth of crystal meth from the trunk of a parked Cadillac.

The first several blocks were tense. Kitty sat rigidly, her skateboard across her lap, one hand on her phone's screen, ready to dial 911. But it wasn't long before she started to loosen up. Luke was relaxed and engaging. He asked where she was from, what she did for work (she told him she was a courier), then shared a few showbiz anecdotes that made her snort with laughter—physically *snort*, so that she had to cover her mouth and nose.

Kitty had debated getting into the car with him, and asked herself later why she did. Maybe she was drawn to his celebrity, such as it was. Or maybe—and this was more likely—after saving his life, she felt he needed someone in his corner.

He'd dropped her at the intersection of Third and Fairfax. As she skateboarded to the Caddy, she thought how strange it was that, four and a half months into her life in L.A., Luke was perhaps the closest thing she had to a friend.

Time drummed along. Kitty's days were spent chatting with family and friends back home, going to the gym, fluttering through her socials, and attending her yoga classes. Her nights were spent making drops for Sly Boy, hating herself every time she put her hand into a garbage can.

The Viking was right. She deserved better.

On her night off, seven weeks after thwarting Luke's suicide attempt, she joined him for a cold beer, both lazing across the hood of his Caliber, propped against the windshield. It was warm, the heat rising from below after spending the whole day beating down. Crickets chirruped in the weeds along the sides of Luke's house. A neighbor's sprinkler made a tranquil whispering sound.

"I don't care how many industry awards he's won," Luke said, concluding another of his Hollywood anecdotes. "He's still an asshole."

Kitty smiled, guzzled her beer. She stared at the hazy night sky for a beat or two, then turned to Luke. He was looking better. The hotter days had bronzed his skin. He'd trimmed his beard and put on weight.

"You have an agent?" she asked. The question surprised her—her mouth in motion before her brain was in gear. A trait of the exuberant.

"Not anymore." Luke swirled the contents of his bottle, then took a swig. He wrinkled his brow as he swallowed, as if the drink were bitter. "I used to be with Marty Lustbader at Paradigm. A tiny guy, five-foot-zip, but tough as rocks. He was the reason I got *A Bullet Affair*. It was down to me and Timothy Olyphant, but Marty worked his magic, nudged the producers in my direction. It was good to be on his roster. Felt like a goddamn hammer to the gut when he cut me loose."

Kitty inhaled, letting the night chorus fill the silence between them. She peeled one corner of the bottle's label, the moisture making it lift easily. Horns sounded distantly. Luke shifted and the hood voiced a metallic pop.

"Why?" he asked. "You want an introduction?"

"I don't know. Maybe." Kitty drew one knee to her chest and looked at Luke. "I just want a *chance*, you know. I didn't move to L.A. to be a delivery girl."

"You have any acting experience?"

"I modeled in my teens—ball caps for Lids and outerwear for Banana Republic. And I enrolled in summer classes at a performing arts school in Lexington, but had to give it up after my daddy was sent to prison. Mama took on a second job and I had to help look after my little brothers."

"Doesn't get any easier," Luke remarked. "Your first year acting—or *trying* to get paid work—you feel like you've run a marathon. Then you turn around and see you've actually moved about ten yards. And the clock is always ticking. There's always someone younger, prettier, hungrier, ready to take your place."

"I'm not afraid to put in the time," Kitty said. She shrugged and peeled more of her beer label away. "Anyway, just thought I'd ask. And hey, so you know, that's *not* the reason I saved your life."

"Didn't think it for a second." Luke grinned and clinked his bottle against hers. "Shit, you'd be better off getting a job at Chateau Marmont or Spago. Someplace like that. Smiling your smile as you serve those big-league producers their smashed avocado toast."

"First thing I tried when I got to town," Kitty said, and it was true. She'd had a stack of résumés printed off and hit every landmark in Hollywood. There were no takers. "Those places are tough to crack. It's all favors and referrals."

"Well, my name's worth shit in this town, and my referral is worth even less." Luke peeled off his own beer label, rolled it into a ball, and flicked it from the tip of his finger. "But I might be able to work something out. I know a guy, Denny Chick, a makeup artist. Does a lot of horror movies. You ever see *It Came from the Dumpster*?"

"Yeah. At a drive-in in La Grange." Kitty raised her eyebrows. "First and last date with *that* fucking guy."

"Remember the scene where the dude's severed head bounces down the basement steps?"

"Unfortunately."

"*Thonk-thonk-thonk*. Hit every fucking step on the way down. Like a goddamn Slinky."

"Yeah. It's etched into my mind."

"Denny did that." Luke's eyes flared with excitement. "One take. No CGI. You know how hard it is to get the head to hit *every* step? He used ball bearings and raw beef liver. Had to get the weight exactly right."

Kitty frowned and drank her beer, trying not to dwell on Luke's enthusiasm for severed heads.

"Anyway," Luke continued. "I bailed Denny out of a gambling debt to the tune of seventeen thousand dollars. This was back in the day. He'll never be able to pay me back, which means I can always call on him for a favor."

"What can he do?" Kitty asked.

"He's made a shit-ton of pictures," Luke replied. "Knows a lot of people. I can ask him to get you face time with an agent. Hopefully a lunch meeting. That way, the referral comes from Denny, not me."

"You'd do that?"

"I owe you big, Kitty. It's the least I can do."

A grin stretched across Kitty's face. It felt, for a moment, like *all* of her—a Cheshire Cat on the hood of Luke's old Dodge, beaming into the soupy night sky. Something dislodged inside her, too. A tension. A *reserve*. The space around her dreams expanded.

"Thank you, Luke," she said. "Holy shit, *thank* you."

"A referral isn't a guarantee," Luke said. "This is Hollywood. Anything and nothing can happen. And once you're in front of the agent, you're on your own. Just, you know . . ." He shrugged, a touch bashful. "Be your winning self."

"I'm hungry," Kitty said. "I'll do whatever it takes."

"Yeah? Well, you may want to be careful who you share that willingness with." Luke finished his beer, wiped his lips with the back of one hand. "The big bad wolf may be in prison, but there are still a lot of fucking dogs out there."

Kitty quit her "courier" job two nights later, but maintained her working connection to Sly Boy. The possibility of lunch with a talent agent may have encouraged this decision, but it wasn't the only thing. She lingered on what the Viking had said to her. *Hopping between garbage cans. My little raccoon.* She didn't want to be a raccoon. She wanted to fill the sky with light. *You deserve better.*

And maybe she could have shouldered the indignity for a month or three, or at least until she started getting regular auditions, but a couple of things happened that fast-tracked the move.

The first was Angelo Gallo, who'd bumbled toward her from a shadowy doorway, cupping his crotch, high on crystal.

"I'm gonna fuck you one day, Kitty," he slurred. His dirty curls fell across his forehead, bouncing like springs as he twitched and jerked. "Gonna hit every hole in that sweet Black body."

"Fuck you, Angelo."

"Maybe make a few new holes."

The second thing to happen was not as threatening, but it upset her more deeply. She'd just made a drop at a garbage can in Rampart Village, half an ounce of meth in a crumpled Subway wrapper, which she had to push down to keep it from blowing away. She was in the process of doing this when a car horn pipped twice— *hey, you!*—and she turned, her hand still in the garbage can, to see a familiar Mustang grumbling at the light. Johan sat in the passenger seat, one tattooed arm hanging loosely out the open window. He smiled, flicked a finger in salute, then the light turned green and the Mustang pulled away. Kitty groaned, slowly withdrawing her hand, her sense of shame so vast that she stood rooted to the spot for eight minutes.

She finished her rounds, then rode her board to Fusion 44. Sly Boy wasn't there when she arrived. She waited two hours. A nu jazz band played brightly. An old guy with a missing tooth hit on her. Kitty was about to leave when Sly Boy came in. He greeted a few of his regulars before taking the barstool next to Kitty's.

"I'm not doing this anymore," she said to him. "I'm out."

"Maybe we can talk about this some other time."

"No." Kitty shook her head, then borrowed Johan's analogy. "My L.A. dream doesn't involve me hopping between garbage cans like a raccoon—"

"A well-paid raccoon . . ."

"I deserve better."

The band played, hitting a groove that felt like pure improvisation, but sounded tight enough to have been rehearsed a thousand times. The vocalist—white hair, a tight green dress—swayed like an orchid. Sly Boy watched them appreciatively for a moment, then ordered two Cognacs. He gave one to Kitty.

"This won't change my mind," she said.

"Not trying to change your mind."

He had Clooney good looks, close to fifty years old, strong shoulders. There wasn't a worry crease on his brow, and why should there be? He'd amassed a small fortune dealing heroin from the late 1990s to the early 2010s, and had semiretired to the good life. Fine suits, fast cars, a house in the Bird Streets. He owned two clubs: Fusion 44 and E-Five, a rock venue in Santa Monica.

"You have something else lined up?" Sly Boy sipped his Cognac and smiled.

"Maybe," Kitty replied. Her eyes dimmed, then she pulled back her shoulders. "I'm meeting with a talent agent soon. That'll be my new starting point. I'll bartend, I guess, until the roles start coming in."

"Respectfully," Sly Boy said, "that doesn't sound like a carefully considered plan. I think you're being impetuous."

"I'm done working with garbage."

Warm applause as the band wrapped their improv. The singer applauded, too, then whispered into the mic that they had one more number. She nodded to the drummer, who counted them in. Kitty listened for a moment, then wet her lips on the Cognac and grabbed her board.

"I appreciate everything you've done for me," she said. "But I'm done."

"Work here," Sly Boy said, spreading his hands. His cuff links flashed in the soft lighting. "Gracie says she wants fewer hours, so I'm going to need another emcee—you know, someone to introduce the talent, ad lib with the audience. I'd be prepared to give you a shot."

"Hmm. And this won't be that thing," Kitty said, "where I start emceeing, then I do a couple of runs to help you out, then a couple more, and the next thing I know, I'm back to slinging glass for East Hollywood lowlifes?"

"This won't be that thing. I might get you to bartend a couple of shifts a week, since you'll be on the payroll, and a pretty face working the bar is never a bad thing." A lighter expression touched Sly Boy's face. "There's only one catch."

"Yeah?"

"You've got to like jazz."

"I *do* like jazz."

"All right, then." Sly Boy raised his glass. Kitty raised hers. They touched, nodded, and sipped to seal the deal. "Start on Monday. It's a slower night. You can learn the ropes."

"Thank you," Kitty said.

"You'll be good for this place."

The band hit a crescendo and came out of it swinging. Sly Boy finished his Cognac, said good night to Kitty, then retreated to his office. Kitty watched him go, idly spinning a wheel on her skateboard. He was unlawful, crooked, and cowardly, too. But he'd also offered his hand—shown generosity. Despite his shortcomings, Kitty thought he wasn't such a bad guy.

Kitty was wrong.

5
ROCK STEADY

A heat haze blanketed L.A., shimmering from the hills to the ocean. Beyond this, the sky was a scuffed blue, punched through the center by a fat, angry sun. Phone in one hand, water bottle in the other, Kitty jogged around her neighborhood, a three-mile circuit, culminating in the hill that led to her apartment.

Luke was reversing out of his driveway, soul music floating from the Caliber's speakers. Not Lisa Hayes, Kitty noted. This was *old* soul, the kind her nana listened to. Luke saw her and turned it down.

"Hey, Kitty." He dropped the transmission into park—blocking half the street—and motioned her over. "Got your phone?"

"Yeah." It was still in her hand. She held it up.

"Okay. Take this number down."

Kitty nodded, catching her breath, then opened her contacts and punched in the number as Luke read it off his own phone. He did so slowly—had to start over twice. Kitty noticed the tremor in his voice, the wetness around his eyes. Dude had been crying.

"That's Milly Morello." He spelled her surname. "She's with

Sequoia, a new agency. They don't have as much clout as WME or CAA, but Milly is building her list, and looking for actors of color."

"Oh shit, Luke. That's *lit*. That's . . ." Kitty was tired after her run, but suddenly didn't feel it. She beamed, jumped on the spot. "Thank you."

"Think nothing of it," Luke said, wiping a tear from his cheek. "Milly's expecting your call."

"She is? Oh Jesus." Kitty inhaled and her chest filled, the motion lifting her to her toes. "You have any advice?"

"Yeah," Luke said, and tapped the side of his nose. "Snort a line of canary before going in."

"Right," Kitty said, and raised one eyebrow. "I just need to rob a bank first."

Canary was the chic new drug in Hollywood. Dubbed a "power nootropic," it boosted confidence, concentration, and calmed the nerves, and was used primarily as a performance-enhancing drug by celebrities. It was highly sought after, highly illegal, and the price—$800 a gram—kept it exclusive to the Tinseltown elite.

"Just be yourself," Luke said, wiping another tear away. "Do *not* kiss ass. Act like you have every right to be there, but don't be arrogant."

"I won't."

"You have a demo reel?"

"No."

"We'll work on that. In the meantime, get new headshots, if you haven't already. Spend some money on them. It'll be worth it. There's a great guy—Antonio Senza—in Toluca Lake. Make him your first call."

"Got it," Kitty said.

A car approached, having to steer around Luke's Caliber. The driver punched the horn and glared.

"Fuck you, buddy," Luke said under his breath, and then, to Kitty, "I should get out of the road."

"Wait a second." Kitty stepped closer, leaned down, hands on her knees. "Is everything okay?"

"Yeah, I—"

"You look . . . upset."

Luke stared blankly through the windshield. The creases across his brow deepened. "A good friend of mine passed away this morning."

"Oh, Luke. I'm so sorry."

"I was expecting it. He was old. Cancer. Still . . . it's tough, you know?"

Kitty nodded.

"We started out as drinking acquaintances, meeting up every few weeks to share a pitcher and shoot the breeze. But these last few years, he became the most important person in my life." Luke blinked his wet eyes and exhaled from some lonely place deep inside. "Funeral will be sometime next week. I'm heading to Inglewood now to check in with the family, see if there's anything I can do to help."

"I'm sorry," Kitty repeated. She didn't know what else to say. Everything seemed empty, even more so when she was clearly on a high. She stammered for a moment, and was spared further awkwardness when two vehicles approached, one from each direction. They slowed, then made an impatient drama out of navigating around Luke's car. No horns this time, but one of the drivers—a barrel-sized woman—shot Kitty the bird.

"I think that's my cue," Luke said. "Fucking L.A."

Kitty retreated to the opposite sidewalk. She waved with the empty water bottle, and was about to take the steps leading up to her apartment building when she thought of something to say. Something meaningful.

"Luke?"

"Yeah?" He had the car facing east, looking at her over his shoulder.

"If you want some company at the funeral . . . if you need . . . you know, a friend." Kitty offered a small but sincere smile. "I'll be there for you."

His expression illuminated from within, as if all the lights inside his skull had been flicked on at once. "Really?"

"Really."

She'd seen him smile before, but never like this. It was a thing of near-beauty. He turned the music back up—a song Kitty recognized: "Rock Steady," by Aretha Franklin. She used to dance to this at her nana's house in Phoenix Hill, and Nana danced, too, twirling beautifully, endlessly, across the cluttered living room. This memory, and Luke's genuine smile, lifted laughter from Kitty's soul.

"Good luck with Milly," Luke said. "And for God's sake, don't tell her you know me."

He pulled away, soon gone. Kitty ran up to her apartment, still laughing. Once inside, she found "Rock Steady" on Spotify and turned it up loud.

Kitty called Antonio Senza and her luck continued; Antonio had a six-week waiting list, but there'd been a cancelation and she scored an appointment for Wednesday morning. She then took several deep breaths and called Milly Morello—or rather, Milly Morello's assistant, who was succinct and clinical, and who booked Kitty "a slot" (a term Kitty didn't care for—it certainly wasn't a "lunch meeting") at 2:25 P.M. "sharp," on Friday.

The call with Milly's assistant had taken some of the wind out of Kitty's sails, but certainly not all. She video-called her mama next, and squealed all the way to Kentucky.

• • •

Friday, 2:24 P.M.

Kitty sat in the Sequoia waiting room, her eyebrows threaded, her fingernails painted, a dash of makeup accentuating her lips and cheekbones. She wore a jean jacket over a vintage Rolling Stones tee, black jeggings, slip-on Nikes. Cool, comfortable, totally Kitty. She'd left the skateboard at home, though.

Her appearance was only a small part of it. How she conducted herself during the meeting would be make-or-break. Kitty wasn't going in cold; she'd done her homework on Milly Morello (all hail Google), looking to see who she represented (nobody big . . . *yet*) or if there were any red flags to be aware of. She found none. Milly had been in the industry less than a year, barely time to form a reputation, good or otherwise.

There was common ground, though. Milly was thirty-two years old, of Puerto Rican and African American descent. She had moved to Los Angeles from Louisiana when she was twenty-four. Before becoming a talent agent, she'd studied contract law at UCLA and modeled for several well-known fashion companies.

Kitty's strategy was to be cool, be herself, and use their common ground to build rapport. She planned to highlight her ambition—keeping it grounded—and her willingness to work hard. She had envisioned a professional but friendly twenty-minute meeting with a positive result ("*Manifest*," her mama had screeched during their video call. "Manifest the shit out of that, baby girl."). By 2:45, she would have a Hollywood talent agent.

It didn't quite go to plan.

"Don't sit down," Milly said the very second that Kitty—smiling confidently, quaking inside—walked into her office. "I have a meeting in fifteen minutes, which gives you . . ." She clicked her Fitbit. "Forty-five seconds."

"Oh. Okay." Kitty's confident smile cracked and started to slide off her face in small pieces. Her game plan dropped out of her skull, suddenly, and with a whooshing noise, like an elevator with a broken cable. "I'm . . . Kitty . . . Kitty Rae. Twenty-four years old. I'll be twenty-five in two months."

What Google didn't reveal (fuck Google) was that Milly Morello had an aura like jagged ice and a habitual squint, which tinged every expression with impatience. She wore heavy bracelets on her left wrist that jangled distractingly whenever she moved. Her fingernails were filed to points.

"I'm originally from Louisville, Kentucky," Kitty blathered, aware that every word out of her mouth was like rain on an umbrella. "I live in Los Angeles now, in Silver Lake. I've been here for—"

"Skip all that, Kitty," Milly snapped. "What makes you special?"

"Special?" Kitty shook her head. "What—"

"You have no industry accolades, no notable acting credits, and a limited social media presence." Milly shrugged. Jingle-jangle. "So what can *you* bring that no other actor can?"

"I, um . . . well, I—"

"And bear in mind that you're stuttering already."

"Little nervous," Kitty gasped. She held the envelope with her new headshots inside close to her chest, feeling them flex and bend. An interior voice—calling to her from the other end of a long tunnel—urged her to calm down and take control.

"You're nervous now?" Milly leaned across her tidy, organized desk and squinted. "How are you going to feel when you're auditioning in front of David Fincher or Jordan Peele? Or when you've been on set for ten hours, and you're tired, you feel like shit, and you know that every mistake you make—every second you waste—is costing the studio money?"

"I can do this," Kitty said, and chided herself. She sounded so *small*, so desperate.

"I can do this. I've got what it takes. All I need is one chance." Milly held up a finger with each banal assertion. "I've only been in this profession for ten months, Kitty, and believe me, I've heard it all before."

Kitty took a deep breath, already resigned to the fact that this meeting—this forty-five-second "slot"—had gone terribly wrong, that she would have to put it down to a learning experience, and maybe get Luke to pull another favor. She felt frustrated, as if she'd let herself down, when really she hadn't been given the opportunity to do much more than stutter.

But she didn't spend an hour on a stinking city bus, and shell out four hundred dollars on headshots, only to stand shaking by this jangly bitch's door. She stepped forward, showing some personality at last, and tossed the envelope onto Milly's desk. They were *good* photographs. Antonio had spent two hours with her, and had found mannerisms, moments, *lights*, that even Kitty didn't know she had.

"Someone is going to discover me," she said. Her voice still trembled, but there was some fuel beneath it, at least. "If it isn't you, it'll be someone else."

Milly nodded, and was that an approving look in her eye? She picked up the envelope, removed the photographs, shuffled through them—laid a couple out on her desk.

"You're a beautiful woman. Jesus, it'd take makeup an hour to dull those cheekbones." A smile—a distinct hint of warmth—at last. She sat back in her chair. Jingle-jangle. "You *look* like a star. But, sweetie, my roster is full of stars. It's a veritable galaxy."

"I've got more than looks," Kitty said.

Milly's phone buzzed. She glanced at it. "My Lyft is here." She grabbed her MacBook, her phone, her purse, then gathered up Kitty's headshots, juggling everything as she got to her feet. "Walk with me."

They left Milly's office, swept through the waiting room, then down a single flight of stairs to street level. Milly talked throughout, while rearranging her armload of items and texting her Lyft driver.

"Passion. Determination. Talent. All essential qualities, but in Hollywood, all very *common* qualities. Jesus, my *mailman* has a demo reel. Do you hear what I'm telling you, Kitty?"

"I do."

"You need something that sets you apart. You absolutely *have* to be able to take it to the next level."

"I can. I will."

"That's your role in this." They stepped outside. The street was too bright, too loud. Traffic clamored. Music thumped from a bar on the corner, where the weekend was already under way. "*My* role is to find you work, assist you with career decisions, and negotiate contracts. I get paid on commission and my rate is ten percent."

Kitty stopped walking—almost took a step backward. She looked at Milly carefully. Was that . . . an *offer?*

"I assume"—Milly thrust the headshots into Kitty's hands—"you have digital copies of these?"

"Yes," Kitty squeaked.

"Upload them to the Sequoia portal." Milly acknowledged her Lyft driver, then gave Kitty a squinty smile and strutted away. "It's not 1995 anymore."

She took a cramped bus back to Silver Lake, churning through her emotions with every slow mile. There were flashes of optimism, nubs of possibility, but she kept returning to Milly's jagged aura, her forty-five-second method of reducing dreams to ashes. It had not been the chilled, sociable get-together she had been hoping for, but had it been successful?

Her mama texted but Kitty wasn't ready to respond. She curled over her phone and opened Facebook, but didn't linger on her own page. Instead, she went to her second-most-visited profile, that of

Courtney Caruso, a near-perfect American. She and her husband, architect Logan Caruso, owned a $600,000 home in Shively, Kentucky. They could afford more, but committed a portion of their income to community efforts. They were outspoken liberals, gun-control lobbyists, advocates for equality and civil rights. Courtney was presently spearheading a statewide campaign to increase the education budget in low-income areas.

Logan had beaten leukemia in 2011, but could no longer have children of his own. (He'd subsequently raised $474,000 for the Leukemia and Lymphoma Society.) Courtney's profile picture was a professional shot of her and Logan (wearing matching sweaters), their fourteen-year-old biological daughter, Madison, and their adopted son.

His name was Levi, and he was six years old.

Kitty touched the boy in the photograph. She closed her eyes, drifted tearfully, but kept her fingers on the screen.

Passion Hour. The setting sun dressed the street in burnt orange, a touch of pink. The palms chattered busily. Kitty hovered at her window, lost in the moment, given to her thoughts. Before long, she stood in a dark, silent room, only realizing this when her phone buzzed to life and cast its blue light.

It was a text. No name, just a number she half recognized. Kitty read it, wondering if it might be from Milly. It wasn't.

I sent a car 2 pick u up it'll b there in 15

Kitty frowned, read the message twice, then matched the confident—*arrogant*—tone to the number and came up with a face. He flowed through her mind, flaunting his disarming smile, twirling the prongs of his beard.

She texted back: sorry busy

It didn't take Johan long to respond: car is a limo. And a moment later: we're going somewhere special but u don't have 2 dress up. just b kitty

This prompted a smile, as surprising as it was welcome. Kitty's fingers dithered above the keypad. She started to write something, then deleted it. Her thoughts and feelings were at odds. She threw the phone onto the sofa, looked at it for a full minute, then picked it up and, perhaps against her better judgment, texted back:

where r u taking me

The reply came within seconds:

higher ground

6

HIGHER GROUND

Johan had a new tattoo on the back of his left hand, written in the Younger Futhark. He took great pride in his heritage, and felt a savage connection to his Norse ancestors. Other tattoos across his body included Ouroboros, the Horn Triskelion, and the Helm of Awe. Odin's twin ravens—Huginn and Muninn—flew across his chest, and Yggdrasil, the tree of life, spanned his broad back. Women had journeyed his naked body and asked what each one meant. Others had asked about the weapon mounted over his bed, and he told them: it was a replica of Krókr, a bearded ax wielded by his forefathers, and rumored to have opened the skulls of a thousand men.

"This is beautiful," Thiago said, pointing at the new tattoo. "What does it mean?"

He was sitting with his new husband, Enzo, on the opposite side of the limo. Both were dressed in Canali suits, one royal blue, one gray windowpane. They had matching Ivy League haircuts, slick with product. Johan could smell the oils they'd worked into their thin, freshly waxed bodies. Xander Cray—his driver and one-man security detail—was also present, along with Liberty Mendoza, a YouTube star who made headlines last year when, high on coke, she'd driven her Maserati into the *Torso* statue on Rodeo.

There was a magnum of Cristal in an ice bucket on the cocktail bar. There had been molly, too, up until a few minutes ago, but Johan had asked them to clean the colorful little pills away. He had his own product, of course—Xander was holding on to it—but he wasn't going to waste it on these starfuckers.

"It means the hungry wolf will always hunt."

Johan looked at the tattoo, the runes written in a clear, straight line. It was still healing. He ran one finger lightly over the raised, scabby skin, enjoying the cracked feel. It was as if this part of him were emerging from a cocoon. There had been other transformations over the years. The tattoos, yes, but also his body shape, his power. He might have been a chubby, unremarkable young man working at his father's computer hardware company, in the mailroom to begin with—to build character; his old man was so uncreative—and gradually working his way up to the big seat. Johan became a different creature, though, the same genus, but more relentless, more breathtaking.

"You forge," he'd said to his father not so long ago, "I wield, but we both know the sword."

"Wield?" Aksel Fly had laughed and looked at Johan over the top of his computer screen. "You make annoying videos and post them online. You know nothing of the sword."

Johan was content for his father to believe that.

The limo stopped smoothly. Liberty asked, "Who is this girl, anyway?" Johan ignored her. She even ignored herself, flopping back into her seat, grinding her jaw. "Silver Lake fucking *stinks* of skunk. You ever notice that?" The molly was kicking in.

Johan looked out the window, at the light squeezing between the blinds in the third-floor apartment. He smiled, glanced at his phone. Fifteen minutes since he'd texted. Right on time.

"You want me to get her?" Xander asked.

Johan leaned out of his seat and poured two flutes of champagne. "No. She'll come to me."

Her apartment light flicked off a moment later, then she was on the front steps, moving hesitantly toward the limo. The driver stepped out. He opened the rear door for her.

Kitty crouched, looked inside before committing.

"Sweetie!" Enzo said colorfully, and beckoned.

Johan smiled and offered the champagne.

Johan had Xander take the seat beside his so that Kitty had to sit next to Liberty. He did this for two reasons: one, so that Kitty wouldn't feel uncomfortable, and two, so that he could look at her without turning his head.

"I'm sure you remember Xander," Johan said, gesturing toward his mean and muscled assistant. Kitty nodded awkwardly, no doubt recalling the violent incident at Fusion 44, and perhaps surprised to see him riding in the back of the limo, as opposed to behind the wheel.

"I remember," Kitty said.

Johan continued with the introductions, then raised his glass. Kitty nodded, whispered, "Hi," and "Hello," and raised hers. She sipped and sat stiffly in her seat.

"Your *hair*," Thiago gushed.

"I change it up," Kitty responded, a flutter in her voice. "I've had it like this awhile, though. True to my roots."

"What do you do?" This was Liberty.

"For work?"

"Yeah, for work."

Kitty glanced at Johan. He sensed her discomfort, and offered his best nonjudgmental smile. Ruben Osterfeld—Sly Boy's muscle—had run a few jobs for Johan recently, and had told Johan that Kitty was no longer on raccoon duty, that Sly Boy had her emceeing at Fusion 44. A step sideways, as far as Johan was concerned. No garbage cans, but a servant's wage.

As he'd told Kitty before, she deserved better.

"I work at a jazz club," she replied without embellishment.

Johan nodded approvingly. He'd suggested in his text that Kitty be herself, and she was, from her natural hair to her $60 sneakers. Good for her.

"Oh." Liberty was also being herself. "You look like more."

"I'll take that as a compliment." Kitty leaned forward, angling away from Liberty. She looked at Johan. "Where are we going?"

It was Enzo who replied. "A housewarming extravaganza. Barrett Lorne has a new place in Bev Crest."

"Barrett Lorne?" Kitty asked. "The actor?"

Johan replied, "He's a fan of my work."

The limo rolled west on Sunset, the dark, soundproofed windows softening the city's edges. Enzo touched Thiago's chest where his shirt was unbuttoned. Liberty ground her teeth and selected glam metal from the limo's streaming service.

"This?" Kitty smiled at Johan, indicating his beard by gesturing at her own chin.

"This." He ran a hand beneath his jaw, cupping his beard, which he'd woven into a thick, single braid and adorned with a wooden bead. Kitty had never seen it dressed up. He winked at her. "True to my roots."

"And a new tattoo?" She tapped the back of her left hand.

"You've been paying attention to me, Kitty. I'm flattered."

"Tattoo's healing. *Has* to be new." A glimpse of her teeth. She'd relaxed quite a bit. "What does it mean?"

Johan considered his response to Thiago. *The hungry wolf will always hunt.* With Kitty, he opted for a less dramatic interpretation.

"It means never give up."

The limo took a series of switchbacks into the hills, then coasted a private road crowded by California pepper trees, their leaves stroking the bodywork like hands. It ended at a wrought-iron gate that yawned inward. A narrow, S-shaped driveway led to the house: a 1930s Spanish eclectic on half an acre, with an aviary in the garden bristling with multicolored birds, and movie stars smoking weed around a cascading water fountain.

They stepped into a broad foyer, greeted there by Barrett Lorne's assistant, who took a group photo on her phone—"God, you're all so beautiful. I *hate* you!"—before directing them to a long table lined with champagne and pre-rolled joints.

His entourage grabbed their fill, except for Kitty, who hung back. Johan ushered her in. He whispered in her ear, "You belong here." She selected a flute of champagne and a short joint, which she tucked into her pocket. Johan took a glass, clinked it against Kitty's, then snapped a selfie with her in front of the double staircase.

"You mind if I share?" he showed her the photo.

"Go ahead."

He posted it to his socials and watched the likes escalate. "You're famous already." He clinked Kitty's glass again. Paul Rudd stepped into the foyer behind them. Barrett's assistant greeted him, took his photo.

"God, you're so beautiful. I *hate* you!"

They walked through Barrett's new home, full of jungle-like

plants, shiny furniture, and Japanese art. The killer robot from *Fall of Adam*—Barrett's sci-fi spectacular—stood sentinel in the living room, its lights flashing menacingly. There was live music outside, guests in the pool, a fire-breather on the lawn. Servers circled with rich platters balanced on their palms.

Liberty saw someone she knew and sashayed away. Thiago and Enzo were not far behind, leaving only Xander and Kitty. Her eyes shone.

"Okay," she said, turning to Johan. "Color me impressed."

He smiled. "You want a drink? I'm sick of champagne."

"I want you to tell me why you brought me here."

Johan started around the pool and toward the bar, a glittering setup of bottles, glasses, and chilled beers. Kitty and Xander followed. There were A-listers everywhere—actors, directors, musicians. Essie Elliot was onstage with the band. Jennifer Lawrence snapped photos of the fire-breather, standing close enough to shy from the heat.

"My business has expanded over the past twelve months," Johan said, slowing so that Kitty could catch up to him. "I need good people, and people who *look* good. It's rare—in my field—to find someone who's both."

"You don't know me," Kitty said. "You don't know that I'm good."

"I'm willing to take a chance."

He ordered whiskeys for him and Xander, and a mojito for Kitty. They'd each taken only a sip when Barrett Lorne approached. He was jittery—high on the atmosphere. A dark V of sweat extended down the back of his shirt.

"Are we good?" he asked Johan. He didn't so much as glance at Kitty and Xander.

"We're good," Johan said.

"Okay, let's go."

Barrett started toward the house and Johan followed, gesturing for Kitty and Xander to come with. They'd taken only half a dozen steps when Barrett stopped, shaking his head.

"No, fuck that." His unsteady gaze passed over Kitty and Xander, then settled on Johan. "Just you."

"They go where I go." Johan stroked his braided beard and looked around. "Or we can do it right here, if you'd prefer."

Barrett dragged a palm across his face and wrinkled his nose. "Fine." Spittle popped from between his lips. He'd battled a Colombian drug cartel on-screen, as well as predatory robots and Mexican banditos, but he couldn't handle Johan. To have power over the powerful was a fine feeling indeed.

They entered the house, Barrett walking purposefully, pausing only for him to stumble his way through greeting Channing Tatum—"Hey, man, yeah . . . thanks for coming, everything's out . . . you know, out . . ."—and then ascending a back staircase to the third floor. An arched hallway led from there to a small room on the east side of the house. Barrett clearly wanted to do this far away from his guests, as if him being a canary-head were some big secret. He'd cut his teeth on mindless action movies like *The Zero Faction* and *Dynamite City*, in which he did little more than point a Kel-Tec and grunt. His last picture, *A Kind of Truth*, was a box-office sizzler, earning $780 million worldwide. Moreover, Barrett's performance garnered universal praise. Kerry McDaniel from *The Hollywood Reporter* wrote, "I have seen Barrett Lorne in a different light, and it is blinding."

That light had a scientific name: Citromantyl-V4.

Several framed one-sheets were stacked against the wall, ready to be hung around the property. Barrett lifted one of them—*A Kind of Truth*, ironically—and placed it glass-up on a cardboard box. He turned to Johan and made a grabbing motion with his hand.

Johan nodded at Xander, who stepped forward, pulling an ounce bag of yellow powder from the inside pocket of his jacket. Barrett snatched it from Xander's hand. "Fuck, yeah!" He tore the bag open, spilling powder down the front of his shirt and across the glass. "Fuck, *fuck*." He pulled his wallet from the pocket of his chino shorts, plucked out a twenty, and handed it to Kitty. "Roll this." He dropped to one knee, shook out a spoonful of the powder, and used his platinum AmEx card to shape it into a fat rail.

Xander held Kitty's mojito while she rolled the twenty into a tight tube. Once finished, she handed it to Barrett, who took it and bowed servant-like to the glass. He had tough-guy good looks, sculpted features, a body like rock. On-screen, he appeared larger than life. Johan was altogether sold on him being able to dispatch killer robots and gun-toting gangsters. Now, on his knees, snorting a line of yellow chemicals up his left nostril, he looked incredibly small.

"That's what I'm talking about." He blinked, sniffed through his nose, then exhaled easily. "Yeah, there it is."

The change in him was quick, a matter of seconds. His shoulders dropped, his jitters diminished, the muscles in his face and neck relaxed. He got to his feet and blinked again, as if he'd just inserted contact lenses, ready to see the world more clearly.

"You're all very welcome here," he said, and displayed his best Hollywood grin. "Chill out. Stay awhile. It's a beautiful evening."

"Thank you, Barrett," Johan said.

"My pleasure." He brushed the spilled powder from the front of his shirt, then pinched his nose and sniffed a couple of times, clearing the yellow ring from inside his left nostril. There was no longer any sign that he'd taken the drug, and there'd be no negative side effects. No twitching, grinding, or scratching. He was good to go—a new Barrett Lorne, confident and in control—and would be until the party wrapped.

Johan looked at Kitty, who regarded him with questioning eyes. He winked at her, then turned toward the door.

"Oh hey, Nancy, my assistant, will pay you when you leave." Barrett smiled warmly. "You met her on the way in, right?"

"We did."

"She's going to hand you an envelope full of cash, but don't make a show of counting it in the foyer. You'll just have to trust that it's all there."

Johan nodded, tipped an imaginary hat, then he, Kitty, and Xander left the actor to clean up. Out in the hallway, Kitty stepped in front of Johan, placing one hand gently on his arm. Her eyes were beautiful brown circles.

"You're a canary dealer?" she asked.

"No." Johan finished his whiskey in one hit. "I'm *the* canary dealer. It's my product."

They started walking again. On the stairway down to ground level, Kitty said, almost under her breath, "You are full of surprises."

Johan said, "We're just getting started."

Maria Kiszka was the ditzy, gap-toothed star of *Tell Me About It*, a sitcom that ran on CBS for three seasons and was dropped around the time Netflix started making waves. Maria played the part of Tiffany Colt, the neighbor's daughter, who always managed to get involved with the lead family's affairs, and was known for her catchphrase, "Well, *IIIIIIIII* didn't do it!" She was the comic relief in a sitcom, the break-in-case-of-emergency role that Peter Riven at *Key Light* called "the cat litter of acting."

When *Tell Me About It* ended, Maria seemed destined to sink into the dark quicksand of obscurity reserved for former sitcom actors. Not the case. She crossed the pond and appeared in the BBC police drama *Heron Quays*—a left-field decision that saved her career. After this, she returned stateside (met Johan) and put in a head-turning performance as a young mother with HIV in an episode of *Echoes Fade*. Her last role, playing a crooked cop in the movie *A Derelict Life*, was already getting Oscar buzz.

She approached Johan beneath a covered lanai away from the pool area, and thus away from most of the guests. There was a polite hug and air-kiss, maybe twenty seconds of pleasantries, then it was down to business. It wasn't nearly as clandestine as Barrett Lorne's backroom transaction. Maria handed Xander an envelope crammed with cash, he handed her a half-ounce bag of canary, which she placed inside her purse. Before stepping away, she looked at Kitty and her mouth wrinkled—the barest hint of shame.

"It's not cheating," she said, and shook her head, perhaps to re-inforce her fragile words. "The light's already inside me. This just helps it shine brighter."

"It's all good, sister," Kitty said.

Kurt Wilborn was next. He'd nodded at Johan a couple of times during the party but didn't approach until after midnight, when half the guests had said their goodbyes. Johan was checking out the nine-foot robot in the living room. Xander was with him, as always. Kitty had struck up a conversation with Samuel L. Jackson and looked entirely enamored.

"This wasn't even in the movie," Kurt said, sliding up beside Johan, hands in his pockets. "It's a life-size model, used as a visual reference. The movie's all CGI."

"Doesn't surprise me," Johan said. "How are you, Kurt?"

"Conflicted," Kurt said.

Kurt Wilborn's career was successfully average—an eighteen-year run of small parts in big movies. He was the scientist in the superhero flick, the married friend in the rom-com, the deputy sheriff in the western. He had one leading role on his résumé, in the gritty crime thriller *Smoke Street*, which was slated for the-atrical release, but went straight to VOD during COVID-19 and bombed. He'd once told *MovieMaker* that the words "ALSO STAR-RING" would likely appear on his headstone.

"Conflicted?"

"I'm not sure I want to use your product anymore." Kurt squeezed one of the robot's huge metallic fingers. His hand was baby-sized in comparison. "I don't think it's helping. I'll always be that guy, you know. That actor. Doesn't matter how well I read for a main part."

"Hey, man . . ." Johan shrugged. "Your life. Your career."

"There's an ethical dilemma, too," Kurt continued. "An *artistic* dilemma. I mean, even if I land another lead role, will that be down to me—you know, my talent—or down to the canary?"

"Canary is a direct line to your potential," Johan said, tapping one finger against his chest. "It takes away any distractions and enables you to do your best work. It's not a genie in a lamp. It can't make wishes come true. It's a nootropic, which are widely used in all industries. Jesus, even college kids use them at exam time."

"It's more than that," Kurt said, scratching the shelf of his jaw. His designer stubble rasped. "If it was just another focus enhancer, you'd have it approved by the FDA, and I wouldn't need to buy it off you like some fucking street kid buying crank."

Johan smiled. "Kurt, I like you. You have a solid career and always do good work. You should be proud of your accomplishments."

"I can't work out," Kurt said, "if that was an insult or a compliment."

"Hollywood needs actors like you, and actors like you don't need my product." Johan nodded at Xander. They stepped away from the giant robot. "I'll be here a couple more hours. Don't leave without saying goodbye."

Kurt *did* say goodbye, not thirty minutes later. His parting gift was two $5,000 straps in a royal blue deposit bag. Xander checked the money, then handed Kurt a little something in return.

"Fuck ethics," the actor said to Johan. His breath smelled of whiskey where it hadn't before. "In this town, that's like clutching a rosary in hell."

1:40 A.M. The live band had wrapped, the caterers were packing up, there were several guests dotted around the garden, finishing their drinks, their joints. Johan kicked off his shoes, peeled off his shirt and jeans, and dove into the pool wearing only his underwear. The water was a cool remedy.

He glided across the bottom, sleek as a ray, coming up for air and then diving again. Kitty had taken a seat poolside, watching him, smoking the joint she'd tucked into her pocket earlier. She exhaled a ribbon of smoke and smiled.

"Shouldn't swim with a new tattoo," she warned when he stepped out a moment later. "That's what I heard."

"It's mostly healed," Johan said. He gave his head a little shake to get the water out of his ears. "Besides, I couldn't resist."

He grabbed a thick white towel from a caddy, dabbed his new tattoo first, then dried his upper body, working slowly, flexing every exposed muscle. When he'd finished, he wrapped the towel around his waist and took a seat next to Kitty.

She offered her joint. He declined. She took another hit and gestured through squinted eyes at his torso.

"Got some ink, son."

"Yeah." Johan squeezed water from his beard, feeling it flood the gaps between his fingers. "They're a part of me. Part of my heritage."

"So this whole Viking thing . . . it's real?"

"Absolutely. I'm twenty-eight years old, the first Fly to be born in North America, but my lineage is one hundred percent Danish." Johan peeled wet hair from his forehead and smiled. "You just have to look at me to see that."

"Fly." Kitty blew smoke as she said this. "Is that a common Danish surname?"

"No. It was probably anglicized somewhere along the way. My grandfather was able to trace it back eleven generations, to the late seventeenth century. Our DNA goes back further, though. Genetic ancestry testing has us linked strongly to Scandinavia from before the time of the Vikings."

"So you're the real deal."

"Pure Viking blood."

"And you believe in the Norse gods? Odin . . . Thor?"

"They're no less believable than any other god. Here . . ." Johan pointed out the detailed birds inked across his chest. "Huginn and Muninn, Odin's ravens. They were information gatherers, connected to Odin's thought and memory. His consciousness."

"And this one?" Kitty gestured at the tree that covered Johan's back, its intricate branches spreading onto his shoulders and down both arms.

"Yggdrasil," Johan said, leaning forward so that she could see it more clearly. "The tree of life. It holds the nine worlds together, and its branches reach up to the heavens."

"Yeah. Okay." Kitty drew on the joint, held the smoke in, let it out with a small, tight cough. "You are the real deal. No doubt, man."

Voices from behind. More guests were leaving. Johan saw Thiago and Enzo canoodling on a chaise longue, still high on molly. Over by the lanai, Barrett Lorne was in deep conversation with Channing Tatum. Their famous host was cool and comfortable, the best possible version of himself.

"I hear them sometimes, my ancestors, in my blood. They fascinate me." Johan studied his tattoos, then turned his attention back to Kitty. "I'm drawn to their near-mythical quality, something so outrageous and powerful you wonder if it can even be real. That's what I want. That's how I want people to see me."

"So you became a drug dealer?"

"Drugs are a commodity in this town, like real estate, like land, run primarily by Mexican cartels." Johan shrugged and reached for his shirt. "I'm staking my claim, marking my territory. It's a very Viking thing to do."

"That's one way of looking at it." Kitty took a last pull on the joint, then stubbed it out on the sole of her sneaker and dropped it into an empty glass. "And what's the deal with Xander? You boys go back?"

"Not too far." Johan brushed the grass off his shirt. "A few years. He's my . . . security."

"A Viking with a bodyguard." Kitty looked surprised.

"Viking leaders had their warriors, men who fought relentlessly for them, and would lay their lives down without hesitation." Johan grinned, leaning a little closer to Kitty. "Many of them wore bear- or wolfskins. They were known as berserkers."

"Is that what Xander is? Your berserker?"

"He is whatever I want him to be. A driver, a bodyguard, an enforcer. But mostly he's *trustworthy*—a rare and valuable quality."

Kitty nodded. The muscles in her face had relaxed. She stretched out her left leg and rolled her foot, watching the tip of her sneaker make small circles. Johan thought of the girl on the skateboard, the *raccoon*, so cool and resilient. *You're too dangerous*, she'd said to him. And look at her now. He could hold out his hand and she'd hop right in. He could tuck her into his pocket and carry her home.

"Now you." He smiled and slipped into his shirt. "Tell me something about you that I don't already know."

"There's a lot about me you don't know."

"One thing." He held up his index finger. "Just one."

Kitty inhaled deeply. Her eyelids were at half-mast, her mouth tilted into a smile somewhere between stoned and sad. "Okay. One thing." She looked at him for a second, then her eyes flicked away. "I have a six-year-old son."

"A son?" Johan tried not to sound too surprised. "Really? Back in—"

"Kentucky, yeah."

"With his dad?"

"No." Kitty drew one knee onto the recliner, wrapped both arms around it, and hugged it close. "I was eighteen when I had him. Young and stupid. His father was in prison. I lived with my mama. No money, no job. I knew I couldn't offer him any kind of life, and I wanted him to have everything—or at least a shot at everything. So I gave him up for adoption."

Johan buttoned his shirt. Water trickled from his hair, down his back.

"He lives now with a beautiful, wealthy, very white family." Kitty chewed her lower lip and gazed across the pool. "And in every photograph of him I see, he's smiling, which makes my heart ache, and fills it with joy."

"Do you have any interaction with him?" Johan asked.

"I relinquished all parental rights," Kitty replied. "But I chose the family, and they're very nice, super-liberal. The door is open, you know?"

Johan nodded.

"It has to be on my son's terms, though. When *he's* ready. I just . . ." Kitty trailed off, then breathed out slowly and fanned her eyes. After a moment, she looked at him. Her face was still relaxed, but her smile had returned. "This has been one of the greatest nights of my life, you know that?"

"I know that."

Kitty angled her head, cocked an eyebrow.

He said, "I promised you higher ground."

"Sam Jackson, Jennifer Lawrence, Barrett Lorne." She spread her arms. "You delivered."

"Not yet." Johan retrieved his jeans. He dug into one of the pockets and took out a baggie of yellow powder. He held it up and grinned. "You ready for some real star power?"

He shook a little—a bump—into his palm, used his fingernail to group it, then held it out to Kitty. She closed her left nostril and snorted through her right. Johan smiled, feeling her damp mouth against his skin. It was like feeding a sick animal. A lamb, maybe.

Kitty sat up, rubbing her nose. "That . . . that . . ." Her eyes cleared suddenly. She looked slowly from left to right, taking it all in, then up at the sky. "Okay, yeah . . . that feels *good*."

"You're tweeting," Johan said. "That's what the movie stars call it. And the best part: there are no external symptoms. You look perfectly natural."

"Nobody can tell?" Kitty looked down at her body, running her hands over her stomach. "Because I feel like I'm a hundred feet tall."

"And yet in total control," Johan said. "There's no comedown, either. No crash."

"I dig it." She looked at him, frowning. "How did you *do* this?"

His usual vague response: "I know a man."

Kitty stood and walked around the pool, where the ground rose slightly, offering views across Franklin Canyon and the city beyond. Everything winked and flashed. Even the darkness wanted to shine.

"I could pick this whole city up," Kitty said. Her voice was strong and confident. She made an effortless lifting motion. "Like a record. Put it on a turntable and spin it."

"What would it sound like?"

"Whatever I *want* it to sound like." She grinned. It lit a fire beneath her skin. Then she cocked her head, listening. "Talking of sounds . . . can you hear the birds?"

Kitty dashed along the side of the house, whipping through the lilacs and sunflowers. Johan—barefoot, buttoning his jeans—struggled to keep up. She stopped at the aviary, her fingers laced through the wire mesh, gazing at the flecks of color within the dark canopy. The sound was exhilarating.

"I heard Barrett used to own a tiger," Johan said. "Birds are safer."

Kitty scrolled along the side of the aviary until she found the door. A simple hook-and-eye device kept it closed. She flipped it and stepped inside. The birds responded. A flurry of greens, yellows, and blues. Kitty closed the door behind her and spread her arms.

She stood motionless. Johan thought the birds might land on her arms and shoulders but they didn't. After several minutes, their excitement ebbed. A lovebird swooped close to Kitty and she whipped out her hand, quick as a cat, and plucked it from the air.

"Everything inside me . . . if it isn't complete, it can be." She cupped the bird tenderly, stroking one thumb along its bright feathers. "Nothing is broken."

The limo took them home. Kitty sat next to Johan, singing along to the music. "I remember every word," she said. Thiago and Enzo slept hand in hand across from them, their hair mussed, their Canali suits wrinkled. Liberty had gone home with one of the stars of *Exit 68*.

It was just after four when they pulled up outside Kitty's apartment. The street moved lazily in the early morning gloom: palm fronds nodding, a gender-fluid pride flag saluting from a fifth-floor balcony. The chauffeur opened the rear door. Johan got out. He offered his hand to Kitty and she took it.

"I'll call," he said.

"You've got my number."

She stepped past him and started up the steps to her apartment. When she reached the top, Johan called out:

"Can I trust you, Kitty?"

She stopped, looked over her shoulder. It was too dark to read her eyes. "You can trust me."

Johan watched from the sidewalk until she was inside her apartment building, then got back into the limo and went home.

He waited three days—just long enough for her to wonder if she'd been cast aside—then texted:

> have 2 deliver a script 2 casey cookmans assistant in w hollywood. U wanna do it???

It didn't take Kitty long to respond.

7

NO CRIME WITHOUT A BODY

Floyd Tallent's funeral service was held at Inglewood Park Cemetery. It was a sweet and soulful affair, comprised of family and friends. Luke was there with Kitty, and he was grateful for her presence. She wore an off-shoulder black dress and her hair was braided, coiled at the back, which opened her face magnificently. Luke wore an old suit with a belt that he had to punch a new hole in—he really needed to put on some weight—and a yellow tie that Val Kilmer had given him one Christmas.

"You might want to walk ahead," Luke had said to Kitty when they arrived, pointing out a small group of photographers that had assembled outside the chapel. "Being seen with me would not be good for your burgeoning career."

"I came here to support you, Luke," Kitty had responded, and had looped her arm through his. "And that's what I'm going to do."

Floyd's great-niece sang Otis Redding's "Pain in My Heart" with a second cousin accompanying on guitar. Every note rang hauntingly throughout the chapel, punctuated by sobs and snivels—Luke's among them. There followed a gospel rendition of "The Old Rugged Cross," then a reading from Thessalonians.

The pallbearers carried Floyd's casket to a hearse lined with white roses. A winding train of mourners then proceeded to a plot in the northeast of the cemetery grounds, where Floyd was laid to rest within singing distance of his old friend Ray Charles.

Floyd had four ex-wives and no regrets. One of these exes—Doris, with a voice that could crack stone—invited everybody back to her house for a drink in Floyd's memory. "We'll play his music. We'll cut some rug."

"Sounds more like a party than just one drink," Kitty observed quietly.

"Yeah," Luke agreed, loosening his tie. "Won't end till late, probably with the LAPD banging on the door."

Kitty plucked her cell phone from the small purse she carried, checked the time, then pressed her lips together and looked at Luke.

"You have to be somewhere?" he asked.

"Not right away, but yeah . . ." She gestured at her black dress and heels. "I got a new job. I should probably go home, lose the funeral clothes."

"Right, yeah." Luke nodded. "A new job, huh? Anything exciting?"

"No. Still couriering." She dropped her phone back into her purse, then lifted her sunglasses to wipe a bead of sweat from beneath one eye. "Different company. Better . . . benefits."

"That's great," Luke said. They walked toward the parking lot, their surroundings keeping an air of serenity, despite the roar of aircraft out of LAX. "I should go raise a glass to Floyd, but I can run you home first, if you want."

"No need." Kitty dismissed the idea with a wave of her hand. "Metro, Uber. I'll manage."

The mid-afternoon sun dropped a dry, inescapable heat. Luke

fanned his shirt collar, trying to circulate the air across his chest. Kitty had produced her cell again, shielding the screen as she pulled up her Uber app.

"Listen, thank you," Luke said. They'd pulled abreast of where he'd parked his car—his crappy, dented Caliber, looking decidedly low-income within a row of newer, shinier vehicles. "I really appreciate you being here today."

"Don't mention it," Kitty said. "I'd go for that drink, but—"

"Hey, no. You've done more than enough." He fanned his collar again. "Hope the new job goes okay."

They embraced briefly, a touch awkwardly, then Kitty headed toward the main gates. Luke dug his keys from his pocket and started for his car. He was lost in thought, trying to remember where Doris lived, so didn't notice the platinum-haired woman getting out of the vehicle parked two away from his.

"Got a thing for Black women, huh?"

Luke fumbled his keys—nearly dropped them. He looked up, surprised, as the woman approached. She wasn't as tall as Luke, but it was close.

"Does she know," she said, motioning in Kitty's direction, "that you're a homicidal maniac?"

Luke wanted to turn and walk away—heck, *run* away—but held his ground, maintaining eye contact as the woman stepped to the very edge of his personal space.

"Hello, wife killer," she said.

"I guess you're still not ready to join the fan club," Luke returned bitterly, gripping his keys so tightly that the notches sawed into his skin. "How've you been, Detective Montecino?"

If being an inch shy of six feet wasn't enough, Tera Montecino was also stocked with muscle that came from buckets of whey protein and a longtime Gold's membership. Luke had firsthand knowledge of that muscle. She'd pushed and shaken him around on multiple occasions. One time, growing impatient with his responses, she had lifted him out of his chair in the interrogation room and pinned him to the wall. "Lying is more painful with a broken jaw," she'd growled. She had an alligator's sleek strength and ferocity.

Her eyes were primer-gray, as if waiting for a color to be applied. A small defect, maybe a scar on the inside of her lip, wrinkled her mouth on one side. Even smiling couldn't iron it out, which, in Luke's experience, she didn't do often. Her hair was her most striking feature (and arguably a more effective weapon than the Beretta 92FS tucked into her side holster). She wore it pinned back on the streets—rigidly, like an old schoolmarm—but let it down in the interrogation room. It was mirror-bright and touched the bottoms of her shoulder blades. Luke had been quite captivated, watching it ripple and shine, and had wondered how many confessions it had coaxed from the mouths of vulnerable suspects.

He loosened his grip on his keys and took a step backward. Montecino followed, as close as she could get without touching.

"You notice anything different about me?" she asked, hands on her hips.

Luke looked her up and down. Brown boots, blue jeans, a red checked shirt beneath a gray sport jacket, and of course the sidearm holstered to her left side.

"You still look like a Tolkien character and dress like Chuck Norris," he said, and managed a dry smile. "So no, I don't notice anything different about you."

"Funny guy." She tapped the right side of her belt. "No shield."

Luke dropped his gaze to where she'd tapped, and saw no LAPD badge. As much as he wanted to show indifference, he couldn't keep the question out of his eyes.

"I'd always planned to retire early," Tera said. "So here I am. New freedom. New adventures."

"I'm thrilled for you," Luke said stiffly. He moved to step around her but she followed again, cutting him off.

"I recently acquired my private investigator license." There was a glint of intent in her otherwise dull eyes. "It's a simple process for an ex-cop; I have a police science degree and the requisite hours of investigative work. I have my PI firearm permit, too." She lifted the left side of her jacket. "A lot of scumbags out there. I'd rather be prepared than sorry."

"Yeah, best way to be," Luke said. "Now, whatever it is you *really* want to say, make it quick."

Montecino sneered—her wrinkled mouth had no problem with that—and finally took a step away from him. He fetched an unsteady breath and held her gaze, breaking it only to blink.

"I'm not *famous* like you." She all but spat the *f*-word. "But I closed my share of high-profile cases—got my name in the *L.A. Times* on more than one occasion."

Luke had never been to Tera Montecino's home. He had no idea where or how she lived, but an image popped into his mind at that moment: a small, lonely apartment, an alcove dressed with police commendations and framed cutouts from the *Times*, a retirement watch in a display case, next to a novelty mug with I SEE GUILTY PEOPLE printed across the front.

"*You* were the one I always wanted, though," she said, jabbing her finger at him. "And *you* were the one that got away."

"No." Luke shook his head. "I lost everything."

"You didn't." She narrowed her eyebrows. "But I have all kinds of time on my hands now. I'm my own boss, without any departmental red tape or bureaucratic bullshit holding me back. And I'm going to use that newfound time and freedom to find out what happened to Lisa Hayes."

"By harassing me?"

"By getting to the truth," Montecino vowed. "And when I do, when you're wearing an orange jumpsuit and eating slop with a paperboard utensil, then you'll know what losing everything feels like."

Luke swallowed hard, uncomfortable in the heat, but more uncomfortable in Montecino's presence. He dragged sweat from the back of his neck and looked at her.

"A good cop will keep an open mind," he said. "I learned that when researching my role for *Out of Midnight*. So I'm curious: Does any part of you believe I *didn't* kill my wife?"

Tera held her thumb and forefinger half an inch apart. "I have this much doubt."

"Okay," Luke said. "*Some* doubt, then."

"Not enough to make a difference," Tera said, and sneered again. "Occam's razor: the simplest explanation—"

"Yeah, I know how it goes." Luke sighed and gave his collar another tug. "Believe me, I want an explanation more than you do, whether it's simple or not."

"I doubt that very much."

"Just let me know if I can help." He stepped around her, jangling his keys as he headed for his car. "This isn't the best time, though. I know you're not great at reading clues, but . . . the suit, the cemetery . . . I'm actually at a funeral right now."

"Floyd Tallent. Pancreatic cancer. Eighty-one years old. The funeral ended"—she checked the time on her cell phone—"sixteen minutes ago. And talking of death, a little bird tells me you tried to kill yourself a couple of months back."

Luke had reached his car door but stopped short of opening it. He looked at Montecino over his shoulder. She stood straight and cool, not a drop of perspiration on her face.

"Did you know that almost half of all mass shooters turn the gun on themselves, or commit suicide by cop?" She shrugged her broad shoulders. "Maybe it's self-loathing, or the fear of infamy—of shame. But some forensic psychologists believe it's the guilt, that they simply cannot live with what they did."

"I'm depressed and lonely," Luke said, surprised to hear himself speaking out loud; Tera Montecino was not a woman with whom he would ordinarily share such truths. "I don't know where I'm going, or what I'm doing. I can't see a future for myself."

Montecino showed nothing. She was unaffected. A piece of flint.

"It was a cry for help."

"That doesn't always work, does it? Crying for help." She stepped forward and dropped her ass onto the hood of his car. She wasn't finished with him yet. "If it did, your wife might still be alive."

Lisa had been missing for 1,134 days. Luke had counted every one of them, and had relived the first several days—sleepless, surreal stretches of time—over and over again.

For him, the nightmare began when he woke up in the woods to find the front of his shirt covered in blood. He'd thought it was his—a nosebleed, perhaps, even though there was no dried blood around his nose. The gaps in his memory were cavernous, but this seemed the most likely explanation. Or maybe he'd gotten into a fistfight and the other guy had bled all over him.

Sure. Why not?

It was only later, when the crime lab had done its work and the blood came back as Lisa's, that Luke began to realize the extent of his trouble.

The volatile nature of their relationship was in full effect on the night she went missing. They were at a party at Uncle Lizard's, a biker-style roadhouse in the Los Padres Forest. It was either a launch or album-wrap party. Luke didn't know which, only that it was busy and loud, and that he and Lisa were drunk when they arrived. They'd gotten a head start at their hotel in Santa Barbara (where they'd also had their first fight of the day), and had downed a bottle of red wine during the twenty-minute limo ride to Uncle

Lizard's. Luke remembered arriving—he'd met Axl Rose outside and they'd stumbled in together. There were a few other celebs present but mainly it was music industry peeps and starfuckers. He remembered doing tequila slammers with the band—whoever the fuck they were—and posing for photographs. Things started getting blurry around midnight. He had vague memories of dancing on a table and snorting vodka out of a spoon . . . of drinking Knob Creek directly from the bottle and flirting with some chubby goth chick outside the men's restroom. Then there was the second fight with Lisa. He had no idea how it had started or who was at fault. His only recollection was of calling Lisa a talentless whore, and of her trying to break a bottle over his head.

This no doubt appeared shocking to their fellow partygoers—and indeed, many would later communicate their shock to the authorities—but it was just another night for Luke and Lisa.

Did they kiss and make up? Luke couldn't say for sure, but he had an imprecise memory of being outside with her . . . close and hot . . . the smell of the forest and of her perfume.

"I don't think it's working," Lisa had said, or maybe he'd dreamed that. Either way, he didn't think she was talking about their marriage. There was something else, something in her eyes . . .

The next thing he remembered was waking up at the foot of a tree, thirty yards from Uncle Lizard's. Morning light sloped through the pines. A jogger crouched over him, plum-faced and wide-eyed.

"Jesus Christ, mister," he said. "I thought you were dead."

"Hnnh . . . whuuggh?"

"Thought you'd taken one to the chest." The jogger gestured at the blood down the front of Luke's shirt. "A bullet, that is."

Luke looked down at his shirt. "Whufuggdat?" He tried sitting up, then shuddered as a thunderclap of pain reverberated through his skull. Instinctively, he reached for the back of his head and felt a good-sized goose egg. No blood, but the skin was tight and tender. He must have gone for a walk in the woods, passed out, and bumped his noggin on the tree trunk.

Getting to his feet was a gradual, painful process. Luke brushed pine needles from his ass, examined the blood down the front of his shirt again, then looked dazedly around.

"What the fuck?"

He tried to remember the night before. There were only glimpses . . . embarrassing flashes . . . indistinct puzzle pieces. Maybe the blow to the back of his head had caused some short-term memory loss. Or maybe it was the disgusting quantity of alcohol he'd consumed.

Okay, yeah, it was *probably* the alcohol, but still . . .

"My wife," he groaned, looking around again, one hand plastered to his forehead.

"Say, you're that actor fella," the jogger said unhelpfully, and snapped a photo on his phone. It was either a lucky shot, or the jogger had a knack for capturing people at their most murderous-looking: Luke, sneering crookedly, standing in a gloomy forest with blood splashed across his shirt. The jogger would later post the shot to social media. Multiple news sources would comment on his impressive camerawork skills, and ask if they could use and distribute the photograph across all media. The jogger said, sure, go right ahead, to the first dozen or so, then wised up and started requesting payment—a decision that made his bank account very happy.

Luke, blessedly unaware of the U-turn his life was about to take, flapped a dismissive hand at the jogger, then staggered off in the direction of Uncle Lizard's. He took out his cell phone and called Lisa. Straight to voice mail. She was probably back at the hotel, he thought, sleeping off her hangover. He then navigated Uber—slowly, through bleary eyes—and ordered a car. It took twenty minutes to arrive. During that time, Luke had the good sense to turn his bloodstained shirt inside out. It wasn't perfect, but it was better.

Lisa wasn't at the hotel, either. She hadn't been back at all. The room was exactly as they'd left it: one bed made, the other (the one they'd had sex in) all messed up, the heavy sheets drooping to the floor. The curtains were pulled closed. Lisa's bathroom shit was still assembled around the sink. Her toothbrush was bone-dry.

He called her cell again. Okay, *now* he was starting to worry. Had she bypassed the hotel and gone directly home? Had she gone to someone *else's* home?

Straight to voice mail.

"Hey, hon . . . it's, umm . . . it's eleven-twenty, and I don't . . . I don't know where you are. That was . . . Christ, that was one hell of a night. Fucking Jesus. I woke up in the . . . Shit, I'll tell you later. Anyway, I'm at the hotel. Give me a call or drop me a text when you get this. Okay? Love you, babe."

He showered, brushed his teeth, and changed into clean clothes. It felt heavenly. He called Lisa again. Voice mail. He packed up their stuff and checked out, but waited in the lobby for two hours. He tried Lisa's cell yet again and still nothing. He texted her:

I tried CALLING you. Waited at the hotel until 2. where the FUCK are you??? I'm going home. CALL ME PLEASE!!

Luke's concern increased as he drove the one hundred miles back to their house in Sherman Oaks. He ran through dozens of possibilities. Maybe she'd finally left him and was cooling off with a sister or friend. Maybe some fucker had roofied her martini and she was tied up on a couch somewhere. Maybe she was still partying, snorting coke in the back of a stretch limo, on her way to Vegas.

He called her name as he opened their front door, not expecting a response and not getting one. He walked through their spacious house, then out to the pool. No sign of her.

His anxiety grew. It crawled onto his shoulders and pressed down. He couldn't eat. He could barely breathe. Desperate, he called Lisa's best friend, her producer, her manager. Nobody had heard from her. Not a single text, and *that* was unusual.

Something had happened to her. Something bad. Luke became more certain of this with every passing minute.

His agent called a little before six. It was Friday. Luke recalled that they'd scheduled a call for that afternoon to talk about the Netflix original he'd signed on to, but that wasn't what this was about.

"What the fuck, Luke?"

"Yeah, sorry I missed our call. I've got other shit on my mind."

"Forget the damn call. You've gone viral. Again."

Marty sent the photograph that the jogger had taken that morning, which had already been picked up by national news groups and speculated upon widely.

"This is nothing," Luke said to Marty, an irritated note in his voice. "I got blind drunk last night and woke up in the woods. Some douchebag took a picture of me. Big fucking deal."

"But the blood," Marty said.

"Yeah. Nosebleed, I guess. I don't know." Luke turned a slow circle, gazing around his lonely living room. His heart thumped heavily. "Listen, I can't talk right now. I haven't seen or heard from Lisa all day. I don't know where she is and I'm starting to freak."

"She's missing?" Marty drew a sharp breath, which was followed by three or four seconds of edgy silence. Maybe Luke was too emotional to grasp the significance of a missing wife and a bloodstained shirt, but Marty was not. He connected the two ominous dots quickly, then stuttered something about having to feed the cat and hung up.

Luke called the police at nine P.M.

Two uniformed officers came to his house. They asked all the right questions and took notes, but Luke expressed dismay at the muted response. He wanted *action*, dammit—search parties, sniffer dogs, fucking helicopters. Lisa was a *celebrity*, for God's sake. The senior officer pointed out that Lisa had been missing for fewer than twenty-four hours, and that she would, in all likelihood, return voluntarily. He suggested Luke get in touch with all of Lisa's family, friends, and associates, and inform the Van Nuys Division of any developments.

"That's it?" Luke asked. "You guys are done?"

"Not quite," the senior officer replied. "The shirt you were wearing. The one in the photograph. Do you still have it?"

Luke dragged a hand down his face, then gestured in the direction of the driveway. "I packed it up with the rest of our shit at the hotel. The bags are still in the Tesla."

"We'd like to take it with us," the senior officer said.

"The shirt? What do you—" Luke stopped abruptly, interrupted by the cold, metallic chime of the penny touching down. "Oh right. Yeah . . . yeah, of course."

Thirty-six hours later, Lisa still hadn't returned and Luke sat in an interrogation room with two detectives, one of them—Tera Montecino—assigned to Van Nuys from LAPD's Detective Support and Vice Division. Montecino had earned a reputation narrowing the gap between unsolved homicide and missing persons cases, and with the blood on Luke's shirt being matched to Lisa's, she was intent on adding to her résumé.

"Lisa is strong, beautiful, and successful. Two platinum albums, two Grammy Awards. After working the club circuit for nine years, she finally has the career she's always dreamed of." Montecino had leaned closer to Luke, her iridescent hair pooling on the table between them. "A woman like that . . . spirited, ambitious . . . she doesn't simply walk away, leave it all behind."

"No," Luke agreed, his voice just above a whisper.

"So . . ." The detective lifted one side of her wrinkled mouth. "What happened to her?"

She showed no sympathy, despite Luke's tears. On the contrary, his damage and confusion fueled her. She circled the table ravenously, pulling and picking at everything he said. She had him go through his version of events multiple times, and asked the same questions from different angles.

"Does Lisa's success threaten you?"

"No."

"I read in an interview that she wants to get into movies. Does *that* threaten you?"

"No."

On and on. Around and around. The minutes crawled into hours, and each increment of time had its own threatening shape and feel. Luke fought to keep his cool, but resisted asking for a lawyer. That would only make him look more guilty. Besides, he wanted to work *with* the police, not against them.

The other cop—Kraemer, a homicide detective—took his turn. He arranged several surveillance-video stills on the table in front of Luke. They showed Luke and Lisa leaving Uncle Lizard's. The time stamps in the top right-hand corner read 1:52 and 1:53.

"This one." Kraemer tapped his finger against a grainy black-and-white shot showing Luke and Lisa heading across the parking lot. From the angle of their bodies, it looked like they were staggering, propping each other up. "You're clearly walking toward the back of the lot. No lights that way. No roads. Nothing except the Los Padres Forest."

"I think we were going to make out," Luke said.

"What are you, sixteen?"

Luke closed his eyes, half remembering the smell of Lisa's perfume, the tangy, Arcadian aroma of the pines. *I don't think it's working.* Had Lisa really said that? Luke shrugged, touching the bump at the back of his head. It was still sore.

"You weren't seen again," Kraemer continued, "until you were photographed the following morning with Lisa's blood all over your shirt."

"Why didn't you destroy the shirt?" Detective Montecino asked, leaning casually against the wall with her arms folded. "You knew it would be incriminating."

Luke wiped tears from his eyes and said, "Because I didn't do anything wrong."

Kraemer asked Luke about his and Lisa's fight at the hotel. He mentioned that the manager was called to their room at 4:24 P.M.

"Loud fight," the detective said.

"Unh . . . kind of average."

"You broke a lamp."

"Lisa broke a lamp."

Kraemer stroked his graying goatee and asked about their *second* fight, at Uncle Lizard's. He showed Luke a video of the altercation that some turd had uploaded to YouTube. "You'll like this bit," he said, turning up the volume in time to hear Luke call Lisa a talentless whore.

"Sounds like true love to me," Montecino noted. Her hair swayed and flashed.

The pressure continued, more of the same questions, the detectives pecking at his answers like hungry birds. Eventually they vacated the interrogation room, leaving Luke to stew. He paced and prayed. He thumped his fist on the table and swore at Lisa, wherever she was.

There *was* something, though. The video clip of their fight at Uncle Lizard's had dislodged a memory. It wasn't complete, but it had substance.

"There was a guy," Luke said when the detectives returned. They appeared fresh and smelled of coffee.

"A guy?" Montecino took the seat opposite him.

He'd looked out of place, Luke remembered. Uncomfortable,

even, standing with his shoulders drawn in and his small mouth pinched closed. Luke would have dismissed him as a socially inept freak, except Lisa had spoken to him, and something about her body language suggested a familiarity, an intimacy.

"Can you describe him?" Detective Montecino asked.

Luke sighed, propping his whiskery jaw up with one hand. "Mexican guy, I think."

Montecino's dull eyes reflected a beat of personality. "Jesus, this motherfucker's as good as caught. Adrian, put out a BOLO for a *Mexican guy*."

Kraemer snickered, shaking his head.

"You don't get it." Luke propped both elbows on the table and linked his hands. "The party was sixty percent white and thirty-nine-percent Black. Not many Latinos. You should ask around. Check the surveillance footage."

"Lizard's is an old biker shithole," Kraemer growled cynically. "Most of the cams don't work, and the ones that do aren't exactly high-definition. You can see that for yourself."

He gestured at the video captures, still arranged on the table. Luke glanced at them. They were black-and-white, low-res. His and Lisa's faces were little more than smudges.

"What else can you tell us?" Kraemer said.

Luke closed his eyes, drawing on his uncertain memory—trying to step into it and see things with a clearer mind. "He was young-ish . . . early thirties, maybe. And kind of shifty-looking. Awkward. Like he'd walked into the wrong place."

"Was he alone?" Montecino asked.

"As far as I could tell." Luke tried to remember if he'd seen the guy earlier that night, talking to anyone else. He didn't think so. It was as if he'd shown up just to talk to Lisa, and had left again.

"What else?"

"Tall . . . for a Mexican. *Tallish*. Five-eleven, maybe six-foot. He was wearing a button-down shirt. Black, I think."

"Distinguishing features," Montecino said, and the tone of her voice suggested she was already bored with this. She tapped her pen impatiently against her notepad. "Was he bald? Did he have facial hair? Scars, tattoos, moles, missing teeth?"

"No, I . . ." Luke closed his eyes again, recalling the familiar way Lisa had leaned in to the guy, her eyes lowered, her mouth close to his ear. Luke's attention had been on his wife, primarily— her jealousy-inducing body language. But yes, he picked out some features. "He had wide cheekbones, but a narrow jaw. And small, close-set eyes. An ugly fucker, really. Kind of . . . bat-faced."

"So we're looking for a shifty, bat-faced Mexican?" Detective Montecino exhaled dramatically and pushed a hand through her elf-like hair.

"Tallish," Kraemer added wryly.

"Okay. We'll bring an artist in, put a sketch together. In the meantime . . ." Montecino pocketed her notepad and pen. "Let's get back to the guy with the blood on his shirt."

And so it continued: the questions, the doubts, the pushing and pressing. Luke took his time and tried to consider every response before speaking, but it got to where he was afraid his words might be unstitched and fashioned into something sinister. Eventually he resorted to answering every question with, "I've told you everything," and, "That's all I know." For Detective Montecino, this wore thin quickly. The gloves came off. She got physical. Kraemer twice had to intervene.

"You killed her and we all know it," she snapped after Kraemer had pulled her off Luke for the second time. Her face burned and her shirt had come untucked at the front. "We just don't know how you killed her, or what you did with her body. But we'll find out."

Luke shook his head and started to cry. He sometimes had to cry on film, but it was nothing like this: large, hot tears bubbling up from his ruined soul, his chest loaded with smoldering rocks, his brain wrapped in gauze.

"No," he whimpered. "No . . . no . . ."

"You think *I'm* tough on you, just wait until you get out of here." Detective Montecino tucked her shirt back into her jeans and flicked the platinum hair from her eyes. "The press, the internet trolls, Lisa's fans . . . there's no limit on how long they can make you suffer."

That was when Luke called a lawyer.

In the eyes of the law, there was no crime without a body. In the eyes of everybody else, Luke was a guilty man. It was exactly how Detective Montecino had predicted: he was tied daily to the trailer hitch of some rumbling black machine and dragged through the hard streets of the press and the internet.

His life collapsed, a magnificent and violent undoing. It was like watching an earthquake in slow motion. Luke saw every building first crack, then crumble. He watched the ground tremble and rift and accept everything that had once been upright.

"Nothing *is* anymore," he'd said to his psychiatrist, the only Hollywood professional who hadn't cut him loose. "Everything *isn't*. My marriage. My career. My fucking Tesla." And it was true. He slept and ate and shat in a crater. Even his friends had stopped calling. No more poker nights with Ben Affleck and the boys. No more movie nights at Tarantino's.

Maintaining his innocence was futile. Luke knew that the only way his life was getting back on track was if Lisa, alive and well, returned home, or if the truth behind her disappearance was uncovered. He made his own inquiries, but to no avail. Lisa's friends and family refused to talk to him. He hacked into her e-mail account (something the police had already done) and worked his way through every correspondence. Too much was at stake for him not to be thorough. He returned to Uncle Lizard's, hoping a critical memory might be jolted into place, but there was nothing.

The press jumped on his "returning to the scene of the crime," but Luke didn't care. There was another reason for going back:

He wanted to ask about the bat-faced man.

It was a long shot, but maybe one of the servers or bartenders remembered him. Maybe they could dig up a credit card receipt, a *name*.

No cigar.

"Cops have already been asking," Vivien said. Vivien was the longtime manager of Uncle Lizard's. Throat tattoos, pierced areola, a sheepdog's mustache. Her claim to fame was putting Evel Knievel on his ass during a bar brawl in Palm Desert. "They spoke to all the staff . . . had one of those, whaddya call 'em, *compost* sketches."

"Facial composite," Luke said. He'd spent two hours with the artist, trying to get the close-set eyes just right.

"Yeah, that." Vivien set her hands on her broad hips. "Didn't help, in any case. Nobody remembered him. Not for sure. It was just too busy that night, and the celebrities outshone everybody else."

Luke wondered how hard Montecino and Kraemer had pushed, when it was clear they didn't believe the bat-faced man even existed. Montecino had even referred to him as *Señor Smokescreen* at one point. Any follow-up—facial composite or not—had been more to cross him off the list than move him up it.

Luke couldn't discount him, though. Maybe the bat-faced man didn't know where Lisa was, but he might have information, and judging by the way Lisa had cozied up to him, Luke believed that was a good possibility.

The investigation continued. Detective Montecino vowed to find Lisa, dead or alive, and bring any guilty party to justice. Five weeks after Lisa went missing, a fire swept across the southwestern region of the Los Padres Forest, leading many to wonder if critical evidence (meaning Lisa's body) had been destroyed. At this point, ironically, things cooled off, but Montecino wasn't ready to let Luke off the hook. She started to follow and harass him—anything she could do to make his life hell. One time she pulled him over for failing to come to a complete halt at a stop sign. She had him exit the car and threw him over the hood to "frisk" him, applying excessive force, leaving bruises on his ribs that didn't fade for weeks.

Luke hadn't seen Montecino for several months—he figured she'd found some other shmuck to persecute—but now here she was, not a detective but a private investigator, with nothing but time on her hands and a cold, bitter box for a heart.

"I checked your IMDb page," she said, shifting her weight across the hood so that his old Caliber creaked on its springs. "Your last credited work was for a video game, *Back Yard Wilderness*. You provided the voice for Wriggles the Caterpillar. Inspiring."

A 737 thundered low, approaching LAX. Luke was grateful for the disruption. He wished that it could hover in place, the roar of its jets melting Montecino's voice into obscurity.

"I must admit," she continued a moment later, when she only had to contend with the hum of the traffic, "it's been immensely gratifying to watch your career implode. It's not justice, but it's something."

"Don't you have any insurance fraudsters to photograph?" Luke asked.

Montecino curled her crooked lip. She got up off the hood, folded her arms, and stared at Luke.

"Okay," he groaned. "What next? How else do you want to beat me down?"

"She looks like Lisa, don't you think?" Montecino gestured at the cemetery gates, where Kitty stood waiting for her ride.

"Because she's Black?" Luke said.

"Because she's attractive. She has the same body type, the same-shaped eyes, a similar facial structure."

"I don't see it."

"Her name is Kityana Rae, but everyone calls her Kitty. Twenty-four years old, originally from Louisville, Kentucky, but now residing in Silver Lake, directly opposite"—Montecino flicked her finger at Luke—"you."

Luke sighed. "She's just a friend."

"A friend. Okay." Montecino stepped toward him—three broad steps and she was in his personal space once again. The finger she'd just flicked in his direction stabbed the air an inch from his nose. "Anything happens to her, Luke, I will chase you down like a hound out of hell. And there *will* be justice. One way or another."

Luke swallowed a gristly knot of emotion, then exhaled shakily and inched backward.

"I'm watching you," the former detective growled, still pointing. She gave her threat a few seconds to sink in, then stepped aside. Luke blinked sweat from his eyes—it hadn't gotten any cooler, that was for sure—and got into his car.

"Always a pleasure," he said to her through the closed window, and then, under his breath, "Fucking bitch."

Montecino kept her eyes locked on him as he gunned the engine and motored away.

8
BIRTHDAY PRESENT

Kitty was a natural in the spotlight. Smooth and comfortable, her delivery exquisite. Sure, it was only Fusion 44, introducing acts like Celsius Seven and Tickles Gabriel, but put a mic in her hand anywhere, shine a stage light on her, and she would rise.

Sometimes, if her body chemistry was out, or if her mood wasn't quite *on*, a pinch of canary gave her the lift she needed. Kitty maintained a small supply, taken from the many bags she delivered for Johan. A dash here, a fingernail there—too insignificant an amount for Johan to ever notice. It wasn't much, and it wasn't often. Kitty knew where the groove was, and usually found it by herself.

Sly Boy had said that she would be good for Fusion 44, and he was right. As well as emceeing, she worked the bar Tuesday and Saturday afternoons. Sly Boy also wanted her to hang out at the place. He'd pay her, he said, just to sit and chill, chat with the patrons. Kitty needed downtime, though, and she was pulling long hours for Johan, zipping between studios, offices, and parties, her backpack lined with bags of yellow powder. It was good work, for the most part, and enlightening. There were more canary-heads in Hollywood than she realized.

Milly landed her an audition to play the "forlorn lover" in the new Otto Lassiter music video. Before going in, Kitty snorted a thin rail of canary. She'd been of two minds about doing this, but it was worth it. She crushed the audition. The only reason she didn't get the gig, Milly explained, was because Otto's latest album hit number one in Japan, and his record company recommended he select an actress of Asian ethnicity.

The long hours were draining, but not without benefit; her bank account was healthier than it had ever been. It occurred to Kitty that she could quit working for Sly Boy altogether and still make enough to get by. She didn't for two reasons. First: She enjoyed working at Fusion 44—loved the high of emceeing to a packed house. It had also become Kitty's social center of gravity. She had started to meet people, and feel that she belonged. The second reason for not quitting was that she needed a legitimate source of income. Being able to hide Johan's "wage" behind her consistent Fusion 44 salary and tips meant that she could pay her taxes, and invite fewer suspicions.

Maybe, if the auditions continued and she scored regular acting work, she could quit *both* jobs. Dreaming big didn't involve introducing jazz acts and running champagne drugs. Kitty aspired to a life that she wouldn't have to quieten—that she could shout from the rooftops, in fact, in a voice loud enough to reach her son's ears.

Ephraim, her former fiancé and the father of her son, had listed ambition as one of Kitty's flaws. "Know your place," he'd said. An unaspiring boor, and what did she *ever* see in him? He'd also said that she was too rash, and while this was not entirely true (she'd carefully deliberated her life's bigger decisions, like moving to L.A., and giving her son up for adoption), she was inclined to moments of impulsiveness. It was all part of her exuberant soul, and she made no apology for it.

Case in point: Eight weeks after she'd started working for Johan—on the morning before her twenty-fifth birthday—Kitty had called her mama, needing to hear a familiar voice and to get a little love from home. Mama had been in good form. She'd explained that she was taking Muncel Stevens to visit with her new baby granddaughter, and later they were all going to Shirley Mae's for barbecued ribs. Kitty had hung up with tears of homesickness stinging her eyes, and before she knew it, she was on a flight back to Kentucky. Spending her twenty-fifth birthday with friends and family seemed not only appealing, but *essential*. Kitty had called Johan and Sly Boy from the airport lounge, to inform them of her impetuous decision. "Yeah, take a couple of days," Johan had said. He sounded stressed, but maybe that was just her. "And happy birthday. I'll get you a little something while you're away."

Kitty spent precisely forty-six hours back home, and they were everything she needed them to be, proving that an impulsive nature was occasionally a good thing. She ate barbecued ribs at Shirley Mae's ("I can't *believe* my baby is here!" Mama kept clucking), then she and a few of the girls hit the town for drinks and dancing. She got happily drunk, shared some of her L.A. stories (omitting her connection to the Hollywood drug scene), and flirted with an ex-boyfriend. On her birthday morning, a flock of them went for breakfast at Shoney's, then for a soul-filling walk in Cherokee Park. Kitty couldn't remember the last time she felt so . . . *replete*. The housewarming soiree at Barrett Lorne's place had been unforgettable, but there was nothing quite like the comfort and familiarity of family.

That afternoon, her sister Connie drove her to Shively, and they parked across the street from a large colonial with tall white columns and a perfectly landscaped yard. A teenage girl with shimmering blond hair shot hoops in the driveway. After a moment, a younger African American boy joined her. The girl was taller and more experienced, but she was kind to the boy, and kept the contest close.

"You okay, sweetie?" Connie asked.

"Yeah," Kitty replied, wiping the tears from beneath her large round sunglasses. "He looks so happy."

"He does. And that's good."

Kitty would never interfere with that happiness, but she vowed to return one day and *add* to it—to be a woman of whom her son could be proud.

She flew back to Los Angeles the following morning, with her heart both empty and full. Her mama had gotten emotional and asked her to stay. "I miss you, baby girl. I *worry* for you out there." A few months ago, Kitty might have been tempted, but L.A. was home now. She was making money, making connections, she had a talent agent.

It was all coming together. Life was good.

And then, in a blink, it wasn't.

Sunday night. She wasn't scheduled to work at Fusion 44 until her afternoon bar shift on Tuesday, but she texted Sly Boy to ask if he wanted her there anyway, seeing as she'd given herself the weekend off. No response from Sly Boy, which wasn't like him. He had his faults, but ignoring texts was not one of them. She gave it thirty minutes, then tried again. Still nothing.

"Netflix and sweatpants, then," she said. "No bad thing." She even had half a bottle of Chardonnay chilling in the fridge. Better and better.

Kitty had just pulled her comfy pants up over her hips when her intercom buzzed. She frowned, wondering who was at her door at this time on a Sunday. Maybe Luke, welcoming her back, although he probably didn't even know she'd gone.

She pushed the talk button in the little box next to her apartment door. "Hello?"

"Happy birthday, Kitty!"

"Johan?"

"I have something for you."

Kitty grinned, pushed the door button, heard the lock disengage downstairs. She checked her reflection in the living room mirror (tired, but passable), picked up her skateboard and leaned it against the wall, then opened her apartment door and waited for Johan to appear. He took the stairs, in no hurry at all—casual, leisurely steps, as if the world would wait for him. Kitty heard those steps getting gradually louder as he ascended from the second to the third floor, then he rounded the corner onto her hallway, carrying a box in his hands—a gift, all tied up with a pretty pink bow.

"Hey," she said.

"Hey."

"That for me?" She pointed at the box, smiling.

"It sure is."

She stepped back into her apartment, holding the door open for him. He entered, looking around as he crossed the living room and placed her gift on the coffee table. Blue paper, a ribbon to match the bow. It was beautifully wrapped.

"Nice place," he said. "Larger than it looks from the outside."

"I use the space well," Kitty said. "And the windows let in a lot of light—makes it look larger than it really is. Can I get you a drink?"

"I'm fine."

"I have half a bottle of white wine in the fridge. I was just about to—"

"I'm fine. Really."

Kitty remembered calling Johan from the airport to let him know that she wouldn't be available for a couple of days. He'd seemed stiff on the phone, not his usual cool self, and that same stiffness was on display now. His shoulders were up, and there was a seriousness in his eyes—his demeanor at odds with the pretty gift he'd brought.

"Okay, well . . ." Kitty gestured at the sofa. "Sit down. Chill."

He took a seat but didn't chill, although his shoulders dropped a couple of inches and he almost smiled.

"Everything okay?" Kitty asked.

"You should open your gift."

"Right. Yeah." Kitty nodded and looked at the brightly wrapped box. She stooped, placed her hands on either side, and tested its weight—even gave it a little shake. She felt something roll heavily inside.

"Did you buy me a watermelon?" she asked.

"It's better than that."

"Ooh, exciting." Kitty pulled the end of the ribbon and the bow came untied. Johan leaned forward, elbows on his knees, his long fingers linked. Kitty looked at him. His shoulders had crept up again, and she wondered if she'd read him wrong. Maybe his stiffness was down to awkwardness and nerves. She'd seen it in men before. They'd danced skittishly around the edges before making their move.

Was that the real reason for this visit?

Kitty had been running canary for Johan for almost two months, and during that time had grown comfortable around him, something she would never have believed possible after their first meeting. He'd stroked her cheek on occasion, or touched her hair, and although this was inappropriate, it never felt *seedy*. Even after Barrett Lorne's party, when she *might* have slept with him if he'd pursued it, he'd dropped her outside her apartment without so much as a peck on the cheek. *I'll call*, he'd said. The perfect gentleman.

Kitty had begun to believe that she wasn't his type, but now here he was, unannounced and out of sorts. Perhaps he felt that, after two months, the groundwork had been established and it was time to push for more.

If so, Kitty hoped her rejecting these advances would not damage their relationship.

She pulled the ribbon from around the gift, then made quick work of the paper, tearing and crumpling. Beneath, the mystery continued: a plain, rigid box with a lid that had been secured with little rectangles of sticky tape. Kitty peeled the first of these away, rolling it into a ball between her thumb and forefinger.

"You really shouldn't have," she said, working on the second piece of tape.

"I really should."

One corner of the lid popped up just a touch and she got her first sense that something was wrong. It was the smell, wafting from inside the box, bloody and thick. The stench of spoiled meat.

Kitty frowned, looked at Johan.

"Don't you just love surprises?" he said.

Kitty lifted the lid and her first reaction was to scream, but there was nothing to scream with. Her airway had collapsed, drawing everything inside her chest into a hard, frosty ball. She gagged and fell backward onto her ass, pushing herself away from the table, from the box.

"You said I could trust you, Kitty," Johan said. "You lied."

She looked at him as he stood up—his knees, his spine unfolding, extending impossibly, twenty . . . thirty feet tall. A Norse god. He wasn't real. *None* of this was real. Then Kitty looked at the box again and saw Angelo Gallo's black curls poking out over the top. She found a fraction of her voice and husked something. Not a word. Not a scream. Just a weak, frightened hiss.

Johan pulled his cell phone from the front pocket of his jeans. His thumb tapped across the screen, texting someone, and without looking at Kitty he said:

"We need to talk."

"*Hsssk*," she said.

Johan returned his phone to his pocket. He walked over to Kitty. She tried getting to her feet, but he knocked her down and planted his foot on her chest.

The intercom buzzed and Kitty jerked beneath Johan's foot as if a gun had been fired. He reached down, grabbed a fistful of her hair, and dragged her across the floor toward the apartment door. Kitty, who still hadn't found her voice, found some fight, at least. She popped to her knees and stumbled along beside him, lashing out with her fists. Johan absorbed her blows—they thumped harmlessly off his arm and thigh—before responding with a strike of his own. It was a crisp backhand slap that came from beyond his shoulder and whipped across her face. Her head snapped to one side. She felt the inside of her cheek split—the taste of blood splashed across her tongue—and the lights in the apartment dimmed for a long second.

Two more yanks, and Johan had reached the intercom. He didn't speak into it, only pushed the button that unlocked the main door downstairs, using his knuckle so that he didn't leave a fingerprint. This small detail fell like a raindrop onto her fear. He meant to kill her. No doubt about it.

"Johan," she managed, gasping his name on half a breath. "Please . . . *please*."

"You stole from me, Kitty."

"Just . . . just a little . . ."

He let go of her hair and she slumped to the floor. She tried to crawl away but he dropped to his haunches, clamped his hand beneath her jaw, and swiveled her head so that she faced him. A perilous light shone in his eyes, and amid all her consternation and fear, Kitty remembered what she'd said to him on the night they'd met: *You're too dangerous.* The blood in her mouth tasted oily and sour.

"You stole from me," he said again.

The apartment door opened and Ruben Osterfeld—Sly Boy's right-hand man—walked in. Kitty blinked, trying to make sense of these illogical pieces. What the *hell* was going on here? Ruben flexed his hands inside leather gloves. He glanced at Kitty, but couldn't look her in the eye.

"What the fuck, Ruben?" she murmured.

He wrinkled his nose and ignored her.

"Check the apartment," Johan said to him, one hand still clasped beneath Kitty's jaw. "Don't mess anything up. If you move something, put it back."

"Got it."

"I'll meet you at Jink's."

Ruben nodded and started toward the bedroom, stepping over Kitty's splayed legs. Johan stroked his braided beard, made a disappointed clicking sound with his tongue, then hoisted Kitty to her feet.

"Okay, Kitty, time to go." He pointed at the box on the table. "Bring your birthday present."

"Please, Johan . . ." In a high, cracked voice. "Don't do this . . . I can . . . can . . . *please.*"

He pushed her. She stumbled, fell to her knees.

"Bring your present, Kitty."

"No, please . . . please don't—"

"*Bring it!*"

Kitty nodded, tears spilling from her eyes. She placed the lid on the box and picked it up, gathering it beneath one arm. Johan gripped the back of her neck and urged her toward the door. Before leaving the apartment, Kitty grabbed her skateboard with her free hand, an automatic action. Walking down the stairway and out into the night, she clutched it to her side. A familiar thing. A comfort.

A black SUV rumbled curbside. Johan opened the back door and pushed Kitty inside. She spilled across the seat, feeling Angelo's severed head roll inside the box and bump against the sides. Nausea swelled from the base of her stomach. She gagged and coughed as Johan climbed in beside her.

Xander was behind the wheel. His hair had been shaved to a dark fuzz, short enough for Kitty to see the tattoos on his skull.

"Jink's," Johan said to him.

The SUV pulled away. Kitty's neighborhood scrolled inexorably beyond the window. It was Passion Hour, she noticed, the sky peach-colored, the buildings painted warmly, the fan palms drawn in jagged silhouette. Kitty locked her skateboard between her knees and moaned.

Silver Lake became the Hollywood Freeway, then Interstate 110, then Compton. Post Malone played on the stereo—music Kitty had always enjoyed, but now it sounded mocking, tortuous. Darkness fell across the city like a coffin lid.

"You know what this is about, Kitty," Johan said. She wasn't sure if it was a question or not.

"I only took a little—a line every now and then." Kitty touched his arm and he shook her off. "For auditions, mainly. I swear."

"That so?" He took out his phone, opened Instagram, not interested in her excuses.

"Please, Johan, please. I'll . . . I'll *pay* for what I took."

"You're damn right."

Kitty pressed the heel of her hand against her forehead and

screwed her eyes shut. Nothing made sense. All of *this* for a few pinches of canary? And Angelo? Jesus Christ, what did any of this have to do with Angelo?

Something bigger was at play here. A deal gone south? An all-out drug war? Kitty had no idea, but she had been swept into the middle of it.

Xander steered the SUV into a scrub lot, then down a narrow industrial track lined on both sides with collapsed fencing. From here, he cut behind a derelict gas station, then crossed another disused lot, bouncing over potholes, pushing through tall weeds, finally stopping in front of a wide brick building with JINK'S WARE-HOUSE painted across the bay doors.

Johan got out of the SUV and when Kitty didn't follow he grabbed her by the hair again.

"Okay, okay. Jesus."

The air smelled garbagy and old. Several stray cats paraded around a pile of bald tires, their crooked tails hoisted. Johan, Xander, and Kitty—still clutching the box and her skateboard—entered Jink's through a side door. They took a metallic, echoey stairway to a basement with a low ceiling and a smooth cement floor. Pipes dripped. Low-wattage lights hummed and flickered.

They walked a short way and then came across Sly Boy, beaten and gagged, chained on his hands and knees to ringbolts in the floor.

9

THE FLOODED WORLD

Do you know what the blood-eagle ritual is?"

Johan walked a slow figure eight, the heels of his shoes clicking off the cement floor. He had his hands behind his back, like a lecturing professor, looking between Sly Boy and Kitty, who'd been pushed to her knees. Xander stood behind her, one hand wrapped in her hair. She wasn't going anywhere.

"Oh Jesus Christ," Sly Boy mumbled. His gag had been removed. It lay on the floor nearby, damp and bloody. "Oh Christ. Oh sweet Jesus."

"So you know?" Johan asked him, a surprised note in his voice.

"Yeah, I know." Sly Boy looked up. His left eye was swollen closed, seeping bright tears. "I wish to hell I didn't."

"And you, Kitty?"

She shook her head, feeling the tug of Xander's strong hand. Johan could have asked a simple question—her name, what birthday she'd just celebrated—and she might not have been able to answer. The sky had been split down the middle, allowing a rain of misery and brokenness. The world's clear shapes had been flooded.

"Then allow me to educate you." Johan stepped toward Kitty,

taking one hand from behind his back to stroke his beard. "The blood-eagle is a Viking execution ritual, a punishment for the loss of honor, or for some grave wrongdoing. First, the outline of an eagle is carved into your back. Then, while still alive, your ribs are separated from your spine, using an ax, and your lungs are pulled out and placed over your shoulders in the manner of wings."

He stopped—let this settle in. Sly Boy squirmed. His chains clanked wretchedly. Kitty whimpered and flinched. She had placed the box on the floor at her knees. The lid was still on, but she noticed blood leaking from a seam at the bottom—such an abhorrent detail, and she averted her eyes quickly. She looked up at Johan, lost and scared.

"Very brutal. Incredibly painful." A cold smirk curled Johan's upper lip. "Some scholars believe that keeping you alive while hacking the ribs from your spine would be impossible without modern medical equipment, that you would die before your lungs were removed."

"Don't do this, Johan," Kitty croaked. She linked her hands like she used to as a child, reciting her nightly prayers. "Please, whatever this is about, we can—"

"*Whatever* this is about? Oh, Kitty, you disappoint me." He stood over her, wisps of blond hair hanging across his face, then turned on his heels and walked over to Sly Boy. "How about you, Kris? You know why you're here?"

"No, I . . . I . . ." Pinkish saliva dangled from Sly Boy's lower lip. "I told you, man. I don't know what the *fuck* is going on."

"One of you is lying. Or both."

The pipes dripped, and for a while this was the only sound, so diminutive compared to how vast everything else had become. Johan stood with his head low, lost in thought—Rodin's *Thinker* in an alternate pose. He then walked beyond Kitty and Sly Boy, out of sight, although his heels could be heard clicking across the floor.

Sly Boy spluttered and spat between his hands. He shifted position, as much as the chains would allow. His good eye rolled slowly toward Kitty. She couldn't read the expression in it.

"I don't know," she said, not to Sly Boy, but in regard to everything: the flooded world. It was impossible to believe that she had woken up in Kentucky that morning, listening to her mama sing while she dressed for church. What Kitty would give to be there now, snuggled up in her childhood bed, the sweet aroma of milkweed blowing through the open windows. Tears filled her eyes and she slumped, but Xander was there to hold her up. His hand was as hard as a bear's jaw.

The sound of Johan's footsteps echoed in the dimness, growing louder as he returned to the patch of damp cement between Sly Boy and Kitty. He walked another dilatory figure eight. The ax in his hand had a glimmering, hooked blade and a long handle, beautifully engraved.

Kitty wiped her eyes and listened to the dripping pipes, imagining she could catch the water in her cupped palms and drink it—take on its smallness until she disappeared.

"A couple of weeks ago, it came to my attention that Mr. Salvador Gallo, aka *Angelo*, was selling a diluted version of *my* product to his tweaker friends." Johan ran the tip of one finger along the ax's swooping blade. "You can see the problem here. Canary is an exclusive focus enhancer, used by the Hollywood elite, and it is priced accordingly. Angelo distributing it to his lowlife cohorts negates that exclusivity, which severely impacts its appeal, and therefore my revenue. More importantly, the inferior quality demeans my reputation."

His shoes were immaculately polished, the brown leather reflecting the basement lights as he stepped toward Kitty. He lowered the ax so that the head almost struck the floor, then used the hooked edge to flip the lid off the box. Kitty caught another glimpse of Angelo's soft black curls before screwing her eyes shut. She then heard a scraping sound, followed by a light thump. When she opened her eyes, she saw that the box had been upended, and that Angelo's head had rolled across the floor, facing Sly Boy.

Johan crouched over it for a moment—admiring his handiwork, perhaps—then stood to his full height and switched his gaze between Sly Boy and Kitty. His voice was steady, despite his obscene anger.

"I asked Angelo how he managed to obtain my canary—enough of it to distribute over a matter of weeks—and he said . . ." Johan let the sentence hang, now swinging the ax head like a pendulum, first toward Sly Boy, then toward Kitty, back and forth, seven or eight times, finally settling on Sly Boy. "*You*, Sly Boy. Angelo said he got it from you."

"And you *believe* him?" Sly Boy stormed. Spittle popped from between his broken lips. "He's a fucking piece-of-shit liar."

"I had this ax held to his throat," Johan said with an eerie degree of nonchalance. "Why would he lie?"

"Because he's a fucking meth-head." Sly Boy's chains dragged, then tightened as he tried to crawl toward Johan. An expression of terrific angst worked every bruised muscle in his face. "I don't know anything about this, Johan, I swear to you. I fucking *swear*."

Johan appeared to consider this, tilting his head, frowning lightly. Kitty clutched her skateboard to her chest. It had been a comfort before, but now it felt like *more*—an embodiment of her freedom. She had a brief, hopeful vision of driving the tail of the board backward, into Xander's balls, making her escape as he fell gasping to his knees.

"Angelo *is* untrustworthy, I'll give you that." Johan turned his attention to Kitty, pointing at her with the head of his ax. "So what, then—or *who*—is the link between my product and Angelo Gallo, who usually digs his drugs out of garbage cans?"

"No, Johan," Kitty wheezed. She shook her head, feeling the tension of Xander's hand in her hair with every small movement. "No, I only . . . only took a little bit. Just a little."

"How much is a little, Kitty?"

"I don't know. A pinch here and there. For personal use."

Again, Johan made a show out of considering this. He walked another figure eight, stepping close to Sly Boy, then Kitty, looping around Angelo's head.

"Someone is lying to me." He raised the ax, regarding the sharpened blade with his jaw pushed out.

"Not me," Sly Boy insisted. His mouth quivered. More tears oozed from his closed eye. "Not me, Johan."

"Are you sure about that, Kris?" Johan placed the ax on one shoulder, lumberjack-style, and stepped casually over to Sly Boy. "Because if you didn't sell my canary to Angelo, that means Kitty *did*. And as punishment, I'm going to have to blood-eagle her."

Kitty screamed and writhed. Xander pulled back on her hair, placing one knee between her shoulder blades to restrain her.

"If you're lying," Johan continued, raising his voice to be heard over Kitty's struggles, "that's going to be on your conscience. A terrible thing to have to carry around."

"I'm not lying," Sly Boy insisted. "I don't know anything about your fucking canary."

"Okay, Kris." Johan crouched beside Sly Boy and patted him affectionately on the shoulder. "This has been enlightening. Thank you."

Sly Boy whimpered and clanked his heavy chains. Johan straightened, the ax still on one shoulder. Kitty watched through the tears in her eyes as he caressed his beard, then nodded at Xander, who pushed down on the back of her head. A whistling breath was pressed from her lungs as she was forced low, the curve of her spine exposed.

Kitty heard but didn't see Johan step toward her.

"Are you sure, Kris?" he boomed. "Last chance."

"I'm sure," Sly Boy blubbered.

Kitty tried to twist her body, but Xander was too strong. She was locked in place—couldn't even get enough air to scream. Johan touched the ax to the top of her spine. He cut through the collar of her T-shirt, then tore it down her back in a wide V.

Kitty saw her son in her mind and ran to him. I love you, she said, taking him into her arms, feeling the weight and realness of him. I love you, I love you. He looked into her eyes and recognized her, even though he had never fully seen her. I love you, my beautiful boy. I love you, too, Mama.

This reverie was knocked from her mind when she heard a vehicle pull up outside, the distinct crunch of its tires on gravel, its engine shutting off. The pressure on the back of her head was relinquished and she popped up, then crawled a little way. Shocked tears spouted from her eyes. Xander tightened his hold and stopped her from going too far. Her torn T-shirt hung off one shoulder.

"Off me," she gasped.

The warehouse's side door banged open. Footsteps chimed in the metallic stairway. The police, Kitty thought hopefully, peering through the flickering light. But no, it was only Ruben Osterfeld. This nightmare would continue.

A confused expression had clouded Sly Boy's face, visible through all the blood and bruising.

"Rube?" he hissed.

Ruben ignored him. He went to Johan, handing him something—Kitty didn't see what—as the two shared quiet words. Johan nodded, pocketing whatever Ruben had given him.

"Thank you," Johan whispered. "Good work."

"Rube?" Sly Boy said again. "What the fuck, man?"

"Oh, you didn't know?" Johan asked Sly Boy, and then, to Ruben: "You didn't tell him about us?"

Ruben lowered his eyes.

"Well, *that's* embarrassing." Johan pulled a mock-awkward face, resting the ax on his shoulder once again. "Ruben's been going behind your back, Kris. He and I have been working together for a few months now."

"Oh fuck," Sly Boy muttered.

"Yeah," Johan said. He walked over to Sly Boy, who tried to back away, chains dragging. "I know all your dirty secrets."

"Johan, please . . . let's just—"

The ax came down in a heavy semicircle. It didn't whoosh or thrum. It was quick and silent. Sly Boy recoiled but couldn't go anywhere. His face flowed with multiple expressions, each canceling out the other. It was a full but featureless oval—a rain cloud. The ax's blade struck the back of his neck, but not cleanly. Johan staggered with the effort. Blood splashed his jeans and his polished brown shoes.

It took two attempts to remove Sly Boy's head from his shoulders.

Kitty didn't know which detail was more gruesome—that Sly Boy's head had rolled across the smooth cement and cozied up to Angelo's, or that his body remained on its hands and knees, kept from falling by the tightness of the chains. She stared, disbelieving, barely breathing. Bizarrely, she thought of the lovebird she had plucked out of the air in Barrett Lorne's aviary, and how hollow its bones had felt.

Johan walked toward her, dragging the ax along the floor behind him. It *scraped.* A sound like winter. Kitty looked up as he approached. There was a scream in her chest, held down by something, and she realized that it might never escape—only bubble away for however long she had left.

"This is Krókr," Johan said. He stooped before her, holding the ax up in front of her whirling eyes. Sly Boy's blood dripped from the tip of its beard. "It means *hook* in Old Norse, and Krókr is a replica of the ax used by the great Danish warrior Gottfrid the Bird. There's no real way of proving it—twelve hundred years have passed—but there is strong evidence to suggest that we Flys are descendants of Gottfrid the Bird."

He stroked her face and smiled. His touch ignited something inside her: a small blue flame. It flickered, the kind of pale light that might only be seen in the dark.

"There! Now you know something else about me." Johan tilted his head, gesturing in Sly Boy's direction. "You know something else about Kris 'Sly Boy' Streeter, too. That he is—*was*—a liar and a coward."

"I knew that already," Kitty said in a cracked, airless voice.

"He lied, Kitty. What's more, he was willing to let you die—to let you get *blood-eagled*—to save his own skin." Johan shook his head. He appeared genuinely insulted by Sly Boy's lack of moral fiber. "What kind of a man does that?"

"Not a man," Kitty said, not sure which of them she was referring to.

Johan stood up straight and paced, avoiding the blood spreading across the floor, the same blood that had splashed onto his jeans and shoes. His clothes would have to be burned, Kitty thought, along with the bodies. No evidence. Only emptiness and questions.

"I know exactly what happened, Kitty, because Ruben has kept me informed. I just wanted to see if Sly Boy could regain some honor, and own his wrongdoing like a man." Johan stopped pacing and shook his head. "He couldn't."

"Please, Johan, let me go."

"I also know," Johan continued, "that you took my canary with you when you went to work at Fusion 44."

"Sometimes," Kitty said blankly. "I guess."

"You did. That's how Sly Boy got it." Johan lifted the ax onto his shoulder again. A drop of blood flicked from the blade and landed inches from her. "He removed it from your backpack while you were front of house. He stole a third, sometimes half, then cut what was left with levamisole and powdered food coloring, and returned it to your backpack. You then took that inferior product and handed it off to my customers."

"Oh," Kitty said. She looked at him and nodded, as if he'd asked if she was enjoying the L.A. weather. That flame inside her grew a little, though, and a tendon in her jaw flexed.

Johan said, "This coincides with complaints I'd received that the quality was not to its usual standard. I asked my manufacturer if he'd changed the recipe, and he assured me he had not. He and I have been partners for years. I know when he's telling the truth."

Kitty lowered her head and Xander raised it again. His hand had been in her hair so long that she barely felt it anymore, like a tight elastic.

"Sly Boy also cut the portion he stole, then sold it to Angelo, who offered it to all his failed actor and loser meth-head friends for a bargain price." Johan sighed and shook his head with disappointment. "This happened five times before Ruben found out and came to me."

"Oh," Kitty said again, and she might say it over and over, until that flame inside her triggered a more volatile response.

"But here's something: Sly Boy didn't know that the canary in your backpack was *my* product." Johan tapped his finger against his chest. "Isn't that right, Ruben?"

"Right," Ruben confirmed. "He thought Kitty got it from one of her new Hollywood contacts—that maybe this talent agent she talked about was actually the dealer."

"I believe that, Kitty," Johan said, "because Sly Boy knew better than to fuck with me. Which means you either lied about your canary contact to Sly Boy, or you had no idea he was taking it from your backpack."

Drip-drip went the pipes, and something rattled through the ductwork. A rat, probably. Kitty followed the sound with her eyes. She imagined herself up there, too, scrabbling through the narrow dark, locked to the scent of fresh air. It was a wholly absorbing fantasy . . . until the sound of the rat faded and reality fell like rain.

"*Did* you know what Sly Boy was doing? Look at me, Kitty. Fucking *look* at me!" He clasped her jaw and angled her head to face him. "There you go. I'm right here."

She rolled her eyes away from him and he slapped her hard. Bright spots flared across the world. That small flame inside her leapt and set something else burning.

"Me. Look at *me*."

She looked at him. Hurt . . . crackling inside.

"Were you and Sly Boy in this together?"

"No."

"Why would you take your backpack to Fusion 44—just leave it lying the fuck around with tens of thousands of dollars' worth of product inside?"

"Working . . . hours. So many hours." Kitty sneered and pulled back, yanking her jaw out of Johan's hand. "It was easier. I didn't . . . didn't always have time to run home. I kept it in a locker upstairs."

"And was the locker *locked*?"

"No."

"So you just trusted these people you worked with but didn't really know . . . you trusted them not to go snooping?"

"The canary was hidden inside the lining."

"Hidden? Is that what you call it?"

Kitty shrugged, a small gesture that managed to encapsulate the hopelessness of everything: her miserable situation, people in general, the state of the world. Johan filled his chest with a deep, angry breath, then walked another figure eight—broader on one side to circumvent the heads and the growing pool of blood. He dragged the ax behind him.

"Let's say I believe you," he said, looping toward her again. "You're a stupid, *stupid* little girl, but sure, I believe you."

He paused, perhaps waiting for Kitty to express her gratitude and fealty. She didn't.

"We still," he continued, "have one matter to address."

"I just want to go home," Kitty whispered.

Johan displayed a dry smile, then dug into his pocket and pulled out what Ruben had given him: half a dozen small baggies, each dusted on the inside with a residue of yellow powder. He tossed them at Kitty. They spiraled like leaves. One landed between the front wheels of her skateboard, which was still clutched in her arms.

"Ruben found these in your underwear drawer."

"Yeah, I told you," Kitty said. "Just a little, right? For personal use."

"A pinch here, a pinch there."

"Right."

"It adds up, though. I mean . . ." Johan waved a hand at the empty baggies. "I'm going to estimate six or seven grams over two months."

"Not that much."

"Three grams?"

"Maybe."

"That's still twenty-four hundred dollars' worth of product, buying by the gram." Johan lifted the ax again and looked at her over the blade. "Would you like it if I stole twenty-four hundred dollars from you?"

"The customers couldn't tell the drops were a tiny bit light," Kitty reasoned. Her words—her thoughts—were clearer now, her sense of self returning as the fire inside her quickened. "They still paid full price. You didn't lose anything."

"That's not the point," Johan said.

"You'd never have found out if this shit with Sly Boy hadn't gone down."

"Again, not the point. Theft is theft, Kitty." He leaned forward and touched her cheek where he'd slapped her, his fingers moving over the raised skin. "Dishonor is dishonor."

Kitty pulled away from him. Xander snagged her hair and held her in place. Again, she imagined driving her skateboard backward: a swift, sudden strike that would drop Johan's jackal—his *berserker*—to his knees, giving her a window in which to escape. The flame that had begun in the small of her belly was now a fire in her chest. It raged across her shoulders and down her arms. Her skin prickled in the heat.

"I'll find a way to pay you back," she snarled. "Then you'll never have to see me again. But if you feel your Viking pride has been dented, and that you have to kill me over twenty-four hundred dollars—which, let's face it, you probably spent more on those shoes—well, what kind of man does that make you?"

Johan ran a hand across his forehead. "I can't let you walk out of here, Kitty. Yes, you stole from me, and yes, your stupidity with the backpack cost me a *lot* more than twenty-four hundred dollars. But you have also witnessed a brutal execution."

"I didn't see anything."

She hadn't been able to look away, and knew in her soul that, should she survive this, Sly Boy's rain-cloud face would haunt her dreams forever.

"I made the mistake of trusting you once before," Johan said, "and it cost me dearly. Letting you live might be the right thing to do, but it's not the smart thing."

He nodded at Xander, who lifted Kitty to her feet. She felt his breath on her neck, too close, too intimate.

"I have many notable qualities, but being a good judge of character is apparently not one of them." A regretful smile touched Johan's lips. He held his Viking ax with his hands at either end of the engraved handle. The ready position. "I thought you were different, Kitty."

. . .

One more time . . . clutching the deck of her skateboard with both hands, driving the tail backward with an unequaled fury. Except this time Kitty wasn't imagining it, she was *doing* it. The fire snapped and crackled inside her. She shrieked—a sound like steam escaping.

Xander was shorter than her by three inches, so the board didn't strike him in the balls, as she'd hoped, but in the gut—in the delicate lacework of nerves below the belly button. The result was similar. He woofed out a breath and doubled over, letting go of her hair to clutch his middle. Kitty turned quickly, still clutching the skateboard, and smashed the deck into the side of his skull. The force reverberated through the board, into her arms, and across her shoulders. She even felt it in her rib cage. Xander felt it more, though. He wobbled gamely, then fell to his knees. Blood ran from his nose.

This happened quickly. Three seconds max. It took exactly this long for Johan to react. He lunged for Kitty, but she ducked and twisted away from him. In the same move, she got her board rolling on the cement floor, then hopped onto it and pushed away.

The lights flickered, disorienting her. It took a moment to locate the stairway. She skated toward it, low on her board. Johan yelled at Ruben to shoot her and a gunshot rang out seconds later. The bullet sparked off the floor inches from Kitty's wheels. She pushed again, splashing through puddles of rusty water, which slowed but didn't stop her. Ten feet from the stairway, she hopped off her board and kicked it—still moving—into her waiting hand. A second gunshot shook the air and the bullet ricocheted somewhere to Kitty's left.

Gasping, blinking tears from her eyes, she took the metal risers two at a time, then threw open the door at the top and spilled out into the night.

10

THREE HORSE SALVAGE

Three spotlights shone above the warehouse's bay doors. They cast a frosty luminance across the frontage, where the stray cats swaggered and the SUV and Mustang were parked at diagonals. As she skated around the vehicles, it occurred to Kitty that she hadn't seen the Mustang outside her apartment, probably because it was so distinctive, the kind of car her neighbors would notice and remember. Such carefulness assured Kitty that Johan had every intention of killing her.

The cats arched their spines and hissed as she stopped close by, her wheels lifting a cloud of dust. She quickly surveyed the front lot: cracked, uneven ground, marred by potholes and weeds. Not good for a quick getaway on her skateboard, and the higher weeds were too few and far between to offer solid cover.

It was tempting to head that way, the obvious exit, but she'd only make it halfway across the lot before Johan and his animals caught up to her. She pulled off her torn T-shirt and tossed it into the weeds—a decoy, to throw them off the scent—then turned her board around and started down the paved track that paralleled the warehouse's eastern wall.

She'd rolled only ten yards when she heard the door bang open on the other side, followed by Johan's booming voice: *"Ruben, take the Tahoe. Xan, in the Mustang with me. You see that bitch, put a bullet in her."*

Kitty groaned and pushed hard. Her wheels jounced over the rough pavement, and she worked every muscle in her core and thighs to maintain balance. Engines growled to life behind her, like two hungry dogs sprung from their cages. She looked over her shoulder and saw headlights swooping over the front lot. Had they noticed her discarded tee and been drawn in the wrong direction?

"Please," Kitty gasped. Tears blurred her vision. Not that it mattered; the light at the front of the warehouse barely reached around the sides. It was *dark*, which was what she wanted, of course—to not be seen—but it meant skating blind. She could just make out the tall chain-link fencing to her left and the warehouse wall to her right, and had to swerve to avoid obstacles as they materialized in the darkness.

The engines rumbled. They were still in the front lot, ripping through the high weeds. Kitty rolled in the opposite direction as fast as she could. She had no idea what was behind Jink's Warehouse. More industrial wasteland, probably, but she might be able to scale the fence and find a place to hide, although what she really needed was a neighborhood—stores, people, *police*. If she could only—

Kitty didn't see the barrel. It was painted black, splotched with rust. She hit it hard, and of course it was empty, so it chimed like a gong—first when she slammed into it, and again when it toppled and struck the ground. Kitty spilled off her board and rolled. No helmet. No elbow pads. No *T-shirt*. She scuffed skin from her arms and shoulders. Her head bounced off the pavement too hard.

"Oh . . . oh shit." Kitty pushed herself to one knee, looking for her skateboard in the gloom. She heard its wheels spinning to her left and crawled in that direction, hoping the sound of the barrel hadn't given her away. She swept her hands over weeds and trash, found her board, and got unsteadily to her feet. Blood trickled into her left eye. Kitty traced the laceration running along her hairline and onto her forehead. It was deep, would need stitches.

She had more immediate problems, though.

The light was sudden and stark, illuminating everything around her. Kitty staggered backward, looking through one eye and one splayed hand.

The Mustang rumbled at the top of the track, low to the ground and predatory. Its headlights pinned her like claws.

"No," she wept.

Three throaty revs of the engine, as if in response: *YES-YES-YES.*

It came at her.

The rest of the world was stripped to its quantum, conceptual parts, and the only gristle was a choice: move or die.

In a blank zone, not aware she was moving, yet watching herself do so, Kitty turned, set her board rolling, and jumped onto it at a run. The narrow track was saturated with light now, and she veered around—or ollied over—the numerous obstructions. A sliver of awareness, of *self*, returned. She felt the breeze on her skin, the tears in her eyes. Her heartbeat filled her body—a loud, fearful rhythm.

The Mustang didn't avoid the obstructions. It went through or over them. It struck the same barrel that Kitty had and sent it flying forward, tumbling end over end ahead of her.

Kitty didn't need to look over her shoulder to know that the Mustang was gaining fast. She heard it, *felt* it. The light swelled. Her shadow grew. She pushed and *pushed* with her left leg—long, powerful strokes, but it wouldn't be enough. The Mustang would be on top of her within seconds.

There was a plastic dumpster up ahead, on wheels, with just enough space between it and the chain-link fence for Johan's death machine to squeeze through. Kitty grabbed it as she skated by, yanking it away from the wall with all the strength she could gather at speed. The maneuver pulled her off her board and she ran for a few steps before she could reset. The Mustang slowed, but still struck the dumpster hard. The sound of the impact crowded the air: a boom, a rumble, the desperate squeal of brakes. Kitty glanced behind her and saw the dumpster toppling, split along two sides, its contents cascading over the Mustang's hood. A sheet of newspaper got caught beneath one windshield wiper, temporarily blocking the driver's view, before flapping away like a gull.

The sudden change of velocity caused the driver—Johan, not Xander—to lose control. The Mustang lurched, its back end fishtailing. Sparks glittered as it scraped the warehouse's brick outer wall, then swerved the other way, crashing through the fence, lifting it out of the ground in whickering, chain-link sections.

This damaged but didn't stop the Mustang. Johan worked the brake and navigated it back onto the track. Windshield cracked, one headlight blown, it charged at Kitty again.

She reached the back of the warehouse and saw there was nowhere to go. Crates and wooden pallets were stacked against the fence. There were shadows, but they wouldn't keep her safe.

Her mind hadn't fully returned, and maybe that was a good thing. She was operating on high-octane animal instinct, without the distraction of self, of emotion. Barely thinking, she leapt off her skateboard, tossed it over the rear fence, then followed it, jumping first onto a crate, then clambering over the chain-link.

The Mustang raced closer. All light and roar.

Kitty threw herself off the fence, not knowing what was on the other side. It was a dirt embankment, strewn with sagebrush and sprawling trees, sloping to a low wooden fence that bordered a parking lot. She landed hard, crying out as she rolled her ankle, then tumbling several feet before slowing.

Johan was a tick behind, not following on foot, as she thought he might, but in the Mustang still. Maybe he hadn't been able to brake in time, or—more likely—he was brimming with Viking rage. Either way, he smashed through the fence away to her right, sending sections of chain-link and splintered wood spinning in every direction. One landed close to Kitty, impaling the ground like an arrow.

The Mustang was airborne for a moment—four wheels off the ground—and came down with an uncomfortable thump. The trunk popped open. A cloud of dirt rose and followed the car as it slid down the embankment, turning slowly before stopping against a tree.

"Jesus . . . Jesus Christ." Kitty picked herself up and made her way down the slope, using the sagebrush for cover where she could. She saw the wheels of her skateboard flashing in the Mustang's one working headlight and diverted her course so that she could grab it. A gunshot cracked the dusty night as she did, and she screamed and fell back on her ass. The bullet ripped through the dirt to her left—way too close. Kitty pulled her board to her chest and scurried away. Two more gunshots echoed in quick succession. The first bullet grooved the trunk of an olive tree as she ducked beneath its branches. The second passed through the fist-sized gap between her right ear and shoulder. She turned instinctively and saw Xander leaning out of the Mustang's passenger-side window, gun in hand. Perhaps if his head were clearer—if she hadn't clocked him with her skateboard—he would have blown her out of her Nikes.

Kitty scrambled as deftly as she was able. She reached the wooden fence and toppled over in ungainly fashion, landing on the other side with a spine-jarring thud. She hissed in pain but didn't stop—*couldn't* stop. She got her knees beneath her, then her feet, daring a glimpse over the top of the fence as she stood. The Mustang was struggling to get moving, its wheels spinning in the dirt.

She threw down her board and moved, her body aching all over, her left eye full of blood. The parking lot was half empty. Kitty weaved between the vehicles, using them to cloak her escape.

Out onto a quiet industrial street, keeping to the shadows.

Just when Kitty began to believe she might be in the clear, the black SUV came sliding around the corner, tires smoking.

She got close enough to see Ruben behind the wheel—the whites of his wide eyes, his flaring nostrils. Ruben, who had once been Sly Boy's ride-or-die, but had watched benignly as Johan decapitated him with a replica Viking ax. Clearly, he had all the loyalty of a rat snake. Another fractured player in this City of Fucked-Up Men.

He mounted the sidewalk—ballsy now, behind two tons of American hardware—and steered toward Kitty. There was an alleyway on her left, between a tool rental and industrial clothing store. Kitty *just* made it, feeling the heat of the Tahoe's front end as it missed her by an arm's length. The air rippled. Kitty hit the wall and bounced off. Her skateboard flipped away, lost in the darkness again.

The alleyway was too narrow for the SUV to squeeze through, but Ruben, wide as he was, would have no problem. Kitty got to her feet yet again, woozy and slow. She heard the SUV screech to a halt, then the driver's door clunk open. Ruben's voice followed, pumped on adrenaline, gasping into his cell.

"Found the bitch. On Rowes Street, in an alley beside Tuf-Go Clothing . . ."

Talking to Johan, or maybe Xander. Kitty got moving, limping, leaning against the wall. She stumbled over her skateboard and picked it up, but didn't have the strength to ride it. To propel her bodyweight on wheels felt akin to dragging a tree trunk uphill.

Ruben: "No, but I'm on her ass. She won't get far. Rowes backs onto Three Horse Salvage. You can cut her off there."

The alleyway was capped by an apron of dirty cement crowded with garbage bags and flat-packed boxes. A ten-foot fence topped with razor wire—a goddamn *prison* fence—stood between Kitty and the salvage yard. She smeared the blood from her eye and looked between the chain-links at a sprawl of vehicles and appliances picked to their bones.

Ruben started into the alleyway behind her, using the flashlight on his cell phone to light the way. Kitty turned back to the fence. There was no getting over it, but she noticed a section at the bottom that had peeled away from the cement floor, with just enough clearance to crawl under. Dropping to her knees was easy. She sent her skateboard through, then lowered herself to her belly and followed. The wiry ends of the chain-link snagged her bra strap and she backed up—be damned if she was going to lose her bra, too— then inched lower, squirming from the alley to the salvage yard.

Ruben's flashlight bobbed closer. He couldn't follow—no way he could wriggle his two-sixty under the fence—but the son of a bitch had a gun. Kitty was too drained and injured to keep running. She could only hide. And pray.

She hobbled, tucked herself behind the pale shell of a school bus, then crept deeper into the yard. The flashlight faded behind her. Ruben rattled the fence but it held him. Kitty picked her way between the stripped vehicles and came across a carousel that looked both tragic and magical. Its shimmer was long gone, its drop rods dull and matted with cobwebs. Exhausted, Kitty sagged against one of the horses—not a horse at all, in fact, but a winged unicorn.

An alicorn, she thought, pulling this from somewhere—one of the many middle-grade fantasy novels she had read as a child, perhaps. A unicorn with wings is called an alicorn.

A tired, silly fantasy, but she indulged it nonetheless: climbing onto the alicorn's back and galloping away, stomping into the sky above the salvage yard, heading west, where the Pacific crashed, holding on to its horn as they soared yet higher.

Three Horse Salvage had ceased operations some time ago. The office was a low, whistling shack with boards over the windows and a notice on the door that Kitty didn't get close enough to read. There were no security guards or dogs. No need for them; the lot was three-quarters empty, swaying with weeds, oil spots marking the dirt where wrecks had sat for years. Fan palms creaked and rattled in the breeze. Dim light shone through their canopies from the lots of adjacent properties.

There were gaps in the fence at the front of the yard. The razor wire had been snipped away in one part and this was where Johan and Xander entered. Ruben pushed through a suitably sized hole a little farther down. The three men converged. Their voices carried.

Xander: "You think she's still here?"

Johan: "If she is, we'll find her."

Kitty had hidden beneath the dented hood of an old Chevy Impala, curled up in the cavity where the engine used to be. Rust holes in the fender allowed a limited view. She saw three cell-phone flashlights bloom in the darkness, then separate as they started to look for her.

Johan still had his ax. He dragged it along the ground behind him.

Kitty remained as still as possible, thinking that any small movement would make the Impala groan on its springs, or cause one of the few remaining parts to dislodge and fall loudly to the ground. She breathed through her hand, clamped over her mouth and nose, with only a couple of tight air holes between her fingers.

"You may be safe for the next ten seconds, Kitty," Johan called out. He was close, maybe thirty feet away. "Or the next hour. Or a week. But I will find you eventually."

She imagined a life of looking over her shoulder every other minute, expecting to see that sage Mustang snarling at the end of the street.

"Like I told you before." His voice was closer. "I don't give up easily."

Kitty closed her eyes and saw the ax—Krókr, the fucking thing had a *name*—swooping downward, not once but twice, separating Sly Boy's head from the rest of his body. She pushed the memory away but it came back, and back again. "Levi," she whispered into her hand, because her son's face made everything brighter. Would she ever get the opportunity to place herself at the edge of his world, in the hope of being drawn deeper? Would she ever hold him, touch his hair, smell his skin? Would he ever know her?

The ax fell again, but it was Levi's slender neck beneath the blade. Then it was her mama's, then the rest of her family's, one after the other, and finally her own.

This crazy fucking Viking was taking everything away from her.

She heard his footsteps, and the ax dragging through the dirt behind him. The light from his cell phone bled through the rust holes in the fender.

"Here, Kitty." Close enough that he might hear her heart, the insistent little drum that it was. "Here, Kitty-Kitty."

Blood trickled from the wound in her head. It gathered on her cheekbone and dripped—*splash*—onto the dirt below. She trembled from the hips out, the reverberations traversing her curved spine and tucked knees, rattling her skull like the lid of a boiling kettle.

The light through the rust holes grew brighter. Kitty heard his wet, hungry breaths, and was sure, suddenly, that he knew exactly where she was. He would pop the hood any moment, and would chop and chop and chop before slamming the hood closed again. And there she'd stay, for weeks, months, until the last few wrecks in this shithole were dragged away.

She clapped her hand tighter to her mouth, allowing only the smallest gap to breathe through.

"Here, Kitty-Kitty."

Another few steps. He was right next to the Impala. If he simply bent down and peered through the rust holes, he would see her bright, deer-like eyes staring back.

The next moments moved with hypnotic slowness. Johan moved away, then circled back again. He started to strike the various wrecks with the poll of his ax, and each impact boomed like a shotgun blast. He twice whacked the Impala that Kitty was hiding in. Rust fell in lacy sheets. The hood clapped up and down.

Kitty braced herself with her spine and her feet. It took everything not to scream. Johan stomped away. She heard him hammering the vehicles some distance away. Not a *safe* distance, by any means. After what felt like a long stretch, he met up with Xander and Ruben. It was impossible to tell exactly where they were, or how far away. She saw nothing of their flashlights, but heard their voices clearly enough.

Johan: "I don't know, man. Fuck!"

Xander: "She probably got out through another hole in the fence."

Johan: "If she did, then we've lost her. For now. Bitch can't run forever, though."

Xander: "Think she'll go to the cops?"

Johan: "Let her. She's a Black drug runner. I'm a rich white man. What do *you* think will happen?"

Ruben: "*I'm* not a rich white man."

Johan: "I've got your back, Ruben, despite the fact that you let her out of your fucking sight!"

Ruben: "I couldn't follow her skinny ass."

Johan: "Just don't worry. I'll secure us a solid alibi. Xan, head back to Jink's and clean up. We'll keep searching here until you're done."

It continued. The footsteps. The hammering. The flashlights seeping through the rust holes and the half-inch seam where the hood wouldn't latch. Kitty had no idea how long she hid in that cramped engine compartment. Even when the search ended and she heard their vehicles pulling away, she didn't move, certain that Johan had remained behind, and was standing on the roof of the office with the ax across one shoulder, carefully surveying the yard, waiting for her to emerge.

Morning broke slowly, in shades of coral and red, and Kitty wept, suddenly aware that she hadn't expected to see a new day. Her tears were frightened and grateful, but mostly angry. She exited her hiding spot the same way she had entered—not by lifting the hood, but by dropping down through the engine compartment and slithering out from beneath the car.

It took a minute to be able to straighten her spine and legs, to first kneel, then stand. Walking was another matter. She leaned against the Impala, then pushed off and staggered six or seven steps, collapsing against the skeletal frame of what had once been a pickup truck.

Johan didn't descend on her with his ax. The salvage yard was empty. The only sounds were the gently creaking palms and the whoosh of commuter traffic on a nearby freeway.

"Come on, Kitty," she gasped. "Come on."

She took a deep breath—it tasted of oil and grit—and stumbled to the next vehicle, then the next. Sweat dappled her brow. She dropped her skateboard to the dirt, lowered her right knee onto it, then pushed herself along.

There was a water barrel outside the derelict office, one-quarter full. Kitty leaned in and removed the skin of insects from the surface, then rinsed the blood and dirt from her body. The water was warm and foul-smelling, but it did the job. She couldn't bring herself to drink it, though, despite a raging thirst.

Marginally fresher, Kitty moved on. She procured a dirty blanket from the trunk of a rust-eaten Ford, shook out the spiders, and wrapped it around herself.

She tried walking again, and managed, but slowly. Eventually, she found a gap in the chain-link and left the yard.

East Compton Boulevard, an hour later. Kitty sat in the doorway of a dry cleaner's, having been moved on from two other places. "Get the fuck out of here," the owner of an auto parts store had said, and took a swipe at her with his broom. She sat with her knees drawn to her chest. The blanket concealed her partial nakedness, as well as the bumps and scrapes on her arms and shoulders. Kitty raked her hair across the more serious wound in her head, and tried to snag the attention of people as they walked by.

Finally, she did—a Black teen with a spring in his step and a red hoodie tied around his waist by its sleeves.

"Hey, man."

"What's up?"

"I'm in a bad place, that's what's up. I'll trade you this two-hundred-dollar skateboard for that hoodie and ten dollars cash."

"Shit. You can't get much crank for ten dollars."

"I'm not after crank. I just need enough for a bottle of water and bus fare."

"You steal that board?"

"No. It's mine."

"Prove it."

"How?"

"Do a trick."

"I'm not your fucking dog. You want to do this, or not?"

He did.

The police could detain Johan. They could interrogate him, obtain warrants to search his home, his car, Jink's Warehouse. Assuming they took Kitty at her word, they could cross-examine Xander and Ruben until one of them slipped up. But would any investigation get that far? Johan would have his bases covered and the sharpest lawyers in Southern California. The question was not could the police charge him, with his elite white connections and solid alibis, but for how long could—or *would*—they protect Kitty?

She rode the bus north, pondering the best course of action. Other than hiding under a rock for the rest of her life, there appeared only two ways out of this: for Johan to be imprisoned, or killed, and neither seemed likely to happen anytime soon.

Her head started to bleed again. She dabbed at it with the sleeve of the hoodie. Red on red. She needed a doctor. Even better: a hot shower and sleep. Not at her apartment, though. Johan would have eyes on the place. (She imagined Ruben parked on her sofa, eating her snacks, watching her TV.) Her phone was there. Her wallet, too. Even if she ran, how far could she get without a photo ID and a bank card? And if she borrowed some cash, or stole it, where would she go? Louisville—*home*—was out of the question. She couldn't put her family in danger.

"Never," she whispered.

Kitty looked out the window. She didn't see the Mustang, but it prowled along beside her nonetheless, emphasizing what she already knew: that Johan had to be stopped.

But how?

She shook her head. The question was too big, too much. First things first: rest and healing. But even this required the basics—a bed, food, medicine, safety.

"A friend," she said, using the other sleeve to wipe her tears. "I need a friend."

In all of Los Angeles, only one person came to mind.

II

THE WORLD FALLING AWAY

Luke was woken by someone knocking on the back door. He opened one eye. Morning light broke through the blinds and the ceiling fan turned in swift, whispering circles. He sat up, disoriented.

Tap-tap-tap.

"What the fuck?"

There were two Xanax capsules on the nightstand, where he'd placed them before going to bed. He'd been trying to be less dependent on them, but it was a losing battle. Last night, though, Luke had drifted off without their assistance. He'd tossed and turned until three A.M., his mind rumbling with the usual dark thoughts that occurred the moment he dropped his head onto the pillow: Lisa, his career, suicide—around and around, like the ceiling fan above him, but screaming, not whispering.

Luke remembered thinking that he would throw in the towel, take the goddamn benzos, like he so often did, but somewhere between thinking this and actually doing it, his body succumbed. Just his luck, then, to be woken up by some jackass knocking on the back door. And *early*, too.

He checked his phone: 8:56.

"Son of a bitch."

Luke looked at the Xanax and at the half-popped strip of antidepressants beside them. Until Lisa disappeared, he'd been able to avoid prescription drugs, no mean feat in a town where everything—livelihoods, principles, levelheadedness—was so dubiously balanced. He'd never been big on recreational drugs, either. Booze had always been enough (sometimes *too* much). Sure, he'd smoked weed in college, like everybody else with a pulse, but he could take it or leave it. Same with cocaine, when his career started to move and the Hollywood parties became more commonplace. He'd do a line, purely to fit in, but the buzz didn't excite him—*except* when he was with Lisa. She'd turned it into something else.

"It's not really my thing," he'd said to her honestly. They'd been dating two or three weeks at the time.

"Yeah?" Lisa had unsnapped her jeans, pulled them—along with her underwear—down to her knees, and sprinkled half a gram onto the shaved mound of her crotch. "Is this your thing?"

They'd had some godly moments on coke, more so at the beginning of their relationship. They'd left their mark at high altitudes. They'd roared and tussled like cubs. When Luke sensed it becoming *too* casual a thing, he'd reined it in. Lisa wasn't as disciplined. She considered herself a low-key user: occasionally in social environments, and always before performing.

"You're better without it," he'd said to her once.

"Oh, baby," Lisa had replied, and kissed him, her mouth sweet and plush. "You'll always reach higher when you have something lifting you up."

Tap-tap-tap.

The *back* door? Who the fuck came to the back door at *any* time of the day, let alone nine o'clock in the morning?

Trouble, that was who.

Luke owned a gun—a snub-nosed .38 Special—which he kept in a lockbox, like a smart American, but had lost the key, like a goddamn idiot. Maybe that was just as well; if the .38 had been accessible four months ago, he might have used it to pop his brains out, rather than rolling down the garage door with the four-banger running.

He sprang out of bed and into the hallway, where he grabbed his Louisville Slugger—forty-two inches of solid ash—from the shit-pile that served as a coat closet. It wasn't as reassuring as his .38, but it would have to do. Hoisting it to his shoulder, he edged into the living room, which was open plan, an L-shaped breakfast bar separating it from the kitchen. It offered a better view of the back door.

Tap-tap.

Luke cleared a channel through the empty beer bottles and looked over the breakfast bar. The blind in the back-door window was down but only half-closed. Through the cracks, he glimpsed someone on the other side, wearing what looked like a red hoodie. Some meth-head, probably, looking to steal his shit.

Tap-tap-tap.

"I have a gun, motherfucker," Luke called out, "and I know how to use it."

The second part was true, at least. He'd spent six weeks training at Brock's Urban Shooter for his role in *A Bullet Affair.* Couldn't hit a bull in the ass to begin with, but by the end could clear a tactical area with nothing but headshots.

Mr. Red Hoodie lingered for several seconds, as if weighing his chances, then disappeared from view. Luke lowered the baseball bat and ran a hand through his hair, aware only then how keenly his heart was drumming. He pulled in a deep breath and exhaled slowly.

"That's right," he shouted. "Get the fuck out of here."

Luke counted to thirty, then looped around the breakfast bar. He took three long strides across the kitchen and peered out the window over the sink.

Red Hoodie was still there. A female, not a male. Luke could tell from her slender shoulders and hands, and from the wavy black hair hanging down from inside her hood. She sat with her back against a sun-faded planter, knees drawn to her chest, her head low. Her track pants were covered in dirt, and her colorful sneakers—

"Oh shit," Luke hissed. He flashed back to just after his suicide attempt, standing in his driveway with a cloth pressed to his whirling head, watching the girl who'd saved his life lower one colorful sneaker onto her skateboard before rolling away.

"Kitty."

Luke dropped the baseball bat and pounced at the back door. He turned the lock, threw the bolt, and lunged outside in one ungainly sequence. Kitty flinched, then looked up at him. Her eyes were wide, shocked with tears. Blood smeared the left side of her forehead.

"Kitty, Jesus . . . Jesus Christ."

Her mouth opened and closed, but no words came out. Luke reached to take her hand but this obviously wasn't enough, because she scrabbled to her feet and threw her arms around him.

"Okay, Kitty . . . it's okay now."

Her body felt small and hurt but her arms were strong. She held him as if the world were falling away beneath her.

His spare room was a catastrophe. There was a bed in there somewhere, concealed beneath an epic mound of worthless crap: totes crammed with VHS cassettes, a torn sleeping bag, a broken curtain rod, three boxes of headshots that would never be signed and sent out to fans. Clothes and towels were scattered across the top. More clothes—most of them Lisa's—crowded the closet. There was an out-of-tune acoustic guitar in the corner, and a desk with an old TV on it. A thick, feathery dust coated the screen.

Luke had given Kitty a glass of cold water and used a soft cloth to wipe the blood from her forehead. He'd tried leading her into the living room to sit down, but she pulled back, pointing at the window. "They can see in," she said, trembling, clutching at him. So he sat her at the breakfast bar and rubbed her back while she sobbed.

"Kitty, what's going on?" he'd asked. "Do I need to call the police?"

"I don't know," she replied. Her hands shook as she lifted the glass to her lips and drank. "Right now I need a hot shower and a long sleep."

So he showed her to the bathroom, and put a fresh (sort of) towel and some clean clothes—Lisa's—out for her, then began cleaning the spare room. Kitty was a long time in the shower, which was just as well, because there was a lot of crap to clear. He moved most of it to the garage, piling it on top of the useless crap already in there. The rest he reassigned to his bedroom, where it would probably stay until he got his head together enough to deal with it.

He found some clean (sort of) sheets and made the bed, then closed the blinds. Perfect timing. Kitty stepped out of the bathroom wearing Lisa's Lakers top and PJ bottoms. They looked quite alike—the former detective Tera Montecino had been right about that—but not in this moment. Kitty was a fraction of her usual self. Her skin was dull, her body drawn inward, like a plant that needed water.

"Better?" Luke asked. He didn't know what else to say.

"A little." A tired, sad smile. She gestured at the clothes. "These are a good fit."

"Yeah, I thought they would be." He shrugged. "They smell kind of musty, but they're clean, I promise you."

"It's all good."

Kitty climbed into the bed, wincing as she moved. Luke left the room and came back with a glass of water, which he set on the nightstand, along with his prescription bottle of Xanax.

"These'll calm your jitters . . . help you sleep."

"I'll take two."

She took them with a sip of water, then sank her head into the pillow and closed her eyes.

She was out a long time.

Luke looked in on her every now and then. The first time she was eerily still, breathing slowly. The cut on her forehead had started to bleed again—not much, just a trickle—and he took the opportunity to clean it with an antibiotic ointment, then close it with Steri-Strips and tape a gauze over the top.

Kitty had been more animated the next time he checked on her. She rolled her head on the pillow, whimpering, "Please, no," over and over. Her body twitched beneath the sheets.

Luke sat on the edge of the bed and placed a hand on her shoulder. "Shhh," he soothed. "It's okay now. You're safe." And he stayed there until she settled.

He tried watching TV but couldn't focus, so he cleaned the kitchen instead. A deep, into-every-corner clean. It was surprisingly therapeutic.

His mind buzzed with what might have happened to Kitty. Had she been mugged? Raped? Why didn't she go to her own apartment, or call the police? The questions mounted, and the sad truth was there were too many possible answers. In the end, Kitty would either tell him, or not, and he would respect that.

He'd be there for her, whatever she needed.

It felt good to care about something again.

It was almost two A.M. when Kitty woke up screaming. Luke leapt up from the sofa—the TV was on but he hadn't been watching it, not really—and bolted into the spare room. She'd clapped a hand over her mouth by the time he'd thrown the door open, as if aware her voice might alert the neighbors. *They can see in*, Luke thought with a chill. Kitty looked at him over the top of her hand. Her eyes were petrified circles, her chest pumping as she fought to suppress her cries.

"Hey, it's okay . . . it's okay, Kitty."

She shook her head. Nothing was okay.

"You're safe here. No one can hurt you." He moved to touch her, to ease her, but thought better of it, so placed both hands on his own chest, over his heart. "I'm here, Kitty. You're safe now."

She gradually calmed, removing her hand from her mouth and sinking back down into the pillow. Her wet eyes flashed in the light edging in from the hallway.

"Okay, Kitty. It's okay."

He remained by her side, kneeling, both hands over his heart, until she drifted into sleep again—still, quiet, and soon deep.

Luke *didn't* sleep. Or not for long, at least. There were a few smoke-like threads, but the clock on his phone never made any big jumps.

He got up a little before six, brewed a pot of coffee, then poured himself a mug and sat out on the back stoop. Birds occupied the eucalyptus tree in his yard, singing with exuberant break-of-day voices. Luke listened, yawning, his own morning sounds—slurps, grunts, and farts—notably less appealing.

In the glory days, he'd go for a swim first thing in the morning. The best way to wake up. He'd climb bare-ass out of bed, stumble groggily outside, and flop into the pool. So much of the grime that had clung to him the day before would be washed away—the bad press, the smell of alcohol, the arguments with Lisa—and he'd emerge baptized, ready to get dirty again.

"Good times," he said.

"I beg to differ."

He jumped off the stoop and whirled around, coffee slopping over the lip of his mug. Kitty stood in the open doorway, regarding him through her huge brown eyes. She tried to smile but it wasn't quite there.

"Hey, Kitty," Luke said, snapping back to the here and now. "How are you feeling?"

"Not good," she replied. "But coffee might straighten me out some."

"Sure, yeah. Absolutely." Luke nodded, content to have somewhere to apply his mind, if only for the next few moments. He stepped back into the kitchen and Kitty followed. "Cream? Sugar?"

"Please. A little of each." She sat at the breakfast bar and looked around. Her eyes brightened. "You cleaned."

"I know, right? I don't know what came over me." He made her coffee, giving her one of the better mugs. "It's hot. Be careful."

"Thank you."

"You hungry?"

"Yes and no." She sipped her coffee, and the look of simple gratitude on her face was heartbreaking. "I am, but I don't know if I can eat."

"Let's find out," Luke said, stepping toward the fridge. He opened the door and looked inside. "I don't have much. Few eggs.

One lonely sausage. I think there are a couple of bagels in the freezer."

"Sure."

He set about fixing Kitty breakfast—again, content to do anything that didn't involve hovering awkwardly around her, afraid of saying the wrong thing. In his experience, trying to comfort an emotional woman was like trying to defuse a bomb. There were several wires to choose from, but only one that wouldn't go boom.

"I got pickles," he said. "You want a pickle with it?"

"Ugh. No."

Luke looked at her and tried a smile. She tried one back. Yeah, he was doing okay.

He made her scrambled eggs and sausage with a hot buttered bagel on the side. She took it onto the back stoop to eat, clearly feeling more comfortable at the rear of the house, which couldn't be seen from the road. Luke joined her a moment later with a bagel of his own, smeared with peanut butter, and they ate together in silence. Or a *near*-silence, anyway; Kitty made mewling, grateful sounds as she forked food into her mouth. She cleaned her plate entirely.

"Well, I guess that answers *that* question," Luke said.

"I guess so."

"More coffee?"

"Sure. But hey, I can get it."

She took her empty plate and both their mugs into the kitchen, and emerged a moment later with refills. She handed Luke his, then resumed her place on the stoop. They sipped their coffees quietly, letting the morning grow around them.

"You know how long it took me to climb over your back fence?" Kitty asked when just enough time had passed.

Luke stared into his mug, his brow cut with a long frown. He opened his mouth to say something, then closed it again. The birds in the eucalyptus chattered inanely. He wasn't about to join them.

"You want to know what's going on," Kitty said. It wasn't a question.

"Only if you want to tell me," Luke replied. He scratched his beard and fixed her with an honest stare. "But first, you need to know three things."

"Okay."

"Number one: Whatever you tell me, you can trust me. Number two: I won't judge you, because heaven knows we've all done things we regret. Number three: I have lived with my fair share of injustice and pain. That gives me a jaded but realistic perspective, and if I can use that to help you, I will."

Kitty nodded. She drank from her mug and sighed, looking around Luke's modest backyard, perhaps wondering where to begin. Finally, she said, "Have you noticed anybody unusual hanging around outside my apartment? A stocky white guy with a shaved head and skull tattoos? Or a tall guy . . . looks like a Viking?"

Luke gave it a moment's thought, then shook his head. "No, but I didn't leave the house yesterday, and I bet I didn't look out the front window more than three or four times."

Kitty sighed again, and this went deep, all the way to the base of her belly, and out in a hard rush of air.

"I told you I was a courier," she said, "and that was true. But what I used to courier was drugs. First meth and ecstasy, then canary."

"Canary?" Luke bit his lip, but couldn't get the surprised note out of his voice. "Oh . . . okay."

"No, Luke. It's not okay."

Kitty started at the beginning and talked for a long time, and Luke realized there were occasions when you didn't have to say anything at all.

Sometimes it was better to just listen.

12

IN A BAD PLACE

The dude with the shaved skull entered Kitty's apartment building at 3:13 P.M. The bulky Black dude—Ruben Osterfeld; Luke had seen some of his UFC bouts—exited at 3:17. There was nothing surreptitious about their movements. They came and went as if they lived there.

No sign of the Viking.

Luke had looked him up online, though, and he wasn't hard to find. Johan Fly had two YouTube channels, each with over four million subscribers. One was for video games. The other—*Vibin' Viking*—followed Johan through the streets of Los Angeles, usually cruising in his Mustang, hanging with his homies, or barhopping on the Strip. He came across as a big personality, the life and soul of the party. The kids no doubt loved him, but Luke saw a privileged douchebag who thought way too much of himself, and who likely hadn't struggled for anything his entire life.

"It's a front," he'd said to Kitty, the YouTube video paused on a shot of Johan pumping free weights at Muscle Beach. "All gangsters hide behind a legitimate business. This is his. It's very Gen Z."

"I guess." Kitty couldn't look at Johan for long. She pushed Luke's cell phone away with a shudder. "Doesn't seem very Viking, though."

"That's because Johan Fly *isn't* a Viking," Luke said. "He's a rich, entitled asshole from the Palisades."

"Tell that to Sly Boy."

Kitty was right. Johan was asking his subscribers to "hit the 'like' button" one moment, and beheading rival drug dealers the next. The guy was dangerously charismatic, and seriously unbalanced—a psychosis that could only lead to ruin.

Luke searched beyond the social media persona, looking for evidence of this psychosis. He found nothing. There were numerous pictures of Johan as a chubby preteen: fly-fishing at Piru Creek with his old man, posing alongside the new family Maserati, standing outside a Viking ship museum in Denmark. There was an article in *Three-Tier Online* about Johan's decision to turn down UCLA in favor of developing his YouTube career. The most incriminating thing was a disturbing-the-peace incident in which Johan used "fighting words" with a doorman at the Mondrian. The police were called, the situation was defused, and Johan was sent home with a slap on the wrist.

Perhaps Luke didn't dig deep enough, but bitter experience had taught him that shit had a tendency to float to the top, which suggested that Johan had been extremely careful over the years, or that he had friends in high places.

Probably both.

"The heavy with the skull tattoos just showed up at your apartment."

Kitty was on the back patio, which Luke had made more comfortable for her. He'd set up an Adirondack chair with a couple of soft pillows, and a table with a pitcher of ice-cold water on it.

Alexa streamed R&B through the open kitchen window, just loud enough to hear.

"Xander," she said, sitting up as Luke approached. "The berserker."

"Is that what he is?" Luke brushed dirt off the edge of the planter and sat down. "Well, he just went in, and Mr. UFC came out, so yeah, they've got at least one person in position in case you show up."

"Do they really think I'm that stupid?"

"You remember the scene in *Pulp Fiction* when Bruce Willis goes back for his old man's watch?" Luke asked rhetorically. He scratched beneath his jaw. "You left your cell phone and your wallet at home, right?"

"Right."

"Johan's not taking any chances."

The backyard was a safe zone, with wooden fencing and trees providing sufficient privacy. They kept their voices low, though, in case they somehow carried around the front and across the street. There was no harm in being careful, Luke reasoned. Similarly, Kitty wouldn't sit in the living room, even in a chair that couldn't be seen through the window. Luke offered to pull the blinds, but she said that might look suspicious during the day. She also suggested Luke work on a "natural response" in case Johan's boys came knocking, asking if he'd seen the girl from across the street. He did so, practicing in the bathroom mirror, the way he used to practice his lines. *Which girl? Kitty? I haven't seen her for . . . shit, I don't know, three or four days, maybe.* It wouldn't win a SAG Award, but it'd be good enough to fool those jackasses.

"My phone's not up there anymore," Kitty said after a moment. She'd poured herself a glass of water. The ice cubes rattled as she drank. "Johan has it. He will have hacked the password, and now has access to everything—names, telephone numbers, texts, e-mails, photographs, social media. My entire *life*."

Luke shifted position on the edge of the planter and nodded. This was extremely likely. The question was, how could Johan use that information?

"I'm scared, Luke," Kitty said, clearly asking herself the same question. "I'm scared for me, and I'm scared for my family."

She was in a bad place, walled in on all sides. Luke had spent most of the afternoon thinking of ways to sledgehammer through the brickwork, to let in a shaft of natural light and clean air. Or, better yet, to reach through, grab both of her hands, and pull her free.

"I'll find a way to help you," he said, recalling what Floyd had said on their final afternoon together: *You need to rediscover your sense of purpose.* And here was something he could sink his teeth into—that could offer a sense of value after three destitute years.

This was important, but there was another reason, one of self-preservation. Tera Montecino had seen Luke and Kitty together. If Kitty's brutalized corpse were discovered in a dumpster, or—far more likely—she disappeared without a trace, it'd be Luke's head on the chopping block. Shit, Montecino had warned him about this very thing. *Anything happens to her, Luke, I will chase you down like a hound out of hell.*

Luke's throat was uncomfortably dry. He refilled the pitcher, poured a glass for himself, and drained it in one hit.

"Okay," he said to Kitty. "What are the options?"

"There aren't many, and none of them are good." Kitty closed her eyes for a moment, her fingers lightly pressed to the gauze taped across her forehead. "I'm increasingly thinking that going to the police might be the best approach. Just tell them everything and hope they can protect me."

"I don't know," Luke said. "I haven't had the best experience with the police in this city. You'd be putting all of your trust in a system that doesn't run as effectively as it should, especially for African Americans."

"Sad but true."

"And remember," he continued, "Johan is a slippery son of a bitch. You'll need evidence to take him down, and I guarantee his bases are covered."

"Also true," Kitty said. "I heard him talking about cleaning up and putting an alibi into place. He is *not* afraid of the police."

"One of the benefits of being a privileged asshole."

"I know, right?" Kitty rolled her eyes. "But I was looking at this from an insurance point of view."

"What do you mean?"

"Will Johan still come after me if I involve the police?" Kitty winced and shifted her weight in the chair, finding a more comfortable position. "They won't have enough evidence to take him down, but he'll know that if something happens to me, he'll be prime suspect number one."

"He'll only be a suspect if there's a crime," Luke pointed out. "And there's no crime without a body. Do you hear what I'm saying?"

"That he'll tie a concrete block to my ankles and dump me in the Pacific?"

Luke shrugged, thinking the means of disposal would be more . . . *graphic*.

"But he knows *someone* would report me missing," Kitty said, looking for any chink of light. "That might be enough to deter him."

"It won't." Luke shook his head. "Think about it, Kitty. The police would bring him in for questioning. He'd shrug and say he hadn't seen you, then remind them that you were a drug runner, involved with all kinds of shady people."

Kitty covered her eyes and sighed.

"Given Johan's status, skin color, and resources," Luke continued, "I don't see how going to the police can work favorably for you."

"I have to do *something*," Kitty hissed. She removed her hand from her eyes, smearing a tear across her cheek in the process. "I can't run for the rest of my life, always looking over my shoulder. I want to stay in this town, Luke. I want to make something of myself."

Luke nodded, acknowledging both the unfairness and the ambition. But it was this hunger for success that had landed Kitty in such hot water. Her new talent agent had said that she needed something to set her apart from the competition, and Kitty had taken this very seriously. Listening to her story, Luke asked himself if he would've done the same thing. Young, new in town, with access to canary, would he have appropriated a pinch here and there to help elevate him to a higher level?

Damn right he would.

"You have to lie low for a while." Luke leaned closer to Kitty, measuring his tone so that it was both forthright and kind. "Give Johan some time to cool his jets, and to prove to him that you're not bringing in the cops."

"Run away, you mean." More tears spilled down Kitty's cheeks and she used Lisa's shirt to wipe them away. "Hide from the big bad man."

"Not forever."

"How long? A few months? A few years?"

"Maybe a year."

"And what if—while I'm working on some potato farm in Idaho—Johan goes after my family? What if he kills them to get back at me?"

"I don't think that will happen," Luke said, although he was far from certain. "Johan Fly isn't the Colombian cartel. He's a drug dealer to the rich and famous. Dangerous? Yeah. Protected? No doubt. But that protection only stretches so far, and it sure as hell doesn't stretch all the way to Kentucky."

"You don't know that."

"No," Luke conceded. "But Johan has been careful so far, which tells me he's smart, which further tells me that he isn't going to take his brand of malice to the other side of the country. He's an L.A. boy, born and bred. Everything he knows is right here."

"Maybe," Kitty said. "Maybe not."

"I know. It's all conjecture." Luke spread his hands and sighed. "All guesswork."

Kitty touched the gauze on her brow again, looking at him through a haze of emotion. "I appreciate everything you're doing, but I can't depend on guesswork. I need a solid plan of action, and I need it quickly."

Luke topped up their glasses. The sound of pouring water, amid this dialogue of desperation and fear, was altogether lovely. He handed Kitty her glass—gave her a moment to drink and regain a thread of composure. They welcomed other sounds: birdsong, the breeze, Alexa playing Marvin Gaye. Beyond the backyard, two neighbors quarreled in Spanish and a FOX 11 news chopper hovered over Echo Park.

"I need to get this psycho off my back," Kitty said, once the moment—all too brief—began to fray at the edges. "It's the only way."

"You know any hit men?" Luke asked wryly.

"No. Do you?"

"Unfortunately not," Luke replied. "Although I used to go on motorcycle rides with Keanu."

"John Wick?" Kitty cracked a smile. "I wish."

"So, hey, I don't know . . ." Luke threw up one hand. "Why not hang here for a few weeks, let the dust settle? Then . . . shit, maybe reach out to Johan, see where his head is at, convince him you're not going to be a problem."

"Yeah, I tried reasoning with him—right after he decapitated Sly

Boy." Kitty pressed a hand to one side of her head, perhaps trying to push the memory away. "The bottom line: I stole from him, and I've got serious dirt on him. That makes me a threat."

This was true. Johan was, above all, a star-soaked narcissist, bathing in the adoration of his followers. He'd likely wriggle out of prison time, but Kitty could still throw shade on his reputation. These days, it didn't take much to get someone canceled.

"And the only way I'm *not* a threat," Kitty added, "is if I'm dead."

With these words, something dropped into Luke's mind. It fell heavily, with weight and heft, a way—*possibly*—to hammer through the brickwork. He looked at Kitty, his eyes widening with a kind of desperate hope.

"What if you *were* dead?" he asked.

"Huh?" Kitty shrank back into her seat, her lips trembling. "Luke, I don't like the way you're looking at me."

He stood up with a flourish and whirled on his heels. A grin surfaced just above his chin and reached all the way to his cheekbones.

"I have an idea," he said.

PART II

STRAY BULLETS

13

DEAD KITTY

The full-length mirror displayed an old companion, a man he'd become intimate with—had embodied—for fourteen full weeks of principle photography, and another six days of reshoots. His neck was scrawnier and his shoulders not quite as broad, but this was him: Colton Stone, with his focused, steely gaze and cleanly shaved jaw.

"Better tell me what I want to know, *ese*, or my friends Smith and Wesson will start asking the questions."

A sad, surprised breath caught in Luke's throat. He reached out one hand and walked closer to the mirror, almost as if he could step through, back into a life of autographs and red carpets. A feeling of longing overwhelmed him—an acute, immersive déjà vu. It was in everything, from Colton's wide, cowboy-like stance (which Luke had adopted without even thinking) to the odor of the silicone adhesive keeping his blond wig in place.

"Jesus, you look the part," Kitty said.

"Yeah," Luke said, using Colton's gravelly, Texas-tinged voice.

He hadn't stepped onto a TV or movie set for over three years. His last real acting gig was in the Hulu original *Bleeding Out*, in which he'd played a punch-drunk boxer. It was a supporting role, maybe a dozen lines, but the writing was strong and he was able to demonstrate some range. The audience never saw this, though, because his scenes were cut from the movie after everything with Lisa went down.

And sure, voice acting was still *acting*. He told himself this all the time. But it wasn't the same—certainly not the dogshit he'd been churning out these past three years. For Luke, there was nothing like stepping onto a set in full costume and makeup, becoming so absorbed in the role that the lights and cameras disappeared.

He missed it. God, he missed it so *much*.

"You're going to crush this," he vowed to his reflection. This was the positive mantra he would recite before every performance. "You are the man. You are the fucking *man*."

There were no cameras rolling, no director, but even so, it felt good to be back.

Luke rented a '78 Camaro from Hooper's Movie Cars on Holly-wood Boulevard, partly because he didn't think Colton Stone would ever drive a 2007 Dodge Caliber, but mainly because Johan had likely seen the crappy little car, with its distinctive dents and rust patches, parked in the driveway opposite Kitty's apartment.

This performance *had* to be convincing, from top to bottom. One errant detail could condemn him—and Kitty—to the cutting room floor.

The three-hour rental set Luke back two hundred and eighty bones. Not cheap, but if it helped sell the illusion, it was money well spent. Besides, the Camaro was a blast to drive, with its worn leather interior and gator-like V-8. Luke couldn't resist a moment to cruise, growling up and down the Strip with the windows down and the radio way too loud.

He stayed on Sunset, taking it southwest to the Palisades, stop-ping only once to buy a bottle of water and a calming supplement for his nerves. (What he would give for a pinch of canary.) He sat on the hood of the Camaro, mentally reciting his mantra, giving the remedy time to kick in. He wasn't recognized as Luke Kingsley or Colton Stone, which didn't surprise him. *Out of Midnight* was a competent crime drama that—like all of Luke's movies—failed to make an impact at the box office. It had something of a cult following, but for the most part could be found in the bargain bins at Walmart and Target, or streaming on services like Popcornflix and Tubi.

Johan's family home was in a guard-gated community in the Palisades Highlands, but Kitty said that Johan kept a crib close to the Village, and this was where he could be found when he wasn't engaging in his social media or canary-dealing exploits. Luke used the GPS on his phone to find the place—an uber-modern glass box surrounded by willow and palm trees. A curved driveway distanced it from the street, enclosed by a wrought-iron gate that managed to be both elegant and imposing.

Luke pulled up to the gate, then took a deep breath and pressed the button on the intercom. A security camera positioned on the adjacent wall challenged him with its single, deprecatory eye.

No response.

"Come on, motherfucker," Luke hissed. Despite the supplement he'd taken—Indian ginseng and B12 with some other shit thrown in—his heart still ran at an agitated clip. He looked through the gate at the drooping willow branches and discerned the back end of a black SUV parked at the top of the driveway. *Someone* was home.

He pressed the button again, waited, then pressed it a third time, and this was the charm. A male voice came through the intercom's speaker—one staticky word, but irrefutably impatient.

"Yeah?"

Luke dropped into character. "Detective Colton Stone. Los Angeles police. I'd like a few words with Johan Fly."

Five seconds of heavy silence, then: "What do you want with Johan?"

"What are you, his fucking mommy?" Colton was not a cop of infinite tact. His approach was often coarse, but effective. "Open the goddamn gate."

Another brief silence, then: "Johan's not home."

"Where is he?"

"Out. Filming. I don't know where."

Luke's turn to pause. He'd wanted to talk to Johan—to get all up in his shit, put a scare on him—but this wasn't essential to the plan. In fact, it might work better this way, provided the information he divulged was passed along to Johan (which it *would* be). It'd doubtless be more convincing if relayed via a trusted source.

"Well, I'm not leaving here until I talk to someone, so I guess it'll have to be you." Luke clicked his tongue, as if encouraging a horse, and used his left hand to gesture at the gate. "Let's go, muchacho. Open up."

Luke counted five seconds, waiting for the gate to slide open, showing nothing but cool despite the jitters he still felt inside. He was about to punch the button again when the voice came back.

"I'm going to need to see some ID."

Luke nodded, surreptitiously wiping a thread of sweat from his brow. He leaned to one side and yanked Colton Stone's ID from the ass pocket of his jeans, not issued by the Los Angeles Police Department, but by Sparx Movie Props & Magic. It was good work, with the detective's photo on one side and his shield on the other. A little souvenir from the shoot.

Luke held it up to the security camera, one eyebrow raised impatiently. His hand was unnaturally steady, as if an invisible scaffold supported it from beneath.

He waited seven (very) slow seconds before, finally, the gate beeped twice and rolled back on its tracks. Luke pocketed his

ID, removed his foot from the brake pedal, and started up the driveway.

"Okay," he whispered. "Quiet on the set."

That was the rehearsal. Now it was showtime.

The voice belonged to the stocky dude with the shaved skull. Xander Cray. The berserker. He stepped outside as Luke parked the Camaro next to the black SUV, poised on the front steps with his arms folded. He looked older than Johan, closer to forty, but with the broad shoulders and cut biceps of a man half his age.

Luke killed the ignition, pulled a manila envelope from inside the glove compartment, and stepped out of the car. Xander didn't move to greet him. He'd rooted himself to the front step, forming a barricade between Luke and Johan's domain.

"And you are?" Luke said as he approached.

"Alexander." There was a yellowing bruise on the left side of his head, probably where Kitty had whacked him with her skateboard. Good for Kitty. "Everyone calls me Xander."

"Xander Cray?" Luke hooked his right thumb into his back pocket, the move opening his jacket in front and briefly exposing the pistol strapped just above his hip. He'd bought the holster that morning. The pistol was his .38 Special snub, finally liberated from its lockbox by way of Jay's Lock & Key Service in Echo Park.

This move—flashing his sidearm—was deliberate, of course. Colton Stone did it twice in *Out of Midnight*, and both times the schnook he'd confronted spilled the beans. Luke didn't need Xander to spill anything, only squirm a little. It worked.

"Yeah," Xander said. His gaze had flicked to the sidearm the moment it came into view, and his shoulders dropped slightly. "Yeah, that's me."

"Right." Luke nodded, thumb still in his back pocket, legs

slightly spread, the full cowboy stance. "Your name has come up a few times."

"In regard to what?"

"We'll get to that." Luke fanned himself with the manila envelope, then nodded at the double-wide front door. "Any chance we can step inside? It's hotter'n a stepmother's kiss out here, and I'll bet that big glass house has one heck of an air-conditioning system."

Xander considered this request for a moment, the thoughts zipping across his face like buzzing insects. He decided, though, that cooperating was the wisest course of action. A slight nod, then he turned and entered the house. Luke followed, his bootheels clipping off the marble steps.

"What's this about?" Xander asked once they were both inside. He stood in the foyer, his arms folded again, not prepared to go any deeper into the house.

Luke inhaled the cooler air, ignoring Xander for now. Let him wait. Let him writhe. The foyer was a bright space with a water fountain, several tall plants, and a broad white wall decorated with Norse art. There were various runes and symbols, a painting of Yggdrasil, the tree of life—Luke had done his homework—and two crossed swords that looked as if they might have been wielded by Ragnar Lodbrok.

"This is all very Nordic," Luke remarked, gesturing at the wall.

"Johan is descended from the great Norse warriors," Xander replied with total conviction.

"Really? He traced his family tree all the way back to the tenth century? That's impressive." Luke whistled through his teeth, looking from the wall to Xander. "Mind you, those Viking men put their dicks in just about anything that moved. That is one wide DNA pool. We've probably all got a little Viking inside us."

He winked, then drew a couple of horns out of the sides of his head and growled. "Grrrr."

"Vikings didn't wear horned helmets," Xander said with a gray expression. "That's a fallacy."

"Yeah, well, I'm not exactly up on my Norse history. I'm more concerned with the present."

"Me, too. So what do you want?"

Luke reverted to the cowboy stance, letting his jacket flap open again—another flash of the sidearm, just to remind Xander who was in charge. His jitters had subsided. There were still a few resolute butterflies fluttering around in his stomach, but not enough to affect his performance. Maybe the calming supplement had kicked in. Or—and this was more likely—it was because he'd *become* Colton Stone. This happened all the time on set. His performance anxiety dissipated the moment the tape started to roll and he dropped into character.

"I'm investigating a homicide," he said, walking over to a potted olive tree, letting this statement percolate while he studied the plant's dull green leaves.

"Okay," Xander said, and swallowed awkwardly. He obviously thought this was about Kris "Sly Boy" Streeter—that Kitty had told the cops everything—and was readying whatever script Johan had given him. "If I can help in any way . . ."

"This is a *nice* place," Luke said, hands on his hips, craning his neck to look at the tall windows and swaying palms beyond. "What, exactly, does Johan Fly do?"

"He's, umm . . ." Xander blinked and shook his head, the stark change of subject catching him off guard. This was another Colton Stone tactic. Don't let the suspect get into a groove. "He's a YouTuber."

"I know that, but what does that entail?"

"He uploads videos to YouTube and gets paid for advertising, product placement, and affiliate links."

"Jeez, he must get paid a *lot*."

"He does."

"And what do you do for him?"

Xander shuffled his feet and pulled his left earlobe, probably a nervous tic. "I'm his . . . assistant."

"You're his assistant," Luke said, frowning, "but you don't know where he is right now—where he's filming?"

"I don't live in his pocket," Xander said. He let go of his earlobe and folded his arms, reestablishing his rigid body language. "Johan's a high-energy guy. He doesn't stay in one place on a shoot. It's tough to keep tabs on him."

"Right." Luke nodded and stepped a little closer to Xander, but not so close that he might reveal the lining of his wig. "So what *do* you do, exactly?"

"I drive for him sometimes," Xander replied. "I facilitate meetings and provide security when necessary."

"Well, you sure look like a bodyguard," Luke said, taking in Xander's muscled shoulders and broad neck. "But an assistant? Nah . . . I don't think so."

"What does an assistant look like?"

"It's probably not very *PC* of me to say." Luke spread his hands and pushed out his lower lip. "But I would think a young, good-looking heterosexual man like Johan would employ a young, good-looking heterosexual woman to oversee his administrative needs."

"Yeah, no." Xander rolled his eyes. "Get your head out of the fifties, boss."

"I know, right? I'm such a terrible male." Luke pulled a wry face. "But I was thinking, you know . . . someone like Kitty Rae."

Xander tried not to react to Kitty's name but couldn't manage it. He touched the bruise on his head, then went back to his left earlobe, giving it a couple of firm tugs.

"You know her, right?" Luke asked coolly.

"I, umm . . ."

"African American? Twenty-five years old?"

"Right. Yeah." Xander flared his nostrils. "I think she did a couple of small jobs for Johan. I'm not sure what, exactly."

"Okay." Luke nodded and stepped over to the fountain, walking slowly, enjoying the way his bootheels echoed in the wide space. He ran his hand beneath the cold water, waiting for Xander to speak just so that he could cut across him.

"Listen, I don't—"

"Have you seen her lately?" Luke's lips twitched. It felt good to be someone else, even an asshole cop like Colton Stone.

"Kitty?"

"Yeah, Kitty," Luke said. He took his hand from the cascading water, wiped it down the front of his jacket, and walked back over to Xander. "When was the last time you saw her?"

Xander pressed his lips together, creasing his brow, pretending to give this some thought. "I, umm . . ." He made a vague gesture with his hand. "A week ago? Maybe?"

"Someone matching your description was seen entering Kitty's apartment building in Silver Lake at approximately three P.M. on Tuesday." Luke ran a thumb across his freshly shaved chin. "What can you tell me about that?"

"Three P.M.?" Xander's mean little eyes shifted as he considered how best to tackle this. "Right. Yeah. Johan wanted her for a job, I think. She wasn't answering her phone so I went to her apartment. There was nobody home."

Luke snorted. He could make this little shit tie himself in knots for the next hour—it was fun, too—but that wasn't what he came here for, and he didn't want to push too hard. He had one objective: to sell the ruse. The first part of this was to walk and talk like a real homicide detective—to be *convincing*. Now it was time for part two.

He held up the manila envelope, but paused before opening it. "Hey, you're not squeamish, are you?"

"No." Xander shook his head.

"Good," Luke said, reaching into the envelope and handing Xander the photos of Kitty's corpse.

Luke had pulled another favor with Denny Chick, his makeup-artist buddy from the good old days. Denny, though, hadn't exactly been thrilled about doing unpaid work.

"I'm a fucking *artist*," he'd stormed. "I don't do shit for free."

"*Free?*" Luke had retorted. "Motherfucker, you owe me seventeen thousand dollars. If it wasn't for me, you'd be walking on fucking crutches right now."

"Ah Christ! Are you going to hang that shit over my head forever?"

They were in Denny's studio in Santa Monica, a brightly lit space with an ocean view and jazz-funk playing on the stereo. Everything was mellow, except for Denny—although he probably *had* been until Luke showed up. A filtration system sucked up the smells of solvents and paints. Latex masks and a menagerie of alien-like creatures crowded shelves and hung from the ceiling on strands of nylon.

"I don't want to hang anything over your head, brother. I just need your help." Luke gestured at Kitty, who stood awkwardly by the door. He had cleared out his garage and backed his car in, so that he could smuggle her out of the house without being seen. "We *both* do."

"I get it, man. I *do*. But I'm swamped right now. I just . . . I . . ."

"You do this for me, Denny, this one big favor, and we are square." Luke drew an invisible square in the air and nodded. "I fucking promise you, man. That seventeen K . . . history."

"Yeah?"

"Yeah."

"Well, shit. What is it you want?"

Luke took a deep breath and gestured at Kitty again. "She needs to look dead. Bullet holes in her head and chest. A realistic amount of blood."

Denny shrugged. "Sure, man. Whatevs."

"No, not fucking *whatevs*. This needs to look like the real fucking deal."

"Cool, man, yeah. I can do that."

"Good," Luke said. "And I want you to dress me up like Colton Stone."

"Colton Stone?" Denny frowned. "Who the fuck is Colton Stone?"

"He's the character I played in *Out of Midnight*. The cop." Luke spread his hands in an affronted fashion. "You know, with the blond hair."

"That was Don Johnson played that guy."

"It was fucking *me*."

"Shit, really?" Denny scratched the back of his head and glanced briefly around his studio. "Okay, well, I think I've got a wig that'll work . . . somewhere. I don't have the wardrobe, though."

"I've got the wardrobe," Luke said. "I've got the sidearm. I've even got Colton Stone's ID."

"Then we're all set." Denny nodded. "You want to do this now?"

"Yeah," Luke said. "Right fucking now."

"Jesus Christ," Xander said. His shocked expression was extremely satisfying. He didn't doubt the authenticity of the photographs. Not for one second. "Jesus, what . . . what happened?"

"She got shot is what happened."

"I can *see* that, but . . . but . . ." Color had risen from inside Xander's collar, spreading across his throat in pink blotches. "I don't . . . I don't know what to say."

There were two photographs. One was a full shot of Kitty slumped in some dim concrete corner (Denny's garage), dressed in the same dirty blue bra and sweatpants she'd been wearing when Luke found her in his backyard. Only one strap of the bra was still blue, though; the rest was dark with blood. More blood covered her body and pooled across the concrete around her. The entry wound in her chest was small but distinct. One grubby sneaker lay on the ground nearby.

"The coroner pulled a forty-caliber slug out of her temporal lobe," Luke said, pointing at the other photograph—a close-up of Kitty's face. "It was in the part of her brain that made her feel emotions. You know, like fear."

This second shot was the winner. The hole in the middle of Kitty's forehead looked deep enough to slot a pencil into. Dried blood caked the skin around it and painted her face in zigzag lines, but she was still identifiable. This, Luke told Denny, was all-important. She had one eye open, staring at nothing. Denny had used an opaque contact lens to make it appear as if all the light behind had been snuffed out. The effect was so convincing that Kitty shuddered when she saw the close-up. "Too real," she'd said, and Luke had to agree. The severed head bouncing down the stairs in *It Came from the Dumpster* was great, but this was Denny's best work.

"Christ," Xander said under his breath, and handed the photographs back to Luke.

"She died instantly," Luke said, studying the photos himself, shaking his head sadly. "So there's that."

"Yeah." Xander cleared his throat and pulled his shoulders square. Luke could almost hear his brain ticking, perhaps thinking of ways to break this news to Johan.

The foyer dimmed as a blanket of cloud drifted across the late afternoon sun. Luke turned his face to the tall windows—letting the gravity of the moment carry, then settle into a bleak silence. He sighed, glanced at the photographs once again, then slipped them back into the envelope. They'd worked perfectly. So far, this whole act had gone according to script. He just had to walk in Colton's boots a little longer, then split.

"Listen, Detective, I . . ." Xander ran one hand over his skull, then—tug-tug—pulled on his earlobe again. "I want to help you, but—"

"Is that Yggdrasil?" Luke asked, pointing at the painting of the tree on the wall. "It *is*, right? It's that big-ass mythological tree. *Igg-drah-sill.* Am I pronouncing that correctly?"

"Uh, yeah." Xander stiffened, wrinkling his nose like a bulldog.

"Man, that is a beautiful painting." Luke nodded appreciatively. "I would love something like that in my crib, but I don't have a large enough wall."

Xander smiled coldly. "Johan bought it at auction for three hundred thousand dollars."

"Well, shit, I guess I don't have a large enough wallet, either," Luke said, and barked an ugly laugh. "Maybe I should start my *own* YouTube channel, chasing down freaks and psychopaths."

"Maybe," Xander said. His impatience was building, one tic at a time. He drummed tattooed fingers against his thigh. Luke returned to the script. Just a few lines left.

"I worked vice for three years. Made a lot of contacts on the street." Luke exhibited Colton Stone's characteristic steely gaze. "Multiple sources have informed me that Kitty was involved with some real lowlife assholes, running drugs for them. Meth, mainly."

"I don't know anything about that."

"I also heard that Johan had a score to settle with Kitty, which is why he was looking for her." Luke stepped closer to Xander, holding the envelope up to indicate its contents. "I heard he was *real* pissed off."

"That's news to me." Xander had a steely gaze of his own.

"Remind me again," Luke said, "why you were at Kitty's apartment on Tuesday."

"Johan was looking for her. For a job, I think."

"You think?"

"Yeah, I think." Xander flashed his teeth, then gestured at the envelope. "Listen, I know what you're driving at, but Johan didn't have anything to do with this."

"How can you be so sure?" Luke asked. He assumed the cowboy stance again, his head cocked. "You said yourself that it's tough to keep tabs on him."

Xander opened his mouth to respond, then thought better of it. His nostrils flared as he took a deep, centering breath. Luke held the stance another ten seconds, then stepped backward. He consulted the script in his mind: *Colton moves easily. He's confident but not cocky, strong but not implacable. A cool smile touches his lips and he nods once. Morricone could score his every move.*

"Coroner estimates the time of death to be around midnight last night," Luke said somberly. "Any idea where Johan was at that time? Or what *you* were doing, for that matter?"

"Okay." Xander nodded, held up both hands. The muscles in his face relaxed and he breathed easier. "I was with Johan. We were clubbing in Nueva Vida until three A.M. Slept in the limo all the way home."

"Nueva Vida?"

"It's a town out in the desert, close to the Nevada state line. The club's called Stray Bullets. It's a refurbished saloon. You know, like in the Old West. Some big bands play there. Foo Fighters. The Chili Peppers. It's dope."

"And if I were to take a drive out to Nueva Vida," Luke said, with no intention of driving anywhere but back to the rental company, then home, "the staff at Stray Bullets would confirm this?"

"No doubt," Xander replied. "We were in the VIP area. Johan signed us in. There'll also be a credit card transaction to the tune of three thousand dollars. And you can check with the limo company, too."

"Oh, I will," Luke said seriously.

"Sorry to roadblock your line of inquiry," Xander said smugly, "but we're rock-solid."

Yeah, they were. A perfect alibi for a crime that never happened. But truly, the most rock-solid thing here was Luke's performance. He'd just removed Kitty from Johan's most-wanted list. Maybe they could celebrate later with beer and nachos.

He gave Xander a tight, capitulating smile, tipped one finger, and prepared to exit the shot. *You'll be seeing me*, he'd growl theatrically, or perhaps something more Colton-esque: *If I need to come back, muchacho, it ain't gonna be pretty.* He edged toward the door, deliberating between the two, when Xander decided to ad-lib.

"Hey, you *could* drive out to Nueva Vida, if you want, but I can save you the trip." He tugged his cell phone from his back pocket and held it up. "PictoShark. Welcome to the information age, Detective."

"Huh?" Luke froze mid-step, trying to hold his cool pose.

"It's a photo-sharing app, like Instagram." Xander accessed the app, swiped and scrolled, then turned the screen toward Luke. "These were taken last night. Look. There's a date and time stamp."

Luke stepped forward, adding a hint of swagger to stay in character. The photo on Xander's phone—a selfie—showed Xander sitting at a table loaded with colorful drinks, with Johan in the background, one arm looped around a beautiful woman. The date and time beneath the shot supported their alibi.

"Yeah." Luke scratched his jaw and sneered, affecting doubt. "That could have been taken anywhere."

"Check out the novelty powder keg behind us." Xander zoomed in. "Says STRAY BULLETS right on it."

It did.

"And here, look." He scrolled through a few more photos: Johan with some other long-haired dude, sticking out their tongues; a close shot of an elaborate cocktail; another pretty woman dressed in a cowboy hat and Stray Bullets T-shirt. "That's Tanika, our server. Notice the tee."

"Already did."

"Here's the stage." A small raised area loaded with musical instruments and a Stray Bullets backdrop. "A band called Mean Heat played last night. They rocked it. And wait, one more . . ."

Xander zipped through several more photos, a blur of lights, bodies, and faces, and Luke was about to say that he'd seen enough when one of those faces leapt off the screen and almost knocked him onto his ass.

"Whoa, shit! Wait a second, back up, back the fuck up." He wanted to grab the phone out of Xander's meaty hands. "Go back . . . no, not that one. Keep going."

Xander flicked through the images until he reached the right one—

"That's it. Stop."

Luke's heart plunged and his lungs filled with a heavy, unbreathable air. Memories surfaced, incomplete but colorful: slamming tequilas at Uncle Lizard's; wild, woody aromas mixed with Dolce & Gabbana perfume; the softness of Lisa's kiss. Luke clenched his jaw, trying to keep his cool, but the script he'd been following had burst into flames and Colton Stone had left the set. Now it was just Luke, with all his fears and failings.

"What's the big deal?" Xander asked.

"Him," Luke said, and pointed.

Three people in the photo: Xander, Johan, and—standing between them—a tall (*tallish*) Latino with a narrow jaw and close-set eyes.

"Him," Luke said again.

It was the bat-faced man.

. . .

Luke was late returning the Camaro. There'd be a $200 minimum charge but he didn't care; rental company policies were not a point of concern at that moment. He was parked on a residential street just off Sunset Boulevard—and had been for the past hour—lost in the depths of his phone. He'd signed up to PictoShark using a fake name and had tried following Xander but his account was private. It didn't matter. Luke found the photo he wanted using the Stray Bullets hashtag. He found other shots of the bat-faced man under the same hashtag, going back several years. He was obviously a regular.

"There you are," Luke whispered. He'd dropped the relevant snaps in a favorites file and swiped quickly between them. "There you fucking are."

Xander hadn't given him a name, despite the way he and Señor Bat Face were cozied up in the photo. He claimed not to know him—that he was just some guy who'd jumped in on the shot. No surprise there, Xander had said. A lot of people wanted their picture taken with Johan.

"On *your* phone?" Luke had asked.

"I don't know. We were drunk." Xander had shrugged—no big deal. "It just happened."

Maybe he was lying. Luke didn't want to press too hard. He'd slipped out of character and this unrelated matter might undo all his good work. But he had something now. Something to work with.

He ran a hand through his hair—his real hair; the blond wig was in the passenger seat—then exited PictoShark and brought up Google Maps. Nueva Vida was two hundred and fifty miles away. He could be there before dark—in time, perhaps, to watch the bat-faced man pull up a stool at Stray Bullets and order a shot of mescal.

Luke remembered the way Lisa had sidled up to him at Uncle Lizard's, the intimate way they'd spoken. There was *something* between them. No doubt about it.

"They knew each other," Luke whispered with certainty.

He wiped sweat from his throat and breathed deeply. It occurred to him that he could off-load this information on Tera Montecino. But would she follow up on it? She didn't like Luke—fucking *despised* him, in fact—but was she big enough to look beyond that and chase down a genuine lead? Luke wasn't sure. Perhaps if he had more information—a name, an address . . .

He looked at the map again.

"Nueva Vida," he said.

It was Spanish for New Life.

14

WHAT FRIENDS DO

Kitty had used Luke's phone to send a text to Connie (having to dig the number from the recesses of her brain—she couldn't remember Mama's number at all), warning her not to reply to any messages.

> My phone was STOLEN!! If u get a text it is NOT from me. DO NOT RESPOND!!!
> Tell mama and everyone else. I will call u when I have a new cell (sending this
> via a friend!!)

The idea that Johan might be exchanging texts with her family—pretending to be her—filled Kitty with a cold and miserable gloom. This, hopefully, would sever that line of communication.

It had been Luke's idea. She would have thought of it herself, and probably a lot sooner, except her brain was only functioning at about forty percent power. The drugs had something to do with that. The painkillers. The Xanax. Mainly, it was the memories— the vivid flashbacks of that terrible night, everything from Sly Boy's rain-cloud expression to the sound of Johan's ax scraping across the cement floor.

. . .

Kitty waited for Luke to return home, trying to distract herself by sleeping, listening to music, or watching Netflix on the dusty TV in the spare room. None of it worked, and she didn't like being in the house by herself. She took a long shower and that helped a little, although the worst of the grime was on the inside. The easiest—and certainly most healing—part of her afternoon was when she sat on the toilet and had a good, deep cry.

Phase one of the plan was to make Johan believe she was dead, which would get him off her back and keep her family safe. It was a stroke of genius from Luke, and his commitment to realism was off the charts, but it wasn't a long-term solution. Not if she wanted to stay in Los Angeles (which she did), and certainly not if she planned on getting into TV and movie work.

Phase two was to defame Johan—to use the internet against him. This was a more tenuous procedure, but Luke was confident he could make it work.

"Discrediting celebrities is all the rage," he'd said. "Trust me, I know what I'm talking about. The internet goes from being a golden, robust structure that supports and celebrates you, to a cancel culture that'll burn your shit to the ground."

"But any kind of smear campaign will be traced to its point of origin," Kitty had said, unable to keep the concern from her voice. "Then it'll be *you* in Johan's crosshairs."

"No, it won't, because I'll be six degrees of Kevin Bacon removed from it." Luke nodded assuredly, then drummed one finger against his temple. "I know people. Shitty Hollywood sharks that circle constantly for a single drop of blood. They'll take this and fight over every scrap. The canary, the celebrities, the Viking imagery . . . it'll be a goddamn feeding frenzy, and I'll be the little fish swimming in the opposite direction."

Kitty covered her mouth, perhaps to hide the hopeful smile that had snuck onto her face. It didn't feel right to hope when so much was broken, but it was *there*, a nebulous cluster of energy, too small to truly shine, too real to be ignored.

"You really think this will work?" she asked.

"Yeah, I do. But I need you to tell me everything you know. I want names, dates, and addresses. Credible information." Luke linked his hands across his chest and leaned forward. "I'll start out slow. Just a little drop of blood here and there. But as soon as the sharks begin sniffing around, Johan's contacts and clients—all those do-good celebrities—will get the fuck out of the water. They won't want *anything* to do with him."

"He won't like that," Kitty said. "The hit to his pride, to his status. He'll begin to unravel."

"Yeah, and then I'll add the *real* meat." Luke grinned and snapped his fingers. "The big guy, Mr. UFC—"

"Ruben."

"You said he turned on Sly Boy, right?"

"Yeah. He was working for Johan behind the scenes—told him everything Sly Boy had been doing."

"Okay, so Ruben has proved himself to be about as loyal as a wet piece of toilet paper." Luke sat back in his seat and shrugged. "I'll find a way to credit at least some of the leaks to him, and Johan won't look any further."

Kitty scrunched her hands into fists and pressed them to her eyes. Everything felt larger than she could comfortably hold. She didn't know if Luke's plan—*any* of it, including faking her death—would work, but she wanted to hug him, if only for his willingness to bear the load.

"Thank you," she said, but the words were enveloped in a rush of emotion, and all she managed was a grateful sigh.

"This might take a few months," Luke continued. "But it'll

hopefully culminate in Johan being sent down for a very long time, and he won't have the same level of protection because his name will be shit in this town."

"Yes," Kitty said. Another sigh.

"The best part, the *key* part: he won't suspect you in any of this, because he's going to think you're dead. So you can go home to Kentucky, be with your family. Then, when you see on the news that Johan has blown his brains out or gone to prison, you can return to L.A. and pick up where you left off."

Kitty shook her head. That little cluster of hope swelled inside her, but she was afraid to encourage it. The possibility of getting her acting career off the ground, of prospering in L.A. and making her family—her *son*—proud, seemed ridiculously far away. These were the aspirations of a different person. Someone carefree . . . unbroken.

Still, she had something now—a *chance*, albeit fragile, to turn this around.

Tears streamed from her eyes. Luke handed her a Kleenex but it wasn't enough. She got out of her seat, went to him, and hugged him as tightly as her aching body could manage.

"Shhh . . . hey, it's okay," he said. "I'll get you through this. I promise."

Kitty wondered how this man could be behind his wife's disappearance, her murder. The negativity and vitriol directed at him may or may not be justified. How could Kitty know for certain? She only had her own experience to go on, and where everyone else saw darkness, she saw light.

It seemed the only thing she'd done right the entire time she'd been in L.A. was save Luke's life.

Luke had said that the Camaro he'd rented was due back at six P.M., and that he'd be home by six-thirty at the latest. Kitty tried not to watch the clock, but this became increasingly difficult as the day wore on. Six-thirty came and went. No sign of Luke. Kitty paced the backyard. She watched ten minutes of *The Umbrella Academy*. She redressed the wound on her head. Seven o'clock. Still nothing. Her anxiety ramped up. Had it all gone terribly wrong? Had Johan recognized Luke—or Colton Stone, for that matter—and driven him out to Jink's for a hands-on demonstration of the blood-eagle ritual?

She popped a Xanax, curled up on the bed in the spare room, and managed a light sleep despite her elevated anxiety. There were no nightmares, only sensations: falling, flying, running. She woke unrested—8:42 P.M., according to the clock on the nightstand—and walked through to the kitchen.

Johan sat at the breakfast bar, looking at her through Nordic-rune eyes.

Kitty shrieked and reached for one of the glasses on the kitchen counter—something she could throw, use as a weapon. Johan got up off the stool and stepped toward her.

"Kitty," he said, his hands raised defensively. "*Kitty . . .*"

She was about pitch the glass when she realized that it wasn't Johan's voice.

"Hey, Kitty. It's cool. It's me." Luke lowered one of his hands and pressed it against his chest. "It's me . . . Luke."

The strength went out of Kitty's legs and she slumped to the floor, crying and trembling. Luke went to her, moving slowly.

"It's okay," he said. "I'm here. It's all good."

She caught her breath and after a long moment said, "Jesus, Luke. You scared the shit out of me."

"I know. I'm sorry." Luke inched closer. "You were sleeping. I didn't want to wake you."

"Jesus Christ."

He reached out and carefully removed the glass from her hand.

"I was going to throw that at you," Kitty said.

"Yeah," Luke said. "I'm glad I didn't leave you the gun."

"You said six-thirty at the latest. I was worried."

"Right, yeah." Luke rubbed his eyes. "I lost track of the time."

They were in the living room. Luke had assured her it was safe, but she made him pull the blinds anyway. She sat on the sofa, sipping a valerian tea—good for the nerves, apparently—looking at Luke over the rim of her mug. He was in the armchair, hunched forward, swigging from a bottle of Bud.

"Did it work?" Kitty asked.

"Better than I could've hoped," Luke said, and told her how it went down—everything from how good it felt to be back in character, to the nervous way Xander kept plucking at his earlobe. She had never seen Xander nervous. He'd always been rock-like, mostly expressionless. That Luke had gotten him agitated spoke to how convincing his performance—not to mention those awful photographs—had been.

"You're in the clear," Luke said. "Now you just have to get out of town, keep a low profile."

"I can do that."

"Maybe give it a few weeks before heading to Kentucky—"

"In case Johan has someone sniffing around?"

"Right, but I don't think he will. He'll call off the dogs, and pretty soon he's going to have bigger problems to deal with."

"Phase two," Kitty said. She *did* feel calmer. Maybe it was the tea, or maybe it was the fact that this plan—so far—was working.

"Yeah," Luke said. "Some people deserve to be ruined."

She showed her gratitude with an earnest smile, and they sat without talking for several minutes, a silence disrupted only by the hum of the refrigerator and the air conditioner whirring to life.

Kitty finished her tea, set her mug down on the coffee table, and looked at Luke. His eyes were glazed and distant. Tiredness, perhaps, or something else.

"What is it?" she asked.

"Huh?"

"Your body language. You're distracted. There's something you're not telling me."

"Oh right, yeah." He pressed a finger to the middle of his forehead, then shrugged. "It's a different thing. Don't worry."

"Different?" Kitty leaned forward, encouraging him to open up. "Good or bad?"

"Maybe good. I don't know." So many emotions crossed his face that Kitty couldn't keep up with them all. "Fuck, I don't know."

"I'm listening," she said. "I could do with something maybe good."

He made a sound that was almost a laugh, mostly a sigh, then finished his beer and looked at her through bloodshot eyes. "I may have inadvertently stumbled upon a person of interest—someone who might provide information about my wife's disappearance."

"Holy shit!" For one second, all of Kitty's hurts and woes disappeared, eclipsed by the hope she felt for Luke. It was bright enough to lift her in her seat and touch her eyes with delight.

"It might come to nothing," he said. "Or it could be everything."

"Tell me," Kitty urged. "Shit, Luke, tell me all about it."

The gratitude was in his eyes now. He got up from his seat, grabbed Kitty's empty mug from the table, and walked through to the kitchen.

"You want another tea?"

"I'll take a beer," she said.

"How many Xanax have you had?"

"Not enough."

Luke laughed, his face illuminated by the light inside the refrigerator. He reached past the yogurt and the orange juice—he'd been shopping—and came back with two bottles of Budweiser. He popped the top on one and handed it to her.

"Okay," Kitty said, and took a drink. The beer was bitter and not exactly enjoyable, but it didn't matter. She drank again.

"Okay," Luke echoed, and started talking.

He told her about the night that Lisa disappeared, leaving nothing out. Kitty knew some of it, what she'd seen on the news and read online, but this was the first time she'd heard his side of things. She sensed the weight of his grief, and counted his pains, like crows on the roof of some rusty old truck. It was a wonder he hadn't completely broken down. By the time he'd finished his story, there were four empty beer bottles on the table and the clock on the DVR read midnight.

"So what do you think?" he asked.

"I think you might be on to something," Kitty replied. "I don't know where it will lead, but you need to find this guy—find out who he is."

"Yeah." Luke nodded. "All those photos of him at Stray Bullets. He *has* to be a regular. He probably lives in Nueva Vida."

"I think so, too."

Luke scratched his jaw, where the dark of his beard had started to grow back in. "I keep thinking that I should involve the police. This is *their* job, after all. But they've branded me guilty, like the rest of the world. I don't know how diligently they'll follow up."

"I get it," Kitty said. "You don't want to take any chances."

"It's too *big*," Luke said. His eyes flooded with emotion and his shoulders trembled. "I've lost everything, Kitty. My wife, my friends, my career, my reputation . . . everything I know and love, *gone*. And if there's a chance I can get even some of it back, you'd better believe I'm going to take it."

"Damn right," Kitty said.

"I'm going to Nueva Vida, and I'm going to find that bat-faced son of a bitch." He dragged his hands through his hair, lifting it into wild tufts. "I'm leaving first thing in the morning."

"Sounds good," Kitty said.

"Listen, I don't know how long I'll be gone, but you can chill here, if you want. There's plenty of food in the fridge, and you can—"

"To hell with that," Kitty said. "I'm coming with you."

He looked at her questioningly.

"After what I've been through, I am *not* staying in this house by myself, jumping at every shadow." She wagged her finger. "No way, son. Not happening."

"I hear you," Luke said. "But this is my shit to deal with. Why would you want to get involved?"

"The same reason you got involved with my shit." Kitty patted her chest and blinked. "You said you lost all your friends, but you didn't. You have *me*. And this is what friends do."

Luke smiled in a way that was both heartbreaking and uplifting, although he also looked like he was about to cry.

"No arguments," Kitty said. "I'm coming with you."

"Good," Luke said, and covered his eyes.

Kitty caught maybe an hour's sleep, in total. She got out of bed a little after five A.M. and sat in the kitchen drinking coffee. Luke joined her a short time later, having not slept, either. They barely spoke. But that was fine. They didn't need to.

By six forty-five, they were on their way to Nueva Vida. The westbound 210 was already getting busy with commuter traffic, but it was open road in their direction. Nothing between them and the new day.

15

THE HUNGRY WOLF

The ability to concoct on-the-spot, believable bullshit was one of Xander Cray's (few) talents. He had told the detective investigating Kitty's murder that Johan wasn't home because he was filming for his YouTube channel. Not true, of course. Johan had, in fact, spent the day personally distributing two hundred thousand dollars' worth of free canary samples, reassuring his wealthy customers that his product was back to its former quality. Damage control was expensive and exhausting, but it needed to be done.

He'd been in Barrett Lorne's trailer, on the set of *Crisis Alert*, the first time Xander called.

"My rule: You fuck me over, we're done," Barrett had said, not taking his eyes off the baggie of yellow powder that Johan had just handed him. "I don't believe in second chances."

Johan had glanced at his phone, seen Xander's name on the screen, and swiped to reject the call.

"We have that in common," Johan replied, easing back into his seat and crossing his legs coolly. "I can assure you that the issue has been addressed and it won't happen again. Still, if you don't want to do business anymore, I completely understand."

Barrett took a thumbnail of canary and vacuumed it up his left nostril. Within seconds he was purring like a big, rich cat.

"We're good," he said.

Xander called again forty minutes later, and this time Johan answered. For him to call twice in the space of one hour, knowing the delicate nature of Johan's work, it had to be important.

"Kitty's dead," he said.

Johan was on his way to West Hollywood, to meet with and win back the trust of a certain Academy Award–winning actor and director. He hit the brakes and pulled his car over—a Tesla Model S he'd appropriated from his father's multi-car garage. The Mustang was too beaten up to make the right impression.

"She's *dead*?" Questions bottlenecked in Johan's mind, none of which he wanted to ask over a cellular network, but one found its way through: "How do you know?"

"Cop came to the house looking for you," Xander replied. "He wanted to know where you were last night."

"What did you tell him?"

"That we were partying in Nueva Vida, and we could prove it, too."

"Okay. Good."

"He was a real hard-ass," Xander continued. "Showed me the photos."

"Photos?"

"Of Kitty's dead body. You should have seen her, man. All shot up." Xander clicked his tongue and exhaled. "What a fucking mess."

"We'll talk about this later," Johan said. He shook his head, snapping back to the task at hand. "I've still got work to do."

Five meetings in three hours, then a party at Boardner's. Johan put the work in. He shone, got the job done, but Kitty was on his mind throughout. Dead Kitty. *All shot up*. It was almost two A.M. by the time he got home. He went straight to bed but couldn't sleep. Something nudged the underside of his brain. The mental equivalent of sitting on his car keys.

Cop came to the house looking for you.

A cop? Singular? Didn't homicide detectives usually work in pairs?

A real hard-ass.

Johan tossed and turned, trying to find a comfortable spot, but that pressure on his brain remained. He finally climbed out of bed, poured himself a glass of water, then accessed the home security app on his computer. Within moments he had zipped through footage from the previous afternoon and paused the tape on a shot of the homicide detective holding his ID up to the cam at the main gate.

One cop. No partner. Johan frowned. Unusual, but not impossible. Maybe the department was shorthanded—and the cop only came by to ask a few questions, not make an arrest.

It was an HD feed, no sound, but a clear picture. Johan looked at the detective. Blond hair. Chiseled jawline. He looked familiar. Maybe they'd crossed paths at some other time. Johan zoomed in on the ID. The shield and photo were unobstructed, but the cop's index finger partially blocked out his name.

Stone. *Something* Stone. Anton? Barton?

Johan studied the freeze-frame a moment longer, then shut off his computer and returned to bed. The cop's face accompanied him like some odd balloon, bopping insistently against the inside of his skull.

Sleep came, finally, sweet while it lasted, which was all of four hours. At 7:42 A.M., Johan snapped awake and sat upright in his bed. "Jesus Christ," he hissed, throwing the sheets off his body. He flew from his bedroom, down the hallway, to the TV room. He had a cabinet packed with old DVDs, mainly westerns, pulp horror, and low-budget action flicks. Johan rarely watched them, but he had a vested interest in might-have-been celebrities.

He ran his finger along the DVD spines until he found the movie he was looking for.

Johan ate breakfast, then called Xander and told him to get his ass over ASAP. Xander showed an hour later, muttering about the traffic while brushing donut sugar off the front of his T-shirt.

Johan growled from deep in his chest, then curled his finger in a "come with me" gesture. They passed through the foyer, into the hallway, then down to the TV room. A paused shot of Colton Stone—standing like a cowboy, one thumb hooked into the back of his jeans—adorned the eighty-two-inch screen. Johan had placed his MacBook on the snack table in front of the TV, its much smaller display frozen on another shot of Detective Stone, this time showing his ID at the front gate.

Xander looked from one screen to the other, his eyes darkening with confusion.

"Take all the time you need," Johan said.

Xander frowned, shook his head. He also had donut sugar around his mouth.

"What the fuck?" he said.

Johan picked up the DVD remote and fast-forwarded through a few scenes, pausing again on an action shot of Colton popping some crackhead in the jaw. His hair was slightly different—longer and blonder—than it was in the security cam footage, but it was the same person. No doubt about it.

It took a few seconds, but Xander finally got there.

"That fucking cocksucker," he said.

"You were duped, Xan." A grin brightened Johan's face, although it wasn't entirely good-humored. There was a hint of murderous rage in it, too. Just at the edges, perhaps, or in the flash of his teeth. "Duped by a two-bit fucking actor. Which means Kitty isn't dead at all. She's alive and well, and still a threat."

"Motherfucker."

"His name is Luke Kingsley. He's made a handful of shitty movies, even a couple of decent ones. This is *not* one of them." Johan gestured at the TV screen. "He's most famous for killing his wife."

Xander shook his head. His eyes were extremely large. There wasn't much in the way of intelligent life behind them. Johan took out his phone, hit the Google app, and typed LUKE KINGSLEY into the search field. It brought up a series of images, including the notorious photograph of him with blood all over his shirt. He showed this to Xander, then showed him another shot of Luke on the set of *A Bullet Affair*, and finally, from a couple of months before, him and Kitty at a funeral in Inglewood. This had caused a minor flurry online because Kitty was young and Black, and not dissimilar in appearance to the wife Luke had killed. Johan recalled asking Kitty about it at the time, and she'd waved it off. "I was doing the guy a solid," she'd said. Now Johan sneered. The sight of them together—best fucking friends forever—raised his core temperature by several degrees.

"Jesus Christ," Xander said, looking at Johan's phone. Not touching, though—not with those sugary paws. "I'm sorry, Johan. I guess I fucked up. But damn, the guy was *convincing*."

"In the same way Chris Hemsworth is a convincing Thor?"

"No, he seemed . . . *real*. Like a cop." Xander's eyebrows flared and he pointed at the security cam shot on the MacBook. "He had an ID, for Christ's sake."

"He had a movie prop."

"And photos, Jesus, those *photos*."

"Staged," Johan said.

"Fuck." Xander gritted his teeth. "I mean, that was a ballsy fucking move. He didn't know for sure we wouldn't recognize him."

"It was a desperate move. A *scared* move. It also shows that they knew involving the real police wasn't their best option." Johan looked at the photo of Kitty and Luke again, then dropped his phone back into his pocket. "That's good for us, of course. And smart on their part. Although it's safe to assume Kitty will have told the actor everything she knows. That makes me very . . . anxious."

"We'll take care of him," Xander said. "He can't be hard to find."

"If we get to him, we'll get to Kitty."

"Leave it to me."

Johan hit play on the remote and the movie resumed: a fight scene, followed by a car chase, in which Colton and his partner—a Black guy—drove their Corvette onto the deck of a drug dealer's luxury yacht.

"This is a fucking *Miami Vice* rip-off," Johan said, flaring his lip with disdain. "Only set in L.A."

"Cocksucker," Xander reiterated, watching as Colton slipped out through the driver's-side window and bustled—pistol drawn— through a cluster of swimwear-clad extras.

"He even looks like Don Johnson."

"I'm going to kill him."

Johan kept *Out of Midnight* playing and exited the room without another word. He had demonstrated commendable calmness, defying how he *truly* felt. He needed a moment to cool down and clear his head. Only then could he think his way through this.

He went to his bedroom, peeled off his tee and basketball shorts, and spent some time with his body, not touching, just looking, following the lines, dips, and ridges in a journey-like, meditative way. The contrast between his pale Scandinavian skin and black tattoos was remarkable. He was stark and storied, light and dark, modern and medieval.

You can trust me, Kitty had said, lying to his face. Was she laughing at him now, believing him stupid? She and that actor. That piece-of-shit-actor . . .

A fiery coal of rage climbed Johan's chest and he studied the tattoos on his upper arms until it shrank to a dimly glowing ember.

Better. He then followed the intricate artwork down his left forearm, to his most recent tattoo—the inscription in Younger Futhark on the back of his hand.

He breathed easier.

The hungry wolf will always hunt.

His ancestors were with him. They communicated through his DNA, his blood. Johan often thought that if he were to cut himself, he would smell them—their thick, coarse bodies. His dreams were often loud and brutal.

It started when he was a boy. The voices were foreign, but he interpreted them nonetheless. They told him that he was special, and that he would do great things. Johan announced this to his parents one night at dinner, expecting them to be proud that he'd been chosen. Instead, his father sent him to therapy. His mother's solution was to not care, to let him eat and do whatever he wanted. He weighed 180 pounds by the time he was twelve. A fat, pink-faced boy with long blond hair and mole-rat teeth. He played video games and scoffed empty calories and uploaded tutorials to YouTube: how to beat this boss, how to get past this level, how to unlock this cheat. His channel was a hit. He used his father's money to amp the production value. A kid in Pale Bone, Nevada—older than Johan, a Venezuelan immigrant living in his uncle's basement—produced music, graphics, and sound effects for a modest fee. Johan had met him playing *Call of Duty* online, and it turned out the kid was a genius. "I can make anything," he'd said to Johan, and it was true. If he'd stayed in South America, he might have earned a scholarship to a prestigious college, and maybe gone on to become an astrophysicist or chemical engineer. As it was, he fixed appliances for his uncle Omar and developed computer viruses for fun.

His name was Ramón Sojo Aparicio. He and Johan would go on to form a long and profitable relationship.

Johan and his family lived in a huge house in the Palisades, although his father was rarely present. Aksel Fly's customers included Microsoft, Apple, and IBM. He spent most of his time flying between his offices in Los Angeles and Santa Clara. Johan's mother, Lesley, was ineffectual. She painted her nails and did Zumba and threw money at him. Buy this, buy that, get out of my sight. Johan knew she was repulsed by him.

Johan was fifteen the first time he tried amphetamines. He'd been poolside, sunning his broad belly, when Francisco, the groundskeeper's son, approached with his idiot amigo.

"*Bola de manteca*," Francisco said. He was nineteen years old, pigeon-chested, thin wrists, but large hands. His friend—cut from the same cloth—laughed.

Johan squinted in the sunlight. "What does that mean?"

"Means you are a fat little fuck." Francisco grinned, his mouth full of gaps. "Like a ball of butter. Like a piggy. *Wheee-wheee.*"

"Get the fuck out of here," Johan snapped. Color climbed into his face. His belly blushed. "I'll get your ass fired. I'll get you fucking deported, you fucking cholo piece of shit."

"Hey, calm down, little piggy. Calm the fuck down."

"Don't call me piggy."

"Okay. I come. I want to help, *sí*? I help you." Francisco grabbed his own flat stomach and shook. "You want to lose this big fucking belly? You want to lose? Uh?"

Johan wiped his sweaty face and shrugged.

"This . . ." Francisco removed a folded square of paper from his jeans pocket. He opened it up, showed Johan the white powder inside. "You know this? Uh? Know this? *Anfeta*. Speed. You know this?"

Johan shook his head.

"You take this. You run and run." Francisco made a circling gesture with his finger, winding it faster and faster. "Twenty dollar, *sí*? I give. You run like a fucker."

"Speedy Gonzales," the friend offered.

"*Sí.*"

Johan gave him the money, if only to get rid of him. Francisco showed him how to take the drug. He licked his finger, mimed dipping it into the powder and rubbing it around his gums. Johan did exactly that. It tasted *bad*, like the shock solution he sprinkled into the hot tub to keep the water clean. Maybe it *was* that. Then again, maybe not; twenty-five minutes later, Johan was running laps around his large back garden, his fat jouncing from stem to stern, his blond hair rippling behind him. This sight was obviously amusing to Francisco and his friend. They sat on their asses, laughing and pointing.

"*Ándale,* Speedy!"

"*Ándale!*"

Humiliated, angry, but still buzzing, Johan exited his property and ran to the end of his street, then down to the bluff overlooking the ocean. He found a dead dog in a patch of sagebrush, hidden from the road. It had broken legs, teeth smashed in, a missing eye. Johan wrapped it in a garbage bag, lifted it onto his shoulder, and trudged back to his house. He stuffed the decomposing animal beneath the passenger seat of Francisco's pickup truck, where he wouldn't find it until it really started to stink.

Johan didn't tell his therapist about this. In fact, he hadn't told his therapist anything real since he was a little kid. He had soon learned to lie about the dreams and the voices in his blood, because that was easier. The semimonthly sessions were futile. It was like drawing circles on a page. They looked like something, but they went nowhere. Neither his father nor mother objected (or perhaps even noticed) when he stopped going. Besides, Johan had shown progress in other areas. His YouTube channel had given him a degree of celebrity. He was more outgoing, had started to socialize. At age seventeen, he was five inches taller and thirty pounds lighter than he was at fifteen, and not all of that was down to the Adderall he occasionally swiped from his mom's overflowing medicine cabinet.

In lieu of therapy, Johan had started to study his ancestry more deeply. He'd spend hours reading about the great Viking warriors, and was particularly drawn to Gottfrid the Bird—known as Godafrid Who Flies, in some sagas—who would leap several feet into the air and descend on his enemies from above. There being a connection between the anglicized surname "Fly" and the Old Norse for "Who Flies" was entirely possible, and Johan wasn't the only Fly to think so. A long genealogy document written by his great-grandfather suggested a link to the Danish warrior, and that was good enough for Johan.

The more he studied, the more he liked the idea of staking his claim and taking no shit. It sang to him like . . . well, like a bird.

Johan got a Corvette for his eighteenth birthday. He drove four hours to Pale Bone and met with Ramón, then they headed out to the Mojave Desert and shot at anything that moved—hawks and gopher snakes, mostly—with a Ruger that Ramón had reconditioned, using an old oil filter to suppress the reports. They didn't hit anything, but it was a grand old time nonetheless.

"Check this out," Ramón said once they'd run out of ammo. They were sitting on a rock, drinking a couple of cheap, warm beers that Ramón had brought along. He set his bottle down and pulled a cloudy white shard from his pocket, the size of a bear's tooth.

"Meth?" Johan asked.

"Yeah. Crystal." Ramón's English was excellent, like everything else he turned his hand to. He was twenty-two, tall, with distinctive features. Living in his uncle's basement for the past ten years, the one thing he lacked was street smarts.

"Where'd you get this?" Johan held the shard up to the sunlight, as if he could determine its purity that way.

"I made it," Ramón replied, smiling. "I can make more. You know anyone in Los Angeles who'll buy it?"

Living in the Palisades, playing video games all day, Johan didn't have much in the way of street smarts himself. But he knew someone who did.

"Maybe," he said.

Ten days later, he and Francisco were in a stinking, squalid house in the frenzied heart of South Los Angeles, negotiating with three Mexican drug dealers. Chico, Benito, and Miguel. They were elaborately tattooed, strapped with weapons, wearing Dickies with white socks pulled up to their knees. Johan, with his blond hair tied back and his belly poking out from under his Super Mario Bros. T-shirt, looked embarrassingly like what he was: a pale jellyfish swimming with the sharks.

Business was conducted in Spanish, with Francisco translating. Johan—trying not to shake too much—handed over a quarter of glass. "*Una muestra*," Francisco explained: a sample. Chico smoked it up. He nodded.

The deal: $9,000 for a pound, $16,000 for a kilo.

Johan was out of his depth, but he wasn't going to let these fucking cholos walk all over him. He didn't *think* they'd kill him. He had a line on what they wanted. He was the hand that feeds.

"No," he said to Francisco, knowing he had to stake his claim, take no shit. It's what Gottfrid the Bird would do. "This is good ice, and they know it. Tell them fifteen and twenty-seven. I'll consider a deeper discount if they buy in larger quantities."

Francisco told them. They laughed. There was a rapid-fire exchange in Spanish, more laughter. Francisco's grin was wide and ugly.

He said, "They want to know where you get this. You suck a big dick? Uh? A dick?"

Johan was green but not stupid. He'd done his homework. With a little footwork, selling in small quantities with the kind of profit margin good meth can fetch, they could turn fifteen K into thirty-five easily. Probably more.

"Tell them it doesn't matter where I got it," Johan said. "Only thing they need to know is that I can make them a lot of money."

The negotiation continued. Johan spoke only to Francisco, shouldering the jibes and laughter. He was asked twice who his manufacturer was. At one point, Miguel threw a lit cigarette at him, but that was as hostile as it got. The Mexican thugs were enjoying themselves, playing with the rich *güero*. Johan had what they wanted, though. It didn't feel like it, but *he* was in control.

They eventually agreed on a price. Benito, who'd done most of the talking, spat into his palm and held it out. Johan shook his head and made a fist. They bumped. Welcome to the USA.

Five months later, Francisco got arrested for drug possession and was deported back to Mexico. Johan started to make the drops alone—he knew the deal: two kilos of crystal flat-packed into three pizza boxes; $48,000 in twenties slotted into the insulated pizza bag. Easy money. See you in two weeks.

Johan gave Ramón thirty percent and kept the rest. He stashed most of it, but spent some on video games, computer systems, new tech, clothes, a neon kit for the 'Vette, bling, hookers, a big-ass TV, shit he didn't even need. Nobody asked where he got the money, because he'd always had it.

It was perfect. But nothing perfect can last forever. On Johan's fourth solo drop, he handed over the three pizza boxes, just like always, but the Mexicans didn't hand anything back. Miguel was slouched across a dirty sofa with a .45 in his lap. Chico smoked weed, leaning against the wall. Benito just looked at him, his lips turned down beneath his pencil mustache.

"Problem?" Johan asked.

"No more with you," Benito mumbled, and gestured toward the door. "We finished. You go."

Johan frowned, spread his hands: *What the fuck?*

"Go," Benito insisted.

"You owe me money." Johan nodded at the boxes he'd placed

among the detritus on the coffee table. Benito smiled. Miguel laughed. A girl—no older than eighteen, clearly high on the product—stumbled into the room, wearing only a pair of discolored underwear. She fell bonelessly across the sofa, nuzzling into Miguel, her head bumping against the .45 in his lap. Chico blew smoke and slurred something in Spanish.

Johan took all this in, understanding what was happening, but not grasping *why*. He shook his head again. Had he insulted them in some way, or done something else wrong? Was the last batch inferior, or light? Had he inadvertently cheated them?

"There's obviously been a misunderstanding," he said. "I can—"

Benito pulled his own semiautomatic and pointed it at Johan.

"Go." One word, spoken coolly.

Johan raised his hands, took a big step back. He would have turned and run, but the voices in his blood had woken. Anger kept him rooted.

"*I* have the contact." He drummed his forefinger against his chest. "You can't get that ice without me."

"Your man . . . Ramón, in Nevada." Benito dropped a knowing wink. "He is our man now."

A light of understanding flared in Johan's mind. They'd followed him. They'd followed his bright fucking yellow Corvette with its stupid fucking neon underglow to Pale Bone. They'd persuaded Ramón to work with them directly. Cut out the middleman. More stacks for everyone.

"You fucked me," Johan whispered. He'd been fucked before—those big-ass mamas down on South Figueroa Street really knew what they were doing—but this was an entirely different experience, and it didn't feel good at all. "We had a deal."

"This deal," Benito said, using the semiautomatic to gesture again at the door. "Only reason you're not already dead."

Johan left in a rage, tears flooding his eyes. The voices in his blood rose to a war-like cacophony that didn't fade for weeks. There was no respite. He was on a crashing, swaying longship, caught in a storm.

He knew what he had to do, and his warrior DNA assured him he could do it.

Louis Cameron was a blacksmith out of Topanga Canyon who specialized in making medieval weaponry for movies. He'd worked on *The Horns of Hattin* and *26 Cannons*, and was known for his authenticity and attention to detail. Johan visited his workshop in the mountains—it had an anvil and forge, much to Johan's pleasure—and handed him an illustration that he'd removed from one of his grandfather's old reference books.

"Can you make it?"

Sagas described Gottfrid the Bird's weapon as a "hawk's talon" and also a "crushing beak." It was, in fact, a bearded ax called Krókr, meaning "hook." It was wielded to devastating effect by Gottfrid, then handed down to Hroar Godfredson, then Bjorn Three Beards, both fearsome warriors. There were varied depictions of the weapon online and in history books, but all agreed that the handle was long and intricately carved, and that the bearded head was heavy enough that only the strongest of men could swing it one-handed.

"Krókr," the blacksmith said.

"You know it?" It hurt Johan's face to smile, but sometimes he pushed himself.

"I made one for a pilot called *The Flying Viking*." Louis shrugged. "It was never picked up."

"Can you make another? Exactly like this, with the carving in the handle, the hawk's head?" Johan pointed at the illustration and forced another smile. "It's a birthday present for my father. He's from a long line of Danes who believe they are descendants of Gottfrid the Bird."

"That handle is hand-carved," Louis said, scratching his jaw with blackened fingers. "A lot of work. I'll have to contract it out. Won't be cheap."

"Not a problem," Johan said.

It was not a quick job—sixteen weeks—but this gave Johan time to prepare. He put down the game controller and went to the gym—took 'roids and crank and got jacked in a minute. He got his teeth fixed, clean and straight. Vicki, a tattooist on the Strip, became his best friend. She inked his transformed body with Norse runes and symbols. He shaved the sides of his head and grew his beard long, and completed his remodeling by tying it in the middle with a strip of leather.

His mother noticed. "Johan . . . Jesus Christ, you look like a dirty fucking biker."

His father: "You are showing your Danish roots. That is good. Now show your strength and get a real fucking job."

Krókr arrived, more beautiful than Johan could have imagined. Its handle was three feet long, elaborately engraved. The head was thick and heavy. And blunt, of course—it was an ornament, not a weapon—but Johan took care of that. Hours at a whetstone, sharpening over and over, until the swooping blade could cut a butterfly down the middle.

He practiced with it. He drove out to the Santa Susana Mountains and whacked at live oak and black walnut trees, felling one after the other, creating drifts of firewood. His goal was to slice through a trunk with one swing. He never managed this—although he came close—but he could wield the ax one-handed. He could jump with it, and bring fury from above.

It would be a quick, brutal attack. The Mexicans would not see him coming. These were not brilliant people with complicated lives. They were drug dealers. Johan knew their routine. When they weren't slinging rock or cruising Crenshaw in Benito's lowrider, they were fucking teenage tweakers or smoking up (usually both at the same time). Johan just needed the three of them alone.

It was the early hours of a Friday morning. Benito, Chico, and Miguel returned from wherever, probably their corners in Huntington Park, or from outside Alejandro's Stop on Pacific Boulevard, where they were known to hang out. Johan was parked at the end of the block in an old Buick he'd bought for $700. He heard them coming before he saw them; Chicano rock pounded from the speakers of Benito's custom ride. Not ideal. It might wake the neighbors, but then again, this was the kind of place that slept through gunshots.

They were alone. No chicas looking to party. That was good. Johan watched as they sauntered one after the other through the front door. He waited seven minutes for any disturbed neighbors to return to bed, but also for the three of them to get comfortable, lower their guard, maybe unstrap their weapons and blaze up.

Johan grabbed Krókr from the backseat. He wore a long jacket and a baseball cap with his hair tucked up inside—a meager disguise, but better than nothing. He got out of the Buick, hid the ax inside his jacket, and crossed the street to the drug dealers' rundown crib. At the front door, concealed in the shadows of the porch, he took off the baseball cap and jacket. He was shirtless beneath, his new tattoos stark and striking, his new muscles pumped with adrenaline.

The front door opened with one swing of the ax. It may have been bolted and chained—Johan had no idea; he heard the sound of splintering wood and then he was in. Everything after that happened in a shocking blur.

He stormed into a cramped living space. Shit everywhere. The stink of cat piss. Stains across the walls. These cholo bad boys clearly hadn't used any of their drug money on home décor. There was a woman on the sofa, very young, maybe twenty. Johan dimly

registered that these three fucks were supposed to be alone—
there'd been no chicas in the lowrider—but this girl must have
been here all night. She screamed, jumped to her feet. Johan swung
the ax and cut her in half.

Benito and Miguel were standing up from the trash-cluttered
coffee table, rigid with alarm. Johan had envisioned this night
countless times, and had always imagined killing Benito last. Real
life played out differently. Johan hoisted the ax and brought it
down in a flashing arc. He cut off Benito's right arm at the shoulder. Benito fell to his knees, screaming, "Oh, Mami, oh, Mami,"
over and over while Johan reset the ax. He split Benito's skull
down the middle and everything that was inside his head came out
in a glistening splash.

Miguel unlocked. He broke for the window, not to escape, but
to grab the .45 on the sill. He turned with it, aiming. Johan was
one step ahead. Krókr hummed, coming down in a diagonal slash.
Miguel dropped with his chest and stomach open. The .45 fell from
his hand. He turned his whirling brown eyes up to Johan.

"Remember me?"

"*Sí*."

Johan was surprised, given his transformation. He was ten feet
taller than the pale, tubby *güero* who'd stood trembling in this
room. He was painted with blood and tattoos, a god, not a boy,
from Valhalla, not the Palisades.

He removed Miguel's head in a single stroke.

Two down.

He found Chico in one of the bedrooms, passed out in a stink
of weed and tequila. An older woman slept beside him. Johan
didn't hesitate. He brought Krókr down between Chico's shoulder
blades. The mattress springs bowed beneath him. He flipped and
jerked, his nerves in chaos. Johan hit him again and again, chopping into his chest. Chico's blood found the walls, even the ceiling.

The woman continued to sleep. She had likely been passed out for hours, maybe days. Johan never considered letting her live. He swung Krókr twice more and she woke briefly but didn't have a chance to scream.

Everything inside Johan was on fire. His Viking ancestors roared and banged on his bones. He walked from the bedroom to the living room, his ax at his side, surveying the carnage. It had taken just a minute. Maybe two.

Johan left via the front door. He put on his long jacket and baseball cap and walked swiftly to the Buick. He wasn't worried about the police. The South Bureau's Criminal Gang and Homicide Division would be looking at the Armenians, the Salvadorans, maybe a rival Mexican gang. They would never suspect a rich white kid from the Palisades.

He got home just before three A.M. and showered the blood from his hair and body. It took an hour. He couldn't sleep, so played video games and posted a video to YouTube.

The news broke the following afternoon: five undocumented Mexicans butchered in Watts, South Los Angeles. Police suspected gang warfare. There were images of body bags being carted from a small house on Los Cielos Avenue.

By this time, Johan had already called Ramón to tell him that they were back in business.

His body wasn't perfect—his calves could be bigger, his cephalic veins more pronounced, and his stomach flatter—but journeying it invariably brought a cooler frame of mind. Johan took photos of his chest and jaw, added a filter to accentuate the lines, and shared them across his social platforms. The likes came in, first by the tens, then by the hundreds. He masturbated as he watched the number next to the little heart symbol grow.

Johan thought Xander might have sloped off home with his tail between his legs, but he was still there. He'd moved from the

TV room to the garage, trying to make amends by working on the Mustang. It was coming together. There were still dents and scratches, but over the last couple of days Xander had replaced the exhaust, headlights, and windshield, and had done something beneath the hood to make the engine snarl louder.

He looked up as Johan entered the garage. His teeth flashed in a hungry, excited sort of way, almost catlike.

"Got the son of a bitch," he said, wiping his hands on a rag, then grabbing his phone from the top compartment in his toolbox. Xander looked at home in the garage, with wrenches scattered around his boots and oil on his face. He was a mechanic when Johan recruited him, chopping stolen vehicles for Redline Rikki in Central-Alameda. Rikki had called Xander her animal, because he used to deadlift engine blocks and hammer out dented panels with his skull. "I keep him chained up at night," she'd said. Xander had once won a thousand bucks in a bet after drinking a quart of 5W-30 straight from the bottle. Johan had surmised that someone so simpleminded would be dog-loyal, and he was right.

He swiped through his phone—still with his teeth showing—and turned it toward Johan. The red *TMZ* logo filled the top of the screen, and beneath this a paparazzi shot of Luke Kingsley climbing behind the wheel of a boxy blue car. The caption beneath read: OH, LUKE! FROM A TESLA TO A DODGE!

"This isn't the car from the security footage," Johan said.

"No. He came here in a Camaro. A '78, I think. Custom paint and a Z28 scoop."

"Right. And how many cops have you ever seen driving a car like that—*outside* of a fucking movie, I mean?"

"Okay. Jesus, okay." Xander plucked at his earlobe. "Anyway, that car . . . the Dodge Caliber. Puke-blue. *Marine* blue, they called it, or something like that. It's not *that* common a color, right? I knew I kept seeing one around, and then I remembered where."

Xander swiped his phone again and brought up another app.

Google Maps. He tapped on the screen and zoomed in on Kitty's street. There was Kitty's apartment building. A slightly fish-eyed view of it, at least. Xander whipped the camera around and there was the Dodge, parked in the driveway of the house opposite.

"They're neighbors," Xander said. Tiny beads of spittle had gathered in the corners of his mouth. "We were waiting in her apartment and she was across the fucking street the whole time."

"And she's probably there right now," Johan said.

"Yeah, unless that prick actor has put her on a bus back to Kentucky," Xander suggested. "She can't stay in L.A., right? Not if she's supposed to be dead."

"Only one way to find out," Johan said. He imagined Kitty and Luke with their rib cages open and their lungs flopped over their shoulders. "Is the Mustang ready to roll?"

"The engine's smooth but the body's still rough."

"It's fine; it looks like it's been in a fight." Johan touched the tattoo on the back of his left hand. "Pull it out front. I'm going to get Krókr."

"We're doing this now?"

"Right now."

"I'm down with that. We'll do them like you did Sly Boy."

Johan said, "It won't be that quick."

16
NUEVA VIDA

They rolled east on I-40 with the sun on the windshield and their visors down. It was like driving into a headache. Luke's Wayfarers deadened the glare, but it was still bright enough that he needed to adjust his speed. It didn't help that the air conditioner was broken. They buzzed their windows down, which at least kept the car's interior from feeling so muggy and still. Kitty turned up the stereo to neutralize the wind noise.

Luke stopped for gas outside Barstow—for human fuel, too, in the form of two large coffees. He also selected a pair of cheap shades for Kitty from the spinning rack next to the beef jerky.

"I was okay with my hand over my eyes," Kitty said, but she took the shades gratefully and put them on.

"They were twelve bucks," Luke said. He hooked his cell phone and other assorted crap—coins, candy wrappers, hand sanitizer—from the cup holders, making room for their coffees. "Besides, I wouldn't want you to miss the breathtaking scenery."

"You mean the arid wastelands of southeastern California?"

"Exactly." Luke grinned and cranked the ignition.

They drove across the High Desert, colorless and dry all the way to the horizon. It was punctuated by dusty towns, skeletal scrub, and volcanic rock. Road signs announced exits and attractions in lackluster tones. The distant mountains were as dark as lead, drawing a serrated line between the pale land and paler sky.

"How long before we get there?" Kitty asked.

"An hour and a half. Maybe a little longer." Luke gestured at the clock in the dash. "Should be pulling into Nueva Vida somewhere around eleven."

"That's early," Kitty said. "We're making good time."

"I'd be there yesterday, if I could."

Kitty was in charge of the music. She shuffled through Luke's CDs, then decided that the radio was the way to go, although she changed stations every time a traffic report or commercial came on. Lisa used to do the same thing, Luke remembered with a wistful smile, even though they'd had satellite radio. She just liked pushing those buttons. "It's like hunting for musical treasure," she'd say. Luke didn't mind Kitty hopping between stations, the same way he'd never minded Lisa doing it. There were always bigger things to get into a fight about.

They lost all radio signal on a stretch of dead highway south of the Mojave Preserve. Kitty punched the buttons for a minute and found nothing. "To hell with it," she said, and shut the radio off. She propped her feet on the dash, reclined her seat, and closed her eyes.

The silence was welcome, although Luke tried not to occupy it with thoughts of what lay ahead. Sometimes it was better to *not* think—to simply trust the gears of instinct. He focused on his surroundings, zipping alongside semis and bikers and buses. He looked at the mountains, and at the dry tangles of creosote bush and desert senna. Bugs slapped the windshield. Kitty's foot twitched.

He didn't think she was sleeping, not with the hot air rumbling through her open window, but she snapped awake a moment later, crying out, one hand clutched to her chest.

"You okay?" Luke asked.

"Jesus Christ. She took off her sunglasses and wiped her eyes. "Oh Jesus."

Whatever she'd dreamed, it was obviously tough to shake. She brought her seat upright, drew her knees to her chest, and took several deep breaths.

"Better pull over, Luke. Think I'm going to puke."

She didn't need to tell him twice. He checked his mirrors, then booted the brake and swerved onto the shoulder—oversteering a touch and edging off road. The car rattled and bounced, tires gripping, pulling up rags of grit. For a beat, Luke thought the back end was going to kick around and they would spin out, but he held the line, coming to a noisy, dusty, but relatively undramatic stop.

Kitty unclipped her belt, threw open the door, and spilled outside. Luke watched the back of her green tee fade amid the dust. She broke through waist-high scrub, stumbled down a shallow embankment, and disappeared behind a rock.

Luke wiped his brow and shut off the ignition. The clock in the dash moved from 10:28 to 10:34. He got out of the car to stretch his legs. His knees popped disagreeably. He wasn't old—Jesus, forty-two wasn't *old*, was it?—but sometimes he felt it.

Vehicles ripped by, making the ground shake. Every speeding semi was a minor earthquake. Luke waited. He saw a roadrunner with a rattlesnake in its beak, and watched a hawk swoop to the ground and come up empty.

"You okay, Kitty?"

"Yeah, sorry," Kitty replied, her voice wet and cracked. "Be there soon."

For a brief time there were no vehicles in either direction. The

Mojave silence was vast, disturbed only by large birds cawing and the distinctly heartbreaking sound of Kitty in tears.

They got moving again, the road quieter as they approached the Dead Mountains. Kitty sat crisscross-applesauce in her seat, her hair hanging over her face. She let out a deep sigh every other mile.

"How long was I asleep?" she asked.

"Not long," Luke replied. "Ten minutes, maybe."

"That's all it took." She shook her head, the sunlight winking off the lenses of her shades. "It's like he's waiting just inside my mind. Like a serial killer behind a door. A monster in the closet."

"It'll get easier," Luke said.

"I hope so."

"It will. You may need to talk to someone when you get back to Kentucky. A professional." He nodded encouragingly and tapped his fingers on the wheel. "It'll take time, but the right help, the right meds . . ."

Encouraging words, but he and Kitty were probably thinking the same thing: that only four months had passed since he'd tried to kill himself in this very car.

They took U.S. 95 north, getting closer to Nueva Vida. The possibility of seeing the bat-faced man became enticingly real, and Luke's anxiety ripened accordingly. He was suddenly sure that if he turned on the radio, he would hear one of Lisa's songs—the universe's way of urging him along.

"This heat," Kitty said, and sighed.

"I know."

They entered Nueva Vida fifteen minutes later. The first thing they saw was an elderly cop perched on a stepladder, cutting down a dead coyote that had been strung by its hind legs to the welcome sign.

. . .

Population 880. It was as if the more affluent homes and businesses had stolen away in the night, leaving only the loose and struggling pieces: a gas station with two pumps and a caged mountain lion, a motel called Lazies with a sign that promised only BEDS and TV, a couple of restaurants, a convenience store, a trailer park with a green-water swimming pool and a thousand yapping dogs. Norteño blared from a closet-sized amp set up in the bed of an old pickup truck. Hispanic grandmothers danced around it, their bare feet stirring puffs of dust. Kids threw stones at cans and bottles.

There was a downtown strip with a paved road, no traffic lights, only a three-way stop. The police station was sandwiched between a gun store and a clinic. Store owners sat on crates outside their businesses. Some waved at Luke and Kitty as they drove through.

"How do you think this place survives?" Kitty asked.

"They probably pick up some Dead Mountains tourism," Luke said. "And there are a couple of casinos just across the state line."

A ranch marked the edge of town, advertising horseback adventures and guided tours into the mountains. Several dusty animals—dogs and cows, mainly—dozed in the shade of a sprawling mesquite. It neighbored a trading post with a huge plastic eagle on the roof and a sign that read SNAKE FARM INSIDE $3.

"I don't see this bar or club, whatever it is," Kitty said. "You think we drove past it?"

"No," Luke said. He checked his phone. "Google Maps says it's two and a half miles northwest of here. Looks like we're going deeper into the wilderness."

"Jesus, could we get any deeper?"

They arrived five minutes later, with the Caliber wearing a thick coat of desert grit and a tumbleweed caught beneath one of the rear wheel arches. Luke pulled into an empty parking lot, shut off the engine, and sat looking at the building for a moment. Xander had said it was a refurbished saloon, but Luke thought this particular drinking establishment had been built long after Billy the Kid was shooting 'em dead. It was all too *straight*, too perfect. Its authenticity was further derailed by a neon sign above the door—cold and dark now—and a stuffed grizzly on the veranda wearing a STRAY BULLETS tee. More signage in the windows announced FREE WI-FI and LIVE MUSIC EVERY NITE.

"Looks super-closed," Kitty noted.

"It super-does," Luke agreed. He got out of the car, stepped onto the neatly laid porch boards, and tried the door. Locked tight. He peered through one of the windows. They were heavily tinted, but he could just make out a light shining toward the back. Otherwise, no sign of life.

"Opens at three," Kitty said, stepping up beside him and pointing at a small sign beside the door. "I'm surprised it gets busy enough to open at all."

"It's got that roadhouse vibe," Luke said. "Gets pretty rowdy, judging from its PictoShark account. A real diamond in the rough."

They returned to the car, their heads low, both feeling the gravity of their different and complicated emotions. Luke got behind the wheel. He looked up at Stray Bullets as he did so, half expecting to see the bat-faced man in one of the upstairs windows.

"We'll come back later," he said as Kitty got in beside him. "Are you hungry?"

"Not at all. But somewhere with ice-cold drinks and air-conditioning would be nice."

"I saw a restaurant in town. And you might change your mind about being hungry." Luke's lips barely twitched, although smile lines radiated from the edges of his sunglasses. "They've got barbecued armadillo on the menu."

. . .

Luke thought he was hungry — he hadn't eaten all day — but found, when his sandwich arrived, that he didn't have an appetite, after all. He took a bite, ate a couple of the chips from the side of the plate, and sniffed at the pickle. It all looked and smelled delicious, but he was just too jittery to eat.

"Not happening," he said, pushing the plate aside.

"The root beer is hitting the spot," Kitty said, stirring the ice cubes with her straw. "Cold and sweet. Exactly what I needed."

The restaurant was called June's or maybe Jane's. The sun had faded the lettering in the window, but a sign on the sidewalk advertised AIRCON and BEST FOOD IN TOWN and COLD DRINKS. The décor was functional, with plastic seats and tables, and a desert mural covering one wall. It was no more than Luke expected, with one exception: a soda fountain in back that looked as if it had been extracted from a 1950s drugstore. There were chrome stools, gooseneck soda taps, and posters of long-dead movie icons staring down from the walls. A countertop jukebox played oldies for a quarter a pop.

A few customers dined in the restaurant proper, but Luke and Kitty had the soda fountain to themselves. They could talk without having to whisper, and Luke had free rein on the jukebox. He changed a five into quarters and played the Shirelles and Frankie Lymon and the Teenagers and the Coasters . . . one after the other. He'd just selected Elvis's rendition of "Blue Moon" when Kitty said:

"We may not have to go back to Stray Bullets. If Mr. Bat-Face lives in town, someone around here will know him."

"I had the same thought," Luke said. He picked up one of his chips, considered eating it, then dropped it back onto the plate. "I want to play it cool, though. If we start asking around like a couple of cops, then word might reach him before we do. I don't want to tip him off."

"Makes sense," Kitty said, and tapped one finger against her temple. "You've given this some thought."

"Not really," Luke admitted. "Other than wanting to keep it low-key, I've tried not to think about it too much. I'm going to go with my gut, hope for the best."

"How do you think you'll react when you see him?"

"*If* I see him. I may just get a name and address and hand it over to the cops."

"Really?" Kitty closed her lips around her straw. Her cheeks dimpled as she drank. "You're telling me you're not going to knock on his door?"

Luke shrugged. He wanted to believe he could play this cool from start to finish, but knew himself better than that. "I guess I didn't come all this way for an address."

"That's what I thought."

"So then it'll depend on *his* reaction. Will he recognize me? Probably, and if he had something to do with Lisa's disappearance, I'll know the moment I look into his eyes." Even *thinking* about it caused Luke's throat to tighten. "That's why I want to take him by surprise—get an honest reaction."

Kitty nodded and sipped her root beer. The ice cubes rattled, moving closer to the bottom of the glass. Neither of them spoke for several moments. Elvis sang, filling the small space at the back of the restaurant with a lamenting, ghostly falsetto—a little too apropos, in Luke's opinion. He rotated the wheel on top of the mini-jukebox, looking for something more upbeat.

"And what if we don't find him?" Kitty asked. "Or if we *do*, but you don't get the answers you're looking for?"

"Then I'm no worse off," Luke said. "At the very least, I can get some closure on this guy. He's been haunting me for too long."

"Let's hope for more than that." Kitty held up her hands, fingers crossed, then found a smile that was both melancholic and comforting. "You must miss her."

"Some days I can't think of anything else," Luke said, running his gaze over the song cards on the juke, but not really reading them. "It feels like all of me, even though our relationship . . . well, it wasn't all kisses and candy. We had our moments."

"Yeah." Kitty nodded. "I read about that. The press made it look like you were always at each other's throats."

"They weren't wrong. Our mistake was that we let the false stuff—the alcohol, the drugs, the fame—get bigger than who we were together. Does that make any sense?"

"I guess."

"So yeah, I miss Lisa, but I don't miss the falseness of what we became." Luke slouched, one elbow on the counter, his hand propping up his jaw. "We were in love, though. No doubt about that. And that's the part I try to remember."

A memory surfaced, too sweet not to indulge: a summer weekend, not long before Luke and Lisa were married. They'd gone camping in Oregon, because Lisa—a city girl to her core—had never camped before. She wanted an adventure, she'd said. "I want to go to sleep smelling of smoke, with dirt under my fingernails and pine needles in my hair." So they'd pitched a tent in the Cascades. They hiked long, breathtaking trails and bathed in frigid creeks, and at night they watched the stars outshine the rising embers from their fire. Deep into their third night, Luke had woken to the sound of Lisa's guitar, and he unzipped the tent to find her sitting fireside with her acoustic across one knee.

"Sounds good," he'd said, blinking the tiredness from his eyes. "Pretty."

"Yeah? I just wrote it. Right here, right now."

"Play it again."

She did, and maybe it was the high half-moon or the crystal air, but every line had sounded like poetry. *"Some dreams are found where the lows don't go, this is the cradle that rocks my soul."* It was an astral moment, and when she'd finished, Luke—at a time when silence would have been better—had stroked her cheek and said something hopelessly obtuse.

"You can even make a cradle sound soulful."

"It's a metaphor," Lisa had replied. She'd kissed him, and it was bigger than the night. "You are the cradle."

The memory lingered, accentuated by Luke's emotion: the stars were fuller, the notes rang clearer, Lisa's kiss lasted longer. Finally, it faded. The fifties-style soda fountain swam back into being. The stool swiveled beneath Luke as he shifted his weight. He plugged another quarter into the juke and hit a random number. "In the Still of the Night" by the Five Satins started playing. The universe, no doubt, keeping him honest.

"These past three years have been . . . just the worst." An understatement, and Luke rolled his eyes to indicate as much. "Everything I've been through has caused me to hate and doubt myself, and there have been times when I've wondered if it's really Lisa I want back, or everything else: the money, the big house in Sherman Oaks, the career I worked so hard to get off the ground. Or maybe I just want to be exonerated—to give a big 'fuck you' to every son of a bitch who dragged my name through the dirt."

"It's okay to want all those things," Kitty said.

"Doesn't feel like it sometimes."

Their server came over to see if they needed anything else. Luke shook his head and asked for the check. They'd used up a good chunk of time in this little slice of fifties heaven, but there was still an hour and a half before Stray Bullets opened its doors. Maybe they could drive into Nevada or Arizona, find a park on the river, eat ice cream.

A few quarters remained on the counter in front of Luke. He pushed one over to Kitty.

"Choose a song."

"I don't really know this music."

"Doesn't matter. It's all good."

Kitty shrugged, slotted the quarter in, and chose "Whispering Bells" by the Del-Vikings. The music started—a foot-tapper, for sure, with its irresistible bass line and bubblegum lyrics, but Luke wasn't quite ready to check out of Heartbreak Hotel.

"I don't know what the future holds," he said, "even *if* I find Lisa."

"What do you mean?"

"A relationship that's good fifty percent of the time isn't actually good at all." Luke scratched his stubbly jaw, one eyebrow raised. "I'd like to think we could rediscover the things that made us fall in love to begin with, and rebuild from there, but I just don't know."

Kitty nodded. "One day at a time."

"I've been lost for so long. Confused. Suicidal." Luke covered his eyes for a moment, as if ashamed, then ran his hand down his face. "But what I've come to realize—really, since meeting you—is that I'm not ready to give up, not on anything."

Kitty's eyes sparked from within, as close to vibrant as she'd looked these past few days. She leaned forward, looped a strand of hair behind one ear, and said, "Your seat belt."

"Huh?"

Their server returned with the check. Thirteen bucks even. Luke handed the kid a twenty and waved him off. Seven dollars was too handsome a tip for someone who could barely raise a smile, but maybe his generosity would be rewarded later.

"When I pulled you out of your car," Kitty continued once the server was out of earshot, "I had to unclip your seat belt. Maybe it was muscle memory, but I like to believe it was more than that— that a voice inside was trying to tell you that you still had something worth living for."

"Oh." Luke's face warmed with a combined expression of gratitude, fondness, and hope. "That's . . . actually kind of reassuring."

She angled her head sweetly. That spark was still in her eyes.

"Maybe I'm not such a fuckup," he said.

"I wouldn't go *that* far," Kitty said. She found a grin. It was small and it trembled, but it was lovely.

Luke placed both hands over his heart, feigning woe. "Come on," he said, and winked. "Let's blow this hot dog stand."

"Yeah."

Kitty slurped the last of her root beer and they left the restaurant. The air outside was baked and gritty. They took a moment to acclimate, standing on the sidewalk, putting their sunglasses on.

"We still have some time to kill," Luke said. "This could be a long day."

"Already has been. But maybe you'll look back on this as the day that everything changed." She considered this for a second or two, then dropped her hands onto her hips and added, "For the better, of course."

"Jesus," Luke said. "Things can't get much worse."

17

LUKE'S HOUSE

Thirty minutes to Silver Lake, on a good day, but an accident had backed up Interstate 10 and Santa Monica Boulevard was its usual shitshow of lights and traffic. Xander came off at the 405, looking to loop around and cut south through the hills.

"Ruben, where are you?"

Ruben, on the phone: "Johan . . . hey. I'm at the gym."

"Echo Park?"

"Yeah."

"Okay, good. I need you to do something for me."

"Sure. Almost finished here."

"*Now*. This is important."

A pause. Johan could almost hear the vague clockwork of Ruben's brain. "Oh right, is it about—"

"Yeah."

"Okay, man."

"Head out to Kitty's place. Watch the house opposite. There should be a blue piece-of-shit Dodge in the driveway—"

"Yeah, I know the one."

"Scope the scene. If anybody leaves, follow them. Me and Xan are on our way. Traffic's a bitch, though." The 405 was moving, but volume had them pinned at forty. "We should be there in . . . shit, I don't know . . . whenever."

"I can be there in fifteen," Ruben said.

"Make it ten."

Xander weaved between lanes, finding any car-sized gap that advanced their average speed, flooring it when he could. His flinty eyes flicked between the mirrors. His jaw was locked as tight as his grip on the wheel.

"Fuck this traffic."

"Ruben'll be there in ten," Johan said. "Chill."

The Mustang's engine made animal sounds. Its thumped-up panels rumbled. Xander swerved into the outside lane. The road opened up and he jumped on the gas. They accelerated to eighty before a Jeep cut in front of them, forcing the brakes. The tires moaned and smoked, leaving long prints along the blacktop. Johan surged forward in the passenger seat, bracing himself on the dash.

"Jesus Christ," he said. "You almost put me through the fucking windshield."

"That son of a bitch cut in front of me." Xander tailgated the Jeep, slamming the horn.

"I told you to chill."

Xander did, then, insomuch as he drove less aggressively, but he remained hunched at the wheel, stiff as steel. The miles—getting closer to Silver Lake—did nothing to relax him.

"Remember," Johan said, speaking between full, steadying breaths—he wasn't exactly chill, either. "Finding Kitty is our priority. If she isn't there, we need the actor to talk. Maybe let me handle that."

"I'm going to take his goddamn head off." Flecks of spittle glistened on Xander's upper lip.

"You'll get your chance."

South on the Hollywood Freeway, moving easier. Xander's hands were fixed to the wheel, the whites of his knuckles showing through his tattoos.

Ruben had texted that there was no car in the driveway and the house looked empty.

"What now?" Xander asked.

They had parked on a neighboring street; it was less conspicuous to approach on foot, and the Mustang might alert the actor, should he return. Johan reflected—not for the first time—that his life's pursuits fell into categories of either extremely low or extremely high profile. This would have to be the former.

"Two choices," he said. "We can check the place out, or wait for movement."

"I'm not in a waiting mood," Xander said.

"Me, neither." Johan opened his door. "Let's go."

Ruben was in his vehicle, a Toyota Tundra with twenty-four-inch rims, parked outside Kitty's apartment building. Johan and Xander walked up beside it, rapped on the passenger-side window.

"Still nothing?" Johan asked.

"All quiet," Ruben said. "Doesn't mean no one's home, though. Car could be in the garage, although I only ever remember seeing it parked in the driveway."

"Same," Xander said.

"What's this about?" Ruben asked.

"Kitty's still alive," Johan said. "And we think she's hiding here, with a neighbor. Or at least *was* hiding here."

"What the fuck?" Ruben shook his head. "But I thought—"

"I'll explain later," Johan cut in. "We're going to check the place out. We'll go in through the back. You stay here. If anybody bolts out the front door, stop them."

"Got it."

Johan and Xander crossed the road and started down Luke Kingsley's driveway. They walked confidently, as if they had every right to be there. Johan knew a thing or two about hiding in plain sight.

"We do this cleanly," he said to Xander. "We don't spill blood or leave prints. If anybody's home, we tie them up and take them to Jink's."

Xander grunted something about cutting Luke's balls off.

Neither man, nor Ruben, noticed the silver Buick parked two spaces behind Ruben's truck, its driver watching closely.

They continued along the side of Luke's house, toward the back-yard, following a concrete path crowded by weeds. There were no windows open, but Johan noted the sheet of plywood that had replaced the glass in the garage's side door.

Nobody in the backyard. Xander checked the door. Locked. They peered through the kitchen window, careful not to leave prints on the glass. The house appeared empty.

"Watch the back," Johan said to Xander. "I'm going in through the garage. I don't think anybody's here, but let's make sure. Then we can figure out next steps."

Johan pressed the flat bottom of a rock against the lower right corner of the plywood, gradually—and quietly—pushing the nails loose. He'd soon created a wide enough gap to slide his hand through, twist the lock, and open the door. No car in the garage. That didn't mean the house was empty. Kitty might be taking a shower or tucked up in bed, feeling safe and self-satisfied.

Johan flicked the light switch next to the door. A dusty bulb bloomed toward the back of the garage, throwing a triangle of lu-minance on a shelf arranged with paintbrushes, jars of screws, and several old tools: a claw hammer, a wrench, a chisel, a screwdriver. Johan considered taking one—imagined attacking Kitty in the shower, *Psycho*-style—then remembered what he'd said to Xander about spilling no blood. He sneered regretfully. There'd be time to make a mess later, though, and he'd get Krókr in on the action.

Johan used the bottom of his T-shirt to wipe the doorknob, lock, and light switch—everything he'd touched—then crossed the garage floor, stepping between double-stacked boxes and piles of junk. The door to the main house was unlocked. Good. Johan pushed it open, his tee wrapped around the knob, and stepped into the hallway.

Silence. Johan stood in one spot, listening intently. No tinkling shower. No flushing toilet. No creaking bedsprings. The hallway spilled into the living room and kitchen. Johan walked through and saw Xander's silhouette against the back-door blinds, shifting impatiently. This was the only movement.

He edged back into the hallway, which was L-shaped. A number of doors led off it. One was a closet. It was ajar, jackets and shoes leaking out of it. The others would be the bedrooms, a bathroom. He should check them all.

The first bedroom was small and dim, its blinds drawn tight. Johan turned on the light. The bed was unmade, but had been slept in recently. He could tell from the dent in the pillow, and the long black hair standing out against the white fabric. Kitty's hair. There was a half-finished glass of water and a TV remote on the nightstand. Women's clothes—T-shirts, a couple of pairs of sweatpants—were folded and laid across the bed.

The second bedroom was larger—a shambolic, musty-smelling space. The actor's room. There was a wallet on the dresser. Johan flipped it open, and saw it was actually the fake ID and badge of one Detective Colton Stone. It was less authentic up close.

"Nice try, Luke," Johan whispered. "Sucks for you that I have such shitty taste in movies."

It could easily have gone the other way, though. The security cam might not have picked up a reliable image, or his mind, after such a long day, might not have been so sharp. It was proof that the gods were smiling on Johan, and a reminder that he needed to be more careful moving forward.

Not that he was negligent by nature. Johan lived by a code of honor, orderliness, and value. Kitty was exceptional in that he'd been seduced by her aesthetic, and had trusted her too readily. Even Xander had cautioned that Kitty knew too much, too soon. But Johan wanted her. Not sexually—at least not to begin with—but to enhance his brand. Hollywood's champagne drug scene necessitated a champagne image, and Kitty fit the bill.

Also—and this was important—he had *liked* her. He admired her sass and spirit. And yes, he'd occasionally considered her in romantic terms. They would almost certainly have taken that direction, given time, but of course she'd ruined everything by being disloyal, and showing how unremarkable she truly was. Maybe she hadn't known anything about Sly Boy's operation, but she'd still stolen hundreds—thousands—of dollars' worth of canary. *Just a little*, she'd said. *For personal use.* Johan knew that a little today would turn into a little *more* tomorrow, and really, it wasn't so much that she'd been skimming, but that she thought he was too stupid to notice.

Even so, Johan had considered granting her a stay of execution, and letting her hightail it back to Kentucky with a promise to keep her mouth shut. He decided against it, though. A person was either trustworthy or they were not. There was no gray area, and therefore no second chances.

He glanced in the actor's closet: a Goodwill-style arrangement of old shirts and tees, a few faded pairs of jeans folded on a shelf, footwear scattered across the floor. No sign of Kitty huddled, petrified, in the back corner. Johan left the room. The bathroom was opposite, door ajar. He pushed it with his elbow and entered. A man's bathroom, with a deep smell of urine and the toilet seat up. There were two toothbrushes, one flattened and old, the other one new. The packaging was in the wastebasket. Kitty's toothbrush. She hadn't taken it with her. Was she coming back?

Johan walked through to the kitchen, unlocked the door, and let Xander in.

"Ain't nobody home," Johan half sang.

"How do you want to play it?" Xander asked, glancing around. He had that look in his eye, like he wanted to set fire to something.

"Cool, for now," Johan said. "I have a feeling they didn't go far. Could be back any moment, so we wait."

Xander nodded.

"I'll get Ruben to give us a heads-up when he sees the car approach." Johan removed his cell phone from his pocket. "Until then, just hang, and wipe down any surface you touch. We came here to eliminate a problem, not create a new one."

They waited in the living room, getting comfortable. Johan swiped through his phone, replying to emails and social media comments. After ten minutes or so, Xander got restless and started to nose around. He drifted from room to room, rooting through various drawers, criticizing the décor.

"Thought this guy was supposed to be famous," he said. "This place is a shithole."

"Yeah, well, this is what happens when you don't cover your tracks," Johan commented. "Fucking idiot woke up in the woods with his wife's blood all over his shirt."

"Dumb prick."

"He's lucky he's not getting popped in the ass at San Quentin." Johan checked his Twitter feed. Mostly bullshit, but he "liked" recent posts from Ariana and LDC. "Which reminds me: you'd better be wiping your paw prints down."

"I'm using my sleeves," Xander said.

He sniffed around a little more, then came back with his first

find, reminding Johan of a dog sniffing through the brush, returning to his owner with a dead bird clamped between his jaws.

"Dug these out of the trash," he said. Not a dead bird, but a pair
of filthy sweatpants and a blue bra—the clothes Kitty had been
wearing when Johan took her to Jink's. They triggered a vibrant
memory: Kitty on her knees with her T-shirt torn down her back,
clutching her skateboard, the fear rising off her in stinking waves.

I just want to go home, she'd whispered, broken, but with still
a little fight left in her. Tenacity was a trait that Johan admired.
Under different circumstances, she would have made an excellent
shield-maiden.

"This isn't real blood," Xander said, indicating the deep staining
on the bra cups and down the front of the pants. "It's what Kitty
was wearing in those fake photos."

"Why the fuck are you digging through the trash?" It was all
Johan could think of to say.

"I wasn't. I saw the bra strap poking up and grabbed it. The
pants were balled up underneath."

"Put them back." Johan hadn't touched the clothing, but he still
wiped his hands down the front of his shirt. "They stink, and they
don't help us."

Xander disappeared, but returned moments later with his second find, and this *was* closer to a dead bird.

"Talking of photos." He handed Johan a manila envelope.
"These were in a drawer in the bedroom. They still look real, even
though I know they're not."

Johan opened the envelope and pulled out the photographs of
Kitty's "dead" body. They were full-color, gruesome as hell. The
close-up was particularly effective.

"Jesus Christ," he said, and whistled through his teeth. "This is
good work."

"Right?" Xander thrust out his jaw, somewhat vindicated. "You
can see how they fooled me."

Johan studied the photos, looking for inconsistencies in the blood spatter and the position of Kitty's body. He found none. Her eye *maybe* looked a little more open in the headshot, but it was difficult to be sure. Johan wondered if he would've been fooled, too, if some homicide cop brandishing a badge had shown these to him . . . and thought he probably would. He wasn't going to admit this to Xander, though.

"These don't help us, either." He handed the photos back to Xander. "You want to find something we can actually use? How about a golf club or a baseball bat—something blunt and heavy to knock them out with. Rags, too, to shove in their mouths. Duct tape. Twine."

"On it," Xander said.

He'd taken only a single step, though, when the doorbell rang—two brief, bright trills that, nonetheless, sounded altogether ominous.

"The fuck?" Xander whispered. "I thought Ruben was on lookout."

Johan edged toward the window and scoped the front of the actor's property. No vehicles in the driveway, and he couldn't see Ruben's truck from this angle. Nor could he see the front step, or whoever was at the door.

"Probably just a neighbor," Johan whispered, and flipped through his phone. "I'll call Ruben. See what's going on."

He was beaten to it. His phone buzzed three seconds later and a message from Ruben came through. Johan frowned and turned the screen toward Xander.

"*Answer the door*," Xander read, then looked curiously at Johan. "What the hell?"

"I guess we answer the door."

Johan stepped into the hallway, approached the door, then unlocked and opened it. Ruben stood outside, his face tight and anxious. Next to him, with a semiautomatic pistol tucked beneath Ruben's rib cage, was a tall woman with platinum hair and a crooked smile.

"Oh shit," Johan said.

"Johan Fly, you slimy motherfucker." Former detective Tera Montecino tilted her head, her eyes as blank as stones. "You want to tell me what the hell is going on?"

18

HAPPY HOUR

Rock music thumped from speakers posted outside Stray Bullets—Ozzy Osbourne singing "Crazy Train," loud enough to send a bassy vibration through the boardwalk. And why not? There were no neighbors, only hawks, vivid as checkmarks in the sky, and a couple of gray chuckwallas fastened gamely to a nearby boulder.

"Sounds open," Luke said wryly.

It was only eight minutes past opening but they were not the first customers. A smoky-haired woman had both elbows on the bar, her face plunged into a glass of red wine, and several jock types—all fixed teeth and gym muscle—crowded a booth, selfies every three seconds.

The bartender called out to them. "Sit anyplace." Her voice was cracked and husky, maybe from continually having to be heard over loud music. "Someone'll be right with you."

It was smaller than it looked from the outside, with a horseshoe bar and the stage taking up a broad portion of floor space. Booths lined one wall, and a wooden staircase led to a mezzanine with a cocktail bar and VIP area. There were a few tables arranged on the main floor, which would probably get cleared away once the bands started rocking. Luke and Kitty bypassed these and pulled up stools at the bar. The smoky-haired woman raised her head, regarded them briefly, then went back to her wine.

"Give me a minute," the bartender said. She was dressed in a Stray Bullets cowboy hat and T-shirt (available in the merch store), had three rings through her upper lip and a lower-back tattoo that announced itself when she bent over to finish loading Red Bulls into a refrigerator.

"No hurry," Luke said, mock-cheery, but Kitty could tell how anxious he was. There was a hitch in his voice she'd never heard before, and his eyes scanned every which way, looking for his bat-faced man.

The music changed from Ozzy to Nirvana. Luke took out his phone and opened PictoShark, while Kitty grabbed a handful of nuts from a bowl on the bar and munched them, gazing idly at the Wild West décor. Not everything fit. There were fake powder kegs and spittoons (emblazoned with the Stray Bullets logo) and coatracks fashioned from wagon wheels, but there were also several electric guitars bolted to the wall next to the stage, and a gallery of celebrity photos, all taken at the venue. Kitty recognized some of them: Lenny Kravitz, Johnny Depp, the singer from Pearl Jam. She scanned them all, curious to see if Johan was among them. Kitty didn't know if this place considered social media personalities to be celebrities, but Johan was vain enough to *pay* to have his picture included.

He wasn't there, though. Thankfully. Kitty could go the rest of her life without seeing his face again.

"What can I get you?" The bartender dusted off her hands and curled her pierced lip into a smile. She had a small star tattooed on her right cheekbone. Her name tag read SAVANNAH.

"Too early for firewater?" Luke asked, working a smile of his own.

"Never too early," Savannah responded.

Luke's smile broadened. He was hiding *his* celebrity, wearing an old Raiders cap and a pair of non-prescription glasses—a "disguise" he'd pulled from the Caliber's glove compartment. Kitty had noticed his handgun in there, too, the .38 Special he'd strapped to his side when posing as the homicide cop. Unlike the badge, it wasn't a fake.

"I'd better play it safe," Luke said. He looked good with glasses on, not *entirely* unlike the troubled star of *A Bullet Affair*, but different enough. "A Bud for me."

"Coke. Lots of ice," Kitty said. She wanted a beer, too, but didn't have her ID, and without makeup on and her hair done up, she looked about seventeen.

Savannah wheeled away to get their drinks. Luke angled his phone toward Kitty, showing her the photo on-screen. It was from the Stray Bullets PictoShark account: staff and customers posing happily at the bar. Savannah was among them, and so was the bat-faced man.

"She knows him," Luke whispered.

"Maybe," Kitty said. "But play it cool, remember?"

"Cool. Yeah." Luke dragged a hand across the back of his neck. "I've got this."

"Are you sure? You look . . . *tense*." Kitty bunched her fists to illustrate Luke's body language. "That might send up a red flag. You want me to do the talking?"

"I'm fine."

Luke didn't want to reel off a string of questions. His plan was to get talking to a member of the staff, then casually steer the conversation to the bat-faced man—using the snaps on PictoShark—and find out about him that way. Kitty had agreed that this less direct approach would be more effective.

He forced another smile as Savannah returned with their drinks. "It's happy hour," she said. "Next one's on us. And it's free refills on soda."

"I knew we came to the right place," Luke said.

"Where you from?"

"Colorado." Luke swigged from his bottle, then continued: "Little town called Mancos. We're here on a research trip."

"*I'm* here on a research trip," Kitty cut in. This was the story they'd agreed on, preferring to blur any Luke-and-Kitty-sized footprints. Better safe than sorry. "I'm writing a term paper on the Mojave people, and how COVID affected their livelihoods."

"My sister's kid," Luke said, still with that hitch in his voice. "I offered to bring her, figuring that, while she's researching the rez, I can research a few of the local casinos."

"I hear *that*," Savannah said. Her lip rings flashed in the bright lights around the bar. "We get a lot of people through here, either spending their winnings, or, more often, drowning their sorrows."

"Well, hopefully I'll be in the first camp." Luke took a quick, clumsy drink, then wiped the spillage off his chin. "I've heard about this place. You get some famous bands play here, right?"

"On occasion," Savannah said. "We're part-owned by Tyler Edwin. He's one of the big record company guys out in L.A."

"Ah, so he's got the connections."

"Right. And the bands dig it—they enjoy playing these smaller, intimate venues every now and then. Connects them to the fans."

"That's what it's all about."

"We had Jane's Addiction here last week. Shit got wild."

Luke nodded appreciatively. He was saying all the right things, Kitty thought, but his body language was rigid with tension, as if someone had a pistol pressed to his lower back. When the door behind them opened, Luke swiveled so quickly that he almost fell off his stool. Savannah frowned at this. It was subtle, mostly hidden by the wide brim of her cowboy hat, but Kitty noticed.

A young couple—not the bat-faced man—had entered the bar. Savannah called to them to sit anyplace, that someone would be right with them, and they chose one of the booths. Luke sighed.

He took another deep drink, then gestured at the celebrity photos behind the bar.

"Quite the wall of fame," he said. "Dave Grohl, Anthony Kiedis, Damon Layne. Shit, I would love to have been here *that* night. I'm a big Mustang Kick fan."

"Yeah," Savannah said. "Damon's a super-cool guy."

"He's an asshole," the smoky-haired woman opined from three stools away. She rolled bloodshot eyes toward Luke, her red-stained teeth creeping over her lower lip.

"Jesus, Dawn, you think everyone's an asshole," Savannah retorted, hands on hips, looking indignantly at the woman. "Just drink your wine, dammit."

Dawn muttered something in return, but Kitty didn't hear it beneath the strident power chords of whatever rock song was now playing. Luke and Savannah exchanged bemused looks, then Savannah strolled to the other side of the bar and started slicing limes. Their conversation had been derailed, and Kitty thought this was for the best. Luke needed to take a few deep breaths and regroup.

"You okay?" she asked him.

"She likes to talk," Luke said, nodding toward Savannah. "That's a good thing."

"Yeah, but you need to bring it down a notch. You're twitchy as hell."

Twenty minutes passed. They refreshed their drinks, and a few more customers entered the bar. Savannah was busy for a moment, and by the time she was on top of things, Luke had loosened up. Not all the way, but hopefully enough.

He brought PictoShark up on his phone again. When Savannah came by to top up Dawn's wine and wipe the bar down, Luke flipped the screen toward her.

"Hey," he said. "You're on PictoShark."

"We're on all of them," Savannah said, stepping closer to look at the photo that Luke had pulled up—a couple of bartenders posing with replica Winchesters. "Facebook, TikTok, YouTube. Social media is king."

"I just followed you," Luke said, and grinned.

"Cool. Keep up with the latest news."

He quickly swiped through a few more shots, stopping on one of a middle-aged guy, perched on the edge of the stage, strumming an acoustic guitar.

"Jesus, is that . . ." Luke zoomed in on the photo. "Is that Ethan Hawke?"

Savannah looked and nodded. "Yeah. I wasn't working that day. Apparently he just stopped by for a couple of drinks and got the place rocking."

"How cool is that?" A few more photos of celebrities, customers, and cocktails, but Luke stopped on the group shot that included Savannah and the bat-faced man. "And there *you* are! How long ago was this?"

Savannah looked at the picture. "Hm, I've been here two years, so . . . maybe eighteen months ago."

Luke had been playing it cooler, but now his hand started to tremble and that nervous hitch returned to his voice. A line of sweat trickled down his jaw. Savannah started to walk away but he stopped her.

"Hey, this guy . . ." He zoomed in on the bat-faced man, turned the screen around. "He's famous, right? I totally recognize him."

Savannah looked once, quickly, and shook her head. "No, you must be getting him mixed up with somebody else."

"Really? I could've sworn . . ." Luke frowned and adjusted his ball cap, the phone's screen still angled toward Savannah. "What's his name?"

This was what it had all been leading up to—this "casual" conversation funneled toward obtaining necessary information. Kitty held her breath, feeling just a shred of Luke's nervousness. She noticed Dawn paying attention, too, her gaze locked to Luke's phone.

It looked like she was about to say something, then went back to her wine.

"You want to know his name?" Savannah asked.

"Yeah." Luke swallowed hard. "Just . . . uh, remind me."

"I'm sorry, I can't do that."

"Can't or won't?" Luke smiled weakly.

"Won't."

Luke shrugged, turned the phone toward him, and zoomed in yet closer. "He's just so *familiar*. Does he live around here?"

Savannah cocked an eyebrow. "He's a semi-regular customer. If he happens to walk in, feel free to ask him however many questions you want, and it'll be up to him whether or not he answers them."

"Right, yeah. I just thought . . ." Luke sighed, flapped a hand. "Ah shit, it doesn't matter."

"Would you want me to share *your* information with a complete stranger?" Savannah pressed. There was lightheartedness in her expression, but her voice was no-nonsense. "We respect the privacy of our staff and customers here. It's policy."

"I get it," Luke said, and put down his phone. "It's all good."

Savannah nodded and went about her work. Luke pinched the bridge of his nose, then looked at Kitty with dark, dispirited eyes.

"That was a total fucking bust," he said.

"Not a *total* bust," Kitty said. "You know he's a regular, for sure. You just need to decide what to do with that information."

Dawn vacated her stool and swayed toward the restroom, but not before catching Kitty's eye and gesturing with a coy flick of the head.

Luke said something else but Kitty wasn't paying attention. She pulled her gaze from Dawn's canted walk and smoke-colored hair. "Huh? Sorry, say that again."

"I said this could take a long time."

"Or not." Kitty reached past Luke, grabbed his phone, and slipped off the barstool. "Get me another Coke. I'll be right back."

. . .

She had slept on the two-hundred-and-fifty-mile car ride from Los
Angeles, but only for ten minutes, according to Luke. That might
ordinarily be enough to take the edge off, but not on this occasion.
It had only upset and unsettled her more, because of the nightmare.
In it, Kitty had been trapped in the engine compartment of an old
car, the darkness perforated by numerous rust holes in the hood
and fender. She heard Johan's ax striking surfaces all around her—
dull, echoing blows. And there was another sound: Levi screaming,
crying for her. "*Mommy! Mommy! Mommy!*" Kitty had struggled
and squirmed, and finally managed to free herself. She'd followed
the cries until she came to a small severed arm lying on the ground,
and that was when she snapped awake.

She had told Luke that it was like Johan was waiting just inside her mind. *Like a serial killer behind a door.* This was accurate,
but it didn't convey how it sometimes felt like he was *with* her,
standing over her shoulder, or following only a step or two behind.
Kitty had heard him breathing in otherwise still moments, and
smelled his expensive cologne on puffs of warm air. He touched
her sometimes. He'd take her hand and she'd have to shake it off.
He stroked her cheek.

Johan was *haunting* her. No other word for it.

Luke had advised Kitty to seek professional help, and she intended to. She *had* to exorcise this ghost. Even obscuring it would
bring some relief. This was the main reason she had accompanied
Luke on his quest to find the bat-faced man. She told him that
she was doing it as a friend. True, of course. But what Kitty really
sought was a distraction.

Hearing Luke open up about his wife, sharing his hopes and
concerns, Kitty became emotionally invested (as if she didn't have
enough on her mind). She was rooting for him, praying that he find
some closure, at least. And it was Luke, not Johan, on her mind

when she tailed Dawn to the restroom. In those few moments, Kitty had the distraction she'd been looking for.

She walked across the main floor, following the signs for COW-GIRLS. They led her past a gumball machine, down a short flight of stairs, and to the end of a wood-paneled corridor half-blocked by a cleaning cart. The ladies' room door was denoted by a cartoon of a pistol-toting blonde wearing a ten-gallon Stetson. Kitty pushed open the door and went inside.

Dawn was at one of the sinks. Without looking up, she said, "You a cop?"

"No," Kitty replied. "What makes you say that?"

"I got busted twelve years ago for drug possession with intent to distribute. Three pounds of bouncing powder packed into my cooch. Served four years in County. Since then, I've developed a nose for bacon."

"I'm not a cop," Kitty said.

"No, you don't smell like one. Your *uncle*, though . . ." Dawn shook her wet hands and turned to Kitty with a sly grin. Her teeth were almost purple. "You know you're not the same color, right?"

Kitty ignored this. She held up Luke's phone—still in the Picto-Shark app—and showed Dawn the picture of the bat-faced man. "You know this guy. Who is he?"

The older woman looked at the mirror over the sink, not at the phone. There was, beneath the weathering of abuse, a vestige of attractiveness. Her eyes flared upward at the edges, a dusky blue, and her neck was long. She might once have had the deportment of a graceful woman. Kitty imagined her striding into a courtroom, dressed in a sleek suit, a briefcase at her side, or at the head of a table ringed with older, male executives. As it was, she wore a tube top and a pair of black jeans with a hole ripped in the ass. The tattoo on her inner left forearm read NO REGRETS.

"I've got a nose for drug dealers, too," she said, turning from the mirror, nodding at the phone without looking at it. "This fucking guy . . . he comes here with his pockets full of molly. Thinks he's slick, but I see the way he operates. Watch someone long enough and you learn a lot about them."

"He sells E?"

"This place gets loud. Kids want to party, and there's only one source." She nodded at the phone again. "We got three cops in this dustbowl and not one of them worth a shit. It's the perfect place to open shop, and no one'll say nothing—not until some dumb jackhole ODs in the parking lot."

Kitty lowered the phone and pocketed it. "What's his name?"

"Ramón . . . something." Dawn shrugged. "Don't know his second name."

"Does he live in Nueva Vida?"

"No," Dawn replied. She wiped a damp hand across the front of her tube top. "He's across the state line."

"Nevada?"

"Yeah. About thirty miles from here. Town called Pale Bone."

"You have an address?"

"Fuck, no."

"A street name?"

"All's I know is he lives on a ranch and drives an Econoline van, blue with a red stripe along the side." Dawn tilted her head. The lines around her eyes were deep and storied. "Shit, there's nothing much to Pale Bone. You could spit across it, with the wind blowing right. He shouldn't be hard to find."

"Thank you," Kitty said. For the first time in days, she felt pleased with herself. Pleased for Luke, too. She turned, eager to share this development with him, but took no more than three steps toward the door before looking back at Dawn. "Why are you helping us?"

Dawn cleared her throat and showed her stained teeth again.

"Because I don't like that motherfucker. He's too quiet. Slippery. Fuck that guy."

"You think he's dangerous?"

"All men are dangerous. Some are just better at hiding it."

"Hard to argue with that."

Dawn nodded and turned back to the mirror. She sneered at her reflection. "Good luck to you, honey. You look like you need it."

Kitty mumbled another thank-you and left the restroom. A flush had bloomed from beneath the collar of her tee, and her legs trembled with something close to excitement. She walked past the cleaning cart, bumping it in her haste, turning it sideways, not correcting it. She took the stairs by twos, wincing at the ghost of pain in her bruised ankle, then swept past the gumball machine and across the main floor. Heavy metal drummed from the sound system with a similar urgency.

Luke had just started Bud number four. Kitty whipped it from his hand.

"The hell?"

"No more. You need a clear head."

"Why? What's going on?"

Despite the anguish, the unfairness, the fierce goddamn terribleness of everything, she smiled. It felt good. Uplifting. Wings across her face.

She said, "I found your man."

19

TERA

Tera by name, terror by nature.

That's what her colleagues used to say about her, with an ingenuity befitting their callow brains and oversized egos. Not that she hadn't earned the epithet. Her daddy had been a cop until cancer wheeled him away at the too-young age of fifty-six. He'd learned, on his deathbed, that Tera was going into law enforcement, and the last piece of advice he gave her was to be uncompromising. Male cops, he'd expounded, didn't respect female cops until they'd proved themselves, not with their know-how but with their grit. Tera had been posted to Carver City's Eleventh Street Precinct the week after she'd scattered her old man's ashes in the Ohio River. She'd swallowed a spoonful of them, too, so that he would always be with her, lightly coating her stomach wall. Day one on the job, a steroid-jacked lieutenant had slapped her on the ass with a file folder and demanded she refill his coffee mug. Tera did, then tossed the hot coffee into the lieutenant's lap and grabbed him by the throat. "Slap my ass again," she'd said, squeezing, "and I'll take your fucking hand."

· · ·

Tera had been woken that morning by her Track-U-Gen app, notifying her that Luke Kingsley's vehicle had left Los Angeles County, and was heading east on I-210. She got out of bed, made herself an herbal tea, and scanned the information on her cell phone. Luke had left his house at 6:42 A.M., and there he was in real time, his little red blip on the outskirts of San Bernardino.

"Where are you going, Luke?"

Tera had attached the GPS tracker to the underside of Luke's Dodge Caliber several months ago, believing that he would, one day, return to the scene of the crime and lead her to Lisa Hayes's body. He was of particular interest now, because of his link, through Kitty Rae, to Kris "Sly Boy" Streeter, who'd recently been reported missing. Kitty was missing, too—hadn't clocked in for her shift at Fusion 44 for a few days. Los Angeles police were nosing around other leads; Sly Boy wasn't as squeaky-clean as he liked to portray, and had a lot of friends in low places. Tera knew about the Luke Kingsley connection, though, and decided, as she watched that red blip move farther east, to drive to Luke's empty house and check it out.

It appeared she wasn't the only one with Luke on her radar.

Ruben Osterfeld—not exactly low-pro in his jacked-up Tundra—scoped the actor's residence from across the street. Tera remembered from her cop days that Ruben worked security at Fusion 44. Sly Boy had put up Ruben's bail on more than one occasion, when the big guy had been brought in on assault charges.

Her cop brain (now her private investigator brain) ticked noisily. Had Luke—that wife-killing motherfucker—offed Sly Boy and Kitty in a fit of jealous rage? Did Ruben suspect as much, and was here to exact his own brand of heavyweight justice?

Tera resisted leaping to conclusions, but this was a feasible explanation. Or so she believed, until two wild cards—Johan Fly and

Xander Cray—appeared on the scene. As far as she knew, Johan didn't have ties to any of this.

She watched Johan, Xander, and Ruben engage in brief conversation, then the two new arrivals crossed the street to Luke's house, leaving Ruben in the truck.

"What the fuck is going on here?" Tera whispered. Her investigative brain whirled blankly for a moment, then kicked into a different gear. She plucked her cell phone from the Buick's console and accessed Johan's Instagram account. She scrolled through two months' worth of self-absorbed bullshit before stopping on a photo of Johan and Kitty at some swanky residence, posing in front of a double staircase, champagne in hand.

Okay, so they knew each other. Were they dating? Just friends? Did Johan want in on the Luke Kingsley beatdown? Were they all here—like Tera—looking for proof of the actor's crimes?

Too many questions. Tera watched and waited a little longer, then decided it was time for answers. She got out of her Buick and approached Ruben's Tundra. His window was open. She removed her pistol and locked the muzzle to his head.

"Ruben Osterfeld. You should have stayed getting your ass kicked in the Octagon."

"Jesus Christ." Ruben flinched away from the gun, but Tera kept it in place. "What the fuck?"

"My thoughts exactly. What are you doing here?"

"I don't know. I was told to be here."

"By Johan? You're working for him now?"

"Sometimes."

"And what's *he* doing here?"

"He didn't say," Ruben blurted. His face was strained and greasy with sweat. "I'm just the lookout."

"Okay, big boy," Tera said. "Get out of the truck."

"I didn't do shit."

"Get out now. I'm warning you." Tera tapped the barrel against Ruben's skull. "I haven't shot anybody in a long time and I kind of miss the feeling."

Rafael Montecino raised three tough boys and one very tough girl. He did it alone. His wife—a Swedish dancer, from whom Tera had inherited her striking hair—had walked out when Tera was five. She'd moved to New York City to try her luck on Broadway. The last Tera had heard, she was working as a high-class escort in Chicago.

Tera grew up in Carver City, a bleak, mob-run town in Western Pennsylvania, where tough was all anyone knew. Her old man was no exception. He was an amateur boxer—a Pennsylvania Golden Gloves champion—before becoming a cop, and he taught Tera everything he knew about how to land a punch, take a punch, and, most importantly, how to get up off the canvas. He arranged backyard bouts with her older brothers, who gave her no leeway; they hit her as meaningfully as they hit each other.

It was a bitter upbringing, but not unusual for that time, that place. Tera found respite in her schoolwork. She played piano, wrote short stories, and took photography classes. She also started kickboxing, because she wanted to please her father, and because the thrill of the fight was in her blood. Tera was made for it, too, with her quick hands and long frame. She won the Allegheny Kickboxing Classic three years in a row, and reached the final of the All-State Championship, only to be beaten by a force of nature by the name of Lola Bear.

Her brothers became copies of one another. They looked the same, with their Chilean complexion and Swedish hair. They trained at the same gym, worked at the same steel mill, and were fathers by the age of twenty-five, marrying eerily similar Catholic girls. Tera wanted to take a different path. She'd begun an undergraduate degree at Pitt, eyeing a career in economics, but didn't get out of her freshman year. Her roommate, returning home from a party one night, was raped, stabbed eight times, and thrown into the Monongahela. Another friend was fatally shot for the nineteen dollars in his wallet. These incidents happened within days of each other, and set Tera's head spinning. She dropped out of college and worked one unfulfilling job after another, including a year-long stint at the mill with her brothers. It paid well, but pounding steel, constantly, furiously, was never going to be enough.

It was around this time that her father was diagnosed with throat cancer, which metastasized aggressively to his lungs and bones. He was a hard parent, an even harder cop, but he believed in justice and fairness, and the streets would be less safe without him. Watching him deteriorate, Tera knew that there needed to be another Montecino in blue.

Throwing hot coffee into Lieutenant Ass Slapper's lap would mark the beginning of a dubious reputation in law enforcement. There were numerous written reprimands, two suspensions. Several police psychologists analyzed her childhood, everything from her absent mother to her abusive father. Tera maintained he was not abusive, but of course she knew otherwise. She also knew that her ruthless methods were an attempt to win her dead father's approval. He was with her, after all, in the lining of her stomach. As well, Tera constantly sought justice for her roommate and her friend. She remembered their faces with every pervert and rapist she dismantled, every murderer she kicked in the dirt.

Tera realized something else early on: that there were too many memories in Carver City, few of them good. She felt that a clean slate would make her a better cop. With three years of policing under her belt, she transferred to Los Angeles, North Hollywood Division. It was the change she needed. Tera learned the streets, the people, and the system. She put in her four years on patrol, then—at the age of thirty-three—made detective, working in juvenile crimes.

She also fell in love. Briefly.

Of the fourteen men she had chosen to share her body with over the years, Ash Castro was the first to excite her. He was a military man, eleven years training grunts at Fort Irwin, the last two in explosive ordnance disposal. Ironic, because he triggered detonations across her entire body and set timed charges in her mind, so that she would go about her everyday duties, and suddenly—BOOM—Ash would be there, blasting into her thoughts in a rising ball of fire and smoke. Tera flew headlong into devotion, a silly, schoolgirl breed of love. Unfortunately, Ash liked to discharge his ordnance on other women's bodies, many of them, according to the emails she'd read. When Tera confronted him about this, he turned violent—strapped bombs to his fists instead. A mistake. Tera took his best, then broke his jaw and six of his ribs. She left him whimpering on his living room floor.

There followed a long and ugly tailspin. Tera drank too much, slept around, and devolved into her old, uncompromising style of police work. She moved to Vice, a better fit, because the skulls she cracked needed cracking. Still, there was not a great deal of sympathy for her methods. After several rough years, she took a position—at the behest of her captain—with the Detective Support and Vice Division, Missing Persons Unit.

The Luke Kingsley case was supposed to be the jewel in Tera's crown. He was obviously guilty. It was simply a matter of hammering a confession out of him, or finding Lisa Hayes's body. Then she could lock in the evidence and nail Kingsley to the fucking wall.

The fact that she hadn't been able to achieve this burned her deeply. It felt like an insult. It *demeaned* her. And watching him walk free—alone and ruined, but *free*—was almost too much to bear.

Her work suffered again. She spent angry months chasing shadows, and hounding Luke at every opportunity. Her frustrations culminated during a routine arrest, when some half-witted perp called her a "fucken dumbass lesbo skank," and Tera retorted by busting his cheekbone with the grip of her service pistol.

She was given a choice: immediate suspension without pay, or early retirement. She chose the latter.

Six months in Maui, reclining in the ultra-blue Pacific, riding horses across Haleakalā's otherworldly landscape, and photographing broad, bleeding sunrises. It was the break her body and mind needed. She returned to L.A. and applied for her private investigator's license. The work was as mundane as she knew it would be, but the slower pace was good for her mental health, and being her own boss had its benefits.

On early mornings, though, deadlifting on her rooftop patio while watching the smog ride low and off-color over the Los Angeles Basin, Tera knew two things for certain. One: she wasn't dead at fifty; she still needed excitement in her life, something to make her pulse run faster.

Two: she wasn't finished with Luke Kingsley.

His house bore the unloved frontage of a single man, with its grimy windows, faded paintwork, and several cracked planters strangled with weed. Tera had Ruben ring the doorbell while she screwed the action end of her Beretta into the pad of muscle between his rib cage and hip.

No answer.

"Send your boss a text," Tera snarled into Ruben's ear. "Tell him to open the fucking door."

Ruben did. Seconds later, the front door swung open. Johan and Xander stood in Luke Kingsley's hallway with decidedly suspect looks on their faces.

"Oh shit," Johan said.

"Johan Fly, you slimy motherfucker. You want to tell me what the hell is going on?"

She pressed with the pistol, urging Ruben forward. They edged into the hallway. Tera kicked the door closed behind her, then pushed Ruben toward Johan and Xander. He stumbled. Johan held him up. Tera kept her pistol at the ready, the sights flicking between the three of them.

Xander—holding a manila envelope in one hand—shot a glance at Johan. Tera knew what he was thinking. *Three-on-one. Let's jump this bitch.* Johan gave his head the tiniest shake and made a calming gesture with one hand.

"That's right," Tera said. "Don't try anything stupid. You think I'm on my own, but I've got fifteen amigos in the mag that are faster and tougher than any of you."

Xander's shoulders slumped. Johan stroked his long Viking beard and smiled.

"It's been a while, Detective Montecino," he said. "No, wait . . . it's *Ms.* Montecino now. Word on the street is you got your ass canned."

"I took early retirement," Tera said, and angled her head, willing him to challenge her. He didn't. "This looks like breaking-and-entering to me, Johan. Unless Luke Kingsley found himself a new cleaner."

"So you know who lives here?" Johan asked.

"That I do."

"And you know he's a wife-killing motherfucker?"

"That he is."

A stillness settled among them—several silent seconds in which mutual interest was gauged. Tera took a step back, lowered her gun a few inches, but kept her arms extended. She stared into each hard face, seeing anger, concern, and uncertainty. Johan softened his expression, then raised both hands peaceably.

"I think we're on the same side here," he said.

"I wouldn't count on it," Tera rebutted. Her gaze flicked to the envelope in Xander's hand. It was half-tucked behind his back, as if he didn't know whether to hide it or not. "What've you got there, Xander?"

Xander plucked his left earlobe nervously, then looked at Johan for permission.

"You don't need to ask him," Tera said. "*I'm* the one with the gun."

Johan shrugged. Xander ventured forward, offering the envelope. Tera took it. Still with the pistol in her hand, she pulled the flap and removed two photographs, eight-by-ten, in glossy, miserable, weakening color. She looked at them, the breath hissing from her lungs.

"Christ," she said.

A female vic. Young. African American. Two bullet holes. One through her chest, the other through her skull. At first glance, Tera thought it was Lisa Hayes—she had a similar facial structure and build. But no . . .

"This is Kitty." Tera's voice was cracked and hurt.

"Yeah," Johan said.

"Where'd you find these?"

"A drawer in the actor's bedroom," Xander replied. "In his dresser. There are some porn DVDs in there, too."

Tera had seen her fair share of death—corpses of all ages, genders, and ethnicities, killed in a multitude of terrible ways. But this shook her, and she knew why. Because Luke Kingsley was behind it, and she had known, in the primal, penetrative part of her soul, that he was going to do something like this. *Anything happens to her, Luke, I will chase you down like a hound out of hell*, she had warned him, while all of her cop senses told her that a warning wouldn't be enough. *And there* will *be justice. One way or another.*

"She was my friend," Johan said, and lowered his eyes.

Tera looked at him, her heart clamoring furiously. She shook her head and dropped her gaze to the photographs again. Was this the reason Luke was currently blazing across the Mojave? Did he have

Kitty in the trunk? Was he going to bury her in the dry, desolate heart of the desert?

No body. No crime.

"Not this time," Tera said. She composed herself on the outside—steady hands, a neutral expression—but on the inside she was a running, hungry lioness.

A second stillness descended on the hallway. It was darker, and lasted longer. At length, Tera slipped the photographs back inside the envelope and returned them to Xander. She still had the gun in her hand.

"What about Sly Boy Streeter?" she asked.

"What about him?" Johan frowned.

"He's missing, too."

"I don't know anything about that," Johan said, and turned to his compadres. They returned know-nothing stares. "We're here for Kitty. That's all."

"How do you know her?"

"I met her at Station 1640," Johan replied. "She was new to town, had big dreams. I wanted to help, so took her to a few parties, introduced her to some people. But Kingsley already had his claws in her. She was . . . *enchanted* by him, I guess. A bona fide movie star."

Tera growled from deep in her chest. She could think of some other things to call Luke.

"I warned her. She didn't listen. The lure of fame . . . it can cloud your judgment, and I'm sure Kingsley promised her the world." Johan appeared to ponder this, then cleared his throat and continued. "Kitty called me last week. She said that Luke came on to her—that he'd been pretty rough. She was scared, she said, and was starting to believe that he really *did* kill his wife. I told her to go to the police. I don't know if she did, but that was the last time I heard from her."

Tera had no idea how much of this was true. Certainly not all of it. Johan was slick, a cobra more than a Viking, who could beguile and strike. He came from elitist wealth and moved in all the right circles. His social media activity was a master class in privilege. It was also a veil. Every police department in L.A. knew he was into some crooked shit. They were just waiting for him to irrefutably trip up. And guys like Johan, they always did.

Perhaps sensing her skepticism, Xander ventured, "I found Kitty's clothes, too. The ones she's wearing in the photos."

"Did you handle them?" Tera asked.

"Handle?"

"Did you tamper with evidence?"

"They were in the trash can," Xander said, and yanked his earlobe again. "I just pulled them out."

Tera pressed a hand to her forehead, trying to restructure her shaky emotions into an efficient strip of resolve. The taste in her mouth was cordite and rage.

"You know what?" she said. "It doesn't matter. Kitty's clothes and those photos of her corpse are incriminating, but they don't prove anything."

"No?" Johan cocked one eyebrow.

"He had his wife's blood all over his shirt last time and still walked."

"Okay. So what puts him away?"

"A bullet," Tera replied corrosively, holding up her Beretta. "It's no less than he deserves. Son of a bitch needs to pay for what he's done. Not just to one woman, but two."

"Two that we know of."

"Right."

"Like I said, we're on the same side."

Tera lifted her lip, stood rigidly. She didn't like Johan, but they wanted the same thing here, and it occurred to her that she could use him and his knuckleheaded accomplices to do the heavy lifting.

In effect, she could put a hit on Luke Kingsley—exact the retribution she'd promised—and keep the blood off her hands.

"He can't get away with this," she said, holstering her pistol. "Not again."

"I agree," Johan said.

"He needs to go down."

"Absolutely."

They exchanged tight, knowing smiles. Tera stepped toward Johan. He was three inches taller, but her hair flashed brighter.

"Look at you, Johan, so goddamn righteous, like butter wouldn't melt in your mouth." Tera chewed her lower lip and stepped closer still. She could smell the product in his hair, woody and enticing. "But I've seen your name on the police reports. I've read the witness accounts. It's a good thing your daddy rolls with the bigwigs down at City Hall."

"Don't believe everything you read," Johan said. "I'm just a lowly YouTuber."

"Bullshit. You're shady as hell, and my cop intuition is telling me not to trust you." Tera inhaled sharply, flaring her nostrils. "But what's that saying? *The enemy of my enemy is my friend.* I'm sure that's not always true, but on this occasion . . ."

Johan's smile grew.

"What do you say, Johan? Can we be friends?"

"Sure," he said.

Tera licked her lips and turned for the door. "Wait right here."

She wanted to scream. She wanted to cry. She wanted to hit her rooftop patio and deadlift until her arms were on fire. Physical exertion was the best way to vent, in her opinion, but it would have to wait. For now, Tera took a moment to breathe the hazy air and unlock a thread of calm, then she grabbed her cell phone from the Buick and returned to Luke's house.

"Track-U-Gen," she said, activating her phone's screen and angling it toward Johan and his boys. She pointed at an icon in the bottom corner: a magnifying glass on top of a map. "It costs more than most GPS trackers and asset locators, but it's reliable, it has a longer battery life, and it's precise to the square inch."

"You're tracking Luke?" Johan asked. She detected a hint of admiration in his voice.

"Have been for a few months now," Tera replied. "I get a notification whenever he exits his allocated geofencing zone. I'm looking for a pattern, somewhere remote, the kind of place he might bury a body."

"I get it," Johan said. "You were hoping he'd lead you to his wife."

"I wondered if he might."

The three men looked at each other, communicating without uttering a single word. Through the waves of testosterone, Tera detected distinct notes of anxiety and anger, which she needed to direct toward the task at hand.

"No one will miss Luke," she said. "He doesn't have an agent. His sister, in Wisconsin, has disowned him. His only friend died two months ago. It'll be weeks—months, maybe—before he's reported missing."

"What an epic fucking loser," Xander offered.

"I couldn't have said it better myself," Tera said, then switched her gaze to Johan, the shot-caller, the big boss. "Let's make a deal: I'll tell you where Luke is, and you put him in the fucking ground."

"You want us to kill him?" Johan asked.

"I want the same as you," Tera replied. "Justice."

"Why don't you do it yourself?" Ruben asked. It was the first time he'd spoken since Tera had parked her Beretta against his skull and ushered him from his truck.

"I'm a fifty-year-old woman with arthritis in my left knee." This last part wasn't true, but it sounded convincing. "You are three capable young criminals. Frankly, you have a much better chance of getting the job done. And besides, Kitty was *your* friend, not mine."

Johan regarded her from beneath the ridge of his narrow brow. Tera could tell she had his attention.

"Alternatively, you can turn in the evidence you tampered with, and hope Luke confesses." She spread her hands and sighed. "Spoiler alert: he won't."

"Or we wait here until he gets home. Put a scare on him. Make him talk." Johan demonstrated reluctance, but the truth was in his eyes. "You're assuming we want this guy dead as much as *you* want him dead."

"And don't you?"

A brief silence fell, disturbed only by the discreet industry of the house and the hum of the city beyond. Johan maintained eye contact with her, then nodded.

"Where is he?" He gestured at her cell phone.

The tip of Tera's right forefinger hovered just above the Track-U-Gen icon. "This is a onetime arrangement, you hear me?"

"I hear you."

"I don't care how you do it, and I don't want to know. Just get the job done and get rid of the body."

Johan's faint smile was all the acknowledgment she needed.

"One other thing: We don't *ever* talk about this." Tera lifted her chin and looked at Johan dead-on—the posture of a serious woman. "It never happened."

Understanding flowed between them, as cold and forceful as water.

"Where is he?" Johan asked again.

Tera opened the tracking app, found Luke's little red blip, and zoomed in.

"He's all yours," she said.

20

EL CAMINO DEL PARAÍSO

Near-empty highway, shimmering beneath a close, indifferent sun. A scuffed green bullet headed east.

Xander drove with his right leg extended, foot bolted to the gas pedal. The muscles in his forearms were as tight as wet knots. Johan sat beside him, exploring Krókr's engraved handle with the tips of his fingers. This delicate, meditative practice kept him from breaking.

"Ruben's falling behind," Xander said, his eyes flicking to the rearview mirror. "Fuck slowing down, though. He can meet us in Nueva Vida."

Johan snarled and shot Xander a reproachful look.

"Shit, man, I know you're pissed, and I get it, but we can turn this around." Xander nodded resolutely. The vein in his temple was showing. "We'll find the actor. Kitty, too. We'll bury those fuckers."

"You better hope that happens before they get to Ramón," Johan said. "Or I'll bury *you*."

When Tera had revealed Luke's location, Xander had groaned and given his earlobe several vigorous tugs. On their way back to the Mustang, he told Johan that the actor had asked about Ramón when he saw the photos from Stray Bullets. This ignited a fiercer, blood-thumping anger inside Johan. "You thought he was a cop," he'd breathed into Xander's face. "And you showed him photos of my fucking *canary* manufacturer!" Xander had squirmed and said something about how the cop—the *actor*, whatever the fuck he was—had liked them for Kitty's murder, and how the photos they'd taken at Stray Bullets had reinforced their alibi. This excuse made a modicum of sense, but did nothing to dampen Johan's rage.

It helped, somewhat, to focus on the single positive: his unlikely partnership with Tera Montecino. As they motored out of the city, Johan considered how the intervention of a former LAPD detective might have upended his plans. He had rolled with it, though, using his charm and acumen, and had yielded an extremely fortuitous result. It would have played out differently had Xander not discovered those photographs. His berserker had displayed glaring stupidity recently, but in this he had reinstated some value.

"I'm wondering," Xander said now, steering the Mustang around a strip of grumbling Harleys, "if this is even about the canary."

"Yeah? What the fuck else is it about?"

"I don't know." Xander kept his eyes locked to the road as he spoke—just as well, considering the needle was touching eighty. "But think about it. How would Luke Kingsley know that the guy in the photo was your manufacturer? I didn't tell him. And Kitty wouldn't know, unless you introduced them at some point."

"I didn't," Johan snapped. "Listen, Ramón used to make cocaine for celebrities. Small amounts, but pristine quality. Maybe Kingsley recognized him from some Hollywood party back in the day, then, knowing about the canary, put two and two together."

"That's possible, I guess," Xander said. "I just don't understand why he'd go after Ramón. That seems like a wild target."

"But it's one he can hit," Johan said. "Faking Kitty's death is just a stopgap. He needs to slow me down permanently, and upending my canary business could do that."

"You think he's looking for evidence?"

"That's exactly what he's looking for, then he'll bring in the authorities." Johan shook his head. "Ramón's smart, but he's not strong. If the cops put the squeeze on him, he'll buckle."

"You could be right," Xander said, and shrugged. He didn't look convinced. "Could also be that Kingsley's got a different ax to grind."

"I don't think so," Johan said. "But either way, we've got to get to Ramón."

He tried calling Ramón for the third time since leaving Silver Lake, and for the third time it went to voice mail. Johan hung up. He'd already left two messages telling him not to answer the door if anyone knocked.

"Cell phone reception's for shit in the desert," Xander noted.

"He built his own tower," Johan said, and sighed. "Maybe he's working. He doesn't usually pick up when he's deep into a batch."

Ramón's genius never failed to impress Johan. It was intricate and varied. He composed music, engineered plant life, and repaired everything from diesel engines to computer tech. In 2017, he constructed a high-altitude drone that was shot out of the air by an F-18 scrambled from NAWS China Lake.

Then there were the drugs. He and Johan resumed their crystal meth operation after the incident with the Mexicans, which became more successful, but no less dangerous, as Johan acclimated to the streets. Ramón also produced his own cocaine, called Venezuelan Sugar, which he sometimes sold—but more often gave away—to celebrities. It wasn't a profitable sideline, but Ramón didn't care; his name was added to a string of Hollywood guest lists, and he got to rub elbows with the stars.

The people Ramón met during this time, and the stories he heard, inspired the development of Citromantyl-V4—a product that went through multiple stages of testing, and took several years to perfect. When it was finally ready, Ramón showed it to Johan.

"Think of it as a steroid for your mind," Ramón said. "It deepens concentration, and enhances creative output."

"A focus enhancer," Johan said, holding the baggie of yellow powder up to the light. They were in Ramón's workshop—a converted barn on his ranch in Pale Bone. "How is this different from the nootropics I can buy over the counter?"

"How is an Arturo Fuente different from a stogie?"

"That good, huh?" Johan opened the baggie and took a delicate sniff. "Anybody else, and I'd call bullshit."

"The secret is in the flower," Ramón said, and plucked a beautiful yellow bloom from a propagator on his workbench. "*El Camino del Paraíso*. I engineered it myself. Properties in the seeds open neural pathways and target the hippocampus. The petal gives the powder its distinct color."

"You're a fucking virtuoso, Ramón."

"I call it Citromantyl-*vee-four*."

"Needs a catchier name."

"I know a few celebs, but I don't have the widespread access that you do. You want to take it out?"

Johan considered the streets, the pushers and crooks, the tweakers and junkies. Dirt everywhere. Decay. Desperation. It was just a matter of time before some scumbag pulled a .44 or otherwise tried to fuck him over. The fucking Mexicans had shown him that no motherfucker—*no* motherfucker—could be trusted. How fucking *sweet* would it be to shift to a different product, an *exclusive* product, and cater to a more trustworthy clientele?

"I'll give it a run," he said.

Johan took the Citromantyl-*vee-four* to a couple of actor friends, Lorenza Scialfa, who'd costarred in some movies back in the aughts, but hadn't worked on anything serious since MySpace was a thing, and Mickey Hubbel, the washed-up star of *A Perfect Situation*, whose current situation was anything but perfect. Ramón's yellow powder turned things around for them both. Lorenza scored a regular role in a popular HBO drama, and Mickey returned to prime time as the bumbling dad in Fox's *Robot in the Family*.

Within three months, Johan's client base had expanded. It included actors, musicians, directors, and CEOs. The momentum was building.

"Forget crystal," Johan said to Ramón during one of their regular business meetings. They were poolside at Johan's crib, smoking Arturo Fuentes. "It's a dirty game. We need to focus on canary, and you need to make more of it."

"Canary?" Ramón frowned.

"That's what the celebs call it," Johan said. "For *us*, it's gold dust."

"Okay, man, okay." Ramón had laughed. "I can up production. How much do you need?"

Johan blew a fat ribbon of smoke into the air. "It's Hollywood, amigo. How much can you make?"

They ripped through the desert, the highway a shimmering strip. Johan estimated that the heat beyond the windshield was somewhere in the low hundreds—positively *arctic* compared to the suffocating temperature in the Mustang. He rocked back and forth in his seat and ran his fingers along Krókr's handle. It didn't get any cooler.

East of Barstow, he tried calling Ramón again. Still no reply. He swore—slammed his cell phone down on the dashboard. It rang seconds later and he snatched it up, answering before he even saw the number on the screen.

"Ramón?"

"Afraid not," Tera Montecino said.

Johan growled and wiped sweat from his eyes.

"Listen," Tera said. There was no emotion in her voice. "The market in Nueva Vida isn't so hot. You should try Pale Bone, Nevada."

"Thank you," Johan said. He closed his eyes and saw forest fires.

"Call me when you're close and I'll give you the details."

Johan hung up. He stroked Krókr's handle for a moment, but couldn't suppress the eruption. It came like a tumbling boulder. He unleashed a torrent of expletives, kicking the dashboard, punching the door until the panel popped loose. Xander flinched but kept his eyes on the horizon.

"Son of a *bitch*." Johan's nostrils flared. "Kingsley's in Pale Bone. He's *definitely* after Ramón."

"Oh shit."

"Go faster."

"We're doing ninety already."

"I don't see any cops."

Xander punched it to triple digits, the Mustang spraying a rooster tail of California dust.

21

PALE BONE

The billboard was twenty feet tall but partially collapsed and hammered by the hard Mojave sun. It read RATTLESNAKE HOTEL, 14 MILES, EXIT 9, and depicted an Obama-era family springing for joy outside a Clinton-era establishment. The word CLOSED had been painted across the front in tall red letters.

"Damn," Luke said. "I thought we'd found our digs for the night."

This addendum could have been added to the next sign they came across: WELCOME TO PALE BONE, a collection of dusty shacks and trailers with creosote bushes growing in the street, the same size as Nueva Vida but with half its spirit. There was a convenience store, an auto repair shop, and a withered casino called Top Dogs. A bare-chested kid—no older than thirteen—with an eagle tattooed on one shoulder threw a stone at Luke's car as he drove through. It struck the rear quarter panel with a gong-like chime.

"You little shit!" Luke shouted through the open window.

"Fuck you, man," the kid called back, and shot him the bird.

• • •

Three ranches in Pale Bone, at different points of the compass, but none had a blue Econoline van parked in the driveway.

There was a mid-nineties Ram at the first property they came to. Several gray-snouted dogs slept in the yard, and an old couple sat just inside their garage listening to the radio. She fanned herself with a magazine. He hooked grime from beneath his big toenail with a pair of scissors.

"Looking for a friend of mine," Luke called out. He'd pulled into their driveway as far as the first sleeping dog.

"No friends of yours here," the old man returned, blowing muck from the tip of one scissor blade.

"His name's Ramón," Luke persisted.

"Like I said, no friends of yours here."

The second ranch, at the eastern edge of town, had an old Triumph motorcycle in the cluttered yard, along with several junkers that looked like they'd been stripped for parts. A newish steel barn stood twenty yards from the main house. There were two dogs in cages. Not the gray-snouted, sleeping variety, but muscly, vicious breeds that barked furiously at Luke's car as he stopped at the end of the driveway.

"No blue van," he said.

"Could be parked in the barn," Kitty offered.

"Let's keep looking," Luke said. He didn't like the looks of those dogs. "We can always come back."

They drove twenty minutes, covering Pale Bone, and found one more ranch. Four late-model pickups and a Peterbilt rig crowded the driveway. There were a few cowboy-types on the porch sipping beers. A mangy horse stared at Luke from over a fence.

"Help you?" one of the cowboys asked as Luke approached. He looked nothing like the cowboys that Luke had played on film; he was walleyed and his teeth had been kicked in.

"Looking for a friend of mine," Luke replied. "I haven't seen him for fifteen years, but I heard he lives on a ranch here in Pale Bone. His name's Ramón."

"We don't hire spics here," the cowboy said. "This is an American place of business, and we only put money in American pockets."

"Okay, well . . . thanks." Luke turned to leave.

"Sierra Vista Road," another of the cowboys called out, and pointed east. "Don't know his name, but you'll find your spic there."

Luke saluted the man—a cool tip of the finger. "Don't let the snakes 'tween yer spurs," he said, which was a line from his episode of *Retribution Gulch*. He returned to the car, exhaled nervously, and looked at Kitty.

"Ranch number two," he said.

"Damn," Kitty said. "Those dogs."

"I know."

"They were in cages, right?"

"Yeah," Luke said. He started the car and threw it into reverse. "But I'm taking my gun just in case."

Still no blue Econoline van, but Luke decided to knock on the door anyway. *Someone* might be home, and he needed to know for sure if he had the correct residence.

The dogs jumped and clawed at their cages as he maneuvered the Caliber up the driveway, bouncing over the uneven surface, windows closed against swirls of rising dust. He stopped short of the house (and the dogs) and grabbed his snub-nose from the glove compartment.

"Stay in the car, just in case he's home," he said to Kitty. "He looked pretty chummy with Johan on PictoShark. We don't want him to see you and be able to describe you. You're supposed to be dead, remember?"

"Yeah, but why would he even mention this to Johan?"

"He likely won't, but let's not take any chances. Speaking of which . . ." Luke gestured at the enraged animals. "I'd keep the windows closed, if I were you."

"Right," Kitty said, and then, "Be careful."

It was more junkyard than ranch. There were old TV sets, lawn mowers, desktop computers, and appliances strewn through the weeds along the sides of the driveway. An assortment of automobile parts filled a tumbledown garage. The vehicles they'd been stripped from sat exhausted in the late afternoon sun, skeleton-like and blasted with desert grit. A fenced-in area housed more junk: bicycles, old tools, an engine hoist, refrigerators, propane cylinders, rusty barrels. A complex nest of satellite dishes dominated the backyard, with some kind of cellular or transmission tower erected beyond this, thirty feet tall and creaking in the wind.

Luke approached the house, giving the dogs as wide a berth as possible. One was a German shepherd, the other a rottweiler. Both had wild, frothy jaws and looked like they had been raised with a sharp stick. Luke kept his pistol by his side, lest one of those cage doors spring open. They were secured by only a single bolt, as thin as a pencil. Enough vibration might shake them loose.

"It's all good, pooches," Luke assured them. "You stay right where you are, and I won't have to shoot you."

He hastened up the porch steps to the front door. His heart was pounding, but it had little to do with the dogs. He was—assuming their intel was correct—on the bat-faced man's property. Had Lisa been brought here three years ago? Was she *still* here, chained up in the basement? Might this be an anticlimactic dead end, and Ramón entirely innocent, after all?

"Maybe," Luke whispered, but the atmosphere suggested otherwise. This felt like a heartless, off-center place.

He tucked his .38 into the back of his jeans and knocked on the door.

No answer. Luke waited thirty seconds before knocking again, harder, reenergizing the dogs' frenzy. Still nothing. Luke sighed, took a step back. He then noticed the surveillance camera above the door, and another at the end of the porch, scanning the driveway. These, coupled with the attack dogs, indicated that Ramón took his home security very seriously. What was he trying to protect?

Luke walked across the porch to the nearest window and peered through. A sparse dining area opened into the kitchen. Compared to the outside, it was clean and orderly. It had little character, though. A single plant struggled on the counter, and a flag drooped from a hook on the wall.

"Venezuelan," Luke muttered to himself, recognizing the flag's colors. "Not Mexican. My bad."

Not that it mattered. Would Detectives Montecino and Kraemer have followed up more assiduously if he'd nailed *Señor Smokescreen*'s nationality?

"Nope," Luke said. He moved back to the front door, thumped it firmly, waited another thirty seconds, then descended the porch steps. Navigating the junk in the yard—still maintaining distance from the dogs' cages—he noticed tire tracks in the driveway. He was no expert, but they looked recent, and wide enough apart to belong to a larger vehicle. A Ford Econoline, for instance.

Kitty had not only kept the windows closed, but locked the doors, as well. Luke heard the clunk of the lock disengaging as he neared the car.

"Not taking any chances, huh?" he said, slumping into the driver's seat. He reached across Kitty and slammed his snub-nose back inside the glove compartment.

"I've seen dogs opening car doors on YouTube," Kitty replied, throwing him a sideways glance. "You're damn right I'm not taking any chances."

Luke cracked a smile, despite the nervous tension racing through his body. A sigh followed, deep and worked. He wiped dust from his eyes.

"Nobody home?" Kitty asked.

"Not a soul," Luke answered.

"So, what next?"

Luke sighed again and looked around. Ramón's ranch was exposed on three sides, but sheltered to the east by sandstone outcrops daubed with shadow. They could sit up there unnoticed, and watch the day fall.

"We wait," he said.

Luke went briefly off-road and parked behind a smaller outcrop. He and Kitty got out of the car, taking the large bottles of water they'd bought at a gas station on the Nevada state line. They started to climb. The cuts and ridges in the sandstone formed natural steps, so the going was mostly light. There were only a couple of places where they had to help each other, or grab handfuls of dry scrub in order to heave themselves onto the higher boulders.

"At least it's cooled off," Kitty said.

"Not enough," Luke moaned.

They crested the outcrop, the breeze stronger and laced with dust. Lizards scampered over rocks and along the trunks of dead junipers extending from cracks in the sandstone like giant antlers. Luke palmed fat droplets of sweat from his forehead, then guzzled from his bottle of water. Kitty checked for rattlers and found a place to sit in the shade. Here, twenty-five feet above the desert floor, they had an elevated view of Ramón's property. The shadow of the transmission tower stretched toward them like an accusatory finger. The dogs were still howling.

"You think he'll be back tonight?" Kitty asked.

Luke nodded. "Someone has to feed those dogs."

They sat silently for a moment, catching their breath, drinking water. The sun sank in degrees of deeper color. Luke estimated there was an hour of decent daylight remaining. The idea of approaching that house—and those dogs—in the dark did not appeal in the least.

Kitty screwed the cap onto her bottle, placed it on the rock between them, and asked Luke how he was feeling.

"Nervous," he replied immediately, then thought about it for a few seconds and gave her a more considered response. "Unsettled. That's a better way of putting it. I'm afraid of being closer to the truth, but more afraid of being no closer at all."

"That's understandable," Kitty said. "You're dealing with a lot. Not just recent information, but years of emptiness . . . of hurt."

"I wish I could jump into next week," Luke said. "Or even the week after. Fast-forward through these feelings, then see where I am and deal with it."

"However this works out—whether you get answers or closure—it's a step forward." Kitty nodded encouragingly. "And that's better than standing still."

"You're right," Luke agreed. He picked up a small stone and tossed it from the rise. It bounced twice off the boulders and hit the desert floor in a little Wile-E.-Coyote-like puff of dust. "How about you? How are you feeling?"

"Oh . . . terrible," Kitty replied. "Terrified, mostly."

"Yeah, well, that's understandable, too."

"Johan once told me that he can hear Vikings in his blood. I never knew what he meant, but now I do." Kitty lifted her hair and touched the dressing on her forehead. The gauze was grimy, the tape peeling away on one side. "He's there when I close my eyes. He's there when I open them."

"It's trauma," Luke said. "Your mind is bruised."

"Yeah. And like you, I'm unsettled." Kitty fetched a trembling sigh. "I'm afraid of what I've seen, and more afraid of it not being over."

"It *is* over, Kitty. Johan thinks you're dead. And when we get out of here, I'll book you a hotel up in . . . I don't know, Montana, maybe. Somewhere you can lay low for a month or so. Then I'll start feeding the sharks—the mudslingers."

"Phase two," Kitty said.

"Right," Luke said firmly. "A few juicy leaks here and there, a few celebrity names dropped . . . it won't be long before Johan Fly's world is turned upside down."

"I hope you're right," Kitty said. "But he feels so close. So *loud.*"

A drove of birds passed overhead, with quick wings and narrow bodies. Down on the ranch, the dogs had finally fallen silent. Luke could see them from where he sat, walking tight circles in their cages. He imagined approaching them with his water bottle, up-ending it through the tops of their cages, and watching delightedly as they snatched the cool, clear flow out of the air.

The thought dried his mouth. He took an empathetic drink.

"You have a happy place, right?" he said, turning to Kitty. "I mean, *everybody* has a happy place."

"I'm a born daydreamer, Luke," Kitty said. "I have a thousand happy places."

"I hear you, but there has to be one that buzzes you more than the rest. Either a sweet memory or a fantasy."

The breeze picked up briefly, whipping across the outcrop, drawing dirt from the desert floor in dizzying whirls. An animal— maybe a bird—called from the middle distance. A captivating sound.

"There is one. A fantasy, I guess." Kitty's jaw trembled. She pressed her lips together and swallowed hard. "Holding my son. Being in his arms."

"Your son?"

"Levi. He's six years old." Kitty nodded. The sunlight flashed off her shades. "And he's the most perfect thing in this or any world. More beautiful than the moon . . . than the stars."

"I don't doubt that," Luke said. His brief smile faded into a frown. "But how is being in his arms a fantasy?"

A tear zipped down from behind Kitty's sunglasses and she scuffed it away. "I knew before he was born that I couldn't give him the life that he—that *any* child—deserved. I didn't want him to have the disadvantages that I had, with a daddy who didn't care, living in a neighborhood that would always cut away at his ambitions."

She drew her knees up and wrapped her arms around them. Luke couldn't see her eyes behind her sunglasses, but the somber shape of her mouth relayed more than enough emotion.

"So I found him a new life, a new family—reputable people, with money, but more importantly, with time for him and love in their hearts." She cleared her throat, lifting her chin as she inhaled. "Levi will never want for attention, and he'll have more opportunities than I ever had."

"Even so," Luke said. "That must have been so hard for you."

"He was five weeks old. A tiny bundle in my arms. So beautiful. So pure." Another tear raced down Kitty's cheek. "That was the last time I held him. I whispered in his ear that I loved him, and let him go."

She took a moment, lost in thought. More tears came, shimmering on her face in the fading light.

"I tell myself," she said, "that by *not* being there, I gave him everything."

"You'll always be there," Luke said. "You'll always be a part of who he is."

A vehicle came into view, rumbling east on Sierra Vista. Not a blue Econoline, but a rusty GMC pickup with a dirt bike in the bed. Rising dust marked its passage, as distinct as a vapor trail.

"I guess he'll ask about me one day," Kitty said, once the truck had passed and the sound of its engine started to fade. "Levi has a different skin color than the rest of his family. That kind of thing tends to prompt conversation. And if he ever wants to meet me . . ."

She removed her sunglasses, wiped her eyes, then the muscles in her face relaxed as she slipped into reverie. It lasted only seconds, but it was deep. Even her voice changed, filtered through some dreamier place.

"I have this fantasy of flying him out to L.A., bringing him into my Hollywood lifestyle—my house in the Bird Streets, with its infinity pool overlooking the Strip, introducing him to my celebrity neighbors." She blinked hard and came back, pausing to gather her thoughts. "It's silly, I know, but that's why I moved to L.A. I wanted to give my dreams a chance."

Luke nodded, recalling his younger, unbroken self, with a backpack over his shoulder and a one-way ticket in his hand.

"And that's why I took the canary," Kitty said. She shrugged, as if there'd been no alternative. "I needed the edge."

Luke said, "There are people in Hollywood who've done a lot worse to get ahead."

Another vehicle passed—a sporty Mazda, blaring Aerosmith at a distorted volume. On Ramón's ranch, the dogs had stopped circling their cages and were sprawled on their sides, still and dark, possibly sleeping. The shadow of the transmission tower had grown longer.

"It's all I think about—or all I *used* to think about, before Johan: seeing my son again, and being a part of his life. And the *feeling* that rushes through me. The hope, the anxiety, the all-consuming love." Kitty put her sunglasses back on, looking directly at the setting sun. "He's my baby, you know?"

Luke drank his water. Some splashed onto his chin and trickled down his throat. It felt cool and good, unlike the emotion that had risen through his chest: a sudden pang of melancholy. He and Lisa had discussed starting a family on numerous occasions, but the time had never been right. Their careers always came first—this movie or that North American tour. He imagined, now, the child they would have made, holding him or her forever close, watching them flower, an achievement that no script or melody could come close to.

Kitty continued, "When the day comes that Levi wants to meet me, *if* it comes, I won't attempt to impose myself or replace his new family. I just want to hang out, get to know him."

"Yeah," Luke grunted around the lump in his throat.

"I want to see him as the child he is, not the child he might have been." Kitty's voice cracked again. Her shoulders hitched as she inhaled. "And I want *him* to see a woman he can be proud of."

"Are you kidding me?" Luke said. "Listen, I've only known you a few months, but that's long enough to know that you're kind and strong, and that any kid would be lucky to have a mom like you."

Kitty wiped more tears away. "You don't know how much I needed to hear that."

"Just telling it like it is."

She threw her arms around him—a brief, slightly awkward hug, but quite the loveliest he'd had in some time. He smiled over her shoulder.

"Thank you," she whispered.

"Right back atcha," he said.

They chatted idly for a few minutes, blithe conversation, cut short by the sound of another vehicle motoring along Sierra Vista. It came from the west, appearing from behind a distant outcrop.

Luke lifted his sunglasses and squinted. As the vehicle drew closer, he identified it as a Ford Econoline van, blue with a red stripe along the side.

"There he is." Kitty saw it at the same time.

They watched as it continued along the cracked strip of road, then swung a left into the ranch's driveway. The dogs woke and went crazy again, springing at their cage doors. The Econoline stopped close to where Luke had seen those tire tracks. His heart jumped and snapped—not unlike the dogs—as the driver's door opened and the bat-faced man stepped out.

Even at this distance—seventy yards or so—seeing him again brought that night at Uncle Lizard's back with startling clarity. Luke could smell the booze, hear the music, feel the closeness of so many lively, dolled-up bodies. He saw the intimate way in which Lisa and Señor Bat Face had interacted. In the years since, Luke had often wondered if he was grabbing at straws, but seeing him again now, he knew beyond doubt that there was a connection between this man and Lisa's disappearance.

"Are you okay?" Kitty asked.

"Yeah," Luke replied. And he was. Despite the nerves and the tension, he felt charged inside—a snarling, quaking engine, ready to redline. "Better than I've been in a long time."

22

THE BAT-FACED MAN

Ramón started unloading bags of soil from the back of his van into his barn, stacking them inside the doorway. "*Cállate carajo,*" he shouted at his dogs. He didn't notice he had company until Luke had drawn to within fifteen feet of him. "Whatever you're selling," Ramón said, raising one hand against the sunlight, "I don't want it." The barn door was on a track and he stepped backward to slide it closed, as if he didn't want anyone to see what was inside. Luke had glimpsed crowds of yellow flowers inside propagators, but these were of no interest to him.

"I'm not selling anything," he said.

"Then get the fuck off my property."

"You know who I am?"

Ramón took a step forward, looking from the shadow of his raised hand. Luke's description—bat-faced—was even more fitting up close, although there was a shimmer of intelligence in those shifty little eyes.

"No," he said. "I don't know who you are."

Luke had lost weight over the past three years, his hair was longer and grayer, and he was standing, partially, in silhouette. He circled to one side, so that Ramón didn't have to squint to see him.

"My name is Luke Kingsley."

The reaction was immediate. Ramón lowered his hand. His jaw clicked loose and his expression darkened. He stuttered something, then regained composure with a deep breath.

"Never heard of you," he said.

"Maybe you've heard of my wife." Luke's voice stiffened with emotion. "Lisa Hayes."

Ramón shuffled his feet and shrugged vaguely. "No, man, sorry."

A lie, of course, but it made no difference. Luke knew he had to act, either by playing it cool, backing off, and bringing in the police, or by acceding to his elevating rage and pummeling some answers out of this sketchy motherfucker.

The decision was taken out of his hands; Ramón bolted, his left shoulder dropping as he swiveled, sneakers kicking up dust. His intention was clear. He wasn't heading left for the house or straight ahead for the barn, but for the patch of yard directly between them.

He was going for the dogs.

Luke considered the snub-nose tucked into the back of his jeans. Putting one in Ramón's leg was a decent option, and he was a good enough marksman—thanks to his prep for *A Bullet Affair*—to nail a moving target. He didn't have a clear shot, though. Ramón darted between the junked vehicles on his way to the cages, moving in and out of sight. His haste was such, however, that he stumbled into a stripped-down Pontiac, bounced off it, then recovered his feet and staggered on.

Luke, giving chase, saw his opportunity. He didn't go around the Pontiac, he went *over* it. His stuntman, Rocco Villeneuve, had pulled off this move in *Out of Midnight*—one foot on the hood, one on the roof, then launching himself through the air to bring down the perp from above. Rocco had done it in one take and made it look easy. Luke was less adept. He landed short of his target and twisted his ankle as he touched down. Momentum carried him forward, though. He lunged, whipped out one hand, and managed to snag Ramón's ankle. It was enough to knock him off balance, and he sprawled to the ground just in front of the dogs' cages.

"Son of a bitch." Luke pushed himself to one knee, then scrabbled forward and jumped on Ramón from behind. This accelerated the dogs' mania. They thrashed and snapped. They boomed and clawed. Luke was all too aware of how close they were, but his focus was on Ramón, who wasn't going down without a fight.

"*Me cago en la madre que te parió.*"

"Fuck you, motherfucker!"

"*Vete a la chingada.*"

"Fuck you."

Luke exerted his weight between Ramón's shoulder blades, but Ramón squirmed, gave himself some room, and drove his elbow backward. It was a blind shot, and frustratingly lucky. It caught Luke clean on the jaw and he flopped to one side. He was too amped to feel any pain, but his equilibrium was momentarily displaced by a sprinkling of tiny white stars.

Ramón swore again and wriggled free. He got to his feet with Luke right behind him. They wrestled—their bodies pressed together, their shoulders tucked, each man trying to upend the other. Luke was taller and broader, but Ramón was younger and wiry with muscle. They canceled one another out, until Luke worked his fist into Ramón's stomach, not once but three times. Ramón spluttered and backed away. Luke followed with a stinging jab that snapped Ramón's head backward. He teetered sideways, then overbalanced and went to one knee.

"Where's my fucking *wife*?" Luke stormed. He hobbled forward, meaning to grab Ramón by the throat and choke out the truth, but Ramón rose quickly, drawing power from the ground and channeling it into his attack. He thrust one shoulder into Luke's middle, knocking the wind from his lungs and driving him backward, slamming him into the side of a junked-out minivan. Still no pain—only one-hundred-proof adrenaline—but Luke's upper body tingled with a loss of feeling and his breaths came in tight rasps.

Ramón threw two quick punches. The first gashed Luke's lower lip. The second bounced off his forehead and sent him sprawling. He hit the ground, pushed himself up quickly, but his legs weren't there and he went down again. Ramón loped forward, his fists raised, his angular face bright with exertion.

"I fucked your wife and killed her," he said, perfect English, "and my dogs drank her blood."

Luke scrambled backward, pushing at the ground with his feet while trying to work the .38 Special from the waistband of his jeans. He had stowed it in the Caliber's glove compartment only as a precaution, and every round he'd loaded was a round he'd hoped not to have to fire. Now, though . . . *now* he wanted to empty the cylinder, bang five circles through this dirty bat-faced bastard.

He tucked his fingers beneath the pistol's grip, and was about to hook the gun free when his right shoulder bumped against the German shepherd's cage. The dog seized its opportunity. It threw itself at the steel mesh, biting through it, grabbing the sleeve of Luke's T-shirt and yanking vigorously. His hand was snatched from the pistol's grip. He tried to pull away but the shepherd held fast, shaking its head, rumbling with bloodlust. Next door, the rottweiler howled and clawed at the ground, wanting in on the action.

Ramón cackled at Luke's plight. He lurched closer, kicked a cloud of grit into Luke's face, then muttered something in Spanish and cackled again. Luke heaved forward, trying to tear his T-shirt from the shepherd's jaws—and it *did* tear, but not enough. The shepherd adjusted its grip with a couple of quick snaps, caught hold of fresh material, and kept Luke pinned to the front of the cage.

The dust cleared. Ramón stood over him. He raised his foot

and brought it down on Luke's face and shoulder—two chopping, painful blows that caused the vivid desert light to dim for just a second. Luke slumped. Blood dripped from his busted lower lip, pattering onto his T-shirt in bright red flowers. He watched as Ramón walked to the rottweiler's cage.

"There are two things my dogs don't like," Ramón said, raising his voice to be heard over their snarls and howls. "Intruders, and being hungry. It is good when I can solve both problems at once."

The rottweiler set its powerful body, growling impatiently as Ramón reached for the bolt.

Kitty attacked in a bright, silent flash. She came from the side, stepping around an old Eldorado, throwing herself at Ramón and tackling him to the ground. They landed in a dusty tangle with Kitty underneath, her right arm looped around Ramón's throat. He bucked and rolled, reaching backward, trying to claw at her face and hair.

"Luke!" she cried, weaving her head to avoid Ramón's snatching hand. "Get your ass over here! Luke . . . *Luke!*"

He gasped, woozy from the knocks he'd taken, and struggled forward. His tee stretched and ripped even more, but the shepherd was not about to relinquish its prize. It dug in, lowering its head, holding Luke in place.

"*Luke!*"

"Trying," he groaned, and pulled again, twisting at the waist, getting nowhere. Kitty, meanwhile, had lost her advantage over Ramón; he'd writhed into a position in which he could elbow her in the ribs, which he did—over and over, not hard strikes, but enough to weaken her headlock. He slipped out of her grasp and got to his feet. Kitty followed. They faced one another, poised to strike.

Luke mustered every ounce of his resolve and lunged forward once more. His tee ripped to the collar, giving him sufficient slack to arch away from the cage and reach for the gun with his left hand.

The shepherd jerked its neck, snatching and growling, leveraging the ground with all four paws. Luke's fingertips danced across the grip of his snub-nose. He couldn't quite get the angle to snatch it cleanly.

Kitty glanced in his direction—a momentary loss of focus. Ramón seized the opening. He leapt forward, flailing both fists. Kitty dodged and countered, catching Ramón with a hook that wobbled but didn't stop him. He muscled closer, wrapped his arms around her, and wrestled her to the ground.

They tussled in the dirt, knotted together. Ramón freed one arm and rang his fist against Kitty's jaw. She grabbed a handful of his thick black hair and pulled. Her efforts—her strength—fueled Luke. He cried out, twisting his upper body enough to yank the revolver from the waistband of his jeans. Within seconds, he had it aimed over his right shoulder. He pulled the trigger, a weak-handed shot, but accurate enough. The shepherd's left ear disappeared in a splash of blood and fur. It yelped, let go of his sleeve, and whirled away from him.

Luke clambered to his feet, his tee hanging off his shoulder in rags. He shook the ringing from his ears and the muddiness from his head. Kitty and Ramón had risen, too, still locked in a vicious embrace. Luke viewed them through the revolver's sights. First Kitty, then Ramón.

"Get away from him, Kitty," Luke wheezed, but his voice was lost beneath the dogs' frantic yelps and yowls. He shifted position, his finger on the trigger, waiting for a clear shot.

It was Ramón who forced separation; he twisted free of Kitty, then pushed her toward Luke. She careened into him, and they both toppled backward. By the time Luke had reset his aim, Ramón had rolled over the hood of the Eldorado and ducked from view.

"Bastard," Luke said. He wavered forward with the revolver extended. Weary, painful breaths pounded from his chest. He reached the Eldorado, swung around it. Ramón had already moved. Luke glimpsed him disappearing behind another wreck, then scrambling across to the minivan that bore the dent made by Luke's body. He was exposed for one second. Maybe two. Luke squeezed off a shot and blew out the minivan's passenger window. The report drowned the racket of the dogs for several seconds, then faded into the deep desert air. Luke shuffled toward the minivan, ducked around it. No sign of Ramón.

"I'll find you," Luke growled. He kept moving, staring down the revolver's stubby barrel. Kitty had positioned herself beside a small crate brimming with parts and junk, also looking for Ramón. Luke caught her eye. She shook her head.

He moved on, checking behind the wrecks and piles of crap, edging toward Ramón's van, circling back to the stripped-out Eldorado. Kitty was in the same place. Luke looked at her with a questioning expression but she shook her head again, then started to move in his direction. She took two steps, then stopped cold. Luke saw the alarm in her face, her gaze fixed on something over his shoulder.

He whipped around, but too late. Ramón stood in front of the dog cages. He had a grin on his face and one door open.

"Shit," Luke gasped, scuffling backward, lifting the gun.

The shepherd came at a bloodthirsty sprint. All teeth and one-eared fury.

Luke shot the dog but it kept coming.

He'd bought the gun—the "Chief's Special," the salesclerk had called it—when he first moved to L.A. Luke liked its classic look and compact size, but had questioned its stopping power. "Well, it isn't a .357," the salesclerk replied, "but it's a solid self-defense option. As for its effectiveness . . . Jack Ruby used a .38 Special to drop Lee Harvey Oswald. Granted, he was point-blank, but one shot was all it took to send that little Commie bastard straight to red hell."

"I see," Luke said, spinning the empty cylinder. "So I'd have to be up close and personal to do any real damage?"

"Depends on the type of ammo you use, and the accuracy of your shot. But yeah, with this caliber, closer is always better."

This conversation flashed through Luke's mind as the dog continued toward him. The bullet he'd put into its shoulder had slowed it, but not by much. It was a primal, single-minded force, packed with strength and a vicious, drumming energy. It leapt at Luke from twelve feet away and knocked him to the ground. The revolver spilled from his hand, but this was of little concern compared to the shepherd's jaws, snapping and clashing inches from his face.

Luke kept it at bay, but only just. He had his left forearm braced against the animal's throat, and his right hand directly beneath, grasping the thick fur on its chest. Saliva whipped and flew. Blood, too, from the gristly gash where its left ear used to be, and from the bullet hole in its shoulder. Luke—his survival instinct fully dialed—recognized what might be his only opportunity. He pushed up with his left forearm, creating just enough clearance to shift his right hand to the shepherd's shoulder, then plunged his thumb into the ragged little hole he'd made with his .38.

The dog howled and thrashed but held its advantage. Luke howled, too, and pressed his thumb deeper, all the way in, feeling flecks of ruined cartilage and bone. This did it. The dog whirled away with a piercing cry, giving Luke room to grabble sideways and retrieve his gun. When it attacked again, he was ready. He threw his left arm up to shield his face. The shepherd clamped onto it at the same moment that Luke locked the revolver's barrel to its throat.

"Die, you Commie bastard," Luke hissed, and pulled the trigger.

The report was blanketed but still loud. The shepherd staggered sideways, blinking its eyes confusedly. Blood darkened the golden brown fur on its throat and dripped between its paws. It wheezed and whined, then—remarkably—came at Luke again. It managed several erratic steps before its front legs folded and it slumped to the dirt. Luke watched the animal try to get back up. It pawed at the ground and its hindquarters shimmied, then it flopped onto its side, tongue lolling.

All this happened in a matter of seconds, maybe twenty, certainly no more than thirty—time enough for Ramón to react to the gunshots, make his way to the other dog's cage, and begin to work the bolt loose. Time enough, also, for Kitty to have plucked a dented hubcap from the crateful of junk she'd been hunkered next to, then sneak up behind Ramón and ring it off the back of his skull.

Ramón stumbled forward, dropped to one knee. He touched his head, as if he couldn't work out what had hit him, then turned to look at Kitty as she drew her hand back for another shot.

"*Ay de mí,*" he mumbled.

"That's right, motherfucker," Kitty said, and knocked him clean out.

I fucked your wife and killed her and my dogs drank her blood.

Luke had one round remaining in the cylinder but one round was all he needed. He glanced at the German shepherd—still alive, but panting in tight bursts—then got to his feet. This proved more challenging than he'd anticipated. He teetered and reeled, taking numerous head-clearing breaths before achieving something close to verticality. Blood trickled from his busted lip and from the puncture wounds the dog had put in his left forearm. He assessed the damage—could have been worse, *much* worse—and, still reeling, made his way over to Kitty.

"Luke," she said as he approached. The wound on her forehead had reopened, spilling a rill of blood onto the bridge of her nose. There was bruising on her face and her T-shirt was dark with dirt. "Jesus, Luke . . . Jesus Christ."

"You okay?" His voice was a dim crackle.

"I think so."

She didn't look okay, though. More fuel for the nightmare fire, no doubt. More sessions with the shrink.

"You?" she asked.

"No," he said, and looked down at Ramón, still on his back in the dirt. His eyelids fluttered. He groaned. One side of his face was swollen. It looked like Kitty had broken his jaw with that second swing of the hubcap.

Luke kicked him in the ribs. Not hard, but hard enough.

"Hey. Motherfucker. Wake the fuck up."

Ramón groaned louder, opened his eyes a crack. He coughed, and blood spurted from his mouth. "Ngggh," he said. Luke kicked him again, then again. When, finally, Ramón opened his eyes fully, Luke crouched and pressed the revolver's stubby little barrel to his forehead.

"You killed my fucking wife."

"Ngggh."

"And now I'm going to kill you."

The revolver was double action, which meant that Luke didn't *have* to cock the hammer, but he did anyway, for dramatic effect, because he was an actor, and he was all about the drama.

"*Nggggggghh.*"

"Fuck you," Luke said, curling his finger around the trigger.

"Luke, *NO!*"

Kitty placed her hand on his shoulder and Luke glanced up at her, a sad, pleading look in his eyes. In hers, too.

"Don't," she said.

"He killed Lisa."

"Please, Luke. This isn't who you are." She was almost in tears, trembling at the idea of more bloodshed. "You'll never live with yourself."

"I don't care," Luke said, staring into Ramón's beady, frightened eyes. "Nothing matters anymore, only this guy, and making him pay for everything he took away from me."

"No," Ramón croaked, and shook his head.

"Yeah. Oh hell, yeah." Luke exhaled shakily. He felt the adrenaline everywhere, even in his soul. "You killed my wife, and you're going to pay."

"I didn't," Ramón said, his voice cracked and tight. He blinked, and tears bloomed in his eyes. "I didn't . . . didn't . . ."

"Didn't what?" Luke tapped the muzzle against his skull. His finger was still on the trigger. "You've got three seconds to talk."

"I didn't kill her."

"I don't fucking believe you."

"She's alive. I swear. I fucking *swear* to you, man."

These words dropped like pebbles into the vast lake of Luke's grief, so small, making almost no sound, but producing ripples that spread across the surface and reached the lonesome shore on which he had been standing these past three years. He gritted his teeth, afraid to hope, but those ripples had symmetry and breadth.

"Alive?" Luke sobbed. He eased his finger off the trigger. "How do you know that?"

Ramón nodded, and the tears rolled from his eyes. He moved his right hand, dragging it through the dirt, slowly lifting it until he was pointing behind him.

"Because she's locked in my basement," he said.

Kitty pulled a six-foot power cord from the crate of junk and used it to tie Ramón's hands behind his back. "Make it tight," Luke had said, and she did, wrapping it four times around Ramón's wrists, then tying a double-knot that pinched his skin. Luke kept the revolver to his head the entire time. He'd lowered the hammer, though.

They grabbed an armpit each and heaved Ramón to his feet. Luke kicked the seat of his pants, not as hard as he wanted to.

"Okay, muchacho. Move your ass."

They walked to the house. The rottweiler's howls and remonstrations followed them. (The shepherd had fallen silent at last.) Kitty pulled Ramón's keys from his front pocket and used them to unlock the door. An alarm sounded—a rapid-fire synth blast, like something from a sci-fi movie. Luke gestured at a keypad beside the door that looked like it had been made from an old push-button phone.

"Code," he snapped.

"Five-six-four-two-six."

Kitty punched it in. The alarm fell silent. They continued through the house, Ramón leading the way, all of them limping and wheezing. They passed through the dining area where the Venezuelan flag hung, into the kitchen—clean, with lingering aromas of garlic and cooked meat—then through to a small room stacked with old Spanish-language newspapers and magazines. A desktop computer hummed on an antique bureau. There was a portrait on the wall of an elderly Latino with distinct angular features. *Papi*, perhaps. Dried garlands and a rosary drooped off the frame. Luke looked at it briefly, but his attention was on a door in the wall opposite. An austere door, with steel plates riveted across the front and thick bolts set top and bottom.

"The basement, I presume," Luke said.

Ramón nodded, slumping dejectedly. Luke pulled him upright, tapping the back of his skull with the revolver to let him know it was still there. Kitty stepped forward. She threw the bolts. There was a dead lock beneath a short strip of chain that served as a handle. Kitty rattled the keys in front of Ramón's face.

"Save me some time," she said. "Which one?"

"Bronze-colored," Ramón mumbled. "SCHLAGE stamped on the head."

She found the key, pushed it into the lock. It turned easily. She grabbed the chain and pulled. The basement door opened slowly, heavily.

Kitty went first, taking each step down with a degree of trepidation. Ramón followed, with Luke clutching his arm from behind, the gun in his other hand.

"Stinks," Kitty muttered, pulling her T-shirt up over her mouth and nose. It was the smell of human waste, uncleanliness, and airlessness. It grew thicker as they descended. Luke felt a wave of revulsion and sadness, but these were obscured by a more aggressive rush of feelings. The idea that he was within moments of seeing Lisa was too huge to grasp. He stood in its shadow, waiting for it to either topple and crush him, or provide elevation to the top.

The main basement room was large and windowless. Luke took in certain details—cockroaches skittering across a cracked linoleum floor, water dripping from an overhead pipe—at the same time as he noticed the four women. They were drab-faced and pale, dressed in loose clothes, their hair long and dirty. One slept on a pile of laundry in the corner. Two were slumped across a stained green sofa, watching a *Friends* rerun on an old TV. The other woman sat at a small table, weighing yellow powder on a precision scale. She wore latex gloves and her red hair was pulled into a tight ponytail—minor hygiene considerations in an otherwise filthy environment.

Lisa was not among them.

Three Latinas and a redhead. Ghosts, all of them, void of life and reaction. The redhead glanced up as Kitty approached the table. She tilted one eyebrow, then went back to her work. This was the only acknowledgment of their presence.

"Jesus, Luke," Kitty said, grabbing a half-pound baggie of yellow powder and holding it up for him to see. "This is canary. Now we know the connection to Johan. This is his manufacturer."

"You know Johan?" Ramón asked, then sneered. "Anything happens to me, or this operation, he'll kill you."

"I've got enough dirt to bury that motherfucker twice," Luke said, and slotted the barrel of the gun into the hollow at the back of Ramón's neck. "Now where's my fucking wife?"

That was when a door behind Luke opened and a heartbreakingly familiar voice said, "There you are."

23

CITY WOMAN DREAMIN'

Luke met Lisa at the Melody Bar & Grill, and their first date had been at Taix a week later. He thought he'd fallen in love with her that night; Luke had pushed the boat all the way out—champagne, rack of lamb, a variety of delicious hors d'oeuvres—after which Lisa had smiled appreciatively and said, "Nice, Luke, real nice, but now take me to a place where they serve nasty cocktails and play loud music." The mischievous little wink she'd offered made Luke wonder if this sweet Black angel had fallen unto him from the heavens.

He *truly*, unquestionably fell in love with her four months later, in a way that made him realize that he hadn't, until then, known what love was.

He'd taken a spill—drunk off his ass, of course—and fallen down a short flight of stairs outside a Japanese restaurant in Los Feliz. It wasn't the stairs themselves, but the way his head thumped off the wall at the bottom that put him into a coma. He was out for five days, during which a CT scan revealed a small bleed on the brain—an acute subdural hematoma, to give it its fancy name. A surgeon drilled a burr hole in Luke's skull to drain the blood, and he rose from his unconsciousness to see Lisa standing over him.

"There you are," she said, and there'd been such a spirited and certain light in her eyes, as if she never doubted that he would return to her. It was exactly what Luke needed to see in that moment. This light defined Lisa as an individual, and them as a couple.

His head buzzed and his arms were too weak to lift, but he reached out to her with his soul—wrapped it around her eight or nine times, like a long, colorful scarf.

"You're everything to me," he said, and he meant it.

Luke didn't remember too much about his hospital stay, and *nothing* about his five days in a coma, but he always remembered the overwhelming love he felt when he saw that light in Lisa's eyes, and those three short words, like three musical notes forming a chord—a perfect harmony.

Lisa spoke them numerous times in the years to come—when Luke returned from shooting on location, when he appeared onscreen in a movie or TV show, when they made love and he moved his firm, wanting body into hers.

There you are.

Soft at times, more aggressive at others, but always spoken with that strong, remarkable light in her eyes.

The words were there but the light had gone. Lisa stood like a human shadow, detached from the things that gave her depth and verve, starved of the nutrients that once fed her soul. Her eyes were dark pits, no glimmer at all. She was thin, horribly thin, maybe ninety pounds, whereas before she had been a comfortable one-twenty. Beneath her clothes—a dirty T-shirt and leggings with holes in the knees—every bone would be showing, stark points and ridges instead of appealing muscle and curves. Her hair had been cut into a short, lusterless Afro that framed her face unevenly. Luke might not have recognized her, except for the tattoo on her right forearm: CITY WOMAN DREAMIN', the title of her first studio album.

She smiled weakly. Her mouth was the same, too, he realized, the shape of her lips, the slightly crooked front tooth.

"Lisa," he said, but his voice wasn't there, only a frail, sibilant breath. He took a single shaky step toward her, then fell at her feet and cried.

Luke rose through a fog that was mostly gray with grief but turned red with anger the higher he climbed. He pushed himself upright, touched his wife's face, then turned on Ramón and cracked the grip of the revolver off the top of his skull. Ramón went down heavily, unable to break his fall with his arms tied behind his back. His swollen jaw hit the linoleum with a wet sound.

This caught the attention of the women in the room. The redhead stood up quickly. "Baby," she said. Her mouth was full of crooked brown teeth. One of the Latinas had swiveled away from the TV, blinking slowly, like someone waking from a faint. Lisa clapped her hands over her ears. "No, no, no," she said, and backed away.

Luke half dragged Ramón up, threw him against the sofa, slapped his face to get his attention.

"What did you *do* to her?" Luke slapped him again and pressed the gun into the soft pocket of his left eye. "Start talking, mother-fucker."

The redhead said, "Baby," again and began to cry. Kitty went to her, touched her gently on the shoulder. "It's going to be okay," she said, then announced to the other women in a more strident voice, "We're going to help you all. We're going to get you out of here."

Luke looked around the basement fleetingly, then recentered his attention on Ramón. "I don't know what the hell you've got going on here, whether these women are your sex slaves or just bagging your product, but it's over for you."

Ramón whimpered. Blood appeared at his hairline and trickled down the left side of his forehead.

"Maybe I call the cops. Maybe I put a bullet in your eye." Luke pressed a little harder with the gun. "I guess that depends on you."

"Please, man, please—"

"*Talk*, you son of a bitch. I want to know what you did to my wife. Why she's locked up here, and why she looks like a goddamn ghost."

"I was . . . was trying to help her."

"Help her?" Luke said incredulously. He looked at Lisa, who stood plain, shallow, and silent. "*Help* her?"

"Canary," Ramón said.

Luke lifted the gun from Ramón's eye and straightened up, grimacing at the little pops and aches in his body. His gaze panned from Ramón to the baggies of yellow powder on the table, then to Lisa. He saw a shimmer of who she used to be in the angle of her hips, the twist of one shoulder. A shimmer—that was all. He looked at Ramón again.

"I've waited three years for answers." Luke's mind was a logjam of thoughts and fears. "Tell me everything."

Ramón's jaw worked stiffly, but only gasps and grunts came out. He took a breath, appeared to compose himself, but it was Lisa who spoke first.

"I tried to fly," she said. "But it didn't work."

Lisa's arrangement with cocaine had been "low-key" and "social." That's how she described it, and Luke saw little reason to challenge her. *You're better without it*, he'd ventured once, regarding her need to use before performing, to which Lisa had replied, unforgettably, *You'll always reach higher when you have something lifting you up.* A contestable logic, he'd believed, in a person with so much natural talent.

She'd met Ramón at a launch party at the Whisky. Her producer, Moon Child, had made the introductions, getting directly to the point: "Ramón, this is Lisa Hayes, aka the second coming of Aretha. Lisa, this is Ramón Sojo Apa . . . Apa . . . oh fuck, I don't know, but he makes the best blow this side of the Big River. Calls it Venezuelan Sugar. How *cute* is that?" Up until then, Lisa had procured her coke from a dealer out of West Hollywood—called himself the Bounce. Her first question to Ramón had been: "What makes your product so good?"

"I told her it was sleek," Ramón said, blinking the blood out of his left eye. "A smoother up, a smoother down. No shade."

"Sugar," Lisa said. She smiled, so familiar—a shot to Luke's solar plexus.

"When was this?" he asked.

"Four, five years ago." Ramón squirmed, his face turned sideways with discomfort. "Motherfucker, I'm *hurting* here."

"Yeah. Shame." But Luke hoisted him—threw him onto the sofa. "Better?"

"*Joder!* No. *Dios mío!*"

"Too bad. Talk."

Lisa had dropped the Bounce and switched her coke allegiance to Ramón. Her assistant, Jazmine, handled transactions. This was a side of Lisa's life of which Luke had little knowledge, and no influence. She did her thing. Luke rolled with it.

"She invited me to Uncle Lizard's. I didn't want to go. Too far from home." Ramón shook his head again. "But she said . . . she said I was the emperor of the high—"

"Emperor," Lisa said.

"She said I needed to be there. She wanted to introduce me to some people. Spread the love. The sugar."

Lisa had, by this time, shared with Ramón how she wanted to get into movies, and Ramón had shared with Lisa how he was working on a new product, one that accentuated natural ability, and elevated the user to the best possible version of themselves.

"Canary," Luke said.

"A prototype," Ramón said. "It wasn't ready. I told her it wasn't ready, but she insisted."

"First," Lisa said.

"*Sí.* She was the first person to test it," Ramón said. "It . . . it didn't go well."

Luke flashed back to that night, so much of it a drunken blur, but he had honed the memory of Lisa and Ramón talking to one another. He'd been her dealer for at least a year at that point, long enough for her to believe that whatever he—the emperor of the high—gave her would be of a certain quality, including a canary prototype.

I tried to fly. But it didn't work.

"You took it that night?" Luke asked her. "At Uncle Lizard's?"

Lisa looked at him through her sunken eyes. She shrugged, then nodded. "First," she said again.

"I think," Ramón said, "the prototype, together with the coke she'd already taken . . . it had an adverse effect—"

"No shit," Luke growled. "Fucking genius."

"I told her to take it easy." Ramón closed his eyes and moaned. The left side of his jaw was twice the size of the right. Broken. No doubt about it. He talked through his teeth, like a ventriloquist. "She didn't listen. She took too much."

Luke looked at Lisa. This rang true. Her impatience and impetuousness had led to many arguments during their time together. She didn't like to wait for anything.

"Why did you even bring it"—Luke turned back to Ramón—"if it wasn't ready?"

"I'd turned her down on other occasions, with earlier batches."

Another runnel of blood crept from his hairline. "She was beginning to doubt it was real. I brought it to save face. She pushed me to try it."

Again, remembering their intimate exchange, evoking jealousy in Luke, when all Lisa had been passionate for was a new high. He shook his head, this surfeit of information vying for space with the emotion. On some level, he registered the upshot of all this: the exoneration, and perhaps the rebirth of his career. But how could he indulge such an ideal conclusion, when Lisa herself was so far from the woman she had been?

This would take time. Months. Maybe years. The road to healing—for both of them—would be uncertain.

"Your arm," Kitty said.

Luke looked at it. "Oh," he said, and dragged it across his tee. It was bleeding freely, dripping on the linoleum. He hadn't noticed.

"I'm going to get something for it," Kitty said, and to Ramón: "You got a first-aid kit? I'll get something for you, too."

"To hell with him," Luke said.

"You want him to pass out on you?"

Luke groaned. Ramón blinked more blood out of his eye and told Kitty there was a first-aid kit beneath the sink in the bathroom, and a cold compress in the freezer. She swept from the basement, thumped up the stairs. As the basement door swung open, Luke heard the rottweiler woofing and howling out in the yard.

He looked at Ramón, felt a rush of intense anger, then cooled it by looking at Lisa.

"What's my name?" he asked her.

It didn't come immediately. She frowned and blinked her broken brown eyes, then uttered, softly, "Luke."

"Luke. Yeah. And who am I to you?"

"You are the cradle."

Tears pricked the backs of his eyes and he might have held them back, except she sang, distantly, but with a soulfulness that hadn't been touched: "*Some dreams are found where the lows don't go, this is the cradle that rocks my soul.*" This brought back all the feelings—every last one—and his tears fell brightly, as heavy as coins on his face.

"It's going to be okay," he sniffled. "I promise you."

Kitty returned with a first-aid kit, painkillers, and a cold compress wrapped in a thin towel. "This will help with the bleeding," she said to Ramón. She placed the compress on top of his head, then gestured for the redhead to hold it in place. "Give him these," Kitty said, and shook three Advil into her palm. "I don't want my hand anywhere near his mouth."

"You take any of those?" Luke asked as Kitty tended to him.

"Two," she replied. "I'm fine. A little bruised up, is all."

"You saved my life out there," he said.

"I'm getting used to it."

Luke dry-swallowed two Advil while Kitty cleaned and dressed his arm.

"It'll do for now," she said, "but you'll probably need a tetanus booster. Those dogs were filthy."

He nodded gratefully, looked at Lisa, then switched his focus to Ramón. "My friend is kinder than I am. But then, you didn't kidnap her loved one and ruin her fucking life."

Ramón exhaled tiredly. The redhead held the cold pack to his head and whispered, "Baby, oh, baby," into his ear. In the background, yet a thousand miles away, the TV switched from *Friends* to *Frasier*. Both Latinas watched it. One of them—zero-eyed—hadn't looked at Luke once. A crust of saliva circled her mouth.

"Let's keep it going," Luke said. He kicked the bottom of the green sofa between Ramón's legs, making him jump. "What happened after Lisa took the prototype?"

Lisa looked down at her bare feet, twisting her hands together. Ramón cleared his throat and winced.

"Baby, oh, baby—"

"Shut the fuck up, Christine," Ramón barked, and she did—her mouth snapping closed, as if pulled by a string.

He sighed, either with relief or pain, and resumed talking.

He kept his eye on her. That's what he said. Lisa went to the ladies' room and came out after seven or eight minutes. She caught Ramón's eye, nodded, then started talking to one of her music-industry friends.

"She looked fine. Fresh-faced. She was smiling." Ramón's gaze drifted as he remembered, taking himself back to a night Luke had relived a thousand times. "I watched her from across the room, looking for any negative side effects. She moved from person to person, fully engaged. I couldn't tell if that was the coke or the prototype, but I felt cautiously optimistic."

"I guess that didn't last long," Luke said.

"It didn't." Ramón shook his head and sighed again. "Things turned bad soon after."

Lisa had glided across the dance floor, stopping occasionally to interact with associates and fans—an air-kiss here, a selfie there—before shuffling up alongside Ramón.

"How are you feeling?" he asked her.

"Good . . . yeah, good."

"Any nausea? Head pain?"

"No, I . . . no pain, but my left eye is ticking." She blinked a few times, her painted lashes flashing up and down. "Does it look like it's ticking?"

"No," Ramón replied. "You look good. Any positive effects, aside from what you would normally feel with the sugar? Clear-headedness? A heightened focus?"

"No, I . . . maybe, I don't know. I'm having a good time." She smiled at him. "Listen, I'm going to go find my husband. We had a fight earlier and I want to make it up to him."

Lisa swished away from Ramón, skirting the bar to find Luke on the other side. She sprawled into his arms, whispered in his ear. They laughed, kissed, then downed a shot of tequila each. Ramón watched, paying close attention to Lisa's movements. She jerked once—an abrupt twitch of the shoulders. She also pressed the heel of her hand into her left eye, perhaps to suppress the mysterious ticking sensation.

"You left the bar shortly after that," Ramón said. "This was somewhere around two in the morning."

"One fifty-two," Luke said, recalling the time stamp on the grainy surveillance photo that Detective Kraemer had shown him.

"I followed you outside," Ramón said. "I wondered if you were leaving for the night, but you crossed the parking lot and went into the woods."

Luke's throat clicked dryly. He looked at Lisa, grasping at foggy memories: the sweet, woody fragrance of the trees, the smell of Dolce & Gabbana perfume. A kiss? He thought so, yes. Long, warm, and soft, and the words she'd spoken—just above a whisper: *I don't think it's working*. She hadn't been talking about them, their marriage. No, it was the drug she had charging through her brain, the one for which she had just become test subject number one.

"You didn't go far into the woods," Ramón said. "I could see you from where I stood at the edge of the parking lot, next to my van. I saw you stumbling around a little, ducking beneath the branches. I watched you kiss."

Luke nodded.

"Then Lisa made a gurgling sound and started to convulse. You hugged her close, as if she were cold, and clapped her on the back. She had her head against your chest, rolling it from side to side. That was when her nose started to bleed. Not just a trickle. It poured."

"All over my shirt."

"She pushed you away and stumbled deeper into the woods. You followed, saying her name over and over. I lost sight of you and had to follow the sound of your voice." Ramón hissed and twisted his neck. "Jesus, Christine, that's enough. My head is freezing."

Christine lifted the cold compress and said, "Baby."

"*Que ladilla eres*," he said to her, and then, to Luke: "She was a crack whore. Found her in the gutter in Vegas. Brought her here. Saved her life."

"And what a life," Luke said, stepping away from a cockroach as it skittered across the linoleum in front of him. "Now keep talking."

Ramón did: "Lisa didn't get far. You caught up to her, took her by the arms. She was still convulsing. I was maybe fifteen feet away. It was too dark for me to see everything, but I *did* see her collapse. She jerked away from you, then slumped to her knees and fell backward."

"So dark," Lisa chimed in. She looked at Luke, her mouth angled downward. "And cold, baby. *Cold.*"

Luke remembered none of this, an absence of mind that offered no reprieve. On the contrary, he felt hollowed out, emasculated—a spectator at his wife's undoing. Lisa mumbled something else, still looking at him through the dull stones of her eyes. He wondered if there was a way back for her.

The .38 Special was still in his right hand and it still felt good. The temptation to aim, fire, and put his last bullet through Ramón's skull was great indeed.

"Go on," he said instead.

"There's not much left to say." Ramón rolled his shoulders, flashing his teeth with the discomfort. "You crouched over Lisa, trying to get her to wake up, then you took out your cell phone—to call for an ambulance, I suppose, although you never made it that far."

"You hit me from behind," Luke said, touching the back of his head. "Knocked me out."

"I found a heavy branch," Ramón said. "You went down. I put your phone into your pocket and dragged you to the nearest tree. You were so still. I thought you might be dead."

Not quite, Luke thought. Just a few critical memories erased.

"I picked Lisa up and carried her to my van." Ramón looked at her while he spoke. She returned the gaze, smiling vacantly. "I had to wait for some people to leave the parking lot, then I put her in the back and drove away."

Luke gritted his teeth. He had the answers he wanted—to the most important questions, at least. But he felt no relief, no peace.

"You dirty son of a bitch," he said.

"I did what I had to. I knew that, if Lisa went to hospital, or if she died, the prototype would be discovered in her bloodstream, and the police would start asking questions." Ramón lowered his eyes. "Maybe they'd track me down, maybe not, but I couldn't take that chance."

"So you were willing to let Lisa die," Kitty said, "to save your own ass?"

"My hope was to bring her back here," Ramón said. "Flush the prototype out of her system, nurse her back to health, then let her go."

Kitty: "And why *didn't* you do that?"

"She was unconscious for ten days. Stable, but unresponsive. And when, finally, she did wake up, she was not the same." Ramón's voice was slurred, his jaw somewhat looser. The painkillers were kicking in. "There were clear signs of brain damage: cognitive impairment, motor slowing, severe memory loss."

"You couldn't leave her outside a hospital and drive away?" Luke asked.

"At the risk of her talking? No."

Again, the urge to aim the revolver and fire was monumental. Only Lisa, and these other mistreated women, kept him from doing it. They'd seen enough horror.

"These past two years, she has shown real improvement," Ramón said. He looked at Lisa, curling his upper lip into an unappealing smile. "She gets better every day. Isn't that right, *mi cielo*?"

"Every day," Lisa said.

"She has a long way to go, though." The ugly little smile faded, replaced by an ugly little frown. "She can remember the words to all her songs one moment, then forget how to use a fork the next."

"And these other women," Kitty said, gesturing around the room. "Are they your guinea pigs, too?"

Ramón shook his head and gestured at the Latina sleeping on the pile of laundry. "Only Angelica. I thought I had it right with her, and *I* controlled the dosage. But no, there were still detrimental side effects."

"Jesus Christ," Kitty hissed.

"The others are here because they want to be," Ramón added.

"Bullshit," Luke snapped. "They're prisoners. They may not know it, but they are."

"And those bolts on the door prove it," Kitty said.

"They're safe down here," Ramón said. "Those bolts are for their own protection."

Kitty put her hands on her hips, shaking her head angrily. She walked around the basement, stepping over trash, discarded clothes, and empty plates, looking with grief at each of the women, imprisoned in their own heads as much as in this room. The TV chattered in the background, the laugh track absurdly inappropriate.

"I've heard enough," Kitty said, stopping at Luke's side. "It's time to call the police."

"No," Luke said, and flared his nostrils. "I'm pretty sure Vegas cops serve this whole area. They've probably got substations here and there, but how long will it take them to get to us? They might even dispatch a part-timer from Pale Bone, probably poker buddies with this motherfucker"—he kicked Ramón's heels—"and with all the cop savvy of a goddamn watermelon."

"So what do you want to do?" Kitty leaned in to him, speaking out of the side of her mouth. "We can't just take Lisa and leave."

"No, we can't," Luke agreed. "But I don't want to be here for one second longer than I have to be. So we're going to load everything up—the canary included—and hit the road. We're, what . . . forty, fifty miles from Vegas? We'll find the biggest, *glitziest* police department in town, and drop this shitshow at their door. Then I'm going to call Aster Aarons at the *L.A. Times*, and drop one hell of a story at *her* door."

"I'm down with that," Kitty said. "We can take Ramón's van."

"Exactly." Luke clicked his tongue and smiled. "You can drive. I'll sit in the back and entertain."

"*Chamo*, hey, I told you everything. I did what you asked me to." Ramón wriggled his shoulders, his face fraught with desperation. "You can take my girls, but please, no police. Just let me do my thing here."

"Are you out of your goddamn mind?" Luke said.

"Please. My father died six years ago. I have family in Venezuela who depend on the money I send them. It's bad for them there." More blood trickled from Ramón's hairline. "They will die. They will be killed."

"You took *everything* from me," Luke stormed, flinching as the anger rocked his body. "You took everything from my wife. And these women . . . these poor women have been imprisoned down here, living in filth. What about them? What about their families?"

"I didn't want *any* of this." Ramón twisted and struggled, trying to work his hands free. Tears welled in his eyes. "It just . . . happened. I'm not a bad person."

"You might be able to work a deal, keep your family safe," Kitty said, "if you offer up Johan Fly."

Ramón groaned and looked up at the ceiling, his narrow chin already quivering. If what he said about his family was true, Luke had no doubt he'd throw Johan to the dogs.

"I guess phase two just got a kick-start," Luke whispered to Kitty, then spread his arms wide and announced in a strident, actorly voice: "Okay, ladies. You're out of here. We're taking a road trip to freedom."

They didn't move. It was as if they didn't hear. Kitty rolled her eyes and snapped into action. She turned off the TV and all but hoisted the two women off the sofa, then woke up Angelica, curled like a kitten on top of the laundry. Christine stood back, nervously twisting her ponytail. She looked sad and confused.

"Let's go!" Kitty clapped her hands, rallying them along. "Come on, girls. It's time to haul ass."

Luke sprang into action, too. He stepped toward Lisa, cupped the back of her neck, and kissed her firmly on the lips. She shrank back at first, surprised, then relaxed—*responded*, her mouth, the same as it had always been, shaping itself to his, so full and warm and utterly, wonderfully familiar.

Luke pulled away slowly, his head turning a dizzy circle. He looked into Lisa's eyes and saw something there, deep but distinct: a spark of her old self.

"Goddammit, I missed you," he said.

Kitty found a backpack in a pile of junk beside the water heater. There were a couple dozen cockroaches living inside it. She shook them out, then loaded in the canary. Twenty-seven half-pound baggies. She knew Hollywood prices, and given the discount for buying in bulk . . .

"Jesus, Luke, there's over three million dollars' worth of product here."

"Bring it all," Luke said. "Let's make headlines."

They left the basement in a somewhat orderly line, Ramón first, still with his hands tied behind his back, then Luke and Lisa. They walked side by side, fingers touching. Luke had the revolver in his other hand. "Try anything smart," he warned Ramón, "and I'll put a bullet in your back." The other four women followed, looking around apprehensively as they emerged first from the basement, then the house. They whispered in Spanish. Their eyes were large, but dull. Kitty brought up the rear, encouraging the women with gentle words. She had the backpack looped over one shoulder.

They crossed the yard toward Ramón's Econoline, meandering between the junked-out cars and stacks of debris. The rottweiler observed their passage with a cacophony of rumbling barks. Two turkey vultures—unperturbed by the noise—snapped ravenously at the dead shepherd, only taking wing when Luke and company approached. This was the only disagreeable sight. It was dusk, and the desert sky was a magnificent swirl of purples and oranges. Luke sighed reverently and looked west, his eyes full of burning, hopeful color. He thought it was the most beautiful sunset he'd ever seen.

Then everything changed.

The snarling, booming rottweiler masked the sound of the speeding vehicle. Luke saw it before he heard it: an aggressive splash of headlights racing along Sierra Vista, then sliding onto Ramón's property. It bounced and fishtailed, filling the yard with dust and light, before screeching to a stop not far from Luke's Caliber.

There was a beat—a shadowy, unsettled moment—then everything became clear with Kitty's chilling scream. She had recognized the car, the dented sage panels and squat, muscular stance.

The passenger door opened. Luke saw a swish of blond, braided hair, the flash of an ax.

Johan Fly came at them, a terrible Viking storm.

24
RAGE

The last time Johan saw Kitty, she had been scrambling down the embankment behind Jink's Warehouse. He'd watched her topple over a wooden fence and disappear from sight, but here she was now, locked in the headlights, as small as a rabbit. The rage that had consumed him all day pushed itself out of his throat and his eyes. He exited the Mustang, hoisting Krókr to his chest. His ancestors announced themselves in his blood.

There were other rabbits. The actor was there, his face smeared with blood and dirt. Ramón looked equally beaten. He stood with his shoulders slumped and his hands tied behind his back. Five raggedy-ass women lurked just behind them, almost transparent in the dusty evening air. Johan had no idea who they were, or what the hell was going on here, but none of that mattered now.

It was only as he got closer that he saw the snub-nosed revolver in the actor's hand.

Luke raised the .38 Special, took aim, and pulled the trigger. He did it before the fear could take hold—a reflexive action, almost. It gave him no satisfaction, no sense of power. He would never have believed that shooting to kill could feel so unremarkable.

His aim was true. He knew it before the hammer dropped—a sizzling, deadly projectile on a collision course with the middle of Johan's skull. Johan lifted his ax at just the right moment, though—or the wrong moment, from Luke's point of view—and the bullet deflected off the blade. There was a spark, a brilliant *ping!* that cut through the echoing report. Johan staggered backward, rocked by the bullet's closeness. Xander Cray, who'd stepped out from the Mustang's driver's side, took cover behind the front fender.

Kitty's scream tailed off, and another—Christine's—took its place. Luke stood with the gun extended, trying to process how Johan was still standing. He remained locked in that position for a blink or two, which was as long as it took for the world to rupture and fall.

Ramón peeled away, shouting something in Spanish. The women scattered like birds. Their movement jolted Luke from his stupor. He turned, saw Lisa drifting aimlessly, and caught up to her at a leap.

"Listen to me, listen . . ." He tucked her behind one of the stripped-down vehicles and turned her face up to his. "The house. Go back to the house, okay? And hide. *Hide.* A closet, a crawl space. Anywhere."

He kissed her. She tried to hold on to him, but he pushed her away. It broke his heart.

"Now, baby. Go, just *go!*"

All Kitty could assume was that she'd brought him here. Johan had been inside her mind—a heavy, bulky presence; she'd *felt* him—and when she lowered her guard, dared to hope, he had crept out somehow.

She saw the spark of the bullet strike the ax blade. Johan floundered backward. Xander ducked out of view. Kitty broke to her right, still screaming, and threw herself against the side of the junked Eldorado. She looked through the rectangular gap where the rear windshield used to be and saw Johan advancing again. Behind her, the rottweiler voiced a succession of bass-drum barks, and Kitty considered throwing the bolt and setting it free. It had just as much chance—more, in fact—of attacking one of the stranded women than going for Johan, though.

If she ran, he would catch her. If she hid, he would find her. There was only one possible way out of this.

"Fight," she gasped.

Kitty saw Luke kiss his wife and leave her side, clearly hoping to draw the fight away from her. Kitty recognized an opportunity, thin though it was: if Johan went after Luke, she might be able to weave through the junk and sneak up behind him. She had knocked Ramón out with a hubcap. She'd prefer something heavier, more lethal, to deal with the Viking. A lead pipe. A baseball bat wrapped in razor wire.

There had to be *something* in this shithole of a yard. Kitty peeked through the rear windshield again—didn't see Johan or Xander—then hustled out from behind the Eldorado. She yanked a piece of timber from the crate in which she'd found the hubcap. A good size, about the same length as a baseball bat, but ravaged by termites. It would break too easily. She dug through cables and circuit boards and the skeletons of old appliances. Nothing good. Nothing with heft.

Kitty moved away from the crate, scanning the yard for Johan, although her attention was diverted to something lying in the dust beneath an old wreck. It was an L-shaped lug wrench, heavy and solid enough to do some real damage.

She scuttled toward it, keeping low, grasping the potential weapon. It felt incredibly small, compared to that ax. Still, if she could approach on Johan's blind side—

Pain flared suddenly in her lower back. Kitty reeled sideways, glimpsing Johan's reflection in the wreck's dusty window. He'd achieved what she'd been trying to—had advanced on *her* blind side and struck with the blunt side of his ax.

He caught her arm before she could fall and threw her against the car. His hand found her throat and squeezed. The pain expanded from her back into her limbs, but she struggled against him, kicking her legs.

"You're pretty lively for a dead girl," Johan hissed, then laughed and squeezed harder. His eyes were cold circles. "I'm going to make this slow, Kitty. You'll wish you *did* have a bullet in your head."

Kitty could get no real leverage with the lug wrench, but she lashed out regardless, two quick shots, striking his left arm and shoulder. Her third shot was no harder, but the socket end connected with his jaw and staggered him. His grip on her throat loosened, giving Kitty more room to move. She swung with the wrench again, a purring, violent shot that missed his skull by two inches.

"Bitch," Johan said. Spittle sprayed from his lips. He lifted her at the throat, pressed her up against the car, then turned his ax around and slammed the bottom of the handle between her eyes. The first strike brought a frisson of brilliant stars. The second turned everything dark.

There was no reason for Johan to go after Lisa—she'd done nothing to him—but Luke couldn't take that chance. Johan wasn't a Viking, he was a psychopath, and he wanted blood.

If he, Luke, could sacrifice himself to keep Lisa and Kitty safe, he would do it. But one head would not be enough. Luke realized this, and he arrived at the same conclusion Kitty had only moments before: that the only way out was to fight.

Lisa wandered toward the house, but slowly. Another woman

cowered with her hands over her ears, her eyes large and confused. One gunshot had penetrated her languidness, and Luke wished he could fire another. He recalled, when purchasing the firearm, that he'd also been considering a semiautomatic with an eight-round mag, and how he wanted those extra bullets now.

A burst of Spanish sounded from across the yard. It was Ramón, hollering at Christine. She hastened to him like an oppressed wife and began to untie the power cord from his wrists. Luke wanted to intervene, but a more urgent matter had arisen. He heard Kitty cry out and looked to see Johan strike her in the forehead with the butt of his ax handle. Kitty folded at the knees. Johan lifted her up with one hand in her armpit and dragged her toward his Mustang.

Rage obscured everything. Luke leapt from his crouch and ran at Johan, crossing the cluttered yard in a blur. With twenty feet between them, he lowered his shoulder and braced for impact. His plan: to hit Johan from behind, knock the ax from his hand, then retrieve it and drive the blade into the back of his neck.

It was an outrageous strategy, and one Luke didn't get to see play out. Something struck him from the side. It felt like a wrecking ball. Luke hit the ground in a cloud of dust and hurt. He groaned, looked up, and saw Xander standing above him.

"Colton motherfucking Stone," Xander said, and put his boot into Luke's ribs.

Johan flicked hair from his eyes and boomed laughter. He felt invincible. Unstoppable. Kitty—the little raccoon—moaned and squirmed, turning her black eyes up to his. "*Unghh*," she said. "*Gaaggh*." Blood ran down her face from a wound high on her forehead, an old wound, by the looks, that he'd opened when he'd butted her with Krókr's handle.

"Shut your fucking mouth," he snarled at her. He dug his hand deeper into her armpit and yanked her along. Behind him, Xander drove his boot into the actor's midsection, while Ramón's wrists were being untied by some carrot-haired skank wearing latex gloves. Another woman was screaming, running around like a spooked goose, the dog howled and pounced at its cage door, and turkey vultures dared the madness to tug strips out of the other dog. The only thing missing was an inquisitive town cop showing up to investigate the gunshot.

"We're getting out of here, Kitty," Johan said. He needed somewhere quiet, where he could work without interruption. "This place is a fucking circus."

He reached the Mustang and popped the trunk—a shallow space, barely room for Kitty's narrow ass even when empty, but this had in it a full-sized spare and Xander's toolbox.

"No room at the inn," Johan said, slamming the trunk closed. "Guess you're riding club class."

He started to unbuckle his belt—an upgrade to club also meant tying her hands behind her back—and Kitty saw this as her moment to strike. She threw her shoulder into his middle, then balled her right fist and cracked him in the jaw. It was, to her credit, a good shot, quick and accurate, but lacking any real oomph. Outweighing her by a hundred pounds was always going to play to Johan's advantage. Which was why, when he retaliated, she felt it. He made a fist of his own and drove it into her stomach. Kitty doubled over, coughing in pain, then he grabbed her by the hair and whammed her face off the trunk lid—two solid knocks that put her into a daze.

Johan threw her over the trunk, whipped off his belt, and strapped her hands behind her back. Her backpack had slipped off her shoulder during this exchange. Johan picked it up and looked inside.

"I'll be a son of a bitch."

Canary. Enough of it to turn the HOLLYWOOD sign yellow. *Certainly* enough to take this whole operation down, and Johan with it.

"If you wanted to fuck me, Kitty, all you had to do was ask." He opened the Mustang's passenger door, yanked the seat forward, and threw her into the back. "Now I'm going to kill you *real* slow."

Xander approached. He had the actor in a hammerlock hold—his right arm twisted up behind his back—bullying him toward the waiting car. Luke stumbled and groaned. His T-shirt was a torn, dusty rag, his mouth a red smear. A dirty strip of rolled gauze fluttered from his left forearm.

"Where do you want this fucker?" Xander asked.

"Six feet under," Johan replied, looking at the bullet-sized groove in the cheek of his ax. "But we're not doing it here. It's too busy. Too chaotic."

"No shit," Xander said. "What the hell is going on? What's with all these women?"

"Ramón's bitches, I guess." Johan shrugged. "His crackheads, his whores. I don't know everything he's into, and right now I don't care. I just want to get the fuck out of here."

"Agreed." Xander continued forward, pushing Luke ahead of him, keeping that hammerlock high and tight. "Let's get this piece of shit in the trunk."

"No room," Johan said. "And I got Kitty on the backseat."

"Open the door. I'll throw him on top."

"I don't want them both kicking around back there. Double the trouble." Johan nodded toward Luke's Caliber, its pansy-blue paint job veiled by a skin of desert grime. It had Tera's tracking device attached, but he wasn't concerned about that—he'd deal with it later. "Take *his* car. The keys are probably in his pocket. Just tie him up so he doesn't try anything."

"Got it."

Johan got behind the wheel of his Mustang and fired it up. The engine caught with a deep growl, then ticked and purred. He flicked the headlights on, throwing a bold luminance across the yard and the house beyond. A turkey vulture took wing with a scrap of dead dog in its beak. Ramón clapped his recently freed hands and shouted at his women, herding them into the back of his van.

"I'm heading toward town, then taking Black Valley Road west," Johan said, raising his voice above the Mustang's throaty snarl. "Text me when you're clear of this shithole."

"We need somewhere we can operate," Xander said. His eyes were wild and his teeth were showing. He looked like a dog with a new squeaky toy. "Somewhere I can take my time with Colton here."

Johan dropped into drive. "I know just the place."

Through the tears in his eyes, Luke watched Johan swing his muscle car around, then rumble down the dusty driveway. He saw Kitty's bright sneaker flash briefly through the rear windshield, then the Mustang turned right on Sierra Vista and they were gone.

In the next breath, he turned and saw Ramón grab Lisa by the upper arm and push her into the back of his van. Luke tried calling out to her, but his throat was dry and cracked and all he managed was a husky, spluttering cough. His bruised ribs throbbed.

"Move your ass, and don't do anything stupid." Xander exerted more pressure on his right arm. "I don't want to have to kill you quickly."

An unlikely memory occurred to Luke as they edged toward his car: a scene from *Ventura Knights*, in which Sebastian (Travolta) and Logan Knight (Luke) stood at the perimeter of the bad guys' compound, having had everything they loved burned to the ground. "You sure you wanna do this, little brother?" Sebastian had asked, and Logan had replied, "When you don't got nothin', you got nothin' to lose." It was a cheeseball line, the same tired old shit Luke spouted in most of his movies, but in that moment, with his shoulder threatening to vacate its socket and his entire world being pulled apart (again), it seemed an enlightened philosophy.

Ramón grabbed the last, straggling woman and threw her into the back of the Econoline, then slammed the rear doors and hopped behind the wheel. Kitty had appropriated his keys, but he must have found a spare. The engine wheezed to life. The lights flared.

"Nothin' to lose," Luke groaned. He stopped dead and Xander bumped into him. "Keep moving, ass—" And that was as far as he got; Luke lunged backward, cracking the back of his skull into Xander's mouth. It was a surprising strike, hard enough to stagger Xander. He dropped back a step, relaxing his hold on Luke's arm.

The next ten seconds ticked by as if choreographed, and Luke hit all his marks. He twisted away from Xander, freeing his right arm, swinging his left simultaneously. It was a looping strike that began open-handed, but his fingers formed a tight fist a split second before impact, rocking Xander's head to the side.

He was at least six inches shorter than Luke, but wide—a dense two-twenty, maybe two-thirty. Luke thought it would take a chain saw to cut him down, but this punch did it. Xander slumped to one knee, and that was all Luke needed. He sprang forward, grasping the loose gauze bandage on his left forearm and wrapping it around Xander's throat. There was enough slack to go around twice.

He pulled as hard as he could. Xander struggled, clawing at the thin fabric, trying to work his fingertips between it and his skin.

"*Fuck you*," Luke screamed. His arms vibrated with the effort. Blood sprayed from his open lip, peppering the top of Xander's shaved skull. "*Fuck you . . . FUCK YOU.*"

Xander rolled his shoulders and bucked. A bull of a man. He rained fists behind him, catching Luke a couple of times, but Luke felt nothing. He tightened his stranglehold, the gauze cutting into his hands, turning his knuckles white. He planned on leaving something else for the vultures to feed on.

Light washed over him as Ramón turned his van around and

started down the driveway. At the same moment, Luke's makeshift garrote frayed and snapped. He stumbled off balance, holding a tattered strip of gauze in his right hand. Xander sucked in a huge breath, yanking at the fabric around his throat, pulling it over his face and off Luke's left forearm. Luke bustled forward, kicked Xander in the back, and knocked him onto his ass.

"Lisa," he gasped.

He took a few ragged steps and watched the Econoline swing left out of the driveway. The tears in his eyes magnified the brightness of the taillights.

"Mother*fucker*," Xander wheezed behind him, pushing himself to one knee. His eyes blazed in the dusky gloom. "You are so fucking *dead*."

Luke didn't hesitate. He hobbled toward the rottweiler's cage, holding his ribs, dragging in every hard breath. The dog clawed and snapped. Luke threw the bolt and opened the door in one fluid move. He knew it was risky; the rottweiler could just as easily go for him, but as a wise man once said, when you don't got nothin', you got nothin' to lose.

He ducked, tucking himself behind the cage door as he opened it, removing himself from the rottweiler's sight line. It bolted from its cage with furious purpose, like a greyhound out of its trap. Xander had just regained his feet when the dog leapt at him. It clamped its heavy jaws onto his shoulder, twisted him back to the ground, then planted itself—front paws on his chest. Xander screamed, trying to keep those teeth at bay. His boots kicked up flowers of dust.

Luke swiped a hand across his face, smearing away the blood, tears, and dirt. A weak sigh seeped from his chest. He stood for a moment, watching the rottweiler lunge and snap, then reeled toward his car. The sunset filled his glistening eyes. In the sky opposite, a vastness of stars.

He had lost his gun when Xander tackled him to the ground. Not that it mattered; without bullets, it was useless. Also useless: his cell phone. Luke dug it from his back pocket as he opened his car door. The screen was a webwork of shattered glass. A few shards had fallen out, revealing the hardware beneath. He swore miserably, hit the power button anyway. A light stuttered deep inside, but that was all. Luke tossed it onto the passenger seat and dropped behind the wheel. He patted his front pockets for his keys. Empty. There was a dark moment when he thought he'd lost them, too, then noticed them dangling from the ignition.

He clutched them, eyes closed, wishing they were the keys to something else—a rocket to another world, a doorway to another life, one without wives and friends and Vikings. For a moment everything faded, then he cranked the key and his old car brought him back.

Luke turned the Caliber around, started down the driveway, then jumped on the brake. Sierra Vista waited, two lanes of sun-baked blacktop, the stars on one side, the sunset on the other. He looked left, where Ramón had driven away with Lisa. There was an unfathomable breadth of nothingness out there, all too easy to disappear into. Maybe Ramón would live in a cave and eat rattlesnakes until the heat was off. Or maybe he'd dig a grave big enough for five women, then find a little town east of the Mississippi and start over.

He looked right, toward the sunset, where the Mustang had disappeared with Kitty tied up on the backseat. It was all too easy to imagine what would happen to her. The only question was, would Johan bury her in the desert, or leave her body for the vultures?

Luke screamed and hammered the wheel, knowing he could only catch up to, and *maybe* save, one of them. He remembered Lisa's kiss, how familiar and warm it had been. And Kitty, who had saved his life more than once, and whose happy place was in her son's arms.

His wife, or his friend? His life, his career, exoneration . . . or Kitty's life, her future, her being there for a little boy?

Luke's shoulders hitched. His eyes blinked emptily. How cruel, how obscenely fucking *cruel*. He looked left and right again. The stars. The sunset. His brittle mind was pulled in both directions, then he heard a sound from behind him: a high-pitched whine, full of pain. Luke looked in the rearview, and in the red glow of the taillights he saw Xander kneeling with his right arm looped around the rottweiler's throat. The dog scrabbled and cried, then fell silent when Xander squeezed and twisted at the same time, breaking its neck. The sound was crisp and upsetting. Xander dropped the rottweiler. It slumped to the dirt. He got to his feet—bleeding from bite wounds across his face and arms—then ran at the Caliber.

Luke hit the gas, kicking up a screen of dust as he ripped down the driveway, still looking left toward Lisa, and right toward Kitty.

By the time he reached Sierra Vista, he'd made his decision.

PART III

SHOWDOWN AT THE RATTLESNAKE HOTEL

25

CHASE

The Caliber had a trembling four-cylinder engine, built for economy, not power. Luke pushed it nonetheless. His foot hit the metal and stayed there. Nothing on these desert roads, and little more to either side. It was an empty, ghostly landscape, even during the high heat of day, but within the headlights it was interstellar. Luke could imagine hitting the brakes, getting out, then floating away among other stars.

He touched eighty-seven and the needle stayed there. It was all this old car had, and it had to be enough. The engine struggled. Everything else rattled and knocked. He remained focused, his hands locked on the wheel, making incremental adjustments every time he hit a bump and shimmied.

Nothing but nothing, for mile after mile, then finally, in the distance, taillights.

Was it them? Was he catching up?

He considered his decision, second-guessed it, hated himself. Lisa's and Kitty's faces swirled through his mind. It felt not so much like he was trying to save one, but outwardly condemning the other. He wondered—assuming he had a future—how long his soul would be at war with itself.

A pack of coyotes skulked at the edge of the road. They scattered as he rushed by, eyes flashing green in the headlights. There was a billboard just beyond, hanging in the darkness in faded colors. Like the one on the outskirts of Pale Bone, it was for the Rattlesnake Hotel. Only seven miles away now, but still CLOSED, according to the aggressive red lettering stenciled across the front.

Luke glanced at it, then concentrated on the taillights up ahead. They had grown larger. He was closing in, within half a mile.

Moments later, he saw the low shape and scarred green body of the Mustang.

I'm heading toward town, then taking Black Valley Road west, Johan had said to Xander, believing his man-ape would soon be following. Did knowing this aid Luke's decision? He didn't think so. It removed some of the hard work, certainly, but he would have gone after Johan regardless—albeit blindly.

It came down to this: Ramón would very likely disappear with Lisa and the other women. He *might* kill them. Kitty's fate was more certain; Johan had brought his ax for a reason.

Luke hunched over the wheel, willing his car to go faster. Gradually, he got close enough to determine certain details: the width of the Mustang's tires, its chrome accents, the branding between the taillights. He saw Kitty's sneaker zip into view through the windshield again, there and gone in a second. The Mustang veered left, crossed the center line, then swung right again. Was Kitty kicking around too much, causing Johan to lose focus? Or was he scanning his cell phone? Had Xander texted to let him know that Luke had slipped the leash?

Maybe, but it changed nothing. Luke was all in.

One hundred feet . . . sixty . . . twenty . . . Luke thumped into the

Mustang's back end, hard enough to explode one of its taillights and crease the Caliber's hood. The Mustang wobbled, slowing down while Johan got it under control. Luke knocked into it again and his front left headlight went out in a quick shower of glass.

This was a rash, dangerous course of action, but he saw no other way. He'd quickly dismissed the idea of driving into Pale Bone, rousing the auxiliary cops—if they even existed—from the dust, or hunting down a phone to call the main police department in Vegas. By the time they'd asked their questions and dispatched units, Ramón and Johan would have disappeared.

If there was a better way, Luke couldn't see it. He *had* to run that goddamn Mustang off the road. Then, with the more urgent problem solved, he could turn every cop in the country on to Ramón, and hope like hell it wasn't too late.

Luke crunched into Johan's back end again. Tires screeched. Metal buckled. He didn't have his .38 Special, but his Caliber packed a bigger punch. He'd assessed the risks—the dangers to Kitty and himself—and concluded they were worth taking. This way, at least, she stood a chance.

Eighty-seven, bumper-to-bumper, tearing through the wide and empty night. The Mustang had all the horses and started to pull away, but it slowed for a curve in the road and Luke saw his chance. He kept in the high eighties and maneuvered into the oncoming lane. His back end fanned out precariously and for one loud heartbeat he thought he was going to lose it, but the Caliber found its line and held the road. Luke drew alongside Johan. The two men looked at each other through their windows. Johan's upper lip was flared, his teeth stained green in the dashboard lights.

Luke edged right. Their doors kissed with a dull bang. Both cars weaved, rocking on their springs, then came together again. Luke's side mirror shattered and the passenger window cracked. His hope was to slow Johan down, then clip his back end and spin him out. He had to outmuscle the muscle car, which could be achieved with technique rather than brute force. He'd learned some tactical driving skills during a two-week course in prep for *Out of Midnight*. He was about to see how effective they were when the cameras weren't rolling.

Johan *did* slow down—eighty-seven was too fast to play bumper cars—but not by enough. Luke matched him, watching the needle drop to seventy, but spinning him out at this speed would probably result in the Mustang flipping multiple times. Not good for Kitty, tied up on the backseat. Luke had accepted that she might be injured in this exchange, but he wanted to avoid it, if possible.

"Come on, you son of a bitch." Luke's tongue was thick with the taste of blood. His entire body drummed with pain—a loud, constant percussion from the cap of his skull to the balls of his feet. He refused to let it in, riding his adrenaline as hard as he drove his car. They raced out of the curve and Luke was greeted by headlights—an oncoming vehicle, moving fast. He nudged Johan again, trying to squeeze into his lane, but the Mustang held its ground. Luke went the other way, swooping onto the eastbound shoulder and avoiding a head-on collision by a matter of feet. For one deathly second it was all light and sound, then the vehicle's taillights were in his rearview.

"Jesus fucking *Christ*." Luke's lower body flushed ice-cold. His scalp stiffened, lifting every hair. He experienced a single tick of relief, then the Caliber's tires started to lose traction. Hands soldered to the wheel, he steered a hard right, onto the road again. Momentum carried him all the way over and he punched hard into Johan's door.

The impact rocked Luke in his seat—Johan, too, who struggled to keep control. The Mustang's back end slewed left and right. Smoke rippled from the wheel arches. Suddenly he was gone, straying off-road in a thick pall of dust. He hit a low bank and floated airborne for two seconds, then touched down with a crunch that popped the passenger door open.

He didn't stop—couldn't risk giving Luke the speed and force. The Mustang dug at the dirt, sliding wildly, then regained its wheels and boomed across the desert.

Luke hit the same bank. He was airborne for longer, and touched down harder.

He didn't stop, either.

It was slower over the desert's uneven surface, bouncing over small rocks and tearing through creosote bushes. Luke followed the Mustang's single taillight as Johan steered around outcrops and ragged trees. The Caliber clonked and protested. Luke felt the desert floor through the steering wheel, through the seat. His head thumped off the roof numerous times. The dashboard lights flickered.

Johan hit the brakes, drifted one-eighty, then churned at the dirt and got moving again. Luke was right behind him. He turned a broader circle but maintained a higher speed. Smoke had started to leak from under the hood. Something was broken under there. This had to end soon.

He swept into the Mustang's driver's side again, hard enough to ripple the A-pillar and knock the glass out of the window. Johan's blond hair flew wildly. He yanked the wheel and clobbered into Luke. Their fenders met in a spray of sparks. They parted to steer around a cluster of boulders, then came together again. The impact threw Luke sideways and his head banged off the window. For a moment everything dulled, then he thought of Kitty on the back-seat—of everything that would happen to her—and the edges came back hard and sharp.

He touched the brake, allowing Johan to pull ahead, then jerked the wheel and nudged his back end. The Mustang whipped this way and that, slowed to twenty, then spun out. It turned three dusty circles before coming to a stop, engine grumbling.

Luke looped around quickly, his rear tires sliding. He looked at the Mustang, bathed in its own flickering light. It started forward again, trembling on its shocks. Scrub crowded the wheel arches. There was another sprig caught beneath the windshield wiper. Luke jumped on the accelerator, aiming his front end at the dented driver's door. He intended to hit it so hard that he would knock Johan's skeleton right out of his skin.

The Caliber jumped forward, sluggish at first but picking up speed. Luke flexed his hands on the wheel and braced himself.

In all the dust, pain, and frenzy, he didn't notice the Tundra's headlights until they were on top of him.

It struck the Caliber's rear passenger side like a tank, removing the quarter panel, buckling the wheel. The glass on that side spider-webbed. Luke screamed, thrown first against the driver's door, then into the passenger seat. He had no idea what had just happened—not until he looked up and saw a Toyota Tundra swinging around behind him. Ruben Osterfeld—Mr. goddamn UFC—was behind the wheel, with Xander riding shotgun.

"Kidding me," Luke groaned. A delirious cackle broke from between his lips. He had been so *close*—twenty feet away from broadsiding Johan, liberating Kitty, then delivering to the authorities one hell of a story.

The Caliber, remarkably, was still running, chugging along doggedly on three and a half wheels. Luke glanced at the speedometer. It read 120, but that wasn't right. It was fucked, just like the rest of the car, just like Luke himself.

The Tundra rolled alongside him. Xander leaned out the passenger window. His face was a red map, detailed with dog bites. He'd have some memorable scars to go with that charming demeanor.

"Fuck you, man." Luke flipped him the bird.

Xander responded by pulling out a semiautomatic pistol, something fat and mean and with a decidedly more serious payload than Luke's .38 Special. Before Luke could make any kind of evasive maneuver, Xander aimed at the Caliber's front tire, squeezed the trigger, and blew the rubber off the rim.

Luke pumped the brake, worked the wheel, but couldn't keep his gutsy old Dodge from skewing out of control. It veered blindly through the scrub, clipped the trunk of a dead juniper, then slammed into a boulder that appeared so suddenly in the darkness that it could have been magicked into existence.

There was a riot of sound: metal crumpling, glass breaking, the airbag discharging with a loud, powdery bang. The Caliber flipped onto its left side and skimmed across the desert floor, leaving a long scratch mark behind it. The engine ticked and spluttered, then gave up the ghost.

Luke pried his hands from the wheel. He was still alive, but he didn't care.

The ax came through the windshield only seconds later.

The laminated glass—already shattered into a meshwork of tiny squares—sagged inward, split in a broad line where the ax had punched through. Its bearded bottom hooked to the inside, and when Johan pulled back, he lifted the entire windshield out in one flexible piece.

Luke managed a cracked and helpless yell, twisting in his seat. Johan bent down and peered through the open windshield. He was grinning, but his eyes relayed a deeper, more ferocious energy.

"Hey, are you that actor guy?" He curled a tress of blond hair behind one ear. "Any chance of a selfie?"

He reached in, grabbed the front of Luke's T-shirt, and started to yank him out of his seat. He met the resistance of the safety belt, though, just like Kitty had four months before. She had been saving his life then. Johan was intent on doing the opposite.

The car was on its side—one wheel still spinning slowly—so it was not a stretch for Johan to reach up and unclip the belt. It retracted across Luke's body and he slumped against his battered door. Johan grabbed his tee again, pulled him over the steering wheel, over the dash, and out through the rectangular opening where the windshield used to be.

Luke collapsed to the desert floor, coughing up dust and blood. Johan clutched the back of his neck and lifted him to his feet. He sagged, half leaning on Johan, who had his cell phone in his other hand. He extended it for a selfie. Luke saw himself on-screen—a blackish scrawl of blood across his mouth and chin, his eyes bright and tear-struck in the dirty mask of his face. One of his early roles had been playing an earthquake survivor in the medical drama *Lion's Ward*. He'd spent eighty minutes in makeup, and looked then exactly as he looked now.

Johan duck-faced and snapped the pic. He showed it to Luke, who turned away from the screen.

"What do you think? Should I post it to my socials?" Johan's grin was blade-like. "I don't know, man. Maybe being associated with you will tarnish my spectacular reputation."

"Just fucking kill me," Luke said.

"Oh, I will. Don't you worry about that. And I'm going to kill her, too." He gestured at his battered Mustang, indicating Kitty, helpless on the backseat. Xander and Ruben stood close by, both with guns drawn. Xander mopped his face with a balled-up hoodie.

"Let her go," Luke said. "Please. She's only here because of me."

"Bitch stole from me, Luke. *You* know that. She tried to make a fool of me." Johan pocketed his cell phone and pulled Luke a little closer. "Then you *both* tried to make a fool of me. Faking her death? That was almost pretty smart, especially for a shit-for-brains like you."

Luke sighed, which turned into a painful splutter. He held his ribs and winced.

"What's more, I have a backpack full of canary in my car that leads me to believe you were trying to fuck me over. And you know something, Luke? You *would* have. The canary by itself may not have been enough, but my manufacturer, too?" Johan whistled through his teeth. "Ramón's the smartest motherfucker I know, but he's got no spine, no fucking *balls*. He'd cut a deal, and that would make things extremely uncomfortable for me."

"That was the plan," Luke said.

"I'd deny everything, of course, and let my father's lawyers work it out in court. Then I'd sue for defamation of character. But really, who needs the headache?"

Luke drew a dry breath. Pain radiated from his ribs and spine.

"Either way, it would have meant the end of my lucrative canary enterprise." Johan shook his head, as if the mere thought of this were an affront. "And all because of you and Kitty. You two make quite the team."

"Crockett and Tubbs," Xander quipped.

Johan laughed at that. He pointed at his berserker and nodded appreciatively. "Right? Because he looks like Don Johnson. In that fucking movie."

"And because Kitty's Black," Xander added.

"Good, Xan. Good."

Luke straightened, pulling his shoulders square. He met Johan's gaze and tried to find whatever steel he had inside. "Let her go. This is all on me."

Johan's laughter ebbed to a mirthless hiss. He stroked his woven beard and narrowed his eyes. "Noble. I admire that. And such an *unusual* quality for a wife-killer."

Luke shook his head. A coyote howled somewhere to the south, a lone cry that filled the night for a moment, then faded to nothing.

"How did you find us?" Luke asked.

Johan removed his hand from the back of Luke's neck and walked around to the exposed underside of the Caliber. He crouched, craning his head this way and that, then grabbed something close to where the pummeled muffler hung by one strap. He examined it for a few seconds, turning it this way and that, before returning to Luke.

"These things really stick, huh?" He held it up—a small black box with a winking green light and the word TRACK-U-GEN printed on one side. "You know what this is?"

"You were tracking me?" Luke asked.

"Not *me*," Johan replied. "This little doodad landed on your shitbox courtesy of Tera Montecino, formerly of the LAPD. You know her?"

"Fuck."

"Yeah, she doesn't like you much, either." Johan flicked his attention from the tracking device to Luke. "She gave us your location—just in the nick of time, I might add—on the promise that I enforce my own brand of justice. I assume she didn't want to get any blood on her hands. But that's okay; it washes off my Scandinavian skin quite easily."

"Justice," Luke echoed grimly. "For my wife's supposed death."

"Yes, but also for Kitty's death." Johan displayed his blade-like grin again. "You really shouldn't have left those staged photos lying around your house."

"Jesus Christ," Luke said. He looked at the stars, as if they were all gods, every one of them laughing at him.

"That was excellent work, by the way. My compliments to your makeup artist."

Luke lowered his eyes and gazed beyond Xander and Ruben, at the Mustang, envisioning Kitty on the backseat. He couldn't see her, but she was there, tied up and terrified. He called to her on some hurting, spiritual level, and apologized for letting her down. Similarly, he sent a silent prayer out to Lisa, that she find a way back to her celebrated self, and discover every melody still in her soul.

Johan studied the tracking device, turning it this way and that.

He was too smart to leave it near the car of a soon-to-be missing man, and he wouldn't want it tracking *his* movements, not even for a short while. So he did the only thing he could, and exactly what Luke would have done in that situation: he dropped it in the dirt and brought his bootheel down on it—once, twice, three times, until the casing shattered and the little green light went out. Johan picked up the pieces and put them in his pocket.

"So what's the plan?" Luke asked. "Kill me right here, leave me for the buzzards?"

"I'm a Viking, not a common thug." Johan's ax was still buried beard-deep in the Caliber's ruined windshield. He extracted it with a couple of beefy tugs, and positioned it over one shoulder. "I value honor above all else, and I *will* honor my agreement with Tera Montecino. At the same time, my own need for revenge can't be overlooked. And believe me, Luke, I intend to savor the moment."

"You're not a Viking. You were born in Los Angeles twenty-eight years ago. Your old man is a computer hardware developer."

"I am descended from—"

"You're a murderer, a criminal, and a goddamn *YouTuber*." Luke wrinkled his nose, staring Johan in the eye. "What's honorable about that?"

Johan's tone had been a dissonant blend of chaos and cool, but with this a storm crossed his face. It emphasized his imperfections— his narrow brow and crooked nose. In those few seconds, he looked unnerving. Luke readied himself. He didn't quite know for what—an ax blade, a thunderbolt—then the storm passed and Johan's long grin returned, sharp enough to cut wood.

"Xan, Ruben, we're leaving. Tie this motherfucker's hands behind his back. Use his belt, if you can't find anything else." And to Luke he whispered, close enough to bite, "I'll bury you deep, but I can't promise the coyotes won't get to your bones."

. . .

Johan led the way, cutting a groove across the silent desert, rejoining Black Valley Road west. Tailpipe dragging, bodywork clattering, his Mustang moved at one-quarter the speed it had once been capable of.

The Tundra followed, with Ruben behind the wheel. Luke was propped awkwardly on the backseat, with Xander next to him. The berserker's energy was as live and hazardous as a downed power line. He brandished his semiautomatic pistol, listing all the places that Luke could take a bullet and still die slowly.

"Your foot," he said. "Lots of small bones in the foot. *Real* painful. Or your shoulder . . . your thigh . . . your leg. Hey, how about your kneecap? *Both* kneecaps?"

His face and hands had stopped bleeding. The wounds were dark and puffy. Luke wondered, if Xander were to contract rabies, if anyone would notice.

"I could shoot off your thumbs."

Luke stared through the windshield, and before long the Tundra's one working headlight picked out the dark angles and unwelcoming façade of the Rattlesnake Hotel.

26

SO WRONG

By her own estimation, Tera Montecino's cop intuition operated at seventy-five-percent efficiency. It—and her notable temper—had been the reason for her numerous reprimands during her time on the force. She still trusted it, though, because it was right more often than it was wrong, and because, without intuition, a cop was little more than a badge with a face.

She had gone from Luke's house to a Starbucks in Echo Park, where she indulged in a Frappuccino while monitoring the red blip on her Track-U-Gen app. She'd assumed Luke had ventured into the desert to bury Kitty's body, but his route didn't jive with that. He had kept to the main roads, stopping only a couple of times along the way, once at a gas station outside Barstow, and again, briefly, on Interstate 40. In Nueva Vida, he'd parked outside Jane's Family Restaurant on Principle Street, presumably to eat, then spent close to an hour at a bar called Stray Bullets.

This, Tera opined, was remarkably casual behavior for a man with a dead body in his trunk.

"So he dumped her somewhere else," Tera had said under her

breath, wiping cream from the tip of her nose. "It doesn't change anything."

Right. The time for detective work was behind her. This whole thing had been stripped down to two components: Luke the killer, and Johan the vigilante. Everything else was redundant.

Her intuition would not be so easily dismissed, however. It grew increasingly persistent as her anger quelled, informing Tera that there was *more* to all of this. Luke—and whatever the hell he was doing in the desert—was only a part of it. Aligning herself with Johan was another part. He'd offered a version of the truth to suit his own needs, which was fine as long as their needs ran parallel, but Johan clearly hadn't told her everything. What's more, she hadn't liked Xander's reaction when she revealed that Luke was in Nueva Vida. He had squirmed and tugged his earlobe—a dubious response, if ever there was one.

Something else was going on.

"No doubt about it," Tera had whispered, drinking her Frap. "But you've made your play. Now just let it be."

How could she, though, when everything felt so . . . *wrong*?

Tera shifted in her seat, uncomfortable, agitated. She ordered a calming herbal tea, but it didn't calm her. Eventually she closed her eyes and deferred to the lining of her stomach, where a vestige of her daddy remained. He told her—in harmony with her intuition, which was often the case—that if there was a truth, she wasn't going to find it by scrutinizing a blip on her cell phone. She needed to strap her investigative boots on and go to work.

With that, Tera left Starbucks, got into her car, and took the Foothill Freeway out of the city. She didn't know if this instinctive course of action would amount to anything, but it felt right.

At 4:40, she left Los Angeles County, which put her an hour behind Johan.

. . .

She arrived in Nueva Vida after sunset. A dry throat of a town, musky and pale. Most of the life seemed centered on a trailer park, where a huge fire blazed and residents sat around it on crates and folding chairs. A few children chased each other with burning sticks. Norteño boomed.

Tera pulled up outside Jane's Family Restaurant, not looking for anything in particular, just throwing her cop radar out there and seeing if anything bounced back. Nothing did. Following Luke's route, she headed northwest out of town, and arrived at Stray Bullets five minutes later.

It was a lively, neon-decked establishment, loud enough to hear from half a mile away. Tera stowed her Beretta in the glove compartment and got out of the car. It was like stepping into 1988. Vixen blasted from the club's exterior speakers. A group of old rockers dressed in jean jackets and tight black pants clustered on the veranda, their long hair made big with product. For a beat, Tera felt like she was sixteen years old again, dressed in her Mötley Crüe tee, sneaking out of the house to party with her friends at the Steel Attic in Carver City.

It had been a day of grim emotions—anger chief among them. Tera hadn't smiled often, but she did then.

She let her hair down and went inside.

It was busy but not packed. There was a band setting up onstage—long hair and jean jackets, just like the rockers outside. The booths were full but there were vacancies at the bar. Tera grabbed a stool, ordered a drink, then checked her phone.

She had contacted Johan shortly after leaving L.A. County, informing him that the target had moved from Nueva Vida to Pale Bone. *Call me when you're close*, she had said to him, *and I'll give you the details.* Johan hadn't called her, though, which meant he'd either backed out of the deal—unlikely—or that he knew exactly where to find Luke.

Her drink arrived. A virgin Bloody Mary. She gulped half of it, then swiped to Johan's contact information and sent a one-word text:

Status?

She waited for a response while finishing her drink. A couple of emails came through, but nothing from Johan. Tera waited a little longer, then tapped on her web browser and brought up a recent photograph of Luke Kingsley. It was a paparazzi shot of him and Kitty, taken at Floyd Tallent's funeral—an hour or so before Tera had accosted him in the parking lot and warned him that if any harm came to Kitty, she would chase him down like a hound out of hell.

For all the good *that* did.

The bartender checked in to see if she wanted another drink. Tera cracked a smile. Yes, dammit, she wanted another drink. She wanted to douse herself in liquor and party with the band. That'd be a *much* better way to spend her evening. Instead, she shook her head and dropped a twenty on the bar. When the bartender reached to pick it up, she turned her cell phone toward him and asked, "You see this guy in here today?"

He leaned closer and looked at the photo on the screen. "That's Luke Kingsley. Son of a bitch killed his wife."

"Impossible to prove without a body, but yeah, son of a bitch killed his wife." The music switched to something else that reminded Tera of being young and dangerous, as opposed to old and angry. "I have reason to believe he was here today, between three and four o'clock."

"You a cop?"

"I used to be a cop. Now I'm a private investigator."

"Okay, cool," he said. "But hey, I can't help you. I just got here. Savannah worked the afternoon shift."

"Is Savannah here?"

He pointed across the main floor, to where a woman in a Stray Bullets cowboy hat stood chatting with a long-haired rocker who wore more eye makeup than she did. Tera thanked the bartender, then walked over to the woman. She was attractive, early thirties, with piercings through her upper lip and a star tattooed on her cheek. The muscles in her arms suggested she was quite used to throwing obnoxious drunks out into the desert night.

Tera hovered close by, waiting for her moment, then approached.

"Savannah?"

"Who's asking?"

"Tera Montecino. I'm a private investigator from Los Angeles." She showed Savannah the license in her wallet. "You have time to answer a couple of questions?"

Her mouth twitched unsurely. She looked at the long-hair, who muttered, "Check you later, Sav," and went about his business. Tera had swapped her wallet for her phone in the five or six seconds it took Savannah to swivel back toward her. The same paparazzi shot of Luke and Kitty filled the screen.

"You recognize this guy?" Tera asked.

Savannah tapped her tongue against her upper lip. Her piercings jangled. "That's, uh . . . shit, I can't think of his name. The actor . . ."

"Luke Kingsley."

"Right, yeah." Savannah snapped her fingers, then her eyes grew wide and she pointed at the screen. "Oh shit. I recognize him now. He was *here*. This afternoon."

Tera nodded. She knew that Luke had been there. She knew what time he arrived, and what time he left. Savannah confirming this was no surprise, although what she said next lifted Tera to the balls of her feet and rocked her back a step.

"They were both here—sat right up there at the bar."

"Both?" Tera looked at the shot of Luke and Kitty, then flashed back to the photographs she'd seen only hours before—a bullet hole in Kitty's chest and another in the middle of her forehead. "*Both?* You sure?"

"Hell, yeah, I'm sure. I mean, they looked different. He had on a ball cap, wore glasses." She cocked her hip and pointed at Tera's phone again. "She didn't have all that makeup on, and her hair was down. But it was her, all right. Those cheekbones."

Tera stood perfectly still, afraid that she might spill to the floor if she tried moving. A sick feeling bloomed in her stomach.

"You okay?" Savannah asked. "You look a little pale."

"I'm fine." She wasn't fine, but she had to act like she was. People responded positively to strength, both victims and felons. It was one of the first things she'd learned as a cop. How many interviews had she conducted over the years, having to exist (admittedly, with varying degrees of success) in a space beyond her emotions?

She asked, "Did you speak to them?"

Savannah nodded.

"Did they say what they were doing here? This isn't the kind of place you just happen upon."

Savannah shoved her hands into the back pockets of her jeans. Her T-shirt rode up in front, exposing another piercing through her belly button. "They said they were uncle and niece, that she was here researching the Mojave people for some school project, and that he was going to tour the casinos. Smelled like bullshit to me. Doing this job, you get a nose for it after a while."

Tera nodded. She could relate.

"It was fairly obvious," Savannah continued, "that they were *really* here because they were looking for someone."

"Who?"

"One of our semi-regulars. Name's Ramón."

Tera's eyes narrowed. When she'd called Johan to update him on Luke's location, he had answered the phone quickly—before she even heard the ringing tone. *Ramón?* he'd said, thinking she was someone else, and Tera had detected the desperation and anger in his voice.

Her cop intuition went from tingling around the baseboards to thumping a hammer against the wall.

"A lot of Latinos in Nueva Vida," Tera said. "Probably a lot of Ramóns. What's his surname?"

"I don't know."

"What *can* you tell me about him?"

Savannah screwed her lips together and looked down at the floor.

"You can talk to *me*," Tera pressed, holding up her phone. "Or I can fill this joint with cops and you can talk to them."

"I don't want any trouble."

"Then tell me what I need to know."

Savannah sucked through her teeth, looked at the lights over the stage, then nodded. "Okay, shit, okay." She stepped closer to Tera and whispered so that she couldn't be heard, although there was little chance of that beneath the mad thump of rock music. "Ramón's a dealer, small-time, not exactly El Chapo. He sells party drugs—ecstasy, mostly. Lives out in Pale Bone."

Tera pulled up Track-U-Gen on her phone. Luke's blip had spent two hours in Pale Bone, mostly at an address on the east side of town.

"Sierra Vista Road?" she asked.

Savannah shrugged and ran her thumb across the star tattooed on her cheek.

"What else can you tell me?"

"That's it. That's all I know."

Tera didn't push. This wasn't the time or the place. She thanked Savannah with a stiff nod and left Stray Bullets beneath a cloud of unease. The sick feeling intensified. She stopped halfway across the parking lot—leaning against the hood of a dusty pickup truck—and took several deep breaths to keep from vomiting.

"Jesus," she gasped. "Jesus Christ."

She had colluded with Johan because she believed (or *wanted* to believe) Luke had killed Kitty, but the photos Tera had seen were evidently fake. Kitty had been here, with Luke, only a few hours before. And if Luke was innocent in this, then maybe . . .

Tera recalled her conversation with Luke at his friend's funeral, when he'd asked if any part of her believed he hadn't killed his wife. *I have this much doubt*, she had replied, holding her thumb and forefinger half an inch apart. Some days that doubt had grown to as much as a full inch, but never more than that. Now, though, it expanded, it opened like an old wound, one Tera didn't know she had.

"Don't go there," she chided herself, starting hesitantly toward her car. "Of *course* he killed his wife. Because Occam's fucking razor."

The uncertainty remained, a pall over everything. And what was Kitty's part in this? Why would she pose for those photographs? Was she working with Johan—some elaborate plan to set Luke up?

No, that didn't sound right. But then, nothing did.

Tera reached her car. She flopped behind the wheel and called Johan. Straight to voice mail. She swiped to her tracking app once again. Luke's signal had gone dead, meaning the device she'd attached to the bottom of his car had been destroyed. The last recorded location was approximately ten miles west of Pale Bone. Zooming in revealed it to be in the desert proper, several hundred yards off-road. Had the job been done? If Tera went there, would she find Luke slumped behind the wheel of his Dodge Caliber, a bullet in the back of his skull?

No. The car was there, but Johan was too careful to leave the body where it would so easily be found. Besides, a bullet to the head was too quick and clean for his Viking style. He'd opt for something more . . .

"Brutal," Tera said, breathing deeply. This was, perhaps, the only thing she *was* certain of. Everything else was tangled up in misery and mayhem. What she would give for something solid—a single, dependable truth.

There was small consolation in knowing that her intuition could still be trusted. She had sensed that there'd been more to all of this, and she'd been right.

His name was Ramón.

A picture began to form from the moment her flashlight picked out the two dead dogs in Ramón's driveway. Just a sketch to begin with, but it took shape as she proceeded to the barn (with its rows of yellow flowers and lab equipment), then made her way through the empty house. It was not the picture she expected, and certainly not the picture she wanted.

"No," she said. "Dear God, no."

Tera stood in Ramón's hallway with the front door open and a night breeze blowing dust across the floor. In the space of forty minutes, she had gone from an absence of truth, to having it surround her completely.

She called Adrian Kraemer, her partner on the Lisa Hayes case.

"You at work?" she asked.

"My night off," Kraemer growled, a hint of apprehension in his voice. "First one in ten days. My fella and I just opened a bottle of wine and queued up *The Crown* on Netflix."

"You're going to wish you didn't answer your phone," Tera said. She closed her eyes, fighting to keep her voice even. "I'm going to need you to pull some overtime, dig the Hayes file out of the refrigerator."

"What's going on, Tera?"

The two dead dogs were not the only evidence of a struggle. Tera's flashlight had also shone on a discarded snub-nosed revolver and splashes of blood in the dirt. Luke's blood? Ramón's? At what point had Johan arrived, knowing *exactly* where to go? Tera had proceeded to the house with her Beretta drawn. The front door was wide open, indicating that the property had been vacated in a hurry.

She'd moved cautiously through the darkened rooms, her gun at the ready, and soon arrived at the metal-plated door that led to the basement. It, too, was open, and judging by its adornment of heavy-duty bolts, this wasn't usually the case. This was where the picture in Tera's mind went from an outline to something with depth.

It was not a basement downstairs, so much as a prison—a filthy, roach-infested hole, with a moldering sofa and dripping pipes. Thin mattresses covered the floor in a small sleeping area, strewn with stained sheets and women's clothing. There were piles of dirty plates and drifts of trash. The stench was overpowering, most of it coming from a diseased space that might once have been a bathroom.

Tera covered her mouth and groaned. She populated her picture with half a dozen subjugated women. Perhaps as many as nine.

That wasn't all. There was a precision scale on a table, its stainless-steel platter dusted with a residue of yellow powder. She found a greater amount—an ounce, easily—in a Tupperware container on the floor. Tera had handed in her shield at around the time canary was starting to make waves in Hollywood, but she knew what it was, and what it looked like.

Was *this* the information Johan had been keeping from her? Were he and Ramón partners in crime—canary kingpins? Tera nodded. There were still pieces missing, but this felt right. Johan had the high-rolling connections, after all.

The link between Ramón and Luke was less complicated, but infinitely more distressing.

"Tera?"

"I'm here," she said to Kraemer, walking from the hallway to the kitchen. She had placed two items on the table, procured during a cursory scan of the property. "I'm in Clark County, Nevada. That's Metro's jurisdiction, right?"

"The whole damn county," Kraemer confirmed.

"Who do we know here?"

"There's always somebody." The hint of apprehension was still in Kraemer's voice. "Why? What do you need?"

"What *don't* I need?" Tera sighed, one hand flat on her brow. "This is big, Adrian. I'm going to need forensics, evidence collection trucks, vice and missing persons units. I've got an active drug lab here, as well as signs of false imprisonment and kidnap. We're talking multiple vics, probably female. I'm not ruling out human trafficking."

"Busy night," Kraemer remarked, droll as ever, but the tightness in his voice indicated she had his attention. "I thought you gumshoes only investigated insurance fraud."

"Got that penciled in for tomorrow," Tera replied, equally droll. She looked at the two items on the kitchen table. One was an expired green card, the other a recent vehicle inspection report form. She referenced both now. "Okay, get a pen, write this down."

A brief pause, the sound of Kraemer opening a drawer. "Go."

"I need you to put out a BOLO for Ramón Sojo Aparicio." Tera spoke slowly, then spelled it out. "Venezuelan male, thirty-two years old. He'll probably be driving a blue 2012 Ford Econoline, Nevada plate: two-five-Charlie-six-one-four."

"Give me a starting point, Tera."

"I'm in a town called Pale Bone, fifty miles—give or take—south of Vegas." She guesstimated when Ramón had vacated his property, based on Luke's Track-U-Gen data. "He can't have gone far. Within a one-hundred-mile radius, I'd say."

"That's a lot of real estate."

"Mostly desert, not many roads." Tera flicked hair from her eyes and sneered. "You'll find him."

"On it," Kraemer said. "But first, I want to know why you called *me*, and why I'm pulling the Hayes file."

Tera picked up the green card, studying Ramón's photograph—his close-set eyes and bony, V-shaped face.

An ugly fucker, really, Luke had said, sitting opposite her in the interrogation room. *Kind of . . . bat-faced.*

Quite an accurate description, as it turned out.

"It's your name on the file. Your case." Tera tossed the green card back onto the table. Her stomach and head rolled in different directions. "I was wrong, Adrian. So fucking wrong."

"About?"

"Everything," Tera replied. The word dropped from her mouth like a small, jagged rock. "Find that van, and I'm ninety percent sure you'll find Lisa Hayes."

Her phone chimed moments after she ended her call with Kraemer. It was Johan, finally responding to the one-word text she'd sent at Stray Bullets.

just chill I'm on it

The strength went out of Tera's legs. She flopped into one of the kitchen chairs, her breathing reduced to tasteless sips of air. She thought of all the shit she'd put Luke through over the past three years—the accusations, the excessive force, the harassment—but this was in a different stratosphere.

"Oh Jesus," she gasped. All she'd ever wanted was justice. She'd wanted the *right* thing. "Jesus Christ, what have I done?"

Her phone buzzed again.

I'll let u know when its done

Tera blinked, looking hopelessly at the message. It at least meant that Luke was still alive. Of course he was. Johan would draw this out for as long as he could.

She stood up quickly, but her vision grayed around the edges and she sat down hard again. Tears welled in her eyes. She hadn't cried in sixteen years.

"I have to make this right," she said, wiping a hand across her wet face. She considered texting Johan back, but what good would that do? This had gone too far for him to back down now, and he clearly had his own agenda.

Her head roiled with emotion, offering no clear thought. She consulted the lining of her stomach but found no help there. Desperate, Tera clenched her fist and rocked it hard against her jaw. The pain flared into her skull and jolted several thoughts loose. One of them, at least, was useful. She backed out of her messaging app, accessed Track-U-Gen, and brought up that last-recorded location in the desert.

"Where are you, Johan?"

It wasn't the dead signal she was interested in, but the geography around it. Tera zoomed out and journeyed across the map, looking for isolated buildings within a ten-mile radius. There was a ranch and a gas station, then she scrolled west and saw the Rattlesnake Hotel. She wouldn't have given it a second thought, except it nudged something at the back of her mind. Tera paused, then remembered the sun-beaten billboard she'd seen on her way into Pale Bone, advertising the hotel. Most striking was the signage— CLOSED—splashed across the front in big red letters.

A Google search confirmed this. The Rattlesnake Hotel had closed its doors in November of 2020, another sad casualty of COVID. Tera imagined it, dark and abandoned, the perfect place to kill someone slowly.

She tapped the directions icon. Fifteen minutes away. Ten on these empty roads. But would her confronting Johan turn violent? Tera considered calling Kraemer again, to request backup, but that might resolve badly for her. She was complicit in this. If arrested, Johan, Xander, and Ruben would gladly throw her under the bus, and her tarnished career as a cop wouldn't play to her favor.

Tera spilled from Ramón's kitchen, down the hallway, and out the front door. The air wasn't exactly fresh—it smelled of heat and dead dog—but her breaths deepened and she regained some focus. As she approached her Buick, a Metro police cruiser—light bar whirling—ripped along Sierra Vista and pulled into Ramón's driveway.

Tera checked the clock on her phone. Sixteen minutes had passed since she'd called Kraemer. She'd lost most of that time to her bleak, quicksand thoughts. These uniforms hadn't wasted a second of it.

"You guys were quick," Tera said as they stepped out of their vehicle.

"We're based in Searchlight," the senior officer said. The name above his shirt pocket read CARDONA. He had a good face. "We stick close to Pale Bone after sundown. The locals have a thing for mescal and guns. News flash: they don't mix."

He and the other officer—IZZO—exchanged a smile. Tera nodded. She lifted the left side of her jacket to show that *her* gun was safely holstered, then gently removed her wallet from the back pocket of her jeans. She opened it and handed Officer Cardona her PI license.

"Tera Montecino. I worked this case—or part of it—when I was with the LAPD. My former partner, Adrian Kraemer, called it in." She returned her license to her wallet. Her hands were steady, despite her cartwheeling emotions. "I assume reinforcements are on the way?"

"There's a fleet incoming," Izzo said. "We're here to establish a perimeter."

"That's good," Tera said. She looked from one officer to the next, mirroring their neutral expressions, then continued toward her Buick. "I guess I'll leave you to it."

Cardona: "Where are you going?"

"I have a situation to unfuck." The words raced out of Tera's mouth before she had a chance to hit the brakes. She cupped the back of her neck, inhaled deeply, and glanced back over one shoulder. "I have . . . other business."

"You should probably stay," Cardona said, regarding her from beneath a deeply lined brow. "The detectives will have questions. You know how it works."

"Yeah," Tera said. "I do. And trust me, they'll still be here in the morning. With any luck, I'll be back long before then."

She got into her car before they could say anything else, started the engine, and backed out of the driveway at speed. Within seconds, Ramón's degenerate property was in the rearview, with God-only-knew-what waiting beyond the headlights.

27

THE CALI VIKING

The hotel was aptly named. Luke looked over Johan's shoulder and watched a rattlesnake—a Mojave green—glide from the dark restaurant into the lobby. It moved smoothly, beautifully over the faux-marble tile, the light glimmering across its scales. Luke drew a stuttering breath. His eyes filled with tears and the snake tripled, then faded to a blur before snapping back, clear and long. It slithered behind an overturned luggage cart, where its tail administered a faint warning. Had it caught Xander's animal scent? Had it seen the light reflect momentarily off the head of Johan's ax? More tears welled in Luke's eyes. He blinked them away and watched the rattlesnake emerge from behind the cart, then slip toward the back of the lobby and out of sight.

Luke lowered his head and imagined doing the same: to slide away, unnoticed—just a flick of the tail and gone. He envisioned the cool tile beneath his belly, the taste of freedom on his tongue, and for one vivid second it was there, it felt *real*, then Johan's tattooed fist connected with his jaw and he dropped into a world of red.

· · ·

He opened his eyes to see Xander standing above him. His split tomato of a face appeared overly large, ripe with villainy. He raised his boot and brought it down on Luke's chest. The pain was immense. It felt broad and gray, like the wing of some huge bird, encompassing him and exerting pressure on every bone.

"Pick him up," Johan said.

Xander did, jerking Luke to his feet with a succession of forceful moves. Luke's hands were still tied behind his back and he leaned off balance—would have dropped again if Xander hadn't grabbed his hair to keep him upright.

"What a waste," Johan said, stepping so close to Luke that their chests bumped. They were the same height, yet Johan towered. His arrogance set a cushion of air beneath his heels. "Defamed. Hated. *Broken*. And you started out so hopefully."

"Let him go," Kitty said. She stood several feet to Luke's right, pale and shocked but still on her feet. "He's got . . . nothing to do with this. This is on . . . it's all on me."

This was the first time Kitty had spoken since they'd broken into the hotel. She had groaned and dribbled, and had managed a reedy, desperate scream, but mostly she stared silently at the ground. Now her back was pulled straight and her jaw raised. She looked at Johan imploringly, her eyes shining in the cracked mask of her face.

"On me," she said again.

"Oh, Kitty," Johan said, sparing her the briefest glance. "I'd like to believe you, but you have a history of lies and disloyalty."

"Please, Johan—"

"How should we begin?" Johan lifted his ax, pushing the eye up under Luke's chin and forcing his head backward. "Should we cut off his hands or his feet? What do you think, Kitty?"

She was bound at the wrists with Johan's belt, but she exploded forward nonetheless, lowering one shoulder, intent on driving Johan to the ground. Ruben grabbed her before she managed more than a couple of steps. He wrapped one meaty forearm around her chest and pressed the barrel of his semiautomatic pistol—a Walther PPQ—to her throat. Kitty thrashed, kicking her legs, her lips drawn back over her teeth.

Xander subdued her—a stinging backhand slap that whipped her head sideways. Her right eye darkened and swelled as Luke watched.

"You sons of bitches," he said. His voice was low with emotion, almost unrecognizable. "You're all going straight to hell."

"Not true," Johan said. "I'm going to kill you, then I'll go home, take a long, rejuvenating shower, and grab a few hours' sleep. And later, I'll upload a video to YouTube—me playing *Fortnite* or something—and the kids will laugh and love me, and you'll still be dead, Luke, buried in a dry hole, turning to dust."

The Rattlesnake Hotel had been built in 1996, originally planned as part of the Rattlesnake Complex, which would have included a casino, racetrack, and water park. Financial backing for the complex suffered a setback when a major investor was discovered to have links to a Mexican drug cartel. The hotel had already been built by this point, and for twenty-four years it struggled alone. It survived the Great Recession, and was partially rebuilt after a fire in 2011, but it could not withstand the economic fallout of COVID-19.

It was a midscale establishment, 108 guest rooms and an outdoor pool. The lobby was wide and welcoming, blending seamlessly with the restaurant, gift shop, and a sports-themed bar called Rattlers. Other amenities included a function room and an air-conditioned gym.

At its busiest, the hotel was a whir of activity, sound, and light, never something in itself, but *close* to something, a middle ground for those who wanted to play the casinos in Laughlin or Needles one day, then hike the Dead Mountains the next. Now it was spiritless and dark, accommodating only the whistling desert winds and the wildlife.

Nothing could be done about the emptiness and disrepair, but Xander had dealt with the darkness—at least for now. On arrival, he'd ventured into the mechanical room in search of a generator, and had found two: a main unit, hooked up to the gas line, which had been cut off, and a small diesel-operated backup, with just enough kilowattage to power the emergency systems and very few of the lights. Xander got it running, then he and Ruben had walked the hotel, shutting down anything unnecessary, centering all the power on the lobby.

Xander claimed there was enough diesel to last a few hours, but the lights burned at half their brightness and flickered constantly. There was a contingency plan: park Ruben's Tundra in the lobby and turn the single working headlight on. The battery would last until morning. More than enough time to do what they wanted, as *slowly* as they wanted.

For Kitty, the stuttering lights were in keeping with the erratic nature of her thoughts. She glimpsed memories, faces, dreams, and deaths. In clearer moments—such as they were—she focused on the faintly glowing exit sign at the end of the nearest hallway, trying to convince herself that it was a promise, not a taunt. A tough sell, although she had spent the past hour twisting and flexing her wrists, gradually loosening the knots in Johan's belt.

He stepped toward her now, scraping the ax along the floor behind him, just as he had at Jink's Warehouse. There were so many echoes of that horrific night here, with two big differences: it was Luke (a good man), not Sly Boy (a liar and a coward), tied up next to her, and the Rattlesnake Hotel was in the middle of nowhere. Even if she *did* manage to free herself and throw open the door beneath the exit sign, where would she go?

Johan ran one finger across the swollen skin beneath her right eye. She pulled away from him, pressing backward into Ruben, who tightened his hold across her chest.

"Kitty, Kitty . . . my sweet little raccoon."

"Fuck you."

He pressed his lips together and looked at her. His gaze softened for a beat, as if he were contemplating all the things that might have been, then his nastiness shone through again. He showed his teeth, gesturing toward Luke.

"Your friend here says I'm not a Viking, because I was born in Los Angeles twenty-eight years ago." Johan brushed dust off the shoulder of his T-shirt. "What do *you* say, Kitty?"

"You're a monster," she replied, looking at the exit sign. Was it shining a little brighter now? Were the letters a little larger?

"A monster?" He shook his head. "I simply protect those who are loyal to me, and the things I've worked so hard to achieve."

"You kill people, Johan. Don't make it sound noble."

"I eliminate threats. It's how a business—how *anything*—survives. And, Kitty, you know I want to look good doing it." He struck a pose, raking one hand through his hair. "I'm all about the showmanship."

The lights in the lobby went out for a second, then hummed and clicked back on. The main building was set back from the road, fronted by a parking lot and fringed by unkempt fan palms. Kitty wondered if the blinking lights might be noticed by passing vehicles—a police cruiser, perhaps. This situation could be quickly resolved by a couple of state troopers with good instincts and a precise aim.

"Please," she whispered.

"Your actor friend has a point, though," Johan continued, hoisting his ax and pointing it at Luke. "A Nordic ancestry, by itself, is not enough. A Viking is not defined by who he is, but by the things he does."

He moved away from Kitty, walking a slow, almost predatory semicircle back to Luke. The set of his shoulders, the arrogant tilt of his chin, suggested he was enjoying every second of this.

"So," he said, crouching a little so that he could look into Luke's downcast eyes. "What can I do to convince him?"

Kitty stammered and struggled. Ruben pulled her closer, applying enough pressure to make her ribs creak. It staggered her to think they were friends once—or associates, at least, back in the Sly Boy days. He had given her his number and told her to give him a call if she ever needed some heavyweight backup. What a joke. What a fucking slimeball Ruben turned out to be.

Kitty blinked tears from her eyes and focused on the exit sign once again. She imagined not just reaching it, but bursting through the door beneath and growing wings, flying out across the desert and away. She wondered if she could loop her arm through Luke's on the way out, and how high they might fly together, as hurt and broken as they were.

Johan breathed in, expanding his chest, inhaling this moment, his power, his dominance. It was as if all his Viking dreams were coming true—those things he'd prayed for as a disturbed, spoiled child. He ran one finger along the edge of his ax blade, then stepped away from Luke, surveying their surroundings. He tested the sturdiness of a few nearby fixtures and nodded approvingly.

"I think I know what to do, Kitty." He looked at her with a cruel glint in his eye, stroking his beard. "If he needs to see a Viking, I'll show him a Viking."

"Please," she gasped. "Please, Johan. Don't take this out on him. We can . . . we can—"

"It'll be transcendent, Kitty. *Legendary.* One step from Valhalla. You don't get more Viking than that." Johan flared his nostrils, his chest puffed out reverently. "Ruben, I need you to search the hotel—look for rope, or bedsheets, even."

"Bedsheets?"

"We're going to tie Luke's left arm here." Johan tapped his ax blade against an ornate column close to the front desk, then did the same to the leg of a fixed bench seat, at least fourteen feet away. "And tie his right arm here, to this."

"Johan," Kitty pleaded. "Don't do this."

"He'll be chest down on the floor, cruciform, like this." Johan made a cross out of his body. "And whatever you find needs to be strong. He's going to struggle quite a bit."

"The rooms are stripped, boss." Ruben shrugged. "You could untie him—use his belt."

"That's good for one arm. And *my* belt is staying on her." Johan gestured at Kitty. "She's a slippery little bitch."

Ruben nodded, then let go of Kitty and strode from the lobby, toward the restaurant and guest rooms beyond. Xander slunk forward. He was armed with a semiautomatic pistol, switching the barrel between her and Luke. Blood seeped from a bite wound on his face.

"Just give me a reason," he said.

Kitty lowered her head, but looked up again when Luke spoke to her. His voice rattled and cracked. Kitty couldn't tell if he looked defeated, or had found some measure of peace. The ghosts in his face, which she'd always known to be there, had been chased away.

"Don't watch, Kitty," he said. "Whatever happens, don't watch."

Tera's Beretta was fully loaded and she had a spare magazine in her back pocket. Thirty rounds in total, but she hoped not to have to use a single one of them. Her strategy was to approach under cover of darkness, to first observe, then act. She would only use her gun if there was no other option.

She had detoured briefly—followed her app off-road and located Luke's car, beaten out of shape, lying on its side with its fluids soaked into the desert floor and its windshield removed. There was no sign of Luke, as she suspected, only splashes of blood both inside the car and out. She found multiple boot prints, and two sets of tire tracks heading west. A quick look at the GPS on her phone confirmed they were heading in the direction of the Rattlesnake Hotel.

Tera followed them to the main road. She drove to within two hundred yards of the hotel, then killed the headlights. The night swallowed her car and she proceeded at a crawl, *feeling* the smooth blacktop, adjusting her line whenever her tires rumbled onto the shoulder. Tera continued like this for another hundred yards or so, then pulled over and cut the engine. She could walk from here without being seen.

Advancing across the parking lot, Tera noticed a glimmer of light beyond the main entrance. There were two vehicles parked outside: Johan's beaten-to-shit Mustang, and Ruben's Toyota Tundra, also damaged. (They'd clearly gotten into a fight with Luke's underpowered Dodge, and come out on top.) Tera crept behind them, avoiding the entrance in case she activated the automatic doors and inadvertently announced her arrival. She edged the shadows and approached a tall, narrow window that offered a view across the expansive lobby. The lights were dim, flickering constantly. She saw Johan with an ornamental ax propped on one shoulder, and Xander, aiming a pistol at Luke and Kitty. Not that they were going anywhere. They stood, both of them, bruised and beaten, their hands tied behind their backs.

"Son of a bitch," Tera said.

Johan had said that Kitty was his friend, but this scene told a different story—one that Tera was still trying to piece together. She continued around the building, following the subdued glow from her cell phone, looking for Johan's point of entry. She found it soon after: an open window, its lower pane broken. Tera peered inside, determining what would once have been an office. A few pieces of furniture remained: an overturned chair, a desk, a filing cabinet with two of its empty drawers yawning. She pocketed her phone, climbed through the window, and fumbled her way toward the crack of light beneath the office door. Broken glass crunched underfoot.

There was no peephole in the door through which Tera could assess the hallway beyond, so she did the next best thing: She held her breath and listened. No voices. No footsteps. Judging by how far she'd skulked around the side of the building, Tera estimated that she was between thirty and fifty yards from the lobby. She opened the door a few inches and checked both ways. The emergency lighting hummed hesitantly, just strong enough to reveal an empty hallway. Tera pulled her Beretta and stepped outside.

She moved toward the lobby, walking as softly as she was able in her bootheels. Johan's voice drifted to her. It was deep and aggressive. She heard Kitty, too, pleading, racked with fear. Tera reached the end of the hallway, peeked around the edge of the wall, then crept through the gloom and huddled behind the concierge's desk. A scorpion scuttled across one of its lower shelves, its tail hooked.

"You can consider this retribution for all of your sins," Johan boomed. "Not just the sin of crossing me, and trying to fuck up my canary business."

"Johan, please . . . *please* let us go."

Tera advanced behind the desk—she scuttled, much like the scorpion, her tail also hooked—and moved into the darkness of the adjoining restaurant. She had a better view from here. She watched and listened.

Luke's vision swam. The gaps between the tiles rippled and merged. Johan circled him, dragging his ax. He appeared calm, but Luke heard the agitation in his breathing. Adrenaline? Anticipation? He was like an animal, about to feed.

"Are you familiar with the blood-eagle ritual?" he asked.

Kitty cried out and lunged forward again. Xander halted her with another ringing slap. She rocked on her feet and he pressed the barrel of his pistol to her skull.

"Try that again," he snarled. "Please, I'm begging you."

Johan inhaled, growing a full ten inches, expanding in his savagery as Luke shrank.

"Kitty knows," he said, his voice shaking. "We've been here before, haven't we, Kitty? She *knows* that the blood-eagle ritual is the most brutal of Viking punishments—that it involves prying the victim's rib cage open at the spine, removing his lungs one at a time, and draping them over his shoulders like wings."

Luke swayed on his feet, untethered and numb. He might have floated away for all eternity, but Johan brought him back, whispering in his ear:

"I don't know how long it will take you to die."

He circled once more, then ripped the back of Luke's dog-tattered T-shirt open and dragged a finger down his spine. Luke shuddered. He swayed again, but caught himself before spilling to the floor.

Kitty tried once more, speaking Johan's name over and over, pleading with everything she had. Johan regarded her briefly, then stepped in front of Luke, clasped his jaw, and tilted his head until their eyes locked.

"How about now?" he said, still growing. "Am I beginning to look more like a Viking?"

Tera had seen enough, heard enough. She took aim from the shadows. This would be quick. Two shots. Johan and Xander would drop, and any incriminating link she had to them would drop, also.

Xander first—he was holding the gun. Tera thumbed the Beretta's safety and curled her finger around the trigger. At the same instant, she heard the distinct click of a round being chambered, then felt the muzzle of a pistol against the back of her skull.

She closed her eyes and groaned, remembering the two vehicles parked outside: Johan's Mustang and a Tundra with twenty-four-inch rims.

"Drop the shooter," Ruben said.

Tera hesitated, chiding herself for being so remiss, and wondering how serious Ruben—two hundred and sixty pounds of stupid—was about shooting an ex-cop.

He answered by pressing harder with the pistol and whispering into her ear, "Right now, bitch, or your brains go bye-bye."

Tera opened her hand, allowing her Beretta to spill out and fall to the floor. She hoped it might go off and shoot Ruben between the eyes, but no such luck.

With the pistol locked to Tera's head, Ruben urged her forward, into the flickering light.

Johan heard sounds from the restaurant and turned to see Ruben materialize from the darkness, marching Tera Montecino ahead of him. He had the PPQ rooted to the back of her skull.

"Didn't find any rope," he announced in his big, bouncy voice. "But I found something else."

"Tera?" Johan frowned, holding Krókr close to his chest. "What the fuck? I was going to call you when the job was done."

Ruben pushed her closer. Johan saw no expression in her colorless eyes. He turned to Kitty, beaten and tied up, but who Tera had believed was dead. This was not a good look for him, and tough to explain—a problem that might need to be solved with three graves, not two.

"It's over," Tera said.

"Our deal?"

"Everything. At this very moment, detectives and forensic units from LVMPD are turning over Ramón Sojo Aparicio's house, clearing those canary flowers out of his barn." Tera lifted her lip. Her teeth glistened. "We have more units looking for his van. The 2012 Econoline, right?"

Johan stammered. His insides had turned as cold as a Scandinavian winter. "I don't . . . don't know what . . . what you're talking about."

"You can make this a whole lot easier on yourself if you let me take Luke and Kitty away from here," Tera continued. "You don't need to add murder to your résumé."

"This was *your* fucking idea!" Johan stormed, drumming the cheek of his ax off his chest. "*You* were tracking him. *You* wanted him dead. He's a wife-killer, remember?"

"Our agreement went sideways," Tera said, "when I realized Luke didn't kill Kitty. And guess what, he didn't kill his wife, either."

"Lisa," Luke mumbled, stumbling forward. "Tell me she's okay."

"Shut the fuck up," Johan cried. He rounded on Luke, slapping him hard across the face. If Krókr had been in his right hand, he might have used that instead. "This is all bullshit. It's fucking bullshit."

"No," Tera said. Her voice was a straight line. No emotion whatsoever. "Your canary partner, Ramón, had her imprisoned in his basement, along with multiple other women. He's not a good guy to be associated with."

Johan's shoulders dropped a couple of inches—the wind taken out of his longship sails. He recalled the squealing, raggedy-ass women he'd seen at Ramón's property. Was one of them Lisa Hayes, the actor's wife? And was this the *real* reason he'd gone after Ramón?

"What the fuck is going on, Johan?" Xander asked. He plucked his left earlobe while his gun hand jerked this way and that.

"Relax, Xan," Johan said. He breathed deeply, fighting to show composure. "She hasn't got shit on us."

"Wrong," Tera said.

Her bland tone matched her eyes and he hated it, hated *her*. His blood bubbled and sang—his Viking ancestors, beginning to make a din.

"This . . . this *Ramón* guy you mention. I've never heard of him. Don't know who he is." Johan shrugged and looked at Xander. "How about you, Xan? You ever heard of him?"

"No," Xander replied. "Never."

"Ruben?"

Ruben's eyes were wide and scared but he kept the PPQ locked to Tera's skull. That was a good thing.

"Nope," he said.

"My father's lawyers will be happy to support that claim." Johan drew Krókr close, running one hand up and down its engraved handle. "As for any murders on my résumé . . . well, if Luke here has taught us anything, it's that murder is extremely difficult to prove without a body. And there's a lot of space in the desert to hide three corpses."

For the first time, he saw a flash of emotion in Tera's eyes. Fear or uncertainty, it was difficult to tell. Either way, the voices in his blood sang louder.

"It's over," she said again.

"No." Johan shook his head. "It's not."

"I'm wired for sound. There's a monitoring app on my phone. This entire conversation is being relayed to a police van parked nearby." Tera's lips twitched, accentuating the emotion in her eyes. "You should let us go, Johan."

Xander yanked his earlobe, his escalating heart rate causing his face wounds to bleed. He looked ready to shoot everyone in the room, then fire a round into his own idiot brain. Johan calmed him with a single, cool look, then turned to Tera.

"I don't believe you," he said, his voice raised. "But let's put it to the test. I'm going to have Ruben blow your fucking brains all over the floor in exactly five seconds. If, during that time, the police storm the building and come to your rescue, then I'll know you were telling the truth."

Johan hoisted his shoulders, dragging his ax behind him as he walked a languid circle. He held up one hand, fingers spread.

"Five . . ." He tucked in his thumb. "Four . . ."

Xander wiped blood from his face, looking everywhere at once. Ruben's jaw was cartoon-slack but his pistol hadn't moved. Johan snarled at them in the mad, flickering light, readying them for whatever came next. He lowered his forefinger.

"Three . . ."

The bluff hadn't worked. Nor had she expected it to. Like so much in Tera's life, this would come down to a fight. Just as well, then, that she always excelled with her back against the wall.

There were three targets, but she focused on just one of them: Ruben. Disarm him, and the game would change. It wouldn't exactly be in her favor, but she'd have a fighting chance.

Johan said, "Two," holding up his ring and pinkie fingers, and Tera pressed backward against Ruben. He was jittery, hesitant—she felt it in the closeness of his body and heard it in his breaths. He pushed her forward, as she hoped he would. Tera deliberately stumbled, dropping to one knee, which removed the pistol's muzzle from the back of her skull. A good start.

"One."

Ruben looked from Johan to Tera, then lumbered toward her with the gun foremost. As he closed in, Tera drove her right leg backward in a hard, snapping kick. It connected with Ruben's stomach (which wasn't the wall of muscle it had been during his UFC days). He doubled over, giving Tera the window she needed to spring to her feet and strike more meaningfully.

She cracked his cheekbone with a whistling hammer punch, straight out of the kickboxing handbook, then tried to knock the pistol out of his hand. Ruben was no slouch, though. He slipped the move, rotating his body and countering with an elbow, which staggered her, then a side kick, which put her on her ass. Tera slid backward over the tiles. The weight difference was enormous.

"Zero!" Johan cried, holding up a blank fist. "Zero! Zero! *Shoot that fucking bitch!*"

Ruben got behind his pistol, steadying his aim, and Tera thought this was it, game over, baby, then a high-pitched battle cry sounded from behind her as Kitty entered the fight.

Nothing was over.

28

MOJAVE GREEN

Kitty had never seen the platinum-haired woman before. *Tera*, that's what Johan had called her. She and Johan had spoken like they had an agreement, one that had evidently expired.

The distraction Tera presented was to Kitty's advantage; she was able to stretch and twist the knot in Johan's belt, finally working it loose enough to free her left hand. The rest of the belt unfurled, hanging from her right wrist. Its heavy buckle clinked against the tiles.

All eyes were on Tera and Ruben. Johan's countdown reached zero and he ordered Ruben to open fire. That was when Kitty attacked. She used the belt, but she also used her son, bringing his perfect face to the front of her mind, fueling her resolve. She assembled her anger, fear, and frustration, her hopes and dreams, packing them together like components in a hand grenade.

She went for Johan, lifting the belt up over her shoulder, bringing it down in a humming arc. The first strike whipped across Johan's chest. The second glanced off the left side of his face, but it was enough for the buckle to draw blood and drop him to one knee.

The ax dropped, too, and Kitty was on it in an instant. She grabbed it in both hands and rounded on Xander, who'd turned toward her with his pistol raised.

Krókr. Kitty remembered the ax's name, and it seemed appropriate that it should have one. It had an energy, a certain ill-boding identity. It *wanted* to be used. The blade sliced through the air, hitting Xander's right hand, severing three of his fingers and sending his gun skating into the shadows. Kitty attacked again, bringing Krókr down in a flashing diagonal. This strike was less accurate, but it still caused damage. The blade raked across Xander's left thigh, opening his jeans and the flesh beneath.

He crumpled, screaming, both hands sealed to his thigh, blood spurting. Kitty toppled off balance and Krókr spilled from her grasp. It spun across the floor toward Johan. Both he and Kitty lunged for it but Johan got there first.

Kitty still had the belt, though. She whipped it across Johan's arms, then his back. He dropped again, slumped over his ax. Adrenaline surging, screaming from the corners of every nightmare room he'd locked her in, Kitty struck with the belt over and over, five times . . . six . . . seven. The buckle jangled and snapped.

Exhausted, Kitty dropped back. Her right arm sagged. She hit him once more, but there was no bite to it—no venom.

"Stay the fuck away from me," she cried, then grabbed Luke and urged him from the lobby. She had her eyes on one thing only: the dimly glowing exit sign at the end of the nearest hallway.

"Run," she said to Luke. He shuffled along beside her, fighting for balance with his hands tied behind his back. "Come on, Luke. Run . . . *run!*"

Kitty's attack had derailed Ruben's focus. His gaze flicked away from Tera and the barrel of his pistol dipped. Tera rolled left across the floor, pounced to her feet, then powered forward with a front kick. It connected with Ruben's solar plexus, knocking him back on his heels. Tera saw her opportunity. She ran at him, leapt, and kicked him into the darkness of the restaurant.

Her Beretta was behind her. She turned, looking, edged forward, and saw its carbon steel barrel glimmering in the fitful light. Tera swept toward it, sliding on her knees, then swiveled at the hip with the gun extended.

She closed out everything else—the sounds, the chaos—and zoned in on Ruben. She found him in the shadows at the same time that he found her.

Their gunshots boomed, half a second apart.

Tera missed. Ruben didn't.

Johan slowly got to his feet, easing into his wounds. He smeared blood from his cheek—felt the gash beneath, long and deep. A sound he'd never heard before rumbled from his chest. It was joined by a chorus of Vikings, banging on his bones.

"Bitch," he said, except it came out sounding like a death-metal growl: *Buuurrrrrrrcchhh.* He tore off his T-shirt and examined his body, covered in buckle-shaped welts and crisscross stripes. More blood trickled from grooves across his shoulders.

Back-to-back gunshots went off behind him. They echoed through the large, empty space, punctuated by the sound of Tera Montecino crying out in pain. It sounded like she'd caught a bullet. Something was going their way, at least.

Kill that big ol' whore, Rube, he shouted, or maybe he just thought it. He wiped his eyes and looked toward the restaurant—saw nothing in the gloom. What he *did* see, not too far away, was one of Xander's fingers on the floor, then another. They led like bread crumbs to Xander's .45, wrapped in shadow beneath one of the tables.

Johan retrieved it, aimed groggily, and fired two bullets into the hallway down which Luke and Kitty had disappeared. He blew out the exit sign—lucky shot—and popped one into the door beneath it. Wood splintered.

Xander writhed on the floor, holding his bleeding leg with his bleeding hand. Johan shuffled over to him, wondering if his berserker still had something in the tank.

"Can you aim a gun?" he asked.

Xander gasped and held up his right hand. One finger and one thumb remained. "I'm fucking mutilated."

Johan threw the gun at him. "Use your left hand. Get after them."

"Jesus, Johan, I—"

"How far can they go? They're in the middle of the desert." Johan lifted Krókr and pressed its cool blade to his chest. "I'll take the front hallway—make sure they don't double back."

Xander got to his feet and hobbled in the same direction as Luke and Kitty. Johan watched him—gritting his teeth, his vision doubling—until another burst of gunfire from the darkened restaurant startled him into action. He took a leveling breath, palmed blood from his face, and started across the spacious lobby. His Viking ancestors howled. They banged and crashed. Gottfrid the Bird was among them, the loudest of all.

Yet more gunfire behind him. Everything cranked and violent.

Johan pulled his bleeding shoulders square.

They followed the exit signs and emerged poolside. It was bare and lifeless, with the emergency lighting throwing a hesitant glow at ground level, like a low fog. There were no recliners or tables, only an empty cabana bar and a few creaking palms. An eight-foot wall separated this part of the hotel grounds from the outside world. The pool itself was hollow, a dim green in the meager light.

"Wait," Kitty said. "Let's untie you. You'll move quicker."

Luke nodded and turned around. Kitty started on the tight triple knot in his belt, working quickly, despite her trembling hands.

"You see a way out?" Luke asked.

"There's a gate over there, in the wall."

"Yeah." Luke nodded. "Okay."

"It's probably electric. Let's hope it's unlocked." She pulled the belt free and handed it to Luke, then showed him Johan's belt, still tied to her right wrist. "As weapons go, it's not as good as an ax or a gun, but it's better than nothing."

They continued around the pool. Luke staggered, fell twice—nearly went into the deep end once. Kitty helped him up and he struggled on. He was quicker with his hands untied, but only just.

They reached the gate in the wall. Tall and featureless and very locked.

"Fuck," Kitty said, rattling the handle. "Aren't these things hooked up to the emergency system? They should be unlocked."

Luke stooped and wheezed, hands on his thighs. His eyes fluttered. Kitty took a couple of steps back and assessed the wall.

"We're going over," she said.

"Over? Seriously?" He looked up at the wall. It was coated with stucco. No gaps or ridges to grab hold of. "This thing is eight feet high. I couldn't spit over it."

"You got this."

"No, Kitty. I don't." He wiped sweat from his forehead. "Listen, you do it. I'll boost you over."

Kitty shook her head. "I'm not leaving you."

"You *have* to." Luke hooked a thumb toward the main building. "They'll be out here soon. Run to the road, flag down a car, bring help. I'll find a place to hide."

"Luke, I don't—"

"I'm not getting over that wall, Kitty." Luke tilted on his feet, struggling even to look her in the eye. "This is the only way."

But Kitty couldn't get over the wall, either. She was too beaten up, too exhausted and scared. Luke tried boosting her. He got on his hands and knees, forming a low, shaky step. Kitty clawed and scrabbled, but lacked the upper body strength needed to pull herself over. She tried three times.

"We have to go back through the hotel," she gasped, blinking tears from her eyes. "Find another exit."

They started back the way they'd come, keeping to the shadows. Luke managed only a dozen steps before his legs went from beneath him. He hit the ground like an old drunk, not able to break his fall.

Kitty hooked her arm through his and tried pulling him back up.

"No," he said. "You'll be quicker without me. Just . . . just go."

"Not happening, Luke." She pulled—couldn't shift him. "Help me out here. Move your ass."

"Go, Kitty. Go . . . *please*." He nodded, his lips peeled back over his teeth. "Same deal. I hide. You go for help."

"Luke—"

Gunshots echoed from the direction of the lobby. A volley of them, then more. Kitty considered dragging Luke by the leg, or carrying him on her back—a desperate, manic thought.

"*Now*, Kitty." Luke uncoupled his arm from hers and pushed her away. "And steer clear of the lobby. There'll be plenty of exits on the other side of the hotel."

She nodded, wiped her eyes. "Hide, Luke. Find the best spot you can, and don't come out until a cop shines a flashlight into your face."

He gave Kitty's hand a firm squeeze, then she stepped away from him before she could change her mind. She worked her way around the pool area, moving from one shadow to the next. The first door she tried was locked. The next wasn't. It was the same door they'd exited through.

Kitty glanced over her shoulder. The shadows around the pool were steady and deep. There was no sign of Luke. She eased open the door and turned her attention to both branches of a V-shaped corridor. No sign of Johan or Xander, either.

"Yet," Kitty whispered. She looped her hand around the top of the belt, getting a tighter grip.

She edged inside.

The bullet—a 9mm—hit Tera's side holster, which deflected and slowed it down, but not by much. It blasted through her left hip and knocked her to the floor. Tera cried out, clamping her open hand to the wound as she rolled clumsily to one side. She'd sensed another shot incoming and she was right. There was a thunderous crack, a burst of muzzle flash in the darkness, and a bullet ricocheted off the marble tile where she had been lying only seconds before.

Tera rolled again, then pushed herself to one knee and lunged for cover behind a stainless-steel food counter. Her vision pulsed. A grinding pain spiraled into her pelvis and down her left leg. She'd been shot before—had taken a .38 to the shoulder during a raid on a North Hollywood meth lab. Eight other cops had been with her then, and she'd been in the back of an ambulance within six minutes. That wasn't going to happen now.

Another round zipped overhead. Tera flinched and pressed close to the food counter, then hooked her gun hand over the top and fired blind. Three shots, to keep Ruben on his toes, but also to buy her some time. She crawled to a new position, ripped off another shot.

"Come on," she said shakily. The lights in the lobby dimmed. They stuttered. Or maybe that was her wavering vision. She crawled to the back of the restaurant, propped herself against a wall, and worked on her breathing. In and out, in and out. She bled through the cracks of her fingers.

There'd been a fusillade of sound from the lobby—screaming,

gunshots—but it was all silent now. Tera had no idea what had happened, and couldn't spend time thinking about it. Her initial objective—to disarm Ruben—had not been completed. Tera heard him shuffling in the darkness, but couldn't place him. Maybe if she had a little more blood in her body, and greater clarity in her brain. What she *did* know: his muzzle flash would give him away.

Tera reached a hand into the front left pocket of her jeans—it was warm with blood—and pulled out her car keys. She clutched them tightly to keep them from jingling like little bells, then tossed them into the darkness ahead of her. They landed some fifteen feet away, striking something solid before falling to the floor.

Ruben gasped and immediately opened fire. Four bright, jumpy shots toward the keys. Tera was ready, bracing herself against the wall, but otherwise holding her Beretta like she would at the range. She aimed just beyond Ruben's muzzle flash and squeezed off a succession of rapid-fire shots. The reports were bone-shaking. The silence that followed was deep and clear.

Tera got to her feet, using the wall for support. She staggered a little way, clutching her left side, her shooting hand still extended. The silence continued.

"Did I get you, motherfucker?" she hissed.

Ruben replied with a bullet. It grooved the top of her shoulder, tearing through her jacket and scoring the skin beneath. Tera reeled backward. Another shot rang out, higher and wider than the first.

He materialized in the gloom, lurching heavily toward her. His face was a hurting scrawl—everything drawn big. There was a map of blood across the front of his T-shirt. Tera had hit him, and more than once, by the look of it.

She lifted her gun, pulled the trigger twice. Both shots found their target, but momentum carried him forward. He fell on her and they both spilled to the ground, Ruben on top.

"*Fughaa*," he drooled. Blood bubbled from his mouth. He gurgled something else. Tera screamed from beneath him. She managed to free her gun hand and jam the muzzle into his left eye.

"You big bastard," she said, and pulled the trigger.

Nothing in the chamber. A gutless click, that was all.

Ruben clonked a fat fist down between Tera's eyes. The back of her head bounced off the tiles, and stars appeared in a glittering spread. She blinked hard, squirming beneath Ruben. He steadied himself on one elbow, dragged his right arm into position, and locked the PPQ to her throat.

"*Fugghhhaaa.*"

Tera gritted her teeth. She threw her arm up and bucked her hips, lifting his two-sixty through a mist of hysterical strength. Ruben wobbled. His gun went stray at the same moment he pulled the trigger, and the bullet skimmed across the floor. He tried resetting, but Tera twisted beneath him, managing to free her right knee and drive it up into his balls. He barked and spluttered. Tera lashed out again—with her elbow, with the Beretta's grip. Ruben sagged and flopped off her. She rolled away from him, scrabbling to one knee and reaching for the spare magazine in the back pocket of her jeans.

Ruben lay with his left arm pinned beneath him. His gun hand was still free. He swung the barrel toward her, his eyes burning with shock and pain.

"*Uggaroo,*" he bubbled, not even a word, but it was the last thing he said. It took him a second too long to steady his aim. Tera rammed the fresh mag home, racked the slide, and pulled the trigger.

A single bullet to center mass, at close range. Ruben died staring at her. The light in his eyes didn't flicker. It just went out.

Tera pulled a long, shuddering breath into her lungs and screamed on the exhale. Her wounded side throbbed and bled. She pushed herself to her feet and staggered toward the lobby. Her first objective had been met, but she was still a long way from making this shitstorm right.

She hooked her cell phone from her pocket, dialed as she walked. Now would be a good time to call for backup. An ambulance, too.

Kitty had been gone no longer than thirty seconds before the berserker entered the pool area. He had a gun in his left hand and a cell phone clamped in what remained of his right, directing its flashlight in a jittery arc.

Luke covered his mouth, focusing on silence, on stillness. He was a rock in the shadows. A yucca, growing in the dry dirt between the wall and a fan palm. Xander would pass him by without even a second glance.

"Fucking kill you motherfuckers," he rumbled, dragging his left leg behind him. "Kill you. Fucking *rip* you."

It helped Luke to imagine Kitty busting through one of the hotel's emergency exits, tear-assing across the parking lot, flagging down some good ol' boy who just happened to be passing by in his Chevy pickup. (Even at the direst of times, Luke's thoughts were at least seventy percent movie script.) In reality, it might take *hours* for a vehicle to come this way. And even if Kitty got lucky, how long would it take for the cops—the *real* cops, not some rinky-dink part-timer from Podunk PD—to arrive?

He could hope, though. There was a chance—the very slimmest of chances. And really, the most important thing was for Kitty to escape this nightmare. In separating, he had traded his safety for hers, and he didn't want it to be for nothing.

Xander shuffled closer. His squat, limping form was thrown into mad silhouette by the stuttering ground lights.

"You're here somewhere," he growled. "I can *smell* you."

Luke held his breath. Stillness. Silence. Shadow. He stifled his myriad pains, embodied the role—just a rock—and then heard a rattling sound six or seven feet to his left. Luke was no expert, but he knew a rattlesnake when he heard one. He recalled the Mojave green he'd seen gliding across the tiles in the lobby—one of the most venomous snakes in the world. There was every chance this rattler was from the same family.

Luke breathed through his teeth, trying to remain as still as possible. He was covered in blood and sweat, though, and the smell of dog. Even without moving, how threatening was this to the snake? He imagined its tongue flicking in and out, sampling the air between them, readying itself to strike.

"My fucking fingers," Xander gasped. His flashlight probed the depths of the empty pool. He was twenty feet away, shuffling closer. "Bitch took my *fingers*."

The snake rattled louder, *closer*. Luke had no choice, he *had* to move. He slowly unfolded from his hiding spot and inched away from one threat, but toward another. He clutched the belt tightly in his right hand, remembering what Kitty had said: as weapons went, it wasn't as good as an ax or a gun, but it was better than nothing.

He kept to the darkness, edging along the wall. It wasn't that he didn't breathe, more that he *couldn't*. His internal organs had turned to ice. The snake rattled again, but quieter, less defensively. That was good, but Xander was now only ten feet away. His flashlight swept from side to side, and Luke had no flora to tuck himself behind. He was exposed.

Strike first, he thought. *Be the snake.*

"Rip you open. Fucking *riiiiip* you."

Xander had a gun, but he was injured, bleeding from just about everywhere. He couldn't have much fight left in him, even for a berserker. If Luke attacked suddenly, from the shadows . . .

The snake issued its dreadful, percussive warning once again. At the same time, Xander's flashlight illuminated the wall to Luke's right, scrolling steadily his way. That old movie line recurred one more time: *When you don't got nothin', you got nothin' to lose.*

Luke swore that if he made it out of here alive, he'd get this tat-tooed across his chest.

He pushed himself into a crouched position, his left hand planted on the ground, his right clasping the belt. He muttered some half-assed prayer under his breath, then pushed himself for-ward. There was no athleticism involved. He neither charged nor leapt—more lumbered out of the shadows with all the grace of a jacket falling out of a closet. He directed his energy and effort into the belt, which he brought from behind him in a purring loop. It connected crisply with Xander's shoulder. His gun went off, the bullet sparked off the flagstone around the pool, and Xander yelped in surprise. He turned, most of his weight pitched on one leg, and Luke attacked again—first with the belt, then by grabbing Xander's arm and swinging him into the shadows.

This latter move was all about the direction, and Luke got it right. In the wavering glow of the flashlight, he saw the rattlesnake attack—two vicious, thudding strikes to Xander's right leg—his *good* leg.

"Snakebit!" he cried in a shrill, disbelieving voice. "Christ fuck, I've been snakebit, too!"

He fired his gun twice. The second shot hit the rattler and drove it, twisting, against the wall. Luke came up behind Xander and wrapped the belt around his throat. He'd tried this earlier with a frayed strip of gauze and it had broken before he could do any real damage. That wouldn't happen this time.

He was hurting all over and out on his feet, but he was going to strangle this son of a bitch dead.

Kitty followed the faintly glowing exit lights, from one hallway to the next. She saw a sign for the lobby and headed in the opposite direction—pushed through another door, into another hallway. Was she going in circles?

She might, in her hurt and confusion, have taken a wrong turn and double-backed on herself.

"Don't get disheartened," she whispered. "You've got this."

She hastened down the hallway, to where it intersected another. There were exit signs at both ends. She paused, trying to get her bearings, then went left.

Three steps. She froze.

A sound from behind her, as terrifying as it was familiar: *Screee . . . scrrreeeeeee . . .*

Kitty turned, her heart banging in her throat.

Johan was there, at the other end of the hallway, a man-shaped nightmare in the flickering light. He loped toward her, dragging his ax behind him.

Scrreeeeee . . .

"I see you," he said.

Kitty ran.

29
VALHALLA

There was, on some distant shore, the sense of his world fracturing—of his manufacturer in custody, his canary empire in ruins, and his name potentially being defiled. These concerns were mere whispers, though, beneath the cacophony of voices in his blood. They energized and inspired him. They blanketed his pain. Here he was, in a derelict hotel in the heart of the Mojave, but he might as well be on a blood-drenched field in Mercia, the cries of his Viking brothers and sisters surrounding him.

After the battle, he could regroup. He would stand behind his father's money and defenses. But for now, he needed blood.

Kitty careened through the hallway, screaming. She appeared so small to him. He could pick her up by one ankle and thump her body against the wall until every delicate bone broke.

"I *see* you, Kitty."

She slipped on the smooth floor, went down on her knees, then bumbled back to her feet and pushed through a set of double doors. Johan followed soon after. There was a short, broad hallway on the other side, with several rooms opening off it. Kitty was nowhere to be seen.

"You want to play, Kitty?" Johan stalked forward, dragging his ax behind him. It made music across the tiles, like a needle in the grooves of a record.

"You want to play with me?"

His blood roared and sang.

Xander crackled on the inside, like an overloaded circuit. He planted his feet and pushed backward. Luke fought to keep the belt around his throat but couldn't. Both men floundered, then the ground disappeared beneath them and they fell into the pool—a seven-foot drop to the hard tile below.

Luke—who'd landed on top of Xander—moved first. He had dropped the belt, his one weapon, and spent several fruitless seconds feeling around for it. Deciding escape was a better option, he crawled the incline to the shallow end of the pool. Xander had slipped the other way, down to the deep end. He coughed and groaned. Maybe he had a broken spine to go with everything else.

The poolside lights flickered overhead. Far beyond them, the desert stars were constant, brighter. They were all Luke had and he followed them. He reached the edge of the pool, found the ladder, and heaved his body up one rung at a time.

"When you don't got nothin'," he wheezed. He'd lost his mind—he was certain of it. "You got nothin' to—"

A pistol shot split the air. Luke thought he'd been hit, but it was only shrapnel—fragments of tile spraying him from where the bullet struck six inches away. He fell backward off the ladder and another round pinged off the rung he'd been holding.

Xander limped toward him, dragging his grievously injured body up the slope toward the shallow end. He raised the gun to fire again and Luke moved, drawing on the limited stunt work he'd done in his career. He leapt to his right, intending to hit the ground and roll. Colton Stone would have performed the move while pulling a revolver from the waistband of his jeans. Logan Knight would have pounced immediately to his feet, then followed with a devasting roundhouse kick. Luke Kingsley grunted and staggered, then tripped over his own feet and face-planted like an asshole.

He rolled onto his back, and there were the stars again, but jagged, seen through the tears in his eyes. It was as if the sky had been clawed by some huge, intergalactic cat.

Xander blotted them out. He loomed over Luke, almost unrecognizable in his pain. His gun wasn't unrecognizable, though. It looked ten times bigger. Luke could fall into the barrel like a Bond girl.

"Fuck you," he said. Maybe the snake venom would kick in and Xander would collapse before pulling the trigger.

"Fuck you," Xander returned. Neither man was particularly inspired.

Luke slumped against the tiles and waited for it to be over.

Kitty had the belt looped around her right wrist, and it had proved effective, but she'd ducked into the room because she spotted a better weapon: a rattlesnake, half-coiled, its head and tail raised. It was cast in bronze and set atop a solid wooden plinth.

She supposed it had graced the front desk in a previous life, but had been demoted to this back room, with its assortment of storage crates and desks stacked one on top of the other. Kitty grabbed it in two hands, lifting it by the tail and the head. It was heavy, but not *too* heavy. Maybe fifteen pounds—the weight of a good-sized sledgehammer.

She waited just inside the door, chewed into her lower lip. Her vision throbbed in time with the thudding of her heart. It felt like giant hands were kneading the room from the outside, pressing everything subtly out of shape.

Johan approached. She heard his staggering footsteps, his labored breaths.

"Oh, Kitty," he said, savoring her name, as if it were delicious in his mouth: *Kitteeeeeeee.* He stepped closer to the room, scratching his ax across the floor. "It's so dark, and you're all alone."

She tightened her grip on the bronze rattlesnake. Her rib cage shook with every hard thump of her heart.

"I know you're close."

The emergency lights blinked, went out for three seconds, then came back on. When they did, Johan's shadow appeared on the floor in front of her. He was standing in the doorway, close enough that Kitty could reach around and touch him. With some effort, she hoisted the heavy ornament over her head. Her tired arms trembled.

"So close," Johan said.

He stepped into the room and Kitty attacked. In that second, all of her pain, exhaustion, and fear came together, fused into a cluster of energy intent on connecting the makeshift weapon with Johan's skull. It was perfectly timed, brutally executed. Johan flailed backward, into the hallway. As Kitty watched, a puddle of blood darkened his blond hair and dripped down his face.

He swayed but didn't go down. His mouth drooped into a trembling, inverted V. His eyes clouded for a moment, then snapped into focus, clear and blue.

"I always knew you were a fighter," he hissed.

She screamed and threw the rattlesnake ornament at him. It hit his chest and knocked him back against the wall. She followed with the belt—two quick, stinging strikes. Johan retaliated by swinging Krókr in a heavy arc. It missed Kitty by some distance, but the threat of it unbalanced her. She stumbled and hit the floor hard.

Blood soaked into Johan's plaited beard and splashed onto his chest. He trudged toward her, dragging the hateful ax.

"Bad Kitty," he said.

Scrrreeeeeeee . . .

The poolside lights showed his face: a disfigured mask. They showed his body: a bloodstained rag. Xander pointed with the one remaining finger on his right hand and aimed the .45 with the other.

"Your final performance," he slurred. "And the only one I'm going to enjoy."

The report was deafening, a shuddering clap that opened the night. But it didn't come from Xander's gun.

The bullet entered the back of Xander's skull and exited just above his left eyebrow. It was quick and messy—a splash of blood and bone against the starry sky—then he was gone, dead before his legs buckled.

Luke blinked several times, not breathing but definitely, incomprehensibly, still alive. He wiped Xander's blood from his face and looked up. Tera Montecino, his old nemesis, was perched on one knee at the edge of the pool. A thread of smoke twisted from the barrel of her gun.

"Help is on the way," she said, and collapsed onto her side.

Luke's mouth moved soundlessly. He looked from Tera to Xander, expecting him to leap up for one final jump scare (goddamn the movies). When he was certain that the berserker was dead, he got to his knees, crawled over to the ladder, and dragged himself out of the pool.

"I called for backup," Tera said. She lay, clasping her hip, sheet-pale and reaching for air. "You think you can survive another five minutes?"

"I don't know," he replied honestly. Everything tipped giddily to the left, then the right. He dropped down beside Tera. "My wife . . . did you . . . did—"

"There's a BOLO out for Ramón Aparicio, your bat-faced

man." Tera looked down at her bleeding side, because perhaps that was better than looking him in the eye. "If Lisa is with him . . ."

She continued speaking, but Luke didn't hear. He was caught on an updraft of hope, floating over the hotel, over the desert. There was a possibility that Lisa would be found, that she would be given time to heal, to love, to *remember*. And Kitty . . . if she managed to escape the hotel and flag down a good ol' boy, maybe there were better days ahead for her, too.

A sob bubbled from Luke's chest, and tears—*warm* tears—spilled from his eyes. He wanted to thank Tera, but couldn't bring himself to say those two small words. Yes, she had saved his life, but hadn't she also cut a deal with Johan?

"You were tracking me," he said. "You told that crazy fucking Viking where I was. You asked him to kill me."

"I fucked up, Luke." A look of extreme remorse swam through all the discomfort and tiredness on her face. "Listen, I was wrong, and—"

She was cut off by a scream from the hotel. Luke got to his feet, quicker than he should have. The pain rattled through him and his interior lights dimmed. He puffed out his chest and fought on.

"Kitty," he said.

Tera nodded. She also got to her feet, but slowly, and managed three steps toward to the hotel before her legs buckled and she hit the flagstone.

"I can't," she gasped. "I can't *move*, I—"

"Give me your gun."

Grimacing, she slapped her semiauto into Luke's hand. "You know how to use one of these?"

"Yeah, I did six weeks at Brock's Urban Shooter." He extended the Beretta, looking down the sights. "Training, for *A Bullet Affair*."

"This isn't a movie, Luke." She gritted her teeth and wiped the back of one bloody hand across her forehead. "You shoot someone, they're not getting up after the cameras stop rolling."

"I hope you're right."

Luke started away from her and she called after him, clearly determined to finish what she had started to say a few moments before. Maybe she thought he was going to die and she wouldn't get another chance, and maybe she was right.

"I was wrong about you." Her voice warbled, but it was sincere. "I've never been more wrong about anything in my life, and I'm sorry."

He left her bleeding in the shadows.

Kitty scrabbled backward, the soles of her sneakers pushing at the slick floor. Johan brought his ax down and it cracked off the tile between her feet. He lifted it for another shot, teetered unsurely for a second, then regained himself. Blood streamed down his face, into his eyes and mouth. His beard was red and wet.

He screamed with enough force to make the walls buckle, the floor rise. Kitty clawed herself away from him. He stopped her by planting one boot on her chest.

"Johan," she pleaded, looking into his eyes, but seeing nothing she recognized, only madness and conflict and ego.

"I could have *made* you," he said. "I would have sat you on the biggest throne in Los Angeles."

Krókr's bearded blade flashed in the hesitant light. Kitty readied herself—it would be over quickly—then the doors behind Johan crashed open and Luke reeled into the hallway. He shambled forward, staring down the sights of a lean black pistol.

There were no theatrics. No drama. No Hollywood lines. He pulled the trigger three times and every bullet hit.

One in his upper arm. Two in his back. Johan was lifted off his feet by the force of the bullets. He dropped Krókr, toppled over

Kitty, and turned a full one-eighty before falling. Deep inside, the blond-haired Californian—the rich kid, the YouTuber—cried out, knowing that the sun had set on this bright and privileged life. The voices in his blood believed otherwise. They roused him with all their Viking fury. As long as he had breath to draw, he would fight.

Johan surged to his feet and ran at Luke. Blood rippled across his body. His hair flowed behind him. Luke aimed the pistol, pulled the trigger twice. The first shot missed but the second blew a hole through the right side of Johan's chest.

He dropped to his knees, pushed himself upright, kept going.

Luke shot him again, tearing a piece of his throat away.

The voices swelled. War horns sounded. Weapons clashed. Johan fell against the wall and dragged himself across it. He leapt at Luke, knocking him to the floor. The gun spilled from his hand.

This was it. The end of it all. Johan felt it rushing toward him. A broad, golden light.

"*Valhalla*," he screeched, but all that came out was a soupy gurgle.

He clasped Luke's throat in his bloody hands and squeezed with every fading ounce of his strength, every wild voice in his body.

Kitty made it to her feet. She didn't know how. The hallway sloped and skewed, dark at the edges. One slow step, then another. She dragged Krókr along behind her. *Scrrreeeeeee*. She couldn't remember picking it up.

Johan straddled Luke, his back to her, pocked with bullet holes. Luke shook and struggled beneath him. His legs jittered. He was dying.

Kitty willed herself forward. She got to within striking distance of Johan and lifted the ax, not to her waist, not to her chest, but high above her head, both hands looped around the bottom of the handle. Kitty looked at Johan's shoulders, splashed with blood and crisscross belt marks. Her gaze dropped to his back—to the huge tree tattooed there, its thick trunk following the contour of his spine.

Yggdrasil. The tree of life.

Kitty brought the ax down. She split the tree in two.

Kitty fell against the wall. Her legs went from beneath her and she slid into a sitting position.

"Luke?" She spoke from behind trembling hands.

Nothing for a long moment, then a sigh, a groan. Kitty looked through the cracks of her fingers. She saw Luke crawl from beneath Johan's corpse. He lay still for a moment, catching his breath.

"Luke . . ."

"Hey . . . hey, it's okay, Kitty."

She reached out her hand. He went to her side and took it.

Silence folded around them.

30

WHERE THE LOWS DON'T GO

(SIX MONTHS LATER)

His new ride was a BMW M4 Coupé, five hundred horses under the hood and a custom paint job. It was too much car for the L.A. traffic—this thing needed a launchpad and open sky—but it wasn't too much for Luke. He bought it new, right out of the showroom. He drove it like a boss.

They took Interstate 110 south. It was slow with volume, but that was fine; they were making good time. The radio was tuned to Real 92.3, at Kitty's request, and she sang along to music that made Luke feel old and out of touch. "It helps with my nerves," she had said. Luke had smiled and turned the volume up.

They followed the signs to LAX.

The basketball in her hands was a gift. It was emblazoned with the Lakers logo and covered in signatures. She and Luke had scored courtside seats at the Staples Center—a little thank-you for doing one of the late-night talk shows. They had met the team after the game, and Kitty had passed the basketball around. In the months since, it had become a promise, a symbol of intent, to one day hand it to her son in person. And it was this, as much as anything, that kept her going through the dark times.

"You're going to rub the signatures off that thing," Luke said.

"Oh, right." She'd been rolling the ball between her palms and spinning it in her lap. Despite the music, she was still clearly nervous.

They joined the airport traffic and followed it at a crawl to departures. The constant blare of horns, and the roar of the aircraft, all but drowned out the radio. Kitty reached and turned it off.

"I can't use him as my therapy," she said, looking at Luke. "It's not fair on him. He's only seven years old."

"You're overthinking it," Luke said, looking over his shoulder, easing into the right lane. "Just enjoy the moment. This is what you always wanted."

"Only," Kitty said, "if Levi wants it, too."

"Everything we've been through, Kitty, and are *still* going through . . . trust me, when the good things come along, you've got to grab them in both arms. Hold them close." He touched the brake and pointed at one of the signs "Delta, right?"

Flight 961 to Cincinnati, touching down at 8:26 P.M. local time, then a ninety-minute drive to Louisville. She would sleep tonight at her mama's house, in her old room. Tomorrow, she would meet Courtney Caruso for lunch, then together they would pick up Levi Caruso from his private (and very expensive) Montessori school.

Luke edged into a drop-off spot. He got out of the car, hooked Kitty's luggage from the trunk, and hefted it around to her.

"Jesus, that's heavy," he said.

"Gifts for the fam," Kitty said. "L.A. fashion. My mama's going to be the only one in her church with a hat from Two Rodeo."

"I think the Good Lord would approve."

Kitty smiled and patted the basketball. "I think the Good Lord will probably redirect my luggage to Boise, Idaho, which is the reason I'm holding on to this."

"Smart."

"I don't even know if Levi will like it," Kitty said. "Courtney told me he's a basketball fan, but what if he doesn't like the Lakers?"

"Everybody likes the Lakers," Luke said. "Even if they don't want to admit it."

She curled one arm around him, a loose but affectionate hug. Kitty knew a *lot* more people in Los Angeles now—it was amazing what a little bit of celebrity could do—and considered some of them friends, but Luke was at the top of the pile.

"I'm scared," she whispered, not letting him go. "It's like an audition, but the most important audition of my life."

"No, Kitty. In auditions you pretend to be someone else." He smelled of Dior cologne and his arms felt as strong as branches. "With this, you just have to be yourself."

She beamed, her head against his chest, and held him a while longer.

He was in the neighborhood, so paid a visit to his old friend at Inglewood Park Cemetery. Floyd Tallent's grave was a mound of flowers, many of them wilting in the California sun. A headstone had been added—white marble, etched with musical notes. His epitaph was simple, beautiful, two words: SOUL MAN. For most, this referenced his career in music. For Luke, it spoke to the brilliant light that Floyd had inside him. Here was a man whose friendship had never faltered, and who'd believed in Luke when everybody else had turned their backs. He had entertained, comforted, and counseled. On their final afternoon together, he'd told Luke to stop making excuses, and to rediscover his sense of purpose.

"I've been trying," Luke whispered, running his fingers across that two-word epitaph. "I'm getting closer, but there's still some way to go."

He closed his eyes, drifted away, and heard Lisa's music, not Floyd's, playing at the back of his mind. It came with a pang of emptiness and hurt. *"Some dreams are found where the lows don't go, this is the cradle that rocks my soul."*

He hadn't found everything he'd been looking for.

Sixty-four miles southeast of Pale Bone—at around the time that Luke, Kitty, and Tera Montecino were being loaded into ambulances in the parking lot of the Rattlesnake Hotel—State Trooper Shane Broman of Arizona's Highway Patrol Division made note of a vehicle heading eastbound on State Route 68. He grabbed his radio, gave his unit number, and asked for confirmation of the BOLO alert that had come through NCIC some forty-five minutes before.

Dispatch: "A 2012 Ford Econoline, blue, Nevada plate: two-five-Charlie-six-one-four."

Broman: "In pursuit. Code three."

He flicked on lights and sirens and slammed his boot to the floor. Within seconds he was up behind the vehicle. He expected a chase, but the driver pulled onto the shoulder without incident. Through his PA system, Broman ordered the occupants to step out of the vehicle, slowly, with their hands on their heads.

The driver's door opened. Ramón Sojo Aparicio stepped into the swirling light as instructed.

"On your knees, now. Keep your hands on your head."

Ramón fell to his knees. He was bleeding and bruised. He was also sobbing. *"Lo siento,"* he mumbled, over and over: I'm sorry, I'm sorry. Broman flex-cuffed him and threw him into the back of the cruiser. He was going to wait for assistance before opening the back of the van—the cargo could be hazardous—but went ahead when he heard what sounded like a woman in distress.

Later, State Trooper Broman described to a gaggle of jostling, excited reporters what he found when he opened the doors:

"Five female occupants, aged, at my best guess, between eighteen and thirty. Three Latina, one African American, one Caucasian. All were clearly traumatized, malnourished, and extremely scared."

Mallory Mayflower of Fox 10 news asked State Trooper Broman if he recognized the African American woman as the missing R&B singer Lisa Hayes.

"No, ma'am," Broman said, and smiled. "I'm really more of a country-and-western guy."

Lisa spent eight days at the UCLA Medical Center, where she was treated, evaluated, and questioned by authorities. She was then admitted to Yolanda Grove, a psychiatric care facility in Pasadena. The help (and medication) she received there proved invaluable, from simple exercises designed to redevelop her motor functions and memory, to hypnosis, neurofeedback, and cognitive therapy.

Luke spent as much time with her as he was allowed, although he had his own recovery and mental realignment to consider. He was in the hospital for four days, being treated for various maladies, including concussion and a herniated disc. He and Kitty were discharged at the same time, and a media circus awaited them on the outside. Luke—no stranger to flashing cameras and bleating reporters—blew them all off to be with Lisa. He spent long hours at her bedside, telling her stories, showing her photographs, brushing her hair. At Yolanda Grove, they went for walks in the surrounding gardens, identifying the birds and flowers. He played her favorite music: Etta James, Billie Holiday, Beyoncé, Lady Gaga.

Sometimes she danced, moving her body unsurely, struggling to connect to the inner rhythm that had once coursed through her soul. Luke played *her* music, too, hoping it might unlock those deep, lost places inside her. Lisa recognized the melodies and occasionally sang along, but mostly her eyes shone with sadness.

Her family came down, and that was good for her. They did all the right things, and never pushed. Any interaction with Luke was layered with frost, and he had no problem with that. Maybe there would be conversations and reparations in time, but the handshakes and awkward hugs were enough to begin with.

It was slow, often painful, but Luke watched Lisa's recuperation, like some beautiful building being restored, one brick at a time. She recalled childhood memories, favorite foods, pop culture trivia—nothing monumental in itself, but together they outlined a definite hope. It wasn't all forward progress, though. Increasingly, it became clear to Luke that not everything could be fixed.

Lisa had been at Yolanda Grove four months when he finally accepted this. In keeping with her style—further proof that the woman he'd fallen in love with was finding her way back—it came in the form of a song.

It was early evening. Luke walked into her room to find her sitting at the window with a pen in her hand and a notepad set on one raised knee. The sinking sun cast a warm light across the gardens, and touched her outline with copper.

"Hey," he said.

She turned to him. Sometimes she smiled and said his name. On a couple of occasions she had jumped to her feet and planted a kiss on his cheek. That hadn't happened for a few months, though. Now a wrinkle struck her brow and her chin dimpled. Luke's heart dipped. It was woefully ironic that every forward step she took was a step further from him.

He pulled up a chair and sat next to her. The window was open a crack, and the sounds of the evening eased in. They were varied and clear, complementing the deep light shining through the tree-tops.

Still with the pen clasped between her fingers, Lisa reached across and stroked the back of his hand with her pinkie.

"You don't have to keep coming here," she said.

"I know," he replied. "But there's a part of me that's still looking for you, and every time I walk into this room and see you, it's like finding you all over again."

The furrow on her brow disappeared and she turned back to the window. In profile, she looked like the Lisa of yesteryear. She had put on weight. Her skin shone and her hair fell to her shoulders in full, dark waves. It was only when looking into her eyes that Luke saw the conflict and pain that she was dealing with.

"I still need to find myself," she said.

He wanted to say that they had time, and that he would be there for her, but that wasn't what Lisa wanted. She had grasped the beginnings of a new life, and had no space for fragile or fractured pieces. Their marriage had been many things, but strong wasn't one of them.

"What are you writing?" he asked stiffly, trying to keep the tremor from his voice.

Lisa looked down at the notepad. A hopeful expression flashed across her face.

"Maybe a song." She shook her head. "I don't know. It's just a few lines, but it feels like something."

"Sing it for me."

Lisa tilted her head, as if considering, but she never had, and never would, need encouragement to sing. It was her soul's calling, as natural to her as to a bird.

"*I see the road ahead of me, and every mile is mine.*" Her voice wavered and cracked, partly through trying to nail the melody, mainly because of the passion inside the words. "*But there's a light in my rearview mirror I know will always shine.*"

In the fragrant deep of the Cascades, beneath seven billion stars, Lisa had sung "The Cradle" to him, and maybe it was the moment, but Luke hadn't grasped that she was singing about him.

This time, he was more perceptive.

Luke had dreamt so often of exoneration, but was too preoccupied to notice when it actually came. His healing—Lisa's and Kitty's, too—consumed all of his focus, to the extent that the outside world faded to a vaguely annoying smudge.

The story had made headlines, of course, but Luke shared nothing with the press. Not to begin with, at least. He'd spoken only to the police while in the hospital, and had checked into a hotel after being discharged, where he kept the DO NOT DISTURB sign on his door for the duration of his stay. It was only after Lisa had been admitted to Yolanda Grove that Luke realized that the attention directed at him was largely positive.

He'd walked into a coffee shop in Pasadena, head down, sunglasses on, trying to be invisible, the way he'd walked into every establishment over the past three years. A young woman had stopped him on his way to the counter. She didn't call him "wifekiller" or "motherfucker"—salutations to which Luke had become accustomed. Instead, she smiled, held up her phone, and asked for a selfie.

"Selfie?" Luke had frowned. "Why?"

"Because you're Luke *fucking* Kingsley, man."

It was the inflection in the word "fucking" that won him over. Not hateful, for a change, but laced with respect and reverence. Luke had grunted his consent, and grinned uneasily while the woman held up her phone and took the snap. Other customers joined in, armed with their tech, and for the next thirty minutes Luke posed for selfies and shook hands, and he loved every minute of it.

Furthermore, he noted the hashtags that were used when adding the photos to their socials: #LUKEKINGSLEYISINNOCENT, #LOVE-4LUKE, #HEDIDNTDOIT. Luke hadn't picked up a cell phone since his was destroyed in the fight—the *war*—at Ramón's ranch. That afternoon, while Lisa was sleeping, he went to his provider, and attached his account to a new phone. Over the next few days, he searched for those hashtags (and others) across various social media sites, and reveled in the Luke lovefest.

Another development: 109 missed calls. Many were from press outlets, some were from old friends, a few were from his former agent and management team. Luke called Kitty—convalescing with her family in Louisville—to impart this change of fortune.

"Me, too," Kitty had revealed, and Luke had detected the thread of excitement in her voice. Given what they'd been through, it was beautiful to hear. "My agent's phone hasn't stopped ringing. I've been asked to do *The View* and about six other shows. And one of the top L.A. fashion companies wants me to be the face of their new fragrance. Fortitude, it's called. Or Dauntless. Something like that."

"Jesus, Kitty, that's . . . that's amazing."

"Yeah, Milly wants me to do it—to do *everything*—but I don't know, Luke. It feels too soon."

"I hear you," Luke agreed. "But we'll be yesterday's news before you know it. This may be an opportunity to lay the groundwork for a more deserved future."

Over the next six weeks, Luke and Kitty told their stories on daytime and late-night TV. Five appearances in total, although they could have done fifty. Kitty also signed on to become the new face of Dauntless Eau de Parfum. Her first photo shoot was on Venice Beach. Luke was there to support her. Not that she needed it. Kitty had expanded in front of the lens, a natural, a goddess, a hundred feet tall. Luke watched her with undeniable pride. He would never have guessed that she had so many traumas inside.

The scar curved down from her hairline and she never tried to hide it.

Luke had his own traumas. The ghosts were never far away. His psychiatrist told him that distance would only come from traveling on brighter roads, and Luke was ready to put some miles on the clock. Having Johan and Xander breathing into his ear was bad, but the nightmares were worse—and one in particular: Luke gliding over a landscape of broken pieces, his red wings extended and glistening, a beautiful blood eagle.

The authorities worked to piece together the events at the Rattlesnake Hotel, and everything leading up to it. As well as questioning Luke, Kitty, and Tera, the police also interviewed certain (anonymous) A-listers, Johan's parents, and staff at Fusion 44—the jazz club owned by Kris "Sly Boy" Streeter. Properties belonging to Ramón and Johan were searched, including a warehouse in Compton where "a significant quantity" of Sly Boy's blood was found ingrained in the cement floor. The press chimed in, not so much muddying the water as adding glitter to it. To the general public, the story became part true crime, part movie of the week.

Luke was exonerated, Kitty's fearlessness was celebrated, but it was the fifty-year-old former detective who came out looking like the real hero. According to sources, Tera Montecino had uncovered Johan's canary operation, put the call out to track down Ramón and the missing women, and killed two violent criminals. Nearly dying on the operating table had only added to her renown. The trauma surgeon who removed bullet shrapnel and bone fragments from Tera's left hip had remarked that she was the most determined woman he had ever encountered, a statement to which Luke could attest.

Tera had visited Luke at his new Santa Monica apartment. She looked the same as ever, dressed in blue jeans and a gray sport jacket, her platinum hair pinned back into a tight bun. Apart from a slight limp when she walked, she appeared to have made a full recovery.

"Nice view." She crossed his living room, her long shape framed by floor-to-ceiling windows. Beyond them, the endless sky, the endless ocean, in similar shades of blue. "Beats that dingy crap box in Silver Lake, huh?"

"I guess." He didn't *guess* at all. It was a world apart—in every way, including price—from his old digs in the east-central part of town. He'd rented this place for Lisa, believing the ocean views would help her recovery, when he'd thought that they still had a future together. "I'm doing better these days, all things considered."

"Saw the Bimmer in your parking spot."

"I got a good deal."

"I'm sure you did." Tera's crooked lip twitched. "I'm happy for you."

"Thank you." He folded his arms and looked at Tera closely. "Why are you here?"

"Just to check in," she said. "I thought you might like to know that Christine Flanagan has been reunited with her family in Boston. She has a long road ahead of her, but there are good people by her side."

Christine Flanagan was the "crack whore" that Ramón had apparently found in the gutter in Vegas. The other three women—all undocumented—had been taken to a residential center in Arizona, and were currently awaiting a decision by immigration authorities.

For Ramón, the decision had already been made: a lifetime in High Desert State Prison on a string of charges, including five counts of kidnapping, multiple counts of assault and rape, and the possession, trafficking, and manufacture of various controlled substances.

"You could have told me that in an email," Luke said. "But while you're here, can I get you a drink? I have beer, water . . ."

"A beer with Luke Kingsley." Tera lifted one eyebrow. "Why not?"

The police and the press had a skewed version of events, because Tera had done most of the talking. They didn't know, for instance, that Tera had been tracking Luke for months, and that she had tasked Johan Fly and his cohorts with carrying out an extreme form of justice. If this information were ever to come to light, it would be particularly damaging to Tera's newfound hero status.

This was the *real* reason for her visit. She wanted to get a read on Luke—ascertain whether or not he had any interest in blabbing, and get ahead of it if she had to.

He decided to put her at ease.

"You saved my life," he said, handing her a frosty-cold Bud. "You saved Kitty's life, and you probably saved Lisa's, too."

Tera shrugged, but she knew it was true.

"We're good," Luke said.

"You sure?"

He twisted the cap off his own bottle and angled it toward hers. She considered it for a moment, then held out her hand instead. Luke nodded, drummed his palm into Tera's, and shook. It was every bit the robust, Chuck-Norris-style shake that he'd anticipated, and that pleased him.

Xander Cray was cremated at an unremarkable ceremony in his hometown of Escondido, California. Six people were in attendance, all of whom remained silent. There was no eulogy of any kind, and not a single tear was shed. The entire process was as perfunctory as burning yard waste, and Xander was missed about as much.

Ruben Osterfeld's demise was more widely memorialized, given his large family and MMA background. He trended across social media, and his various accounts exploded in terms of followers before being permanently removed. Ruben was buried in Historic South-Central, with an impressive crowd in attendance, and a soul quartet singing "Stand by Me" as his coffin was lowered into the ground. His father was heard to remark afterward that it was more than he deserved.

The internet had been good to Johan Fly over the years. It had brought him fans and followers, fueled his lavish lifestyle, and displayed his character—the Cali Viking—in an approving light. Johan's online ascent had been swift, but it was nothing compared to his fall from grace. The internet turned on him like an exotic pet. There were streams of hate-filled comments, vicious memes, defamatory blog posts and subreddits. His socials were promptly shut down and his YouTube channels removed.

In the days following the incident at the Rattlesnake Hotel, when the dirty truths began to emerge, Aksel Fly took aggressive measures to clear his son's name. He called his friends at City Hall, hired the best lawyers in Southern California, and threatened to sue just about everybody involved. Within forty-eight hours of throwing his hat into the ring, stocks in Fly Tech Inc. plummeted twenty-nine percent. This prompted a strategic volte-face. Aksel called off the dogs and went back to playing golf with his billionaire friends. Protecting his fortune was obviously more important than protecting his son's name.

There was some debate about Johan's final resting place. One Reddit user claimed that Aksel Fly had paid for a full Norse funeral, complete with a longship and archers with flaming arrows. A more popular theory was that Johan had been cremated in the Hollywood Hills, and his ashes kept among Viking artifacts on the Fly family estate.

Johan had believed in the gods, and he believed in fate, and Luke had to admit, sometimes things had a way of falling into place:

"Luke, Jesus fucking Christ, I've been trying to reach you all morning. What the fuck? You have your phone turned off?"

"Actually, yeah. I took a friend to the airport, and now I'm hanging out with another friend."

Luke looked at the two words etched across the stone: SOUL MAN. He smiled, grabbed a flower, lifted it to his nose.

"You hear the news?" Marty asked.

"I don't know, Marty. Why don't you tell me the news, and I'll tell you if I heard it."

Marty Lustbader, agent extraordinaire. Luke, in his many fantasies, had sworn he'd never go back, even if Marty came groveling on his knees. But he *did* go back, and Marty didn't have to grovel. The truth was, Luke *liked* the old son of a bitch.

"Barrett Lorne," Marty said, breathless.

"What about him?"

"Had a meltdown on the set of *Night City Blues*. Punched Yaron Lewenberg—the head of New Dawn Pictures—in the throat. *In the goddamn throat.*" Marty paused for dramatic effect. "Jesus, Barrett has always been an asshole, but he's been a *raging* asshole since his canary supply dried up. This was the last straw. He's been taken off the picture."

"And?" Luke asked.

"And he needs to be replaced." Another pause. "The producers like *you*, Luke."

"Me?"

"You have the right . . . *beaten-up* look."

"That so?" Luke walked away from Floyd's grave, a little out of breath because his heart was beating so fast. "I guess that's a compliment."

"You're damn right it's a compliment." Marty barked a wheezy laugh. Luke imagined him in his office, reclined in his seat, his grin as long as the HOLLYWOOD sign. "So, you want to talk to them?"

Luke didn't answer right away. He smiled and lifted his face to the sun, sensing—after all this time—a brighter road ahead, the closeness of his dreams.

"Luke?"

"I'm still here, Marty."

And yes, before long he would take that road, but *carefully*. He would savor every step. For now, though, it was enough just to know that it was there.

At three P.M. the following day, on the other side of the country, a school bell rang.

Kitty took a deep breath. Her emotions had been tested recently, in so many ways, but she couldn't remember feeling anything like this. It was an all-new high, a tremendous, stomach-turning excitement. Love pounded from her. It was like music, furious and loud, but full of joy.

"You okay?" Courtney asked.

"Yeah," Kitty replied. She forced a smile. "I'm . . . oh my goodness, I'm so *nervous*."

"You'll be just fine."

Kids began to peel out through the doors, their voices high and beautiful. It was as perfect a day as Kitty could have hoped for. Clear skies, not too hot, the sun slanting through the branches of the surrounding oak trees. Shadows danced everywhere.

"He's usually one of the last out," Courtney said, smiling. "All the other kids are grabbing their bags and booking it, but Levi . . . well, Levi likes to take his time."

"It's all good." Kitty swallowed something roughly the size of the basketball she held in her hands.

"He's a daydreamer," Courtney added.

"That doesn't surprise me."

Other parents waited nearby, or sat behind the wheels of their cars, just another weekday for them. Kitty stood on the sidewalk a few feet from Courtney's Lexus. She scanned each young face as it emerged into the clear afternoon light. Courtney was next to her, dressed in Diesel jeans and Vans, her blond hair cascading down the middle of her back. She was beautiful and kind and genuine—everything that Kitty wanted her to be. Kitty, meanwhile, looked ordinary, but in a strong way. She wore no makeup, her mama had fixed her hair, and the clothes she had on—including her sneakers—cost as much as it had taken for Courtney to fill her Lexus with gas.

She had photos on her phone from the Dauntless shoot, and could have shown up looking like that. But this first time, she wanted Levi to see who she truly was. No pomp. No staging. Not a star or a celebrity, but a powerful woman, scarred and standing tall.

"Here he comes," Courtney said.

Levi shuffled down the front steps, talking to a friend, his Pokémon backpack drooping off one shoulder. Kitty's heart ignited. A bright flash and gone. Her love became something else. It roared at her—a new, beautifully shaped thing.

She clutched the basketball. Doubts, fears, triumphs, dreams . . . they all sailed through her. Tears pricked at her eyes. Her mouth quivered.

Courtney stepped ahead of her, greeting Levi as he said goodbye to his pal and crossed the sidewalk toward her. He lifted his backpack higher onto his shoulder but it slipped right off again.

"Hi, baby."

"Hi, Mom."

"You remember the important conversation we had this morning?"

"Yeah."

Courtney nodded and stepped to one side, and suddenly Levi was looking into Kitty's eyes, and Kitty was looking into his. The lightest frown touched his brow, but it was beautiful. *He* was beautiful, everything about him. She remembered the tiny five-week-old bundle in her arms, and how her heart had ached for him. So much had changed since then, and so much remained the same.

She thumbed a tear from her cheekbone and smiled.

"Hello, Levi," she said.

ACKNOWLEDGMENTS

I have taken a few creative liberties with the city of Los Angeles—certain street names and venues—to better serve the story. Similarly, I sprinkled in the names of real celebrities, to create a sense of time and place, but these are *my* versions of these celebrities, existing in a fictional world, and no inference is intended.

That being said, I wanted the Los Angeles depicted in this novel to feel authentic, and so brought in the expertise of Chris Ryall, my friend, first reader, and a native Californian. Chris took to the first draft with great enthusiasm, and helped me create the right setting and vibe. He did one hell of a job. If anything here does not ring true, that's on me, not Chris.

Tim Lebbon and Christopher Golden also cast their expert eyes over an early draft, and both made suggestions that helped make this a better novel. Moreover, they reminded me how important it is to have beta readers you can trust. They, along with Chris Ryall, have been my go-to guys for many years now, and I owe them so much. An extra shout-out to Tim: *No Second Chances* was written during the long, difficult months of COVID-19, and Tim became my regular Skype companion. His good humor, friendship, and willingness to listen gave me the lift I so often needed. Thanks, pal!

A big thank you to Chris Myles (another Chris) and Mark Muralla, the geniuses who designed and maintain my website. My gratitude is everlasting. And to Sandra and Andrew Marsh, the geniuses who helped me create "canary," the fictional power nootropic described in this book. (As a writer, it's a good idea to surround oneself with geniuses.) Thanks, also, to the staff at the Elora Brewing Company in beautiful downtown Elora, who were happy for me to use their fine establishment as an office every Friday afternoon, and who served me great beer while I worked. (It's a tough job, it really is!) And it was while "working" at the Elora Brewing Company that I met Tera Gillen, who was full of energy, curiosity, and life, and who let me use her name for one of my characters. (Tera would go on to appear in Season 9 of *Big Brother Canada*, and would prove herself to be as strong and ruthless as her namesake.)

Endless thanks to my friend and agent, Howard Morhaim, whose support is so valuable to me. Howard *always* tells me what I need to hear, even when it isn't what I *want* to hear. It really *is* a tough job, and I appreciate him so much.

Huge applause and a standing ovation for the team at William Morrow, and everybody at HarperCollins, with the spotlight focused on Nate Lanman, Brittani Hilles, Andie Schoenfeld, and Ryan Shepherd. The best team in publishing! Which sets the stage for the biggest thank-you of all, this to my brilliant editor, Jennifer Brehl. Her belief in me, her professionalism and support, inspire me to reach deeper and work harder. This is our second book together, and I'm *still* pinching myself.

My deepest appreciation to the friends, family, and readers who have supported me over the years. You're all wonderful. And finally, all the love in the world to my wife, Emily, and our two fantastic children, Lily and Charlie. It sometimes feels like I exist in the branches of a huge, beautiful tree, strong even in the most demanding of storms, and with life and color all around. It's a good place to be.